Our Kind of Traitor

JOHN LE CARRÉ

PENGUIN BOOKS

PENGUIN BOOKS

UK | USA | Canada | Ireland | Australia
India | New Zealand | South Africa

Penguin Books is part of the Penguin Random House group of companies
whose addresses can be found at global.penguinrandomhouse.com.

First published by Viking 2010
Published in Penguin Books 2011
This film tie-in edition published in Penguin Books 2016

009

Copyright © David Cornwell, 2010

The moral right of the author has been asserted

Set in Garamond MT Std by Palimpsest Book Production Ltd, Falkirk, Stirlingshire
Printed in Great Britain by Clays Ltd, St Ives plc

A CIP catalogue record for this book is available from the British Library

ISBN: 978-0-241-97501-5

In memory of
Simon Channing Williams,
film-maker, magician,
honourable man.

Princes in this case
Do hate the traitor, though they love the treason.

Samuel Daniel

I

At seven o'clock of a Caribbean morning, on the island of Antigua, one Peregrine Makepiece, otherwise known as Perry, an all-round amateur athlete of distinction and until recently tutor in English literature at a distinguished Oxford college, played three sets of tennis against a muscular, stiff-backed, bald, brown-eyed Russian man of dignified bearing in his middle fifties called Dima. How this match came about was quickly the subject of intense examination by British agents professionally disposed against the workings of chance. Yet the events leading up to it were on Perry's side blameless.

The dawning of his thirtieth birthday three months previously had triggered a life-change in him that had been building up for a year or more without his being aware of it. Seated head in hands at eight o'clock in the morning in his modest Oxford rooms, after a seven-mile run that had done nothing to ease his sense of calamity, he had searched his soul to know just what the first third of his natural life had achieved, apart from providing him with an excuse for not engaging in the world beyond the city's dreaming spires.

*

Why?

To any outward eye, his was the ultimate academic success story. The State-educated son of secondary-school teachers arrives in Oxford from London University laden with academic honours and takes up a three-year post awarded him by an ancient, rich, achievement-driven college. His first name, traditionally the property of the English upper classes, derives from a rabble-rousing Methodist prelate of the nineteenth century named Arthur Peregrine of Huddersfield.

In the term-time, when he isn't teaching, he distinguishes himself as a cross-country runner and sportsman. On his spare evenings he helps out in a local youth club. In vacations he conquers difficult peaks and Most Serious climbs. Yet when his college offers him a permanent Fellowship – or to his present soured way of thinking, imprisonment for life – he baulks.

Again: why?

Last term he had delivered a series of lectures on George Orwell under the title 'A Stifled Britain?' and his rhetoric had alarmed him. Would Orwell have believed it possible that the same overfed voices which had haunted him in the 1930s, the same crippling incompetence, addiction to foreign wars and assumptions of entitlement, were happily in place in 2009?

Receiving no response from the blank student faces staring up at him, he had supplied it for himself: *no*, Orwell would emphatically *not* have believed it. Or if he had, he would have taken to the streets. He would have smashed some serious glass.

*

It was a topic he had thrashed out mercilessly with Gail, his long-standing girlfriend, as they lay in her bed after a birthday supper at the flat in Primrose Hill that she had part-inherited from her otherwise penniless father.

'I don't like dons and I don't like being one myself. I don't like academia and if I never have to wear a bloody gown again, I'll feel a free man,' he had ranted at the gold-brown hair clustered comfortably on his shoulder.

And receiving no reply beyond a sympathetic purr:

'Hammering on about Byron, Keats and Wordsworth to a bunch of bored undergraduates whose highest ambition is to get a degree, get laid, and get rich? Done it. Been there. Fuck it.'

And raising the odds:

'About the only thing that would *really* keep me in this country is a bloody revolution.'

And Gail, a sparky young barrister on the rise, blessed with looks and a quick tongue – sometimes a little too quick for her own comfort as well as Perry's – assured him that no revolution would be complete without him.

Both were *de facto* orphans. If Perry's late parents had been the soul of high-minded Christian socialist abstinence, Gail's were the other thing. Her father, a sweetly useless actor, had died prematurely of alcohol, sixty cigarettes a day and a misplaced passion for his wayward wife. Her mother, an actress but less sweet, had vanished from the family home when Gail was thirteen, and was reputed to be living the simple life on the Costa Brava with a second cameraman.

*

Perry's initial reaction to his life-decision to shake the dust of academia from his feet – irrevocable, like all Perry's life-decisions – was to return to his grass roots. The only son of Dora and Alfred would put himself where their convictions had been. He would begin his teaching career all over again at the point where they had been forced to abandon theirs.

He would stop playing the intellectual high-flyer, sign up for an honest-to-God teacher-training course and, in their image, qualify as a secondary-school teacher in one of his country's most deprived areas.

He would teach set subjects, and any sport they cared to throw at him, to children who needed him as a lifeline to self-fulfilment rather than as a ticket to middle-class prosperity.

But Gail was not as alarmed by this prospect as perhaps he intended her to be. For all his determination to be at the *hard centre of life*, there remained other unreconciled versions of him, and Gail was on familiar terms with most of them:

Yes, there was Perry the self-punishing student at London University where they had first met, who in the mould of T. E. Lawrence had taken his bicycle to France in the vacations and ridden it until he keeled over with exhaustion.

And yes, there was Perry the alpine adventurer, the Perry who could run no race and play no game, from seven-a-side rugby to pass the parcel with her nephews and nieces at Christmas time, without a compulsive need to win.

But there was also Perry the closet sybarite who treated himself to unpredictable bursts of luxury before hurrying back to his garret. And this was the Perry who stood on the best tennis court at the best recession-hit resort in

Antigua on that early May morning before the sun got too high to play, with the Russian Dima one side of the net and Perry the other, and Gail wearing a swimsuit and a broad-brimmed floppy hat and a silky cover-up that covered very little, sitting amid an unlikely assembly of dead-eyed spectators, some dressed in black, who appeared to have sworn a collective oath not to smile, not to speak, and not to express any interest in the match they were being compelled to watch.

*

It was a lucky chance, in Gail's opinion, that the Caribbean adventure had been planned in advance of Perry's impulsive life-decision. Its inception dated back to darkest November when his father had fallen victim to the same cancer that had carried off his mother two years earlier, leaving Perry in a state of modest affluence. Not holding with inherited wealth, and being in two minds as to whether he should give all he had to the poor, Perry dithered. But after a campaign of attrition mounted by Gail, they had settled for a once-in-a-lifetime bargain tennis holiday in the sun.

And no holiday could have been better planned, as it turned out, for by the time they had embarked on it, even bigger decisions were staring them in the face:

What should Perry do with his life, and should they do it together?

Should Gail give up the Bar and step blindly into the azure yonder with him, or should she continue to pursue her meteoric career in London?

Or might it be time to admit that her career was no more meteoric than most young barristers' careers, and should she therefore get herself pregnant, which was what Perry was forever urging her to do?

And if Gail, either out of impishness or self-defence, had a habit of turning large questions into little ones, there remained no doubt that the two of them were separately and together at life's crossroads with some pretty heavy thinking to do, and that a holiday in Antigua looked like providing the ideal setting in which to do it.

*

Their flight was delayed, with the result that they didn't check into their hotel till after midnight. Ambrose, the resort's ubiquitous major-domo, showed them to their cabin. They rose late and by the time they had breakfasted on their balcony the sun was too hot for tennis. They swam on a three-quarters-empty beach, had a solitary lunch by the pool, made languorous love in the afternoon, and at six in the evening presented themselves at the pro's shop, rested, happy, and eager for a game.

Seen from a distance, the resort was no more than a cluster of white cottages scattered along a mile-wide horseshoe of proverbial talcum-powder sand. Two prom-ontories of rock strewn with scrub forest marked its extremities. Between them ran a coral reef and a line of fluorescent buoys to ward off nosy motor yachts. And on hidden terraces wrested from the hillside lay the resort's championship-standard tennis courts. Meagre stone steps wound between flowering shrubs to the front door of the pro's shop. Once through it, you entered tennis heaven, which was why Perry and Gail had chosen the place.

There were five courts and one centre court. Competition balls were kept in green refrigerators. Competition silver cups in glass cases bore the names of champions of yesteryear and Mark, the overweight Australian pro, was one of them.

'So what sort of level are we looking at here, if I may inquire?' he asked with heavy gentility, taking in without comment the quality of Perry's battle-scarred racquets, his thick white socks and worn but serviceable tennis shoes, and Gail's neckline.

For two people past their first youth but still in the bloom of life, Perry and Gail made a strikingly attractive pair. Nature had provided Gail with long, shapely legs and arms, high, small breasts, a lissom body, English skin, fine gold hair and a smile to light the gloomiest corners of life. Perry had a different sort of Englishness, being lank and at first sight dislocated, with a long neck and prominent Adam's apple. His stride was ungainly, he seemed to topple and his ears protruded. At his State school he had been awarded the nickname of Giraffe, until those unwise enough to use it learned their lesson. But with manhood he had acquired – unconsciously, which only made it more impressive – a precarious but undoubted grace. He had a mop of brown curls, a wide, freckled forehead, and large, bespectacled eyes that gave out an air of angelic perplexity.

Not trusting Perry to blow his own trumpet, and protective of him as always, Gail took the pro's question upon herself.

'Perry plays qualifiers for Queen's and he got into the main draw once too, didn't you? You actually made it to the Masters. And that was after breaking his leg skiing and not playing for six months,' she added proudly.

'And you, madam, if I may make so bold?' Mark the obsequious pro inquired, with a little more spin on the 'madam' than Gail cared for.

'I'm his rabbit,' she replied coolly, to which Perry said, 'Sheer bollocks,' and the Australian sucked his teeth, shook his heavy head in disbelief and thumbed the messy pages of his ledger.

'Well, I've got one pair here might do you good people. They're a sight too classy for my other guests, I'll tell you that right now. Not that I've a vast selection of humanity to choose from, frankly. Maybe you four should give each other a whirl.'

Their opponents turned out to be an Indian honeymoon couple from Mumbai. The centre court was taken, but court 1 was free. Soon a handful of passers-by and players from other courts had drifted over to watch the four of them warm up: fluid strokes from the baseline casually returned, passing shots that nobody ran for, the unanswered smash from the net. Perry and Gail won the toss, Perry gave first serve to Gail who twice double-faulted and they lost the game. The Indian bride followed her. Play remained sedate.

It wasn't till Perry began serving that the quality of his play became apparent. His first serve had height and power, and when it went in, there wasn't much anyone could do about it. He served four in a row. The crowd grew, the players were young and good-looking, the ball boys discovered new heights of energy. Towards the end of the first set, Mark the pro casually turned out to take a look, stayed for three games, then with a thoughtful frown returned to his shop.

After a long second set, the score was one set each. The

third and final set reached 4–3, with Perry and Gail having the edge. But if Gail was inclined to hold back, Perry was by now in full cry, and the match ended without the Indian couple winning another game.

The crowd drifted away. The four lingered to exchange compliments, fix a return and maybe catch a drink in the bar this evening? You bet. The Indians departed, leaving Perry and Gail to gather up their spare racquets and pull-overs.

As they did so, the Australian pro returned to the court bringing with him a muscular, erect, huge-chested, completely bald man wearing a diamond-encrusted gold Rolex wristwatch and grey tracksuit bottoms kept up by a drawstring tied in a bow at his midriff.

*

Why Perry should have spotted the bow at his midriff first and the rest of the man afterwards is easily explained. He was in the act of changing his elderly but comfortable tennis shoes for a pair of beach shoes with rope soles, and when he heard his name called he was still bent double. Therefore he lifted his long head slowly, the way tall, angular men do, and registered first a pair of leather espadrilles on small, almost feminine feet set piratically apart, then a couple of stocky, tracksuited calves in grey; and, coming up, the drawstring bow that kept the trousers aloft, double-tied as such a bow should be, given its considerable area of responsibility.

And above the bow-line, a belly of finest crimson cotton blouse encasing a massive torso that seemed not to know its stomach from its chest, and rising to an Eastern-style collar that if fastened would have made a cut-down version of a clerical dog-collar, except that there was no way it could have accommodated the muscular neck inside it.

And above the collar, tipped to one side in appeal, eyebrows raised in invitation, the creaseless face of a fifty-something man with soulful brown eyes beaming a dolphin smile at him. The absence of creases did not suggest inexperience, rather the opposite. It was a face that to Perry the outdoor adventurer seemed cast for life: the face, he told Gail much later, of a formed man, another definition that he aspired to himself, but for all his manly striving did not feel he had yet attained.

'Perry, allow me to present my good friend and patron, Mr *Dima* from Russia,' said Mark, injecting a ring of ceremony into his unctuous voice. 'Dima thought you played a pretty nifty match out there, am I right, sir? As a fine connoisseur of the game of tennis, he's been watching you highly appreciatively, I think I may say, Dima.'

'Wanna game?' Dima inquired, without taking his brown, apologetic gaze off Perry, who by now was hovering awkwardly at his full height.

'Hi,' said Perry, a bit breathlessly, and shoved out a sweated hand. Dima's was the hand of an artisan turned to fat, tattooed with a small star or asterisk on the second knuckle of the thumb. 'And this is Gail Perkins, my partner in crime,' he added, feeling a need to slow the pace a bit.

But before Dima could respond, Mark had let out a snort of sycophantic protest. '*Crime*, Perry?' he objected. 'Don't you believe this man, Gail! You did a *dandy* job out there, and that's straight. A couple of those backhand passing shots were up there with the gods, right, Dima? You said so yourself. We were watching from the shop. Closed circuit.'

'Mark says you play Queen's,' Dima said, the dolphin smile still directed at Perry, the voice thick and deep and guttural, and vaguely American.

'Well, that was a few years back now,' said Perry modestly, still buying time.

'Dima recently acquired Three Chimneys, right, Dima?' Mark said, as if this news somehow made the proposition of a game more compelling. 'Finest location this side of the island, right, Dima? Got great plans for it, we hear. And you two are in Captain Cook, I believe, one of the best cabins in the resort, in my opinion.'

They were.

'Well, there you go. You're neighbours, right, Dima? Three Chimneys is perched slap on the tip of the peninsula across the bay from you. The last major undeveloped property on the island but Dima's going to put that right, correct, sir? There's talk of a share issue with preference given to the inhabitants, which strikes me as a pretty decent idea. Meanwhile, you're indulging in a bit of rough-and-ready camping, I hear. Hosting a few like-minded friends and family. I admire that. We all do. For a person of your means, we call that true grit.'

'Wanna game?'

'Doubles?' Perry asked, extricating himself from the intensity of Dima's stare in order to peer dubiously at Gail.

But Mark, having achieved his bridgehead, pressed home his advantage:

'Thank you, Perry, no doubles for Dima, I'm afraid,' he interjected smartly. 'Our friend here plays singles only, correct, sir? You're a self-reliant man. You like to be responsible for your own errors, you told me once. Those were your very words to me not so long ago, and I've taken them to heart.'

Seeing that Perry was by now torn but also tempted, Gail rallied to his rescue:

'Don't worry about me, Perry. If you want to play a singles, go ahead, I'll be fine.'

'Perry, I do not believe you should be reluctant to take this gentleman on,' Mark insisted, ramming his case home. 'If I was a betting man, I'd be pushed which of you to favour, and that's a living fact.'

Was that a *limp* as Dima walked away? That slight dragging of the left foot? Or was it just the strain of carting that huge upper body around all day?

*

Was it here too that Perry first became aware of the two white men loitering at the gateway to the court with nothing to do? One with his hands loosely linked behind his back, the other with his arms folded across his chest? Both wearing trainers? The one blond and baby-faced, the other dark-haired and languid?

If so, then only subconsciously, he grudgingly maintained, to the man who called himself Luke, and the woman who called herself Yvonne, ten days later when the four of them were sitting at an oval dining table in the basement of a pretty terrace house in Bloomsbury.

They had been driven there in a black cab from Gail's flat in Primrose Hill by a large, genial man in a beret and an earring who said his name was Ollie. Luke had opened the door to them, Yvonne stood waiting behind Luke. In a thickly carpeted hall that smelled of fresh paint, Perry and Gail had their hands shaken, were courteously thanked by Luke for coming, and led downstairs to this converted basement with its table, six chairs and a kitchenette. Frosted windows, shaped in a half-moon and set high in the exterior wall, flickered to the shadowy feet of passing pedestrians on the pavement overhead.

They were next deprived of their mobiles and invited to sign a declaration under the Official Secrets Act. Gail the lawyer read the text and was outraged. 'Over my dead body,' she exclaimed, whereas Perry, with a mumbled 'what's the difference?', signed it impatiently away. After making a couple of deletions and inking in wording of her own, Gail signed under protest. The lighting in the basement consisted of a single wan lamp hanging over the table. The brick walls exuded a faint scent of old port wine.

Luke was courtly, clean-shaven, mid-forties and to Gail's eye too small. Male spies, she told herself with a false jocularity brought on by nervousness, should come a size larger. With his upright posture, sharp grey suit and little horns of greying hair flicked up above the ears, he reminded her more of a gentleman jockey on his best behaviour.

Yvonne on the other hand could not have been much older than Gail. She was prissy in Gail's initial perception of her, but in a blue-stocking sort of way beautiful. With her boring business suit, bobbed dark hair and no make-up, she looked older than she needed and, for a female spy, again in Gail's determinedly frivolous judgement, too earnest by half.

'So you didn't actually recognize them as *bodyguards*,' Luke suggested, his trim head eagerly switching between the two of them across the table. 'You didn't say to each other, when you were alone, for instance: "Hello, that was a bit odd, this fellow Dima, whoever he is, seems to have got himself some close protection," as it were?'

Is that really how Perry and I talk to each other? Gail thought. I didn't know.

'I *saw* the men, obviously,' Perry conceded. 'But if you're asking, did I make anything of them, the answer's no. Probably two fellows looking for a game, I thought, if I thought anything' – and plucking earnestly at his brow with his long fingers – 'I mean you don't just think *bodyguards* straight off, do you? Well, *you* people may. That's the world you live in, I assume. But if you're an ordinary citizen, it doesn't cross your mind.'

'So how about you, Gail?' Luke inquired with brisk solicitude. 'You're in and out of the law courts all day. You see the wicked world in its awful glory. Did *you* have your suspicions about them?'

'If I was aware of them at all, I probably thought they were a couple of blokes giving me the eye, so I ignored them,' Gail replied.

But this didn't do at all for Yvonne, the teacher's pet. 'But that *evening*, Gail, mulling over the day' – was she Scottish? Could well be, thought Gail, who prided herself on her mynah bird's ear for voices – 'did you *really* not make anything of two spare men hovering in attendance?'

'It was our first proper night in the hotel,' said Gail in a surge of nervous exasperation. 'Perry had booked us Candlelight Dinner on the Captain's Deck, OK? We had stars and a full moon and mating bullfrogs in full cry and a moonpath that ran practically to our table. Do you honestly suppose we spent the evening gazing into one another's eyes and talking about Dima's minders? I mean, give us a break' – and fearing she had sounded ruder than she intended – 'all right, *briefly*, we *did* talk about Dima. He's one of those people who stay on the retina. One minute he was our first Russian oligarch, the next Perry was flagellating himself for agreeing to play a singles with him and wanting to phone the pro and say the game was off. I told him I'd danced with men like Dima and they had the most amazing technique. That shut you up, didn't it, Perry, dear?'

Separated from each other by a gap as wide as the Atlantic Ocean they had recently crossed, yet thankful to be unburdening themselves before two professionally inquisitive listeners, Perry and Gail resumed their story.

*

Quarter to seven next morning. Mark was standing waiting for them at the top of the stone steps, clad in his best whites and clasping two cans of refrigerated tennis balls and a paper cup of coffee.

'I was dead afraid you guys would oversleep,' he said excitedly. 'Listen, we're fine, no bother. Gail, how are you today? Very peachy, if I may say so. After you, Perry, sir. My pleasure. What a day, eh? What a day.'

Perry led the way up the second flight to where the path turned left. As he turned with it he came face to face with the same two men in bomber jackets who had been loitering the previous evening. They were posted either side of the flowered archway that led like a bridal walk to the door of the centre court, which was a world to itself, enclosed on four sides by canvas screens and twenty-foot-high hedges of hibiscus.

Seeing the three of them approach, the fair-haired man with the baby face took a half-pace forward and with a mirthless smile opened out his hands in the classic gesture of one man about to frisk another. Puzzled, Perry came to a halt at his full height, not yet within frisking distance but a good six feet short, with Gail beside him. As the man took another step forward, Perry took one back, taking Gail with him and exclaiming, 'What the hell's all this?' – effectively to Mark, since neither the baby face nor his darker-haired colleague showed any sign of having heard, let alone understood, his question.

'Security, Perry,' Mark explained, pressing past Gail to murmur reassuringly into Perry's ear. 'Routine.'

Perry remained where he stood, craning his neck forward and sideways while he digested this advice.

'*Whose* security exactly? I don't get it. Do you?' – to Gail.

'Me neither,' she agreed.

'*Dima*'s security, Perry. Whose do you think? He's a high-roller. Big-time international. These boys are just obeying orders.'

'*Your* orders, Mark?' – turning and peering down on him accusingly through his spectacles.

'*Dima*'s orders, not mine, Perry, don't be stupid. They're Dima's boys. Go with him everywhere.'

Perry returned his attention to the blond bodyguard. 'Do you gents speak English, by any chance?' he asked. And when the baby face refused to alter in any way, except to harden: 'He appears to speak no English. Or hear it, apparently.'

'For Christ's sakes, Perry,' Mark pleaded, his beery complexion turning a darker shade of crimson. 'One little look in your bag, it's over. It's nothing personal. Routine, like I said. Same as any airport.'

Perry again applied to Gail: 'Do you have a view on this?'

'I certainly do.'

Perry tilted his head the other way. 'I need to get this absolutely right, you see, Mark,' he explained, asserting his pedagogic authority. 'My proposed tennis partner *Dima* wishes to make sure I'm not going to throw a bomb at him. Is that what these men are telling me?'

'It's a dangerous world out there, Perry. Perhaps you haven't heard about that, but the rest of us have, and we endeavour to live with it. With all due respect, I would strongly advise you to go with the flow.'

'Alternatively, I might be about to gun him down with my Kalashnikov,' Perry went on, raising his tennis bag an inch to indicate where he kept the weapon; at which the second man stepped out of the shadow of the bushes and positioned himself beside the first, but there was still not a legible facial expression between the two of them.

'You're making a mountain out of a molehill, if you don't mind my saying so, Mr Makepiece,' Mark protested, his hard-learned courtesy beginning to give way under the strain. 'There's a great game of tennis waiting in there. These boys are doing their duty, and they're doing it very politely and professionally in my judgement. Frankly I do not understand your problem, sir.'

'Ah. *Problem*,' Perry mused, picking on the word as a useful starting point for a group discussion with his students. 'Then allow me to explain my *problem*. Actually, come to think of it I have several problems. My first problem is, nobody looks inside my tennis bag without my permission, and in this case I do not grant my permission. And nobody looks inside this lady's either. Similar rules apply' – indicating Gail.

'Rigorously,' Gail confirmed.

'Second problem. If your friend Dima thinks I'm going to assassinate him, why does he ask me to play tennis with him?' Having allowed ample time for an answer and received none, beyond a voluble sucking of the teeth, he proceeded. 'And my third problem is, the proposal as it stands is one-sided. Have I asked to look inside Dima's bag? I have not. Neither do I wish to. Perhaps you'd explain that to him when you give him my apologies. Gail. What do you say we dig into that great big breakfast buffet we've paid for?'

'Good idea,' Gail agreed heartily. 'I didn't know I was so peckish.'

They turned and, ignoring the pro's entreaties, were heading back down the steps when the gate to the court flew open and Dima's bass voice drew them to a halt.

'Don't run away, Mr Perry Makepiece. You wanna blow my brains out, use a goddam tennis racquet.'

*

'So how about his age, Gail, would you say?' Yvonne the blue-stocking asked, making a prim note on the pad before her.

'Baby Face? Twenty-five max,' she replied, once again wishing she could find a mid-point in herself between flippancy and funk.

'Perry? How old?'

'Thirty.'

'Height?'

'Below average.'

If you're six foot two, Perry, darling, we're *all* below average, thought Gail.

'Five ten,' she said.

And his blond hair cut very short, they both agreed.

'And he wore a gold link bracelet,' she remembered, startling herself. 'I once had a client who wore one just like it. If he got in a tight corner, he was going to break up the links and buy his way out with them, one by one.'

*

With sensibly trimmed, unvarnished fingernails, Yvonne is sliding a wad of press photographs at them across the oval table. In the foreground, half a dozen burly young men in Armani-type suits are congratulating a victorious racehorse, champagne glasses aloft for the camera. In the background, advertisers' hoardings in Cyrillic and English. And far left, arms folded across his chest, the baby-faced bodyguard with his nearly shaven blond head. Unlike his three companions, he wears no dark glasses. But on his left wrist he wears a bracelet of gold links.

Perry looks a little smug. Gail feels a little sick.

2

It was unclear to Gail why she was doing the lion's share of the talking. While she spoke, she listened to her voice rattling back at her from the brick walls of the basement room, the way she did in the divorce courts where she currently had her professional being: now I'm doing righteous indignation, now I'm doing scathingly incredulous, now I sound like my absent bloody mother after the second gin and tonic.

And tonight, for all her best efforts to conceal it, she occasionally caught herself out in an unscripted quaver of fear. If her audience across the table couldn't hear it, she could. And if she wasn't mistaken, so could Perry beside her, because now and then his head would tilt towards her for no reason except to peer at her with anxious tenderness despite the three-thousand-mile gulf between them. And now and then he would go so far as to give her hand a cursory squeeze under the table before taking up the tale himself in the mistaken but pardonable belief that he was giving her feelings a rest, whereas all her feelings did was go underground, regroup, and come out fighting even harder the moment they got a chance.

*

If Perry and Gail didn't actually saunter into the centre court, they agreed, they took their time. There was the stroll down the flowered walkway with the bodyguards acting as guards of honour and Gail holding on to the brim of her broad sunhat and making her flimsy skirts swirl:

'I flounced around a bit,' she admitted.

'And *how*,' Perry agreed, to contained smiles from across the table.

There was shuffle at the entrance to the court when Perry appeared to have second thoughts, until it turned out that he was stepping back to let Gail go ahead of him, which she did with enough ladylike deliberation to suggest that, while the planned offence might not have taken place, neither had it gone away. And after Perry sloped Mark.

Dima stood centre court facing them, arms stretched wide in welcome. He was wearing a fluffy blue crew-neck top with full-length sleeves, and long black shorts that reached below his knees. A sunshade like a green beak stuck out from his bald head, which was already glistening in the early sun. Perry said he wondered whether Dima had oiled it. To complement his bejewelled Rolex, a gold trinket chain of vaguely mystical connotation adorned his huge neck: another glint, another distraction.

But Dima, to Gail's surprise, was not, at the moment of her entry, the main event, she said. Arranged on the spectators' stand behind him was a mixed – and to her eye *weird* – assembly of children and adults.

'Like a bunch of gloomy waxworks,' she protested. 'It wasn't just their overdressed presence at the ungodly hour of seven in the morning. It was their total silence and their sullenness. I took a seat on the empty bottom row and thought, Christ, what *is* this? A people's tribunal, or a church parade, or *what?*'

Even the children seemed estranged from each other. They caught her eye at once. Children did. She counted four of them.

'Two mopy-looking little girls of around five and seven in dark frocks and sunhats squeezed together beside a buxom black woman who was apparently some sort of minder,' she said, determined not to let her feelings run ahead of her before time. 'And two flaxen-haired teenaged boys in freckles and tennis gear. And all looking so down in the mouth you'd think they'd been kicked out of bed and dragged there as a punishment.'

As to the adults, they were just so *alien*, so oversized and so *other*, that they could have stepped out of a Charles Addams cartoon, she went on. And it wasn't only their town clothes or 1970s hairstyles. Or the fact that the women despite the heat were dressed for darkest winter. It was their shared gloom.

'Why's nobody talking?' she whispered to Mark, who had materialized uninvited in the seat beside her.

Mark shrugged. 'Russian.'

'But Russians talk all the time!'

Not these Russians, Mark said. Most of them had flown in over the last few days and still had to get used to being in the Caribbean.

'Something's happened up there,' he said, nodding across the bay. 'According to the buzz, they've got some big family powwow going on, not all of it friendly. Don't know what they do for their personal hygiene. Half the water system's shot.'

She picked out two fat men, one wearing a brown Homburg hat who was murmuring into a mobile, the other a tartan tam-o'-shanter with a red bobble on the top.

'Dima's cousins,' said Mark. 'Everybody's somebody's cousin round here. *Perm* they come from.'

'*Perm?*'

'Perm, Russia. Not the hairdo, darling. The town.'

Go up a level and there were the flaxen-haired boys, chewing gum as if they hated it. Dima's sons, twins, said Mark. And yes, now that Gail looked at them again, she saw a likeness: burly chests, straight backs, and droopy brown bedroom eyes that were already turning covetously towards her.

She took a quick, silent breath and released it. She was approaching what in legal discourse would have been her golden-bullet question, the one that was supposed to reduce the witness to instant rubble. So was she now going to reduce herself to rubble? But when she resumed speaking, she was gratified to hear no quaver in the voice coming back to her from the brick wall, no faltering or other telltale variation:

'And sitting demurely apart from everybody – *demonstratively* apart, one would almost have thought – there was this really rather stunning girl of fifteen or sixteen, with jet-black hair down to her shoulders and a school blouse and a navy blue school skirt over her knees, and she didn't seem to belong to *anyone*. So I asked Mark who she was. Naturally.'

Very naturally, she decided with relief, having listened to herself. Not a raised eyebrow round the table. Bravo, Gail.

'"Her name is Natasha," Mark informed me. "A flower waiting to be plucked," if I'd pardon his French. "Dima's daughter but not Tamara's. Apple of her father's eye."'

And what was the beautiful Natasha, daughter to Dima but not Tamara, doing at seven in the morning when she was supposed to be watching her father playing tennis? Gail asked her audience. Reading a leatherbound tome that she clutched like a shield of virtue on her lap.

'But absolutely drop-dead gorgeous,' Gail insisted. And as a throwaway: 'I mean, *seriously* beautiful.' And then she thought: Oh Christ, I'm beginning to sound like a dyke when all I want is to sound unconcerned.

But once again, neither Perry nor her inquisitors seemed to have noticed anything out of tune.

'So where do I find Tamara who isn't Natasha's mother?' she asked Mark, severely, taking the opportunity to edge away from him.

'Two rows up on your left. Very pious lady. Known locally as Mrs Nun.'

She did a careless swing round and homed in on a spectral woman draped from head to toe in black. Her hair, also black, was shot with white and bound in a bun. Her mouth, locked in a downward curve, seemed never to have smiled. She wore a mauve chiffon scarf.

'And on her bosom, this bishop-grade Orthodox gold cross with an extra bar,' Gail exclaimed. 'Hence the Mrs Nun, presumably.' And as an afterthought: 'But *wow*, did she have presence. A real scene-stealer' – shades of her acting parents – 'you really felt the willpower. Even Perry did.'

'Later,' Perry warned, avoiding her eye. 'They don't want us to be wise after the event.'

Well, I'm not allowed to be wise before it either, am I? she had half a mind to shoot back at him, but in her relief at having successfully negotiated the hurdle of Natasha, let it go.

Something about the immaculate little Luke was seriously distracting her: the way she kept catching his eye without meaning to; the way he caught hers. She'd wondered at first whether he was gay, until she spotted him eyeing the gap in her blouse where a button had opened. It's the loser's gallantry in him, she decided. It's his air of fighting to the last man, when the last man is himself. In the years when she was waiting for Perry, she'd slept with quite a few men, and there'd been one or two she'd said yes to out of kindness, simply to prove to them that they were better than they thought. Luke reminded her of them.

*

Limbering up for the match with Dima, Perry by contrast had scarcely bothered with the spectators at all, he claimed, talking intently to his big hands set flat on the table before him. He knew they were up there, he'd given them a wave of his racquet and got nothing back. Mainly, he was too busy putting in his contact lenses, tightening his shoelaces, smearing on sun cream, worrying about Mark giving Gail a hard time, and generally wondering how quickly he could win and get out. He was also being interrogated by his opponent, standing three feet away:

'They bother you?' Dima inquired in an earnest under-tone. 'My supporters' club? You want I tell them go home?'

'Of course not,' Perry replied, still smarting from his encounter with the bodyguards. 'They're your friends, presumably.'

'You British?'

'I am.'

'English British? Welsh? Scottish?'

'Just plain English, actually.'

Selecting a bench, Perry dumped his tennis bag on it, the one he hadn't let the bodyguards look inside, and yanked the zip. He fished a couple of sweatbands from his bag, one for his head, one for his wrist.

'You a priest?' Dima asked, with the same earnestness.

'Why? D'you need one?'

'Doctor? Some kinda medic?'

'Not a doctor either, I'm afraid.'

'Lawyer?'

'I just play tennis.'

'Banker?'

'God forbid,' Perry replied irritably, and fiddled with a battered sunhat before slinging it back into the bag.

But actually he felt more than irritable. He'd been rolled and didn't care for being rolled. Rolled by the pro and rolled by the bodyguards, if he'd let them. And all right he hadn't let them, but their presence on the court – they'd established themselves like line judges at either end – was quite enough to keep his anger going. More pertinently he had been rolled by Dima himself, and the fact that Dima had press-ganged a bunch of strays into turning out at seven in the morning to watch him win only added to the offence.

Dima had shoved a hand into the pocket of his long black tennis shorts and hauled out a John F. Kennedy silver half-dollar.

'Know something? My kids tell me I had some crook spike it for me so I win,' he confided, indicating with a nod of his bald head the two freckled boys in the stands. 'I win the toss, my own kids think I spike the goddam coin. You got kids?'

'No.'

'Want some?'

'Eventually.' *Mind your own bloody business*, in other words.

'Wanna call?'

Spike, Perry repeated to himself. Where did a man who spoke mangled English with a semi-Bronx accent get a word like *spike* from? He called tails, lost, and heard a honk of derision, the first sign of interest anybody on the spectators' stand had deigned to show. His tutorial eye fixed on Dima's two sons, smirking behind their hands. Dima glanced at the sun and chose the shaded end.

'What racquet you got there?' he asked, with a twinkle of his soulful brown eyes. 'Looks illegal. Never mind, I beat you anyway.' And as he set off down the court: 'That's some girl you got. Worth a lot of camels. You better marry her quick.'

And how in hell's name does the man know we're not married? Perry fumed.

*

Perry has served four aces in a row, just as he did against the Indian couple, but he's overhitting, knows it, doesn't give a damn. Replying to Dima's service, he does what he wouldn't dream of doing unless he was at the top of his game and playing a far weaker opponent: he stands forward, toes practically on the service line, taking the ball on the half-volley, angling it across court or flipping it just inside the tramlines to where the baby-faced bodyguard stands with his arms folded. But only for the first couple of serves, because Dima quickly gets wise to him and drives him back to the baseline where he belongs.

'So then I suppose I began to cool down a bit,' Perry conceded, grinning ruefully at his interlocutors and rubbing the back of his wrist across his mouth at the same time.

'Perry was a total bully,' Gail corrected him. 'And Dima was a natural. For his weight, height and age, amazing. Wasn't he, Perry? You said so yourself. You said he defied the laws of gravity. And really sporting with it. Sweet.'

'Didn't jump for the ball. Levitated,' Perry conceded. 'And yes, he was a good sport, couldn't ask for more. I thought we were going to be in for tantrums and line disputes. We didn't do any of that stuff. He was really good to play with. And cunning as a box of monkeys. Withheld his shots till the absolute last minute and beyond.'

'*And* he had a limp,' Gail put in excitedly. 'He played on the skew and he favoured his right leg, didn't he, Perry? And he was stiff as a ramrod. And he had a knee bandage. And he *still* levitated!'

'Yeah, well, I had to hold off a bit,' Perry admitted, clawing awkwardly at his brow. 'His grunts got a bit heavy on the ear as the game went by, frankly.'

But for all his grunting, Dima's inquisition of Perry between games continued unabated:

'You some big scientist? Blow the goddam world up, same way you serve?' he asked, helping himself to a gulp of iced water.

'Absolutely not.'

'Apparatchik?'

The guessing game had gone on long enough: 'Actually, I teach,' Perry said, peeling a banana.

'Teach like you teach *students*? Like a professor, you teach?'

'Correct. I teach students. But I'm not a professor.'

'Where?'

'Currently at Oxford.'

'Oxford *University*?'

'Got it.'

'What you teach?'

'English literature,' Perry replied, not particularly wishing, at that moment, to explain to a total stranger that his future was up for grabs.

But Dima's pleasure knew no bounds:

'Listen. You know *Jack London*? Number-one English writer?'

'Not personally.' It was a joke, but Dima didn't share it.

'You like the guy?'

'Admire him.'

'*Charlotte Brontë*? You like her too?'

'Very much.'

'*Somerset Maugham?*'

'Less, I'm afraid.'

'I got books by all those guys! Like hundreds! In Russian! Big bookshelves!'

'Great.'

'You read Dostoevsky? Lermontov? Tolstoy?'

'Of course.'

'I got them all. All the number-one guys. I got Pasternak. Know something? Pasternak wrote about my home town. Called it *Yuriatin*. That's *Perm*. Crazy fucker called it Yuriatin. I dunno why. Writers do that. All crazy. See my daughter up there? That's Natasha, don't give a shit about tennis, love books. Hey, Natasha! Say hello to the Professor here!'

After a delay to show that she is being intruded upon, Natasha distractedly raises her head and draws aside her hair long enough to allow Perry to be astonished by her beauty before she returns to her leatherbound tome.

'Embarrassed,' Dima explained. 'Don't wanna hear me yelling at her. See that book she reading? *Turgenev*. Number-one Russian guy. I buy it. She wanna book, I buy. OK, Professor. You serve.'

'From that moment on, I was Professor. I told him again and again I wasn't one, he wouldn't listen, so I gave up. Within a couple of days, half the hotel was calling me Professor. Which is pretty bloody odd when you've decided you're not even a don any more.'

Changing ends at 2–5 in Perry's favour, Perry is consoled to notice that Gail has parted company from the importunate Mark and is installed on the top bench between two little girls.

*

The game was settling to a decent rhythm, said Perry. Not the greatest match ever but – for as long as he lowered his play – fun and entertaining to watch, assuming anybody wanted to be entertained, which remained in question since, other than the twin boys, the spectators might have been attending a revivalist meeting. By *lowering his play*, he meant slowing it down a bit and taking the odd ball that was on its way to the tramlines, or returning a drive without looking too hard at where it had landed. But given that the gap between them – in age and skill and mobility, if Perry was honest – was by now obvious, his only concern was to make a game of it, leave Dima with his dignity, and enjoy a late breakfast with Gail on the Captain's Deck: or so he believed until, as they were again changing ends, Dima locked a hand on his arm and addressed him in an angry growl:

'You goddam pussied me, Professor.'

'I did *what*?'

'That long ball was out. You see it out, you play it in. You think I'm some kinda fat old bastard gonna drop dead you don't be sweet to him?'

'It was borderline.'

'I play retail, Professor. I want something, I goddam take it. Nobody pussy me, hear me? Wanna play for a thousand bucks? Make the game interesting?'

'No thanks.'

'Five thousand?'

Perry laughed and shook his head.

'You're chicken, right? You chicken, so you don't bet me.'

'I suppose that must be it,' Perry agreed, still feeling the imprint of Dima's hand on his upper left arm.

*

'Advantage Great Britain!'

The cry resonates over the court and dies. The twins break out in nervous laughter, waiting for the aftershock. Until now Dima has tolerated their occasional bursts of high spirits. No longer. Laying his racquet on the bench, he pads up the steps of the spectators' stand and, reaching the two boys, presses a forefinger to the tip of each of their noses.

'You want I take my belt and beat the shit outta you?' he inquires in English, presumably for the benefit of Perry and Gail, for why else would he not address them in Russian?

To which one of the boys replies in better English than his father's: 'You're not wearing a belt, Papa.'

That does it. Dima smacks the nearer son so hard across the face that he spins halfway round on the bench before his legs stop him. The first smack is followed by a second just as loud, delivered to the other son with the same hand, reminding Gail of walking with her socially ambitious elder brother when he's out pheasant shooting with his rich friends, an activity she abhors, and the brother scores what he calls a left and a right, meaning one dead pheasant to each gun barrel.

'What got me was that they didn't even turn their heads away. They just sat there and took it,' said Perry, the schoolteachers' son.

But the strangest thing, Gail insisted, was how amicably the conversation was resumed:

'You wanna tennis lesson with Mark after? Or you wanna go home get religion from your mother?'

'Lesson, please, Papa,' says one of the two boys.

'Then don't you make any more ra-ra, or you don't get no Kobe beef tonight. You wanna eat Kobe beef tonight?'

'Sure, Papa.'

'You, Viktor?'

'Sure, Papa.'

'You wanna clap, you clap the Professor there, not your no-good bum father. Come here.'

A fervent bear-hug for each boy, and the match proceeds without further episode to its inevitable end.

*

In defeat, Dima's bearing is embarrassingly fulsome. He's not merely gracious, he's moved to tears of admiration and gratitude. First he must press Perry into his great chest, which Perry swears is made of horn, for the three-times Russian embrace. The tears meanwhile are rolling down his cheeks, and consequently Perry's neck.

'You're a goddam fair-play English, hear me, Professor? You're a goddam English gentleman like in books. I love you, hear me? Gail, come over here.' For Gail the embrace is even more reverent – and cautious, for which she is grateful. 'You take care this stupid fuck, hear me? He can't play tennis no good, but I swear to God he's some kinda goddam gentleman. He's the Professor of *fair play*, hear me?' – repeating the mantra as if he has just invented it.

He swings away to bark irritably into a mobile that the baby-faced bodyguard is holding out to him.

*

The spectators file slowly out of the court. The little girls need hugs from Gail. Gail is happy to oblige. One of Dima's sons drawls 'cool play, man' in American English as he stalks past Perry on his way to his lesson, his cheek still scarlet from the slap. The beautiful Natasha attaches herself to the procession, leatherbound tome in hand. Her thumb marks the place where her reading was disturbed. Bringing up the rear comes Tamara on Dima's arm, her bishop-grade Orthodox cross glinting in the risen sunshine. In the aftermath of the game, Dima's limp is more pronounced. As he walks, he leans back, chin thrust forward, shoulders squared to the enemy. The bodyguards shepherd the group down the winding stone path. Three black-windowed people carriers wait behind the hotel to take them home. Mark the pro is last to leave.

'Great play, sir!' – clapping Perry on the shoulder. 'Fine court craft. A little ragged on the backhands there, if I may make so bold. Maybe we should do a little work on them?'

Side by side, Gail and Perry watch speechless as the cortège bumps its way along the potholed spine road and vanishes into the cedar trees that shelter the house called Three Chimneys from prying eyes.

*

Luke looks up from the notes he has been taking. As if to order, Yvonne does the same. Both are smiling. Gail is trying to avoid Luke's eye, but Luke is staring straight at her so she can't.

'So, Gail,' he says briskly. 'Your turn again, if we may. Mark was a pest. All the same, he does seem to have been quite a mine of information. What extra nuggets can you offer us about the Dima household?' – then gives a flick of both little hands at once, as if urging his horse on to greater things.

Gail glances at Perry, she is not sure what for. Perry does not return her glance.

'He was just so *snaky*,' she complains, using Mark, rather than Luke, as the object of her disfavour, and wrinkles up her face to show how the bad taste lingers.

*

Mark had barely sat beside her on the bottom bench, she began, before he started banging on about what an important millionaire his Russian friend Dima was. According to Mark, Three Chimneys was only one of his several properties. He'd got another in Madeira, another in Sochi on the Black Sea.

'And a house outside Berne,' she went on, 'where his

34

business is based. But he's peripatetic. Part of the year he's in Paris, part Rome, part Moscow, according to Mark' – and watched as Yvonne made another note. 'But home, as far as the kids are concerned, is Switzerland and school is some millionaire internat establishment in the mountains. 'He talks about *the company*. Mark assumes he owns it. There's a company registered in Cyprus. And banks. Several banks. Banking's the big one. That was what brought him to the island in the first place. Antigua currently boasts four Russian banks, by Mark's count, plus one Ukrainian. They're just brass plates in shopping malls and a phone on some lawyer's desk. Dima's one of the brass plates. When he bought Three Chimneys, that was for cash too. Not suitcases of it but laundry baskets, somewhat ominously, lent to him by the hotel, according to Mark. And twenty-dollar bills, not fifties. Fifties are too dicey. He bought the house, and a run-down sugar mill, and the peninsula they stand on.'

'Did Mark mention a figure?' – Luke is back.

'Six million US. And the tennis wasn't pure pleasure either. Or not to begin with,' she continued, surprised by how much she remembered of the awful Mark's monologue. 'Tennis in Russia is a major status symbol. If a Russian tells you he plays tennis, he's telling you he's stinking rich. Thanks to Mark's brilliant tuition, Dima went back to Moscow and won a cup and everybody gasped. But Mark isn't allowed to tell that story, because Dima prides himself on being self-made. It was only because Mark trusted me so completely that he felt able to make an exception. And if I'd like to pop round to his shop some time, he had a dandy little room upstairs where we could continue our conversation.'

Luke and Yvonne offered sympathetic smiles. Perry offered no smile at all.

'And Tamara?' Luke asked.

'*God-smacked* he called her. And barking mad with it, according to the islanders. Doesn't swim, doesn't go down to the beach, doesn't play tennis, doesn't talk to her own children except about God, ignores Natasha completely, barely talks to the natives except for Elspeth, wife of Ambrose, front-of-house manager. Elspeth works in a travel agency, but if the family's around she drops everything and helps out. Apparently one of the maids borrowed some of Tamara's jewellery for a dance not long ago. Tamara caught her before she could put it back and bit her hand so hard she had to have twelve stitches in it. Mark said if it had been him he'd have had an injection for rabies as well.'

'So now tell us about the little girls who came and sat beside you, please, Gail,' Luke suggested.

*

Yvonne was leading the case for the prosecution, Luke was playing her junior, and Gail was in the box trying to keep her temper, which was what she told her witnesses to do on pain of excommunication.

'So were the girls already ensconced up there, Gail, or did they come skipping up to you the moment they saw the pretty lady all on her own?' Yvonne asked, putting her pencil to her mouth while she studied her notes.

'They walked up the steps and sat one either side of me. And they didn't skip. They walked.'

'Smiling? Laughing? Being scamps?'

'Not a smile between them. Not a half of one.'

'Had the girls, in your opinion, been dispatched to you by whoever was looking after them?'

'They came strictly of their own accord. In my opinion.'

'You're *sure* of that?' – becoming more Scottish and persistent.

'I saw the whole thing happen. Mark had made a pass at me that I didn't need, so I stomped up to the top bench to get as far away from him as I could. Nobody on the top bench except me.'

'So where were the wee girls located at this point? Below you? Along the row from you? *Where*, please?'

Gail took a breath to control herself, then spoke with deliberation:

'The *wee girls* were sitting on the second tier, with Elspeth. The older one turned round and looked up at me, then she spoke to Elspeth. And no, I didn't hear what she said. Elspeth turned and looked at me, and nodded yes to the older girl. The two girls had a consultation, stood up, and came *walking* up the steps. Slowly.'

'Don't push her around,' said Perry.

*

Gail's testimony has become evasive. Or so it sounds to her lawyer's ear, and no doubt to Yvonne's also. Yes, the girls arrived in front of her. The elder girl dropped a bob that she must have learned at dancing lessons, and asked in very serious English with only a slight foreign accent: 'May we sit with you, please, miss?' So Gail laughed and said, 'You may indeed, miss,' and they sat down either side of her, still without smiling.

'I asked the elder girl her name. I whispered, because

everybody was being so quiet. She said, "Katya," and I said, "What's your sister's name?" and she said, "Irina." And Irina turned and stared at me as if I was – well, intruding really – I just couldn't understand the hostility. I said, "Are your mummy and daddy here?" To both of them. Katya gave a really vehement shake of her head. Irina didn't say anything at all. We sat still for a while. A *long* while, for children. And I was thinking: maybe they've been told they mustn't speak at tennis matches. Or they mustn't talk to strangers. Or maybe that's all the English they know, or maybe they're autistic, or handicapped in some way.'

She pauses, hoping for encouragement or a question, but sees only four waiting eyes and Perry at her side with his head tipped towards the brick walls that smell of her late father's drinking habits. She takes a mental deep breath and plunges:

'There was a game change. So I tried again: where do you go to school, Katya? Katya shakes her head, Irina shakes hers. No school? Or just none at the moment? None at the moment, apparently. They'd been going to a British International School in Rome, but they don't go there any more. No reason given, none asked for. I didn't want to be pushy, but I had a bad feeling I couldn't pin down. So do they live in Rome? Not any more. Katya again. So Rome's where you learned your excellent English? Yes. At International School they could choose English or Italian. English was better. I point to Dima's two boys. Are those your brothers? More shakes. Cousins? Yes, sort of cousins. Only sort of? Yes. Do they go to International School too? Yes, but in Switzerland, not Rome. And the beautiful girl who lives inside a book, I say, is *she* a cousin? Answer from Katya, squeezed out of her like a confession: Natasha is our cousin but only sort of – again. And still no smile from either of them. But Katya is stroking my silk outfit. As if she's never felt silk before.'

Gail takes a breath. This is nothing, she is telling herself. This is the hors d'oeuvre. Wait till next day for the full five-course horror story. Wait till I'm allowed to be wise after the event.

'And when she's stroked the silk enough, she puts her head against my arm and leaves it there and shuts her eyes. And that's the end of our social exchange for maybe five minutes, except that Irina on the other side of me has taken her cue from Katya and commandeered my hand. She's got these sharp, crabby little claws, and she's really fastening on to me. Then she presses my hand against her forehead and rolls her face round it as if she wants me to know she's got a temperature, except that her cheeks are wet and I realize she's been crying. Then she gives me my hand back, and Katya says, "She cries sometimes. It is normal." Which is when the game ends and Elspeth comes scuttling up the steps to fetch them, by which time I want to wrap Irina up in my sarong and take her home with me, preferably with her sister as well, but since I can't do any of that, and have no idea why she's upset, and don't know either of them from Adam – well, Eve – end of story.'

*

But it isn't the end of the story. Not in Antigua. The story is running beautifully. Perry Makepiece and Gail Perkins are still having the happiest holiday of their lifetimes, just as they had promised themselves back in November. To remind herself of their happiness, Gail plays the uncensored version to herself:

Ten a.m. approx., tennis over, return to cabin for Perry to shower.

Make love, beautifully as ever, we can still do that. Perry can never do anything by halves. All his powers of concentration must be focused on one thing at a time.

Midday or later. Miss breakfast buffet for operational reasons (above), swim in sea, lunch by pool, return to beach because Perry needs to beat me at shuffle-board.

Four p.m. approx. Return to cabin with Perry victorious – why doesn't he let a girl win even *once?* – doze, read, more love, doze again, lose sense of time. Polish off Chardonnay from minibar while reclining on balcony in bathrobes.

Eight p.m. approx. Decide we're too lazy to dress, order supper in cabin.

Still on our once-in-a-lifetime holiday. Still in Eden, munching the bloody apple.

Nine p.m. approx. Supper arrives, wheeled in not by any old room-service waiter but the venerable Ambrose himself who, in addition to the bottle of Californian plonk we have ordered, brings us a frosted bottle of vintage Krug champagne in a silver ice bucket, priced on the wine list at $380 plus tax, which he proceeds to set out for us, together with two frosted glasses, a plate of very yummy-looking canapés, two damask napkins and a prepared speech, which he intones at full volume with his chest out and his hands pressed to his sides like a court copper.

'This very fine bottle of champagne comes to you folk courtesy of the one and only Mr Dima *himself.* Mr Dima, he says to thank you for' – plucking a note from his shirt pocket together with a pair of reading spectacles – 'he says, and I quote: "Professor, I thanks you very heartily for a fine lesson in the great art of fair-play tennis and being an English gentleman. I also thanks you for saving me five thousand dollars of gamble." Plus his compliments to the highly beautiful Miss Gail, and that's his message.'

We drink a couple of glasses of the Krug and agree to finish the rest in bed.

*

'What's Kobe beef?' Perry asks me, sometime during an eventful night.

'Ever rubbed a girl's tummy?' I ask him.

'Wouldn't dream of it,' Perry says, doing just that.

'Virgin cows,' I tell him. 'Reared on sake and best beer. Kobe cattle have their tummies massaged every night till they're ready for the chop. Plus they're prime intellectual property,' I add, which is also true, but I'm not sure he's listening any more. 'Our Chambers fought a lawsuit for them and won hooves down.'

Falling asleep, I have a prophetic dream that I am in Russia, and bad things are happening to small children in wartime black and white.

3

Gail's sky is darkening, and so also is the basement room. With the dying of the light, the wan ceiling lamp seems to burn more glumly over the table, and the brick walls have turned to black. Above them in the street the rumble of traffic has become sporadic. So have the shadowed feet trotting past the frosted half-moon windows. Big, genial Ollie with his one earring but without his beret has bustled in with four cups of tea and a plate of digestive biscuits and disappeared.

Although this is the same Ollie who picked them up from Gail's flat in a black cab earlier this evening, it is by now acknowledged that he is not a *real* cab driver, despite the licence badge he sports on his ample chest. Ollie, according to Luke, 'keeps us all on the straight and narrow', but Gail doesn't buy this. A blue-stocking Scottish Calvinist is not in need of moral guidance, and for a gentleman jockey with a wandering eye and an armoury of upper-class charm, it's way too late.

Besides, Ollie has too much behind the eyes for his menial role, in Gail's opinion. She's also puzzled about his earring, whether it's a sex-signal or just a lark. She's also puzzled about his voice. When she first heard it over the house entryphone in Primrose Hill, it was straight cockney. As he chatted to them through the partition about the dismal weather we were having for May – after that lovely April, and dear me how was the blossom ever going to recover from last night's deluge? – she detected foreign underlays and his syntax began to break up. So what was his home tongue? Greek? Turkish? Hebrew? Or is the voice, like the single earring, an act he puts on to bamboozle us punters?

She wishes she'd never signed that bloody Declaration. She wishes Perry hadn't. Perry wasn't *signing* when he signed that form, he was *joining*.

*

Friday was the last day of the Indian honeymooners' holiday, Perry is saying. They had therefore agreed to play the best of five sets instead of the usual three, and in consequence again missed breakfast.

'So we settled for a swim in the sea, and maybe brunch if we were hungry. We picked the busy end of the beach. It wasn't the bit we normally used, but we had our eye on the Shipwreck Bar.'

His efficient tone, Gail recognizes. Perry the English tutor. Facts and short sentences. No abstract concepts. Let the story tell itself. They chose a sunshade, he is saying. They laid out their gear. They were heading for the water when a people carrier with blackened windows came to a halt in the NO PARKING bay. From it emerged first the baby-faced bodyguard, next the tam-o'-shanter man from the tennis match, now wearing shorts and a yellow buckskin waistcoat, but the tam-o'-shanter still firmly *in situ*. Then Elspeth, wife to Ambrose, and after her an inflated rubber

43

crocodile with its jaws open, followed by Katya – Perry says, parading his fabled powers of recall. And after Katya, exit an enormous red bouncy ball with a smiley face and grab handles which turned out to be the property of Irina, also dressed for the beach.

And finally Natasha emerged, he says, which is time for Gail to cut in. *Natasha is my business, not yours*.

'But only after a stage delay, and just when we're thinking there's no one left in the people carrier,' says Gail. 'Dressed to kill in a Hakka-style lampshade hat and a cheongsam dress with toggle buttons and Grecian sandals cross-tied round her ankles, and she's carting her leatherbound tome. After picking her way *delicately* over the sand for all eyes to see, she then settles herself languidly under the furthest sunshade of the row and begins her *terribly serious* reading. Right, Perry?'

'If you say so,' says Perry awkwardly, and jerks himself back in his chair as if to distance himself from her.

'I do say so. But the truly *eerie* thing, the really *spooky* thing,' she goes on stridently, now that Natasha is safely out of the way again, 'was that each member of the party, big or small, knew *exactly* where to go and what to do as soon as they hit the beach.'

The baby-faced bodyguard headed straight for the Shipwreck Bar, and ordered a can of root beer which he made last for the next two hours, she says, clinging to the initiative. The tam-o'-shanter man, despite his bulk – a *cousin*, according to Mark, one of the many *cousins* from Perm in Russia, the city not the hairdo – scaled the rickety steps of a lifeguard's lookout, hauled a rubber ring from his buckskin waistcoat, blew it up and sat on it, presumably for his piles. The two little girls, followed at a distance by the ample Elspeth with her bulging basket, came walking down the sand slope to where Perry and Gail had made their camp, bearing their crocodile and bouncy ball.

'*Walking* again,' Gail overemphasizes for Yvonne's benefit. 'Not hopping, skipping or yelling. *Walking*, and looking as tight-lipped and bug-eyed as they had at the tennis court. Irina with her thumb in her mouth and a big scowl, Katya's voice about as friendly as a speaking clock: "Will you swim with us, please, Miss Gail?" So *I* said – hoping to loosen things up a bit, I suppose – "Miss Katya, Mr Perry and I will be most honoured to swim with you." So we swam. Didn't we?' – to Perry, who having nodded his assent, again insisted on putting his hand on hers, either in a gesture of support or to steady her down, she wasn't sure which, but the result either way was the same; she was forced to close her eyes and wait several seconds before she was ready to resume, which she did in another gush.

'It was a *total* set-up. *We* knew it was a set-up. The *children* knew it was a set-up. But if ever two girls needed a splash-about with a crocodile and a bouncing ball, these two did, right, Perry?'

'Absolutely,' says Perry enthusiastically.

'So Irina battened on to my hand and practically *frog-marched* me into the water. Katya and Perry came after us with the crocodile. And all the time I was thinking: where on earth are their parents and why are we doing this instead of them? I didn't ask Katya outright. I suppose I had some sort of premonition it might be a bad question. A divorce situation, something like that. So I asked her who the nice gentleman in the hat was, the one sitting on the ladder?

Uncle Vanya, says Katya. Great, I say, who's Uncle Vanya? Answer, just an uncle. From Perm? Yes, from Perm. No further explanation offered. Like: we don't go to school in Rome any more. Have I foot-faulted yet, Perry?'

'Not at all.'

'Then I'll continue.'

*

For a while, the sun and sea do their job, she goes on: 'The girls splash and leap around and Perry is a *complete riot* as mighty Poseidon rising from the deep and making his sea-monster noises – no, honestly, you *were*, Perry, you were *marvellous*, admit it.'

Exhausted, they stagger ashore, the girls to be dried, dressed and sun-creamed by Elspeth.

'But within literally *seconds* they're back, squatting on the edge of my towel. And one *look* at their faces tells me the gloomy shadows are still there, they've just been hiding. Right, I think: ice creams and fizzies. Perry, this is man's work, I tell him, do your duty. Right, Perry?'

Fizzies? she repeats to herself. Why am I sounding like my bloody mother again? Because I'm another failed actress with a six-acre voice that gets louder the longer I speak.

'Right,' Perry agrees belatedly.

'And off he strides to get them, don't you? Caramel-and-nut cones for everybody, pineapple juice for the girls. But when Perry comes to *sign* for them, the barman tells him everything is paid for. Who by?' – she gallops on with the same false gaiety – 'By Vanya! By the ever-so-kind fat uncle in the tam-o'-shanter stuck up on the ladder. But *Perry*, being Perry, you can't be doing with this, can you?'

Awkward shake of the elongated head to say he's out of earshot on the cliff face, but has got the message.

'He's pathologically uncomfortable freeloading on someone else's tab, aren't you? And this is someone you don't even *know*. So up the ladder Perry goes to tell Uncle Vanya, very kind of him and all that, but he prefers to pay his own way.'

She dries. With none of her desperate levity, Perry takes up the story for her:

'I went up the ladder where Vanya was sitting on his rubber ring. I ducked under the sunshade to say my piece and found myself staring at a very large black pistol butt sticking out from under his gut. He'd unbuttoned his buckskin waistcoat in the heat, and there it was, bright as day. I don't know guns, thank God. Don't want to. You people do, no doubt. This one was family size,' he says regretfully, and an eloquent silence falls as he shoots a plaintive glance at Gail and receives no answering look for his pains.

*

'And you didn't think to comment, Perry?' deft little Luke suggests, ever the one to paper over gaps. 'On the gun, I mean.'

'No I did not. I reckoned he hadn't seen that I'd noticed, so I decided it was tactically sensible of me not to have noticed either. I thanked him for the ice cream and went back down the ladder to where Gail was chatting to the girls.'

Luke reflects on this in a rather intense way. Something seems to have got under his skin. Could it perhaps be the tricky question of spy's etiquette that was bothering him? What do you do if you see a chap's gun sticking out of his waistcoat and you don't know him very well? Tell him it's showing, or just ignore it? Like when someone you don't know very well hasn't done their zip up.

The Scottish blue-stocking Yvonne decides to help Luke out of his dilemma:

'In *English*, Perry?' she asks severely. 'You thanked him in *English*, I take it. Did he *reply* in English at all?'

'He didn't reply in any language. However, I did notice that he was wearing a black mourning button pinned to his waistcoat, something I hadn't seen for a long time. And *you* didn't know they existed, did you?' he demanded accusingly.

Puzzled by his aggression, Gail shakes her head. It's true, Perry. Guilty as charged. I didn't know about mourning buttons and now I do, so you can get on with the story, can't you?

'And it didn't occur to you to alert the hotel, for instance, Perry?' Luke asks doggedly. '"There's a Russian with a family-size gun sitting up in the lifeguard's lookout"?'

'Many possibilities suggested themselves, Luke, and that was no doubt one of them,' Perry replies, his bout of aggression not yet run out. 'But what on earth was the hotel supposed to do? There was every indication that, if Dima didn't actually own the place, he had it in his pocket. Anyway, we had the children to consider: whether it was right to make a fuss in front of everyone. We decided it wasn't.'

'And the island's police authorities? You didn't think of them?' – Luke again.

'We had four more days. We didn't intend to spend them making dramatic statements to the police about goings-on they were probably up to their necks in anyway.'

'And that was a *joint* decision?'

'It was an executive decision. Mine. I wasn't about to march up to Gail and say, "Vanya's got a gun stuck in his belt, d'you think we should tell the police?" – least of all in front of the girls. Once we were alone and I'd got my bearings, I told her what I'd seen. We talked it through rationally, and that was the decision we came up with: no action.'

Overtaken by an involuntary rush of loving support, Gail backs him up with her Counsel's Opinion: 'Maybe Vanya had a perfectly good local permit to carry the gun. What did Perry know? Maybe Vanya didn't *need* a permit. Maybe the police had given him the gun in the first place. We weren't exactly up in Antiguan gun law, were we, Perry, either of us?'

She half expects Yvonne to raise a contrary point of law, but Yvonne's too busy consulting her copy of the offending document in its buff folder:

'Could I trouble the two of you for a description of this *Uncle Vanya*, please?' she asks in an aggression-free voice.

'Pockmarked,' says Gail promptly, again dazzled by how it was all there before her in her memory. Fifty-odd. Pumice-stone cheeks. A drinker's paunch. She thought she'd seen him drinking surreptitiously from a flask at the tennis, but couldn't be sure.

'Rings on each finger of his right hand,' says Perry when it's his turn. 'Seen collectively, a knuckleduster. Black, scarecrow hair, jutting out from the back of his hat, but I suspect he was bald on top and that was why he wore the tam-o'-shanter. Lot of blubber on him.'

And yes, Yvonne, that's him, they agree in a shared murmur, their heads touching and the electricity flying between them as they gaze at the full-plate photograph she has slipped under their noses. Yes, that's Vanya from Perm, second from left of four merry, overweight white men sitting in a nightclub surrounded by hookers and paper streamers and bottles of champagne on New Year's Eve 2008 in God-knows-where.

*

Gail needs the loo. Yvonne leads her up the narrow basement stairs to the mysteriously plush ground floor. Genial Ollie without his beret is stretched out in a winged armchair, deep in a newspaper. It's not your ordinary sort of paper, being printed in Cyrillic. Gail thinks she deciphers *Novaya Gazeta* but can't be certain and doesn't want to do him the favour of asking. Yvonne waits while Gail pees. The loo is fancy, with pretty hand towels, scented soap and hunting prints of Jorrocks on expensive wallpaper. They return downstairs. Perry remains stooped over his hands, but this time the palms are upward so he looks as though he's reading two fortunes at once.

'So, Gail,' says little Luke smartly. 'Your shout again, I think.'

Not a shout, actually, Luke. A fucking scream, one that's been banking up in me for some while now, as I think you may have noticed in the course of resting your eyes on me a little more frequently than the spies' *Handbook of Inter-Gender Etiquette* considers strictly necessary.

*

'I simply had no idea,' she begins, talking straight ahead of her, but favouring Yvonne over Luke. 'I just blundered in. I should have realized. I didn't.'

'You've absolutely nothing to reproach yourself with,' Perry retorts hotly from her side. 'Nobody told you, nobody gave you the slightest warning. If anyone was to blame, Dima's lot were.'

Gail is not to be consoled. She is a lawyer in a brick-lined wine cellar at dead of night, assembling the case against the accused, and the accused is herself. She is lying face down on a beach in Antigua under a sunshade in mid-afternoon with her top undone and two small girls squatting beside her and Perry is stretched out on her other side wearing his schoolboy shorts and a pair of his late father's National Health spectacles fitted with his own prescription sunglass lenses.

The girls have eaten their free ice creams and drunk their free fruit juice. Uncle Vanya from Perm is up his ladder with the family-sized pistol in his belt and Natasha – whose name is a challenge to Gail every time she approaches it; she has to gather herself together and make a clean jump of it like horse-riding at school – *Natasha* is lying the other end of the beach in splendid isolation. Elspeth meanwhile has withdrawn to a safe distance. Perhaps she knows what's about to happen. With the hindsight she is not allowed to indulge, Gail thinks so.

The shadows are back in the girls' faces, she notices. The professional in her fears they may share a bad secret. With the stuff she has to listen to in court most days of the week, that's what bothers her, that's what drives her curiosity: children who don't chatter and aren't naughty. Children who don't realize they're victims. Children who can't look you in the eye. Children who blame themselves for the things adults do to them.

'I ask questions for a *living*,' she protests. She is saying everything to Yvonne now. Luke is a blur and Perry is outside her frame, relegated there deliberately. 'I've done family courts, I've had children in the witness box. What we do *in* our work, we do *out of* our work. We're not two people. We're just us.'

In a gesture intended to ease her stress rather than his own, Perry cranes his body upwards and gives a swimmer's stretch of his long arms, but Gail's stress isn't eased.

'So the first thing I said to them was: tell me some more about Uncle Vanya. They'd been so cryptic about him I thought he might be a bad uncle. "Uncle Vanya plays the balalaika with us, we love him very much, and he's funny when he gets drunk." That's Irina speaking. She's decided to be more forthcoming than her big sister. But I'm thinking: a drunken uncle who plays music to them, what else does he play?'

'And the language spoken still *English*, we take it,' Yvonne asks, in her pursuit of every last detail. But gently now, woman to woman. 'We're not into basic French or anything?'

'English was virtually their first language. *Internat* American English with a slight *Italian* accent. So then I asked, is Vanya a real uncle or just an honorary one? Answer: Vanya is our mother's brother and he used to be married to Aunt Raïsa who lives in Sochi with another husband nobody likes. We're doing family tree now, which is great by me. Tamara is Dima's wife, and she's very strict, and she prays a lot because she's holy and she is kind to have us. *Kind? Have us how?* And then I say – I'm being a really clever lawyer now, asking the tangential questions, not the in-your-face ones – is Dima *kind* to Tamara? Is Dima *kind* to his boys?

Meaning: is Dima a bit too kind to you? And Katya says, yes, Dima is kind to Tamara because he is her husband and her sister's dead, and Dima is kind to Natasha because he's her father and her mother's dead, and to his sons because he's their father. Which opens the door to the question I *really* want to ask, and I put it to Katya because she's older: So who's *your* father, Katya? And Katya says, he's dead. And Irina joins in and says, so's our mother. They're both dead. I do a kind of "oh really?" and when they just look at me, I say, I'm very sad for you. How long have they been dead? I wasn't even sure I believed them. There was a bit of me that was still hoping they were pulling some gruesome children's trick. By now it's Irina doing the talking and Katya who's gone into a kind of trance. So have I, but that's beside the point. They died on *Wednesday*, Irina says. A lot of emphasis on the day. As if the day's to blame. *Wednesday* was when they died, whenever *Wednesday* was. So I say – it just gets worse and worse – you mean *last* Wednesday? And Irina says, yes, Wednesday a week ago, the 29th of April: very precisely, making sure I get it right. So Wednesday last week and something about a car smash, and I just sit there staring at them, and Irina takes my hand and pats it and Katya puts her head in my lap, and Perry who I've completely forgotten about wraps his arm round me, and I'm the only person crying.'

*

Gail has wedged the knuckle of her forefinger between her teeth, which is another thing she does in court to protect herself against unprofessional emotions.

'Talking it over with Perry in the cabin afterwards,

everything fell more or less into place,' she says, raising her voice to give it an even more detached ring, but still keeping Perry out of her eye-line, and meanwhile trying to make it sound natural that two little girls should be having a jolly time beside the seaside a few days after their parents have been slaughtered in a car accident.

'Their parents died on the *Wednesday*. The tennis match took place on the *following* Wednesday. Ergo, the household had mourned for a week and Dima had reckoned it was time to get them out into the fresh air: so all snap out of it and who's for tennis? If they were Jewish, which for all we knew they may have been, or some of them were, or the dead parents were, then maybe they'd been sitting shiva, and by the Wednesday they're supposed to be getting back into life. It hardly meshed with Tamara being Christian-holy and wearing a cross, but we weren't talking religious consistency, not with that crowd, and Tamara was widely held to be weird.'

Yvonne again, respectful but firm: 'I hate to press, Gail, but Irina said it was a *car smash*. Now is that *all* she said? Did she say, for instance, where the smash had happened?'

'Outside Moscow somewhere. Vague. She blamed the roads. The roads had too many holes in them. Everyone drove in the middle of the road to avoid the holes, so naturally the cars hit each other.'

'Was there any talk of hospitalization? Or did Mummy and Daddy die instantly? Was that the story?'

'Dead on impact. "A great big lorry came rushing down the middle of the road and killed them dead."'

'Any other casualties at all, apart from the two parents?'

'I wasn't being awfully good at the follow-up questions, I'm afraid' – feeling herself start to waver.

'But was there a driver, for instance? If the driver was killed too, that would be part of the story, surely?'

Yvonne has reckoned without Perry:

'Neither Katya nor Irina made any reference to a driver, dead or alive, direct or indirect, Yvonne,' he says, in the slow, corrective tone he reserves for lazy students and predatory bodyguards. 'There was *no* discussion of other casualties, hospitals, or what particular car anyone was driving.' His voice is mounting. 'Or whether there was third-party insurance cover, or –'

'Cut,' says Luke.

*

Gail had gone upstairs again, this time unescorted. Perry had stayed where he was, head caged in the fingers of one hand, the other tapping restively at the table. Gail returned and sat down. Perry appeared not to notice.

'So, Perry,' said Luke, all brisk and businesslike.

'So what?'

'Cricket.'

'That wasn't till next day.'

'We're aware of that. It's in your document.'

'Then why not read it?'

'I think we've been through that, haven't we?'

All right, it was next day, same time, same beach, different part, Perry grudgingly conceded. The same black-windowed people carrier pulled up in the NO PARKING bay, and out poured not just Elspeth, the two girls and Natasha, but the boys.

All the same, on the word 'cricket' Perry had begun to brighten: 'Looking like a couple of teenaged colts who'd been locked up in the stable for too long and were finally being allowed a gallop,' he said with sudden relish as the memory took him over.

For today's visit to the beach, he and Gail had picked themselves a spot as far from the house called Three Chimneys as it was possible to get. They weren't hiding from Dima and company but they'd had a rocky night of it and woken late with splitting headaches, after making the elementary mistake of drinking their complimentary rum.

'And of course there *was* no escape from them,' Gail cut in, deciding it was her turn again. 'Not anywhere on the *whole* beach. Well *was* there, Perry? Not on the whole *island*, when we started to think about it. Why were the Dimas so bloody interested in us? I mean, who *were* they? What did they want? And why *us*? Every time we turned a corner, there they were. We were getting to feel that. From our cabin, they were straight across the bay, peering at us. Or we imagined they were, which was just as bad. And on the beach, they didn't even need binoculars. All they had to do was lean over the garden wall and gawp. Which no doubt they did a fair amount of, because it was only minutes after we'd pitched camp that the people carrier with black windows drove up.'

The same baby-faced bodyguard, said Perry, taking back the story. Not in the bar this time, but under a shade tree on the high ground. No Uncle Vanya from Perm with his tam-o'-shanter and family-sized revolver, but a gangly string-bean understudy who must have been some kind of fitness freak, because instead of shinning up the lookout he pranced up and down the beach timing himself and stopping each end for a bit of t'ai chi:

'Bubble-haired chap,' Perry said, his grin slowly stretching to its full width. 'Kinetic. Well, *manic* was more like it. Couldn't sit or stand still for five seconds. And beyond skinny. Skeletal. We put him down as a new arrival to the Dima household. We'd decided the Dimas had a high turn-over of cousins from Perm.'

'So Perry took *one* look at the children, didn't you?' Gail said. 'The boys particularly – and you thought, Christ what do we do with *this* lot? Then you had your *one* brilliant idea of the holiday: *cricket*. Well, I mean, not *so* brilliant if you know Perry. Give him a dog-chewed ball and a bit of old driftwood and he's lost to all non-cricketing mankind. Aren't you?'

'We took the game extremely seriously, as one should,' Perry agreed, frowning unconvincingly through his smile. 'We built a wicket out of driftwood, put twigs on top for bails, the marina people found us a bat and ball of sorts, we rounded up a clutch of Rastas and ancient Brits for the outfield, and all of a sudden we had six a side, Russia versus the rest of the world, a sporting first. I sent the boys off to persuade Natasha to come and keep wicket, but they came back saying she was reading some guy called Turgenev they pretended they'd never heard of. Our next job was impart-ing the sacred Laws of Cricket to' – the smile widening into a broad grin – 'well, some pretty lawless chaps. Not the ancient Brits or the Rastas, of course. They were cricketers born and bred. But the young Dimas were *internats*. They'd played a bit of baseball, but didn't take at all kindly to being told they had to bowl a ball and not chuck it. The small girls needed a bit of handling, but once we'd got the ancient Brits batting we could use them as runners. If the girls got bored, Gail swept them off for drinks and a swim. Didn't you?'

'We'd decided that the great thing was to keep them moving,' Gail explained, determinedly sharing Perry's brightness. 'Not give them too much time to brood. The boys were going to have a high old time whatever we did. And for the girls – well, as far as I was concerned, just getting a smile out of them was ... I mean, *Christ* ...' and left the rest unsaid.

Seeing Gail in difficulties, Perry quickly stepped in:

'Very difficult to make a decent cricket pitch out of that soft sand,' he explained to Luke, while she collected herself. 'Bowlers get bogged down, batsmen capsize, you can imagine.'

'I can indeed,' Luke agreed heartily, quick to pick up Perry's tone and match it.

'Not that it mattered a hoot. Everyone had a blast and the winning side got ice creams. We called it a draw so both sides got 'em,' said Perry.

'Paid for by the new presiding uncle, I trust?' Luke suggested.

'I'd put a stop to that,' Perry said. 'The ice creams were strictly on us.'

With Gail recovered, Luke's voice took on a more serious note:

'And it was while both sides were winning – actually quite late in the match – that you saw *inside* the parked people carrier? Have I got that right?'

'We were thinking of drawing stumps,' Perry agreed. 'And suddenly the side door of the carrier opened and there they were. Maybe they wanted a bit of fresh air. Or a clearer look. God knows. It was like a royal visit. An incognito one.'

'How long had the side door been open?'

Perry on guard over his celebrated memory. Perry the

58

perfect witness, never trusting himself, never answering too fast, always holding himself to account. Another Perry that Gail loved.

'Don't know actually, Luke. Can't say exactly. *We* can't' – with a glance at Gail, who shook her head to say she couldn't either. 'I looked; Gail saw me looking, didn't you? So *she* looked. We both saw them. Dima and Tamara, side by side and bolt upright, the dark and the light, the thin and the fat, staring at us from the back of the carrier. Then *wham*, and the door slides shut.'

'Staring, not smiling, as it were,' Luke suggested lightly, while he made a note.

'There was something – well, I said it already – *regal* about him. Yes. About both of them. The royal Dimas. If one of them had reached out and pulled a silk tassel for the coachman to drive on, I wouldn't have been all that surprised.' He dwelled on this idea, then approved it with a nod. 'On an island, big people seem bigger. And the Dimas were – well, big people. Still are.'

Yvonne has yet another photograph for them to consider, this time a police mugshot in black and white: full face and side view, two black eyes, one black eye. And the smashed and swollen mouth of somebody who has just made a voluntary statement. At the sight of it, Gail wrinkles her nose in disapproval. She glances at Perry and they agree: nobody we know.

But Scottish Yvonne is not disheartened:

'So if I put a bit of curly wig on him, imagine for a moment, and if I cleaned his face up a wee bit for him, do the two of you not think this might just possibly be your fitness freak released from an Italian gaol last December at all?'

They think it might well be. Drawing closer to each other, they are sure.

*

Early notice of the invitation was delivered by the venerable Ambrose in the Captain's Deck restaurant the same evening, while he was pouring wine for Perry to sample. Perry the puritan son doesn't do voices. Gail the actors' daughter does them all. She awards herself the part of the venerable Ambrose:

'"And tomorrow night I'm going to have to forgo the pleasure of serving you young folks. You know why? Because you young folks will be the honoured surprise guests of Mr Dima and his lady wife on the occasion of the fourteenth birthday of their twin sons who, so I hear say, you have personally introduced to the noble art of cricket. And my Elspeth, she has made the biggest, finest walnut-whirl cake you ever saw. Any bigger, why, Miss Gail, by all accounts those kids would have you jump right out of it, they love you so deep."'

For his final flourish, Ambrose handed them an envelope inscribed: *To Mr Perry and Miss Gail.* Inside, were two of Dima's business cards, white and deckle-edged like wedding invitations, giving his full name: *Dmitri Vladimirovich Krasnov, European Director, The Arena Multi Global Trading Conglomerate of Nicosia, Cyprus.* And beneath it, the address of his company's website, and an address in Berne styled *Residence and Company Offices.*

4

If it occurred to either of them to decline Dima's invitation, they never admitted it to one another, said Gail:

'We were in it for the children. Two hulking teenaged twin boys were having a birthday: great. That was how the invitation was sold to us, and it's how we bought into it. But for me it was about the two girls' – again privately congratulating herself on not mentioning Natasha – 'whereas for Perry' – she shot a doubtful glance at him.

'For Perry *what?*' Luke asked, when Perry did not respond.

She was already pulling back, protecting her man. 'He was just so fascinated by it all. Weren't you, Perry? Dima, who he was, the life-force, the formed man. This outlaw band of Russians. The danger. The sheer *differentness.* You were – well – *connecting.* Is that unfair?'

'Sounds a bit like psycho-babble to me,' Perry said gruffly, retreating into himself.

Little Luke, ever the conciliator, darted in to intervene. 'So basically, mixed motives on both your sides,' he suggested, in the manner of a man familiar with mixed motives. 'Nothing wrong with that, surely? It's a pretty mixed scene. Vanya's gun. Tales of Russian cash in laundry baskets. Two small orphan girls desperately in need of you – maybe the adults too, for all you knew. *And* it was the twin boys' birthday. I mean, how, as two decent people, could you resist?'

'On an island,' Gail reminded him.

'Exactly. And on top of it all, *dare* one say, you were *jolly* curious. And why shouldn't you be? I mean, that's a pretty heady mix. I'm sure *I'd* have fallen for it.'

Gail was sure he would too. She had a feeling that, in his time, little Luke had fallen for most things, and was a bit worried about himself in consequence.

'And *Dima*,' she insisted. 'Dima was the big lure for you, Perry, admit it. You said so at the time. It was the children for me, but when push came to shove it was Dima for you. We discussed it only a few days ago, remember?'

She meant: *while you were penning your bloody document, and I was a Christian slave.*

Perry brooded for a while, much as he might have brooded over any other academic premise, then with a sporting smile acknowledged the rightness of the argument.

'It's true. I felt *appointed* by him. *Over-promoted* is more like it. Actually, I don't know *what* I felt any more. Maybe I didn't then.'

'But Dima knew. You were his professor of fair play.'

*

'So in the afternoon, instead of going to the beach, we walked into town to do the shopping,' Gail resumed, speaking past Perry's averted head to Yvonne while referring her story to Perry. 'For the birthday boys, the obvious thing was a cricket set. That was *your* department. You enjoyed looking for a cricket set. You loved the sports shop. You loved the old man. You loved the photographs of great West Indian players. Learie Constantine? Who else was there?'

'Martindale.'

'And Sobers. Gary Sobers was there. You pointed him out to me.'

He nodded. Yes, Sobers.

'And we loved the secrecy bit. Because of the children. Ambrose's notion of having me jump out of the cake wasn't so far off the mark, was it? And I did presents for the girls. With a bit of help from you. Scarves for the little ones, and a rather nice shell necklace for Natasha with alternating semi-precious stones.' Done it. She had let Natasha back in, and got away with it. 'You wanted to buy one for me too, but I wouldn't let you.'

'On what grounds, please Gail?' – Yvonne, with her self-effacing, intelligent smile, looking for light relief.

'Exclusivity. It was sweet of Perry, but I didn't want to be paired off with Natasha,' Gail replied, as much to Perry as to Yvonne. 'And I'm sure Natasha wouldn't have wanted to be paired off with *me*. Thanks, it's a lovely thought, but save it for another time, I told you. Right? And I mean *honestly*, try buying decent wrapping paper in St John's, Antigua!'

She plunged on:

'Then there was the business of smuggling us in, wasn't there? Because we were the big surprise. *That* was going to be a blast too. We thought of going as Caribbean pirates – you did – but we decided it might be a bit over the top, specially with people still in mourning, even if we didn't officially know they were. So we went as we were, plus a bit. Perry, you had your old blazer and the grey bags you'd travelled in. Your Brideshead look. Perry isn't exactly what you'd call a fashion freak, but you did your best. And your swimming trunks, of course. And I put a cotton dress over my swimsuit plus a cardigan in case it got nippy because we knew that Three Chimneys had a private beach and there was a chance we might be expected to swim.'

Yvonne writing a meticulous memorandum. Who to? Luke, chin in hand, drinking in her every word, a little too deeply for Gail's taste. Perry gloomily studying a patch of brickwork on the darkened wall. All of them giving her their undivided attention for her swansong.

*

When Ambrose told them to be on parade at the hotel entrance at six, Gail continued in a more measured tone, they assumed they were going to be spirited up to Three Chimneys in one of the people carriers with blackened windows, and let in through a side door. They assumed wrong.

Taking a back route to the car park as instructed, they found Ambrose waiting at the wheel of a 4x4. The plan, he explained in conspiratorial excitement, was to infiltrate the surprise guests by way of the old Nature Path that ran along the spine of the peninsula right up to the rear entrance of the house, where Mr Dima himself would be waiting for them.

She did her Ambrose voice again:

'"Man, they got fairy lights up in that garden, they got a steel band, a marquee, they got a shipment of the tenderest Kobe beef ever came out of a cow. I don't know what they haven't got up there. And Mr Dima, he has it all fixed and prepared down to a fine pin. He has packed off my Elspeth and that whole knockabout family of his to a major crab-racing event over the other side of St John's, just so's we can smuggle you in by the back door, and that's how secret you folks are tonight!'"

If they had been looking for adventure, the Nature Path alone would have provided it. They must have been the first people to use it for simply years. A couple of times Perry actually had to beat a passage through the under-growth:

'Which of course he loved. Actually, he should have been a peasant, shouldn't you? Then we came out in this long green tunnel with Dima standing at the end of it looking like a happy Minotaur. If there is such a thing.'

Perry's bony index finger jerked upward in admonition:

'Which was our first sighting of Dima *alone*,' he warned gravely. 'No bodyguards, no family. No children. No one to watch over us. Or none visible. We were a three, stand-ing at the edge of a wood. I think we were both very much aware of that. The sudden exclusivity.'

But whatever significance Perry attached to this remark was lost in the insistent rush of Gail's narrative:

'He *hugged* us, Yvonne! *Really* hugged us. First Perry, then shoved him aside, then me, then Perry again. Not sexy hugs. Great big family hugs. As if he hadn't seen us for ages. Or wasn't going to see us again.'

'Or else he was desperate,' Perry suggested, on the same earnest, reflective note. 'A bit of that got through to me. Maybe not to you. What we meant to him at that moment. How important we were.'

'He really *loved* us,' Gail swept on determinedly. 'He stood there, declaring his love. Tamara loved us too, he was positive. She just found it difficult to say because she was a bit crazy since her problem. No explanation of what the problem might have been, and who were we to ask? Natasha loved us, but she doesn't say anything to anyone these days, she just reads books. The whole family loved the English for our humanity and fair play. Except he didn't say *humanity*, what did he say?'

'Heart.'

'We're standing there at the end of the tunnel, having this great hug-fest, and he's orating all this stuff about our hearts. I mean, how much love can you profess to somebody you've only ever exchanged six words with?'

'Perry?' Luke prompted.

'I thought he was *heroic*,' Perry replied, his long hand now flying to his brow to form a classic gesture of worry. 'I just didn't know why. Didn't I put that in our document somewhere? *Heroic?* I thought he was' – with a shrug dismissing his own feelings as valueless – 'I thought *dignity under fire*. I just didn't know who was firing at him. Or why. I didn't know anything, except –'

'You were on the rock face with him,' Gail suggested, not unkindly.

'Yes. I was. And he was in a bad place. He *needed* us.'

'*You*,' she corrected him.

'All right. Me. That's all I'm trying to say.'

'Then *you* tell it.'

*

'He walked us out of the tunnel, round to what we realized was going to be the back of the house,' Perry began, and then broke off. 'I take it that you do want an *exact description* of the place?' he demanded sternly of Yvonne.

'We do indeed, Perry,' Yvonne replied, equally efficiently. 'Every last dreary detail, please, *if* you don't mind.' And went back to her meticulous note-taking.

'From where we'd emerged from the woods, there's an old bit of service track covered in some sort of red cinder, probably made by the original builders as an access road. We had to pick our way uphill over the potholes.'

'Carting our presents,' Gail blurted from the wings. 'You with your cricket set, me with the gift-wrapped presents for the kids in the fanciest bag I could find, which isn't saying a lot.'

Is anybody listening out there? she wondered. Not to me. Perry is the horse's mouth. I'm its arse.

'The house as we approached it from the back was a pile of old bones,' he continued. 'We'd been warned not to expect a palace, we knew the house was up for demolition. But we hadn't expected a wreck.' The outward-bound Oxford don had turned field reporter: 'There was a tumbledown brick building with barred windows, I deduced the old slave quarters. There was a high perimeter whitewashed wall, about twelve foot high and capped with razor wire, which was new and vile. There were white security lights stuck up on pylons round it like a football stadium, blazing down on whoever passed. We'd seen the glow from the balcony of our cabin. Fairy lights rigged between them, presumably in preparation for the night's birthday festivities. Security cameras, but pointed away from us because we were the wrong side of them. I assume that was the intention. A shining new aerial dish, twenty foot high, directed northish, as far as I could read it on our way back. Pointed at Miami. Or Houston perhaps. Anyone's guess.' He thought about this. 'Well, not yours, obviously. You people are supposed to know that stuff.'

Is this a challenge or a joke? It's neither. It's Perry showing them how brilliant he is at doing their job, in case they haven't noticed. It's Perry the climber of north-facing overhangs, telling them he never forgets a route. It's the Perry who can't resist a challenge provided the odds are stacked against him.

'Then downhill again through more forest to a bit of grass meadow with the headland sticking up at the end of it. In reality, the house hasn't *got* a back. Or it's *all* back, take your choice. It's a pseudo-Elizabethan hotchpotch of a bungalow built out of clapboard and asbestos, facing three ways. Grey stucco walls. Poky leaded windows. Plywood pretending to be half-timber and a rear porch with a lantern dangling in it. Are you with me, Gail?'

Would I be here if I wasn't? 'You're doing fine,' she said. Which wasn't quite what he'd asked.

'Add-on bedrooms, bathrooms, kitchens, and offices with front doors on them, suggesting that the place had been some sort of commune or settlement at one time. So I mean, overall a shambles. It wasn't Dima's fault. We knew that, thanks to Mark. The Dimas had never lived there till now. Never touched it apart from a crash job on the security. The idea didn't bother us. To the contrary. It had a much-needed touch of reality about it.'

The ever-inquisitive Dr Yvonne is peering up from her medical notes. 'But were there no *chimneys* after all that, Perry?'

'Two attached to the remnants of a sugar mill on the western edge of the peninsula, the third at the edge of the woods. I thought I put that in our document as well.'

Our *bloody document? How many times have you said that now? Our document that you wrote and I haven't been allowed to see, but they have? It's your bloody document! It's their bloody document!* Her cheeks were scorching, and she hoped he'd noticed.

'Then as we started down towards the house, about twenty metres from it, I suppose, Dima slowed us down,' Perry was saying, his voice gathering intensity. 'With his hands. *Slow down.*'

'And would it be here also that he put his finger to his lips in a gesture of complicity?' Yvonne asked, popping her head up at him while she wrote.

'*Yes it was!*' Gail leaped in. '*Exactly* here. *Huge* complicity. First slow down, then shut up. We assumed the finger to the lips was all part of surprising the children, so we played along with it. Ambrose had said they'd been packed off to the crab races, so it seemed a bit odd they were still in the house. But we just assumed something had changed and they hadn't gone after all. Or I did.'

'Thank you, Gail.'

For what, for Christ's sake? For upstaging Perry? Don't mention it, Yvonne, it's a pleasure. She raced on:

'Dima had us on tiptoe by now. Literally holding our breath. We didn't *doubt* him – I think it's a point to make. We were *obeying* him, which isn't like either of us, but we were. He led us to a door, a house door, but a side one. It wasn't locked, he just pushed it and went in ahead, then immediately swung round, with one hand up in the air and the other one to his lips like' – *like Daddy playing Boots in a*

Christmas pantomime, but sober, she was going to say, but didn't – 'well, and this really intense stare, *urging* silence on us. Right, Perry? Your turn.'

'Then, when he knew he had us, he beckoned us to follow. I went first.' Perry's tone by contrast minimal in deliberate counterpoint to hers – his voice for when he's truly excited and pretending he isn't. 'We crept into an empty hall. Well, *hall*! It was about ten by twelve feet, with a cracked, west-facing window with diamond panes made out of masking tape and the evening sun pouring through them. Dima still had his finger to his lips. I stepped inside and he grabbed hold of my arm, the way he'd grabbed it on the court. Strength in a league of its own. I couldn't have competed with it.'

'Did you think you *might have* to compete with it?' Luke inquired, with male sympathy.

'I didn't know what to think. I was worried about Gail and my concern was to get myself between them. For a few seconds, only.'

'And long enough for you to realize it wasn't a children's game any more,' Yvonne suggested.

'Well, it was beginning to dawn,' Perry confessed, and paused, his voice drowned out by the wail of a passing ambulance in the street above them. 'You have to understand the amount of unexpected *din* inside the place,' he insisted, as if the one sound had set off the other. 'We were only in this tiny hall, but we could hear the wind bumping the whole rickety house around. And the light was – well, *phantasmagoric*, to use a word my students love. It was coming at us in layers through the west window. You had this powdery light from the low cloud rolling in from the sea, and then a layer of brilliant sunlight riding in over the top of it. And pitch-black shadows where it didn't reach.'

'And cold,' Gail complained, hugging herself theatrically. 'Like only empty houses are. And that chilly graveyard smell they have. But all *I* was thinking was: where are the girls? Why no sight or sound of them? Why no sound of *anybody* or *anything* except the wind? And if nobody's around, who were we doing all this secrecy stuff for? Who were we fooling except ourselves? And Perry, you were thinking the same, weren't you, you told me so afterwards.'

*

And behind Dima's raised forefinger, a different face, Perry is saying. All the fun had gone out of it. Out of his eyes. It was humourless. Rigid. He really *needed* us to be afraid. To share his fear. And as we stand there bemused – and, yes, afraid – the spectral figure of Tamara materializes before us in a corner of the tiny hall where she's been standing all along without us noticing, in the darkest recess on the other side of the shafts of sunlight. She's wearing the same long black dress she wore at the tennis match, and wore again when she and Dima spied on them from the darkness of the people carrier, and she looks like her own ghost.

Gail grabbed back the story:

'The first thing I saw was her bishop's cross. Then the rest of her, forming round it. She'd plaited and braided her hair for the birthday party and rouged her cheeks, and daubed lipstick round her mouth – I mean, *really* round it. She looked as mad as a bedbug. She didn't have her finger to her lips. She didn't need to. Her whole body was like a warning sign in black and red. Forget Dima, I thought. This is *really* something. And of course I was still wondering what her *problem* was. Because *boy*, did she have one.'

Perry started to speak, but she talked stubbornly through him:

'She was holding this sheet of paper in her hand – A4 typing paper, folded in half – and holding it up to us. For what? Was it a religious tract? Prepare to meet thy God? Or was she serving a writ on us?'

'And Dima, where was he in this?' Luke asked, turning back to Perry.

'Finally let go of my arm,' said Perry with a grimace. 'But not before he'd made sure I was focusing on Tamara's sheet of paper. Which she then proceeded to shove at me. With Dima nodding at me: *read it*. But *still* with his finger to his lips. And Tamara really *possessed*. Both of them possessed, actually. And wanting us to share their fear. But of what? So I read it. Not aloud, obviously. Not even immediately. I wasn't in the sunlight. I had to take it to the window. On tiptoe: which shows you how much we were under the spell. And even *after* that, I had to turn my back to the window because the sunlight was so fierce. Then Gail had to give me my spare reading glasses from her handbag –'

'– because as usual he'd left them behind in our cabin –'

'Then Gail tiptoed up behind me –'

'You beckoned to me –'

'For your protection – and read it over my shoulder. And I suppose we read it, well, twice at least.'

'And then some,' said Gail. 'I mean, what an act of faith! What were they doing *trusting* us like this? What made them think we were the *ones* suddenly? It was such a – such a bloody *imposition*!'

'They didn't have much choice,' Perry softly observed, to which Luke added a wise nod that Yvonne discreetly copied, and Gail felt even more isolated than she had felt all evening.

*

Perhaps the tension in the under-ventilated basement was getting too much for Perry. Or perhaps – Gail's thought – he was having an overdue fit of the guilts. He yanked his long body back into his chair, lowered his craggy shoulders to relax them and stabbed a forefinger at the buff folder lying between Luke's small fists:

'Anyway, you've got her text there in front of you in our document, so you don't need me to recite it to you,' he said aggressively. 'You can read it for yourselves to your heart's content. You have done so already, presumably.'

'All the same,' said Luke. '*If* you don't mind, Perry. For completeness, as it were.'

Was Luke testing him? Gail believed he was. Even in the academic jungle that Perry was so determined to leave behind him, he was renowned for his ability to quote tracts of English literature on the strength of a single read. His vanity appealed to, Perry began reciting slowly and without expression:

'Dmitri Vladimirovich Krasnov, the one they call Dima, European Director of Arena Multi Global Trading Conglomerate of Nicosia, Cyprus, is willing negotiate through intermediary Professor Perry Makepiece and lawyer Madam Gail Perkins mutually profitable arrangement with authority of Great Britain regarding permanent residence all family in exchange for certain informations very important, very urgent, very critical for Great Britain of Her Majesty. Children and household will return in approximately one and a half hour. There is convenient place where Dima and Perry may discuss advantageously without risk to be overheard. Gail will please accompany Tamara to other area of house. *Is possible this house has many microphones.* We will PLEASE NOT SPEAK until all persons return from crab races for celebration.'

'Then the phone rang,' said Gail.

*

Perry is sitting upright in his chair as if he has been called to order, hands as before spread flat on the table, back straight but shoulders on the slope as he meditates on the rightness of what he is about to do. His jaw is set in refusal although nobody has asked anything of him that needs to be refused, except for Gail, whose expression as she stares at him is one of dignified entreaty – or so she hopes, but maybe she's just giving him the hairy eyeball, because she's not sure any more what facial signals she's emitting.

Luke's tone is light-hearted, even debonair, which is presumably how he wishes it to be:

'I'm trying to picture the two of you standing there together, you see,' he explains keenly. 'It's a truly *extraordinary* moment, don't you agree, Yvonne? Standing side by side in the hall? Reading? Perry holding the letter? Gail, you're looking at it over his shoulder. Both *literally* struck mute. You've had this extraordinary proposition thrown at you to which you're not allowed to respond *in any way*. It's a nightmare. And as far as Dima and Tamara are concerned, simply by not speaking you're halfway to being co-opted.

74

Neither of you, I take it, is about to storm out of the house. You're pinned down. Physically and emotionally. Am I right? So from *their* point of view, so far, so good: you've *tacitly* agreed to agree. That's the impression you can't help giving them. Totally inadvertently. Simply by doing nothing, by being there at all, you're becoming part of their big play.'

'I thought they were both totally barking,' Gail says to deflate him. 'Paranoid, the pair of them, frankly, Luke.'

'Their paranoia taking what form exactly?' – Luke undeterred.

'How should I know? Deciding that somebody's bugged the place, for openers. And little green men are listening.'

But Luke is more doughty than she expects. He comes back sharply:

'Was that really so unlikely, Gail, after what you'd both seen and heard? You must have realized by now that you were standing with at least one foot in Russian crime. And you an experienced lawyer, if I may say so.'

*

A long pause followed. Gail had not expected to be locking horns with Luke, but if he wanted a fight he was welcome to one any time:

'The so-called *experience* you refer to, Luke,' she began furiously, 'does *not* unfortunately cover' – but Perry had already headed her off.

'The phone rang,' he gently reminded her.

'Yes. Well, all right, the phone rang,' she conceded. 'It was a yard away from us. Less. Maybe two feet. It had a bell like a fire alarm going off. We jumped out of our skins. They didn't, we did. A mossy, black, 1940s stand-up job

75

with a dial and a concertina flex, sitting on a wobbly rattan table. Dima picked it up and bellowed Russian at it and we watched his face stretch into an arse-kissing smile that he didn't mean. Everything about him was totally against his own free will. Forced smiles, forced laughter, false jollity, and a lot of yes-sir, no-sir, three bags full, and I'd like to strangle you with my bare hands. Eyes fixed all the time on batty Tamara, taking his cues from her. And the finger back in front of his lips, telling us no noises-off, please, all the time he's talking. Right, Perry?' – deliberately avoiding Luke.

Right.

'So these are the people they're afraid of, I'm thinking. And they want *us* to be afraid of them too. Tamara conducting him. Nodding, shaking her head, rouged cheeks and all, pulling a Medusa face for moments of mega-disapproval. Fair description, Perry?'

'Florid, but accurate,' Perry conceded awkwardly – then, thank the Lord, gave her a real full-beam smile, even if it was his guilty one.

'And that was the first of many calls that evening, I rather believe?' nimble Luke suggested, darting from one to the other of them with his quick, strangely lifeless eyes.

'There must have been half-a-dozen phone calls in the time before the family came back,' Perry agreed. 'You heard them too, right?' – for Gail – 'And they were just for openers. All the time I was closeted with Dima, we'd hear the phone go and either Tamara would come yelling at Dima to answer it, or Dima would be jumping to his feet and hurrying off to take it himself, cursing in Russian. If there were phone extensions in the house I never saw them. He told me later that night that mobiles didn't work up there because of the trees and the cliffs, which was why everyone called him on the landline. I didn't believe him. I thought they were checking on his whereabouts, and calling the house on an old landline was the way to do it.'

'*They?*'

'The people who didn't trust him. And he didn't trust in return. The people he's beholden to. And hates. The people they're afraid of, so *we've* got to be.'

The people that Perry, Luke and Yvonne can know about and I mustn't, in other words, thought Gail. The people in *our* bloody document that isn't ours.

'So this is the point where you and Dima retire to your *convenient place* where you can talk without risk of being overheard,' Luke prompted.

'Yes.'

'And Gail, you went off to bond with Tamara.'

'Bond my foot.'

'But you went.'

'To a tacky drawing room that stank of bat-piss. With a plasma television playing Russian Orthodox High Mass. She was carrying a tin.'

'A *tin?*'

'Didn't Perry tell you? In our joint document that I haven't seen? Tamara was carting a black tin handbag around with her. When she put it down it clanked. I don't know where women carry their guns in normal society, but I had a feeling this was her Uncle-Vanya-equivalent.'

If it's my swansong, I'll bloody well make the most of it.

'The plasma TV took up most of one wall. The other walls were decked out in icons. Travelling ones. Ornately framed for extra sanctity. Male saints, no Virgins. Where

Tamara goes, there go the saints, or that was my guess. I've got an aunt like that, ex-tart turned Catholic convert. Each of her saints has a different job. If she's lost her keys, it's Anthony. If she's taking the train, Christopher. If she's stuck for a few quid, Mark. If a relative is sick, Francis. If it's too late, Saint Peter.'

Hiatus. She had dried: another lousy actor, washed up and out of a part.

'And the *rest* of the evening, briefly, Gail?' Luke asked, not quite glancing at his watch, but as good as.

'Simply *scrumptious*, thank you. Beluga caviar, lobster, smoked sturgeon, oceans of vodka, brilliant thirty-minute toasts in drunken Russian for the adults, great birthday cake, washed down with health-giving clouds of vile Russian-cigarette smoke. Kobe beef and floodlit cricket in the garden, a steel band banging away that nobody was listening to, fireworks that nobody was watching, a drunken swim for the last chaps standing, and home by midnight, for a jolly post-mortem over a nightcap.'

*

A stack of Yvonne's glossy photographs is making its positively last appearance. Kindly identify anybody you believe you may recognize from the festivities, says Yvonne, speaking by rote.

Him and *him*, says Gail, wearily pointing.

And *him* too, surely? says Perry.

Yes, Perry, him *too. Another bloody* him. *One day we'll have equal opportunity for female Russian criminals.*

Silence while Yvonne completes another of her careful notes and puts down her pencil. Thank you, Gail, you have been most helpful, says Yvonne. It's randy little Luke's cue to be brisk. Brisk is merciful:

'Gail, I fear we should release you. You've been immensely generous, and a superb witness, and we can pick up on everything else from Perry. We're very grateful. Both of us. Thank you.'

She is standing at the door, not sure how she got there. Yvonne is standing beside her.

'Perry?'

Does he answer her? Not that she notices. She climbs the stairs, Yvonne her gaoler close behind her. In the plush, over-prinked hall, big Ollie of the cockney accent and foreign voices folds up his Russian newspaper, clambers to his feet and, pausing in front of a period mirror, carefully adjusts his beret, using both hands.

5

'See you to the front door, at all, Gail?' Ollie inquired, swivelling in his seat to quiz her through the partition of his cab.

'I'm fine, thank you.'

'You don't *look* fine, Gail. Not from where *I* sit. You look bothered. Want I come in for a cup tea with you?'

Cup tea? Cuppa? Cup of?

'No thanks. I'm fine. I just need to get some sleep.'

'Nothing like a nice kip to see you right, eh?'

'No. There isn't. Goodnight, Ollie. Thanks for the ride.'

She crossed the street, waiting for him to drive off, but he didn't.

'Forgotten our handbag, darling!'

She had. And she was furious with herself. And furious with Ollie for waiting till she was on her own doorstep before charging after her. She mumbled more thanks, said she was an idiot.

'Oh, don't apologize, Gail, I'm completely *worse*. If it was loose, I'd forget my own head. Are we utterly *sure*, darling?'

Not utterly sure of anything, actually, *darling*. Not just now. Not utterly sure whether you're a master-spy or an underling. Not sure why you wear spectacles with thick lenses for driving to Bloomsbury in broad daylight, and no spectacles on the journey back when it's pitch dark. Or might it be that you spies can only see in the dark?

*

The flat she had jointly inherited from her late father wasn't a flat but a maisonette on the two top floors of a pretty white Victorian terrace house of the sort that gives Primrose Hill its charm. Her upwardly mobile brother, who killed pheasants with rich friends, owned the other half of it, and in about fifty years, if he hadn't died of drink by then, and Perry and Gail were still together, which she presently doubted, they will have paid him off.

The entrance hall stank of number 2's Bourguignonne and resounded to other tenants' bickerings and television sets. The mountain bike Perry kept for his weekend visits was in its usual inconvenient place, chained to the downpipe. One day, she had warned him, some enterprising thief was going to steal the downpipe too. His pleasure was to ride it up to Hampstead Heath at six o'clock in the morning and speed-cycle down the paths marked NO CYCLING.

The carpet on the four narrow flights of stairs leading to her front door was in its last stages of decay, but the ground-floor tenant didn't see why he should pay anything and the other two wouldn't pay till he did and Gail as the unpaid in-house lawyer was supposed to come up with a compromise, but since none of the parties would budge from their entrenched positions, where the hell was compromise?

But tonight she was grateful for all of it: let them bicker and play their bloody music to their hearts' content, let them give her all the normality they've got, because, oh mother, did she need normality. Just get her out of surgery and into the recovery room. Just tell her the nightmare's over, Gail dear, there are no more softly spoken Scottish blue-stockings or undersized espiocrats with Etonian accents, no more orphaned children, drop-dead-gorgeous Natashas, gun-slinging uncles, Dimas and Tamaras, and Perry Make-piece my Heaven-sent lover and purblind innocent is not about to wrap himself in the sacrificial flag for his Orwellian love of lost England, his admirable quest for Connection with a capital C – connection with *what?* for Christ's sake – or his homebrewed brand of inverted, puritanical vanity.

Climbing the stairs, her knees began trembling.

At the first poky half-landing they trembled more.

At the second they trembled so wildly she had to prop herself against the wall till they steadied down.

And when she reached the last flight, she had to haul herself up by the handrail to get to the front door before the time-switch cut.

Standing in the tiny hall with her back to the closed door, she listened, sniffing the air for booze, body odour or stale cigarette smoke, or all three, which was how a couple of months back she knew she'd been burgled before she ever walked up the spiral staircase to find her bed pissed on and the pillows slashed and foul lipstick messages smeared across her mirror.

Only when she had relived that moment to the full did she open the kitchen door, hang up her coat, check the bathroom, pee, pour herself a king-sized tumbler of Rioja, swig a mouthful, replenish the tumbler to the brim and carry it precariously to the living room.

*

Standing, not sitting. She'd done enough passive sitting for a lifetime, thank you.

Standing in front of the non-functioning all-pine, do-it-yourself reproduction Georgian fireplace installed by a previous owner, and staring at the same long sash window where Perry had stood six hours ago: Perry on the slant, birdlike and eight foot tall, peering down into the street, waiting for an ordinary black cab with its 'For Hire' light out, last numbers on its licence plate 73, and your driver's name will be Ollie.

No curtains to our sash windows. Shutters only. Perry who likes sheer but will pay his half for curtains if she really wants them. Perry who disapproves of central heating but worries that she's not warm enough. Perry who one minute says we can only have one child for fear of world over-population, then wants six by return of post. Perry who, the moment they touch down in England after the fucked-up holiday of a lifetime, hightails it to Oxford, buries himself in his digs, and for fifty-six hours communicates in cryptic text messages from the front:

> document nearly complete . . . have made
> contact with necessary people . . . arriving
> London midday-ish . . . please leave key under
> doormat . . .

'He said they're a team apart, not run-of-the-mill,' he tells her, as he watches the wrong taxis go by.

'He?'

'Adam.'

'The man who called you back. That Adam?'

'Yes.'

'Surname or Christian name?'

'I didn't ask, he didn't tell me. He says they've got their own set-up for cases like this. A special house. He wouldn't say where over the telephone. The cab driver would know.'

'*Ollie.*'

'Yes.'

'Cases like *what*, actually?'

'Ours. That's all I know.'

A black cab goes past but it has its light on. Not a spy cab then. A normal cab. Driven by a man who isn't Ollie. Disappointed again, Perry rounds on her:

'Look. What else do you expect me to do? If you've got a better suggestion, let's hear it. You've done nothing but snipe since we got back to England.'

'And you've done nothing but keep me at arm's length. Oh, and treat me like a child. Of the weaker sex. I forgot that bit.'

He has gone back to looking out of the window.

'Is *Adam* the only person to have read your letter-document-report-cum-witness statement?' she asks.

'I can't imagine so. I wouldn't bank on his name being Adam either. He just said *Adam* like a password.'

'Really? I wonder how he did that.'

She tries saying *Adam* as a password in several different ways, but Perry is not drawn.

'You're sure Adam's a *man*, are you? Not just a woman with a deep voice?'

No answer. None expected.

Yet another taxi passes. Still not ours. Whatever does one wear for *spies*, darling? as her mother would have said. Cursing herself for even wondering, she has changed out of her office clothes into a skirt and high-necked blouse. And sensible shoes, nothing to stir the juices – well, except Luke's, but how could she have known?

'Perhaps he's stuck in traffic,' she suggests, and again gets no answer, which serves her right. 'Anyway, to resume. You gave the letter to an *Adam*. And an Adam received it. Otherwise he wouldn't have rung you, presumably.' She's being irritating and knows it. So does he. 'How many pages? Of our secret document? Yours.'

'Twenty-eight,' he replies.

'Handwritten or typed?'

'Handwritten.'

'Why not typed?'

'I decided handwritten was safer.'

'Really? On whose advice?'

'I hadn't had advice by then. Dima and Tamara were convinced they were bugged at every turn, so I decided to respect their anxieties and not do anything – electronic. Interceptible.'

'Wasn't that rather paranoid?'

'I'm sure it was. We're both paranoid. So are Dima and Tamara. We're *all* paranoid.'

'Then let's admit it. Let's be paranoid together.'

No answer. Silly little Gail tries yet another tack:

'Do you want to tell me how you got on to Mr Adam in the first place?'

'Anyone can do it. It's not a problem these days. You can do it on the Web.'

'Did *you* do it on the Web?'

'No.'

'Didn't trust the Web?'

'No.'

'Do you trust *me*?'

'Of course I do.'

'I hear the most amazing confidences every day of my life. You know that, don't you?'

'Yes.'

'And you don't exactly hear me regaling our friends at dinner parties with my clients' secrets, do you?'

'No.'

Reload:

'You also know that as a young barrister who is self-employed without a paddle and terrified of where the next job is or is not coming from, I am professionally disposed against mystery briefs that offer no prospect of prestige or reward.'

'Nobody's offering you a brief, Gail. Nobody's asking you to do anything except talk.'

'Which is what I call a brief.'

Another wrong taxi. Another silence, a bad one.

'Well, at least Mr Adam invited both of us,' she says, going for cheerful. 'I thought you'd airbrushed me out of your document completely.'

Which is when Perry becomes Perry again, and the dagger in her hand turns against herself as he gazes at her with so much hurt love that she is more alarmed for Perry than for herself.

'I *tried* to airbrush you out, Gail. I did my absolute damnedest to airbrush you out. I believed I could protect you from being involved. It didn't work. They've got to have us both. Initially anyway. He was – well – adamant.' Lame laugh. 'The way you would be about witnesses. "If the two of you were present, then two of you must obviously come." I'm really sorry.'

And he was. She knew he was. The day Perry learned to fake his feelings would be the day he wasn't Perry any more.

And she was as sorry as he was. Sorrier. She was in his arms telling him this when a black taxi with its flag down appeared in the street outside, last two numbers 73, and a nearly cockney male voice informed them over the house entryphone that he was Ollie and he had two passengers to pick up for Adam.

*

And now she was excluded again. Debarred, debriefed, discarded.

The obedient little woman, waiting for her man to come home, and having another man-sized glass of Rioja to help her do it.

All right, it was in the whole ridiculous contract from the start. She should never have let him get away with it. But that didn't mean she had to sit and twiddle her thumbs, and she hadn't.

That very morning, although he didn't know it, while Perry had been sitting here waiting obediently for the Voice of Adam, she had been busy in her Chambers tapping away at her computer, and not, for once, on the matter of *Samson v. Samson*.

That she had waited until she got to her office rather than use her own laptop from home – that she had waited at all – was still a puzzle to her, if not a cause for outright self-reproach. Put it down to the Perry-generated prevailing atmosphere of conspiracy.

That she still possessed Dima's deckle-edged business card was a hanging offence since Perry had told her to destroy it.

That she had gone electronic – and therefore interceptible – was as it now turned out also a hanging offence. But since he had not informed her in advance of this particular branch of his paranoia, he could hardly complain.

The Arena Multi Global Trading Conglomerate of Nicosia, Cyprus, its website informed her in bad, blotchy English, was a consulting company *specializing in providing help for active traders.* Its head office was in Moscow. It had representatives in Toronto, Rome, Berne, Karachi, Frankfurt, Budapest, Prague, Tel Aviv and Nicosia. None, however, in Antigua. And no brass-plate bank. Or none mentioned.

'*Arena Multi Global prides itself on confidentiality and entreprenurial* [with an 'e' missing] *flare* [misspelled] *at all levels. It offers top-class oportunities* [with one 'p'] *and private banking facilities*' [spelled correctly]. *Note: this web page is currently under reconstruction. Further information available on application to Moscow office.*'

Ted was an American bachelor who sold futures for Morgan Stanley. From her desk in Chambers she rang Ted:

'Gail, sweetheart.'

'An outfit calling itself the Arena Multi Global Trading Conglomerate. Can you dig up the dirt on them for me?'

Dirt? Ted could dig dirt like nobody else. Ten minutes later he was back.

'Those Russki friends of yours.'

'Russki?'

'They're like me. Hot as hell and rich as figgy pudding.'

'How rich is rich?'

'Anybody's guess, but looks mega. Fifty-something subsidiaries, all with great trading records. You into money-laundering, Gail?'

'How did you know?'

'These Russki mothers pass the money around between them so fast nobody knows who owns it for how long. That's all I got for you but I paid blood. Will you love me for ever?'

'I'll think about it, Ted.'

Her next step was Ernie, the Chambers' resourceful, sixty-something clerk. She waited till lunchtime when the coast was clearest.

'Ernie. A favour. Rumour has it that there's a disgraceful chat site you visit when you want to check out the companies of our highly reputable clients. I'm deeply shocked and I need you to consult it for me.'

Thirty minutes on, and Ernie had presented her with an edited printout of disgraceful exchanges on the subject of the Arena Multi Global Trading Conglomerate.

Any asshole got an idea who runs this junk shop? The guys change MDs like socks. P. BROSNAN

Read, mark, learn and inwardly digest the wise words of Maynard Keynes: Markets can remain irrational longer than you can remain solvent. Asshole yourself. R. CROW

What the f***'s happened to MG's website. It's curdled. B. PITT

MG's website is down but not out. B-s rises to the surface. Assholes all beware. M. MUNROE

But I'm really really curious. These guys come on at me like they have the hots, then they leave me panting and unful-filled. P.B.

Hey guys, listen to this! I just heard MGTC opened an office in Toronto. R.C.

Office? You're shitting me! It's a f***ing Russian nightclub, man. Pole dancers, Stolly and bortsch. M.M.

Hey, asshole, me again. Is the office they opened in Toronto the same one they closed in Equatorial Guinea? If so, run for cover man. Run now. R.C.

Arena Multi f***ing Global has absolutely zero hits on Google. I repeat zero. The whole outfit is so über-amateurish I get palpitations. P.B.

Do you by any chance believe in the afterlife? If not, start believing now. You are treading on the Biggest Bananaskinski in the laundering arena. Official. M.M.

They were just so enthusiastic about me. Now this. P.B.

Stay away. Stay far, far away. R.C.

*

She is in Antigua, wafted there by another tumbler of Rioja from the kitchen.

She's listening to the pianist in the mauve bow tie croon-ing Simon and Garfunkel to an elderly American couple in ducks pirouetting all alone on the dance deck.

She's fending off the glances of beautiful waiters who have nothing to do but undress her with their eyes. She is overhearing the seventy-year-old Texan widow-woman of a thousand facelifts telling Ambrose to bring her red wine as long as it isn't French.

She's standing on the tennis court, demurely shaking hands for the first time with a bald fighting bull who calls himself Dima. She's remembering his reproachful brown eyes and rock jaw and the rigid, Erich von Stroheim backward lean of his upper body.

She's in the Bloomsbury basement, one moment Perry's life companion, the next his surplus baggage, not wanted on voyage. She's sitting with three people who, thanks to *our document* and whatever else Perry has managed to bubble to them in the meantime, know a whole lot she doesn't.

She's sitting alone in the drawing room of her desirable residence in Primrose Hill at half past midnight with *Samson v. Samson* on her lap and an empty wineglass beside her.

Springing to her feet – whoops – she climbs the spiral staircase to her bedroom, makes the bed, follows the trail of Perry's dirty clothes across the floor to the bathroom and stuffs them into the laundry basket. Five days since he made love to me. Will we establish a record?

She returns downstairs, one step at a time, one hand for the boat. She's back at the window, staring into the street, praying for her man to come home in a black cab with the last two numbers 73. She's riding buttock to buttock under the midnight stars with Perry in the bumpy people carrier with blackened windows as Baby Face, the short-haired blond bodyguard with the linked gold bracelet, drives them to their hotel at the end of the birthday revels at Three Chimneys.

'You had good night, Gail?'

This is your driver speaking. Until now, Baby Face hasn't

let on that he speaks English. When Perry challenged him outside the tennis court, he didn't speak a word of it. So why's he letting on now? she wonders, alert as never in her life.

'*Fabulous* night, thank you,' she declares in her father's voice, filling in for Perry, who appears to have gone deaf. 'Simply *wonderful*. I'm so happy for those *magnificent* boys.'

'My name is Niki, OK?'

'OK. Great. Hello, Niki,' says Gail. 'Where are you from?'

'Perm, Russia. Nice place. Perry, please? You had good night too?'

Gail is about to jab Perry with her elbow when he comes to life by himself. 'Great, thanks, Niki. Fantastic food. Really nice people. Super. Best evening of our holiday so far.'

Not bad for a beginner, thinks Gail.

'What time you arrive Three Chimneys?' Niki asks.

'We nearly didn't arrive at *all*, Niki,' Gail exclaims, giggling to cover for Perry's hesitation. 'Did we, Perry? We took the Nature Path and had to *hack* our way through the undergrowth! Where did you learn your wonderful English, Niki?'

'Boston, Massachusetts. You got knife?'

'Knife?'

'To cut undergrowth, you got to have big *knife*.'

Those dead eyes in the mirror, what have they seen? What are they seeing now?

'I wish we had, Niki,' Gail cries, still in her father's skin. 'I'm afraid we *English* don't carry knives.' *What gibberish am I talking? Never mind. Talk it.* 'Well, *some* of us do, to be truthful, but not people like *us*. We're the wrong social *class*. You've heard about our class system? Well, in England you only carry a knife if you're lower-middle or below!' And more hoots of laughter to see them round the roundabout and into the drive to the front entrance.

Dazed, they pick their way like strangers between the lighted hibiscus to their cabin. Perry closes the door behind them, locks it, but doesn't switch the light on. They stand facing each other across the bed in the darkness. For an age, there's no soundtrack. Which should not imply that Perry hasn't made up his mind what he's about to say:

'I need paper to write on. So do you.' His I'm-in-charge-here voice, normally reserved, she assumes, for errant undergraduates who have failed to turn in their weekly essay.

He draws the blinds. He switches on the inadequate reading light on my side of the bed, leaving the rest of the room in darkness.

He yanks open the drawer of *my* bedside locker and fishes out a yellow legal pad: also mine. Emblazoned on it, my brilliant reflections on *Samson v. Samson*: my first case as a top silk's junior, my quantum leap to instant fame and fortune.

Or not.

Ripping off the pages on which I have recorded my pearls of legal wisdom, he stuffs them back in the drawer, snaps what's left of *my* yellow pad in two, and hands me my half.

'I'm going in there' – pointing to the bathroom. 'You stay here. Sit at the desk and write down everything you remember. Everything that happened. I'll do the same. All right by you?'

'What's wrong with both of us being in this room? Jesus, Perry. I'm *fucking* scared. Aren't you?'

Setting aside any pardonable desire for his companionship, my question is entirely reasonable. Our cabin contains,

93

in addition to a much-used bed the size of a rugger field, one desk, two armchairs and a table. Perry may have had his heart-to-heart with Dima, but what about me, banged up with bonkers Tamara and her bearded saints?

'Separate witnesses rate separate statements,' Perry decrees, heading for the bathroom.

'Perry! Stop! Come back! Stay here! I'm the fucking lawyer here, not you. What's Dima been telling you?'

Nothing, to judge by his face. It has slammed shut.

'Perry.'

'What?'

'For fuck's sake. It's me. Gail. Remember? So just sit yourself down and tell Auntie what Dima has told you that's turned you into a zombie. All right, don't sit down. Tell me standing up. Is the world ending? Is he a girl? What the *fuck* is going on between you two that I can't know?'

A flinch. A palpable flinch. Enough flinch to give grounds for optimism. Misplaced.

'I can't.'

'Can't what?'

'Involve you in this.'

'Bollocks.'

A second flinch. No more productive than the first.

'You listening, Gail?'

What the fuck d'you think I'm doing? Singing 'The Mikado'?

'You're a good lawyer and you've got a splendid career in front of you.'

'Thank you.'

'Your big case is coming up in two weeks' time. Is that a fair summary?'

Yes, Perry, that is a fair summary. I have a splendid career in

94

front of me, unless we decide to have six children instead, and the case of Samson v. Samson *is set to be heard fifteen days from now, but if I know anything about our leading silk, I'm unlikely to get a word in edgeways.*

'You're the shining star of a prestigious law Chambers. You're worked off your feet. You've told me so often enough.'

Yes indeed, it's true, I'm appallingly overworked. A young barrister should be so lucky, we have just endured the worst night of our lives by several lengths, and what the fuck are you trying to tell me through the orange in your mouth? Perry, you can't do this! Come back! But she only thinks it. The words have run out.

'We draw a line. A line in the sand. Whatever Dima told me is private to me. What Tamara told you is private to you. We don't cross over. We exercise client confidentiality.'

Her power of speech returns. 'Are you telling me Dima is your *client* now? You're as loony as they are.'

'I'm using a legal metaphor. Taken from your world, not mine. I'm saying, Dima's my client and Tamara's yours. Conceptually.'

'Tamara didn't *speak*, Perry. Not one solitary, *fucking* word. She thinks the birds round here are bugged. Periodically, she was moved to offer up a prayer in Russian to one of her bearded protectors, at which point she signed at me to kneel down beside her, and I obliged. I'm not an Anglican atheist any more, I'm a Russian Orthodox atheist. There is otherwise absolutely fuck-all that passed between Tamara and myself that I'm not prepared to share with you in the finest detail, and I've just shared it. My principal anxiety was that I might get my hand bitten off. I didn't. Both my hands are intact. Now it's your turn.'

'Sorry, Gail. I can't.'

'I beg your pardon?'

'I'm not telling. I refuse to drag you any deeper into this affair than you are already. I want you kept clean. Safe.'

'You want?'

'No. I don't *want*. I insist. I'm not to be wooed.'

Wooed? Is this Perry talking? Or the firebrand preacher from Huddersfield that he was named after?

'I'm deadly serious,' he adds, in case she doubted it.

Then a different Perry transmogrifies out of the first one. Out of my beloved, striving Jekyll comes an infinitely less appetizing Mr Hyde of the British Secret Service:

'You also talked to Natasha, I noticed. For quite some time.'

'Yes.'

'Alone.'

'Not alone, actually. We had two small girls with us but they were asleep.'

'Then effectively alone.'

'Is that a crime?'

'She's a source.'

'She's a *what*?'

'Did she talk to you about her father?'

'Come again?'

'I said: did she talk to you about her father?'

'Pass.'

'I'm serious, Gail.'

'So am I. Deadly. Pass, and either mind your own fucking business, or tell me what Dima said to you.'

'Did she talk to you about what Dima does for a living? Who he plays with, who he trusts, who they're so afraid of?' Anything of that sort that you know, you should write it down too. It could be vitally important.'

On which note, he retires to the bathroom and – to his mortal shame – turns the lock.

For half an hour Gail sits huddled on the balcony with the bedspread over her shoulders because she's too drained to undress. She remembers the rum bottle, hangover guaranteed, pours herself a tot regardless, and dozes. She wakes to find the bathroom door open and Ace Operator Perry framed crookedly in the doorway, not sure whether to come out. He is clutching half her legal pad in both hands behind his back. She can see a corner of it poking out and it's covered in his handwriting.

'Have a drink,' she suggests, indicating the rum bottle.

He ignores her.

'I'm sorry,' he says. Then he clears his throat and says it again: 'I'm really very sorry, Gail.'

Chucking pride and reason to the winds, she impulsively jumps up, runs to him and embraces him. In the interests of security, he keeps his arms behind him. She has never seen Perry frightened before, but he's frightened now. Not for himself. For her.

*

She peers blearily at her watch. Two-thirty. She stands up, intending to give herself another glass of Rioja, thinks better of it, sits in Perry's favourite chair and discovers she is under the blanket with Natasha.

'So what does he do, your Max?' she asks.

'He completely loves me,' Natasha replies. 'Also physically.'

'I meant, apart from that, what does he do for a living?' Gail explains, careful not to smile.

It's approaching midnight. To escape the cold winds and amuse two very tired little orphan girls, Gail has made a tent out of blankets and cushions in the lee of the protective wall that borders the garden. Out of nowhere, Natasha has appeared without a book. First Gail identifies her Grecian sandals through a gap in the blankets, waiting to come on stage. For minutes on end they remain there. Is she listening? Is she plucking up her courage? For what? Is she contemplating a surprise assault to amuse the children? Since Gail has not so far exchanged a single word with Natasha, she has no picture of her possible motivations.

The flap parts, a Grecian sandal cautiously enters, followed by a knee and Natasha's averted head, curtained by her long black hair. Then a second sandal and the rest of her. The little girls, fast asleep, have not stirred. For more minutes on end Gail and Natasha lie head to head, mutely watching through the open flap as salvos of rockets are detonated with uncomfortable proficiency by Niki and his comrades-in-arms. Natasha is shivering. Gail pulls a blanket over both of them.

'It appears that I am recently pregnant,' Natasha observes, in groomed Jane Austen English, addressing not Gail but a display of fluorescent peacock feathers dripping down the night sky.

If you are lucky enough to receive the confessions of the young, it is wise to keep your eyes fixed on a common object in the far distance, rather than on one another: Gail Perkins, *ipsissima verba*. In the days before she began reading for the Bar, she taught at a school for children with learning difficulties, and this was one of the things she learned. And if a beautiful girl who is just sixteen confides in you out of the blue that she believes she may be pregnant, the lesson becomes doubly important.

*

'At present time, Max is ski instructor,' Natasha replies to Gail's casually pitched inquiry as to the possible parentage of her expected child. 'But this is temporary. He will be architect and build houses for poor people with no money. Max is very creative, also very sensitive.'

There is no humour in her voice. True love is too serious for that.

'And his parents, what do they do, I wonder?' Gail asks.

'They have hotel. It is for tourists. It is inferior, but Max is completely philosophical regarding material matters.'

'A hotel in the mountains?'

'In Kandersteg. This is village in the mountains, very touristic.'

Gail says she has never been to Kandersteg but Perry has taken part in a ski race there.

'The mother of Max is without culture but she is sympathetic and spiritual like her son. The father is completely negative. An idiot.'

Keep it banal. 'So does Max belong to the official ski school,' Gail asks, 'or is he what they call private?'

'Max is completely private. He skis only with those he respects. He loves best off-piste, which is aesthetic. Also glacier skiing.'

It was in a remote hut high above Kandersteg, Natasha says, that they astonished themselves with their passion:

'I was virgin. Also incompetent. Max is completely considerate. It is his nature to be considerate to all people. Even in passion, he is completely considerate.'

Determinedly in pursuit of the commonplace, Gail asks Natasha where she is with her studies, what subjects she is best at, and what examinations she has fixed her sights on. Since coming to live with Dima and Tamara, Natasha replies, she has been attending Roman Catholic convent school in the Canton of Fribourg as a weekly boarder:

'Unfortunately, I do not believe in God, but this is irrelevant. In life it is frequently necessary to simulate religious conviction. I like best art. Max also is very artistic. Maybe we shall both study art together at St Petersburg or Cambridge. It will be decided.'

'Is he Catholic?'

'In his practices Max is compliant with his family religion. This is because he is dutiful. But in his soul he believes in all gods.'

And in *bed*? Gail wonders, but does not ask: is he still compliant with his family religion?

'So who else knows about you and Max?' she asks in the same comfortable, light-hearted tone that she has so far managed to maintain. 'Apart from his parents, obviously. Or don't they know either, perhaps?'

'The situation is complicated. Max has sworn extremely strong oath that he will tell no one of our love. On this I have insisted.'

'Not even his mother?'

'The mother of Max is not reliable. She is inhibited by bourgeois instincts, also loquacious. If it is convenient for her, she will tell her husband, also many other bourgeois persons.'

'Is that so very bad?'

'If Dima knows that Max is my lover, it is possible Dima will kill him. Dima is not stranger to physicality. It is his nature.'

'And Tamara?'

'Tamara is not my mother,' she snaps, with a flash of her father's physicality.

'So what will you do if you discover you really are having the baby?' Gail asks lightly, as a battery of Roman candles ignites the landscape.

'At moment of confirmation, we shall immediately escape to distant place, perhaps Finland. Max will arrange this. At present time it is not convenient because he is also summer guide. We shall wait one more month. Maybe it will be possible to study in Helsinki. Maybe we shall kill ourselves. We shall see.'

Gail leaves the worst question till last, perhaps because her bourgeois instincts have warned her of the answer:

'And your Max is how old, Natasha?'

'Thirty-one. But in his heart he is child.'

As you are, Natasha. So is this a fairy tale you're spinning me under the Caribbean stars, a fantasy of the dream lover you will one day meet? Or have you really been to bed with a little shit of a thirty-one-year-old ski bum who doesn't tell his mother? Because if you have, you've come to the right address: me.

Gail had been a bit older, not much. The boy in the case wasn't a ski bum but a penniless mixed-race reject from a local grammar school with divorced parents in South Africa.

Her mother had departed the family nest three years ago, leaving no forwarding address. Her alcoholic father, far from being a physical threat, was in hospital with terminal liver failure. With money borrowed from friends, Gail had the baby clumsily aborted, and never told the boy.

And as of tonight, she hasn't got around to telling Perry either. On present form she wonders whether she ever will.

*

From the handbag she nearly left in Ollie's cab, Gail fishes out her mobile and checks it for new messages. Finding none, she scrolls back. Natasha's are in capitals for extra drama. Four of them are spread over a single week:

> I HAVE BETRAYED MY FATHER I AM SHAME.

> YESTERDAY WE BURY MISHA AND OLGA IN
> BEAUTIFUL CHURCH MAYBE I JOIN THEM
> SOON.

> PLEASE INFORM WHEN IS NORMAL TO VOMIT
> IN MORNINGS?

— followed by Gail's reply, stored in her saved messages:

> Roughly first three months, but if you are
> being sick, see doctor IMMEDIATELY, xxxx GAIL

— to which Natasha duly takes offence:

> PLEASE DO NOT SAY I AM SICK. LOVE IS NOT
> SICKNESS. NATASHA

If she's pregnant, she needs me.
If she's *not* pregnant, she needs me.

If she's a screwed-up teenaged girl fantasizing about killing herself, she needs me.

I'm her lawyer and confidante.

I'm all she's got.

*

Perry's line in the sand is drawn.

It is non-negotiable and non-tidal.

Not even tennis works any more. The Indian honeymooners have gone. Singles are too tense. Mark is enemy.

If their lovemaking allows them temporarily to forget its presence, the line is still there waiting to divide them afterwards.

Seated on their balcony after dinner, they gaze at the arc of white security lights hanging over the end of the peninsula. If Gail is hoping for a glimpse of the girls, who is Perry hoping for a glimpse of?

Of Dima, his Jay Gatsby? Of Dima, his personal Kurtz? Or some other flawed hero of his beloved Joseph Conrad?

The sensation that they are being listened to and watched is with them every hour of the day and night. Even if Perry were to break his self-imposed rule of silence, the fear of being overheard would seal his lips.

With two days to go, Perry rises at six and takes an early run. After a lie-in, Gail makes her way to the Captain's Deck resigned to a solitary breakfast, only to find him conspiring with Ambrose to bring forward their departure date. Ambrose regrets that their tickets aren't changeable:

'Now if you was to have said *yesterday*, you could have flown right along with Mr Dima and his family. Except they was all first class and you're plain old economy. Looks like you got no choice but to stick this little old island out for one more day.'

They tried to. They walked into town and looked at whatever they were supposed to look at. Perry lectured her on the sins of slavery. They went to a beach on the other side of the island and snorkled, but they were just two more Brits who didn't know what to do with so much sun.

It wasn't till dinner at the Captain's Deck that Gail finally lost it. Ignoring the embargo that Perry has imposed on their conversations in the cabin, he asks her, unbelievably, whether by any chance she knows anybody in 'the British Intelligence scene'.

'But I *work* for them,' she retorts. 'I thought you'd have guessed by now!' Her sarcasm goes nowhere.

'I just thought, maybe somebody in your Chambers has a line to them,' Perry says in a hangdog voice.

'Oh. And how would that be?' Gail snaps, feeling the heat rise to her face.

'Well' – over-innocent shrug – 'it just occurred to me that, with all the stuff going on about extraordinary rendition and torture – public inquiries, lawsuits and all that – the spies must be needing all the legal help they can get.'

It was too much. With a resounding 'fuck you, Perry', she ran down the path to the cabin, where she collapsed in tears.

And yes she was terribly sorry. And he was terribly sorry too. Mortified. They both were. It was all my fault. No, mine. Let's go home to England and get this whole bloody business over. Temporarily reunited, they grab for each other like drowning swimmers and make love with the same desperation.

*

She is back at the long window, scowling into the street. No bloody taxi. Not even the wrong one.

'*Bastards*,' she says out loud, mimicking her father. And to herself – or to the bastards – silently:

What the hell are you doing with him?

What the hell do you want from him?

What's he saying no-but-yes to as you watch him perform his moral duck shuffle?

How would you feel if Dima had chosen me as his confessor instead of Perry? If instead of man-on-man, it had been man-on-woman?

How would Perry be feeling, sitting here like a bloody cast-off, waiting for me to come back with still more secrets that 'alas, alas, I can't possibly share with you, it's for your own good'?

*

'Is that you, Gail?'

Is it?

Someone has put the phone into her hand and told her to speak to him. But someone hasn't. She's alone. It's Perry in prime time, not flashback, and she's still standing, one hand for the window frame, staring into the street.

'Look. I'm sorry it's late and everything.'

Everything?

'Hector wants to talk to both of us tomorrow morning at nine.'

'*Hector* does?'

'Yes.'

Stay rational. In a mad world, stick to what you know. 'I can't.

I know it's Sunday, but I'm working. *Samson v. Samson* never sleeps.'

'Then call Chambers and say you're sick. It matters, Gail. More than *Samson v. Samson*. Truly.'

'According to Hector?'

'According to both of us, actually.'

6

'His name will be Hector, by the way,' said adept little Luke, glancing up from his copy of the buff folder.

'Is that a warning or a divine ordinance?' Perry asked from inside his spread hands, long after Luke had given up expecting a reply.

In the age since Gail's departure, Perry had not moved from the table, neither lifting his head nor stirring from his place beside her empty chair.

'Where's Yvonne?'

'Gone home,' said Luke, back in his folder.

'Sent or gone?'

No answer.

'Is Hector your supreme leader?'

'Let's say I'm B-list, he's A-list' – pencilling a mark.

'So Hector's your boss?'

'Another way of putting it.'

And another way of not answering the question.

Actually, Perry had to concede, on all the evidence available so far, Luke was someone he could get along with. No high-flyer, maybe. B-list, just as he had said of himself. A bit plummy, perhaps, a bit public school, but a good man on a rope for all that.

'Has Hector been listening to us?'

'I expect so.'

'Watching us?'

'Sometimes it's better just to listen. Like a radio play.' And after a pause: 'Smashing girl, your Gail. Been together long?'

'Five years.'

'Wow.'

'Why *wow*?'

'Well, I suppose I feel a bit Dima-like. Marry her quick.'

This was holy ground, and Perry considered telling him so, then forgave him.

'How long have you been doing this work?' he asked Luke instead.

'Twenty years, give or take.'

'Home or abroad?'

'Abroad mainly.'

'Is it distorting?'

'Come again?'

'The work. Does it warp your mind? Are you aware of – well – *déformation professionnelle*?'

'You mean, am I psycho?'

'Nothing as drastic as that. Just – well, how it affects you over the long term?'

Luke's head remained down, but his pencil had stopped roaming, and there was challenge in his stillness.

'In the *long term*?' he repeated, in studious puzzlement. 'In the long term we'll all be dead, I imagine.'

'I simply meant: how does it grab you, representing a country that can't pay its bills?' Perry explained, aware too late that he was slipping out of his depth. 'Good intelligence being about the only thing that gets us a seat at the international top table these days, I read somewhere,' he blundered on. 'It must be rather a strain on the people who have to provide it, that's all. Punching above one's weight,' he added, in an unintentional reference to Luke's diminutive stature which he immediately regretted.

Their troubled exchange was interrupted by the shuffle of slow, soft footsteps like bedroom slippers along the ceiling before beginning a cautious descent of the basement stairs. As if to order, Luke stood up, strode over to a sideboard, picked up a tray of malt whisky, mineral water and three glasses, and set it on the table.

The footsteps reached the bottom of the stairs. The door opened. Perry rose instinctively to his feet. A mutual inspection ensued. The two men were of equal height, which for both was unusual. Without his stoop, Hector might have been the taller. With his classic broad brow and flowing white hair tossed back in two untidy waves, he resembled to Perry's eye a Head of College of the old, dotty sort. He was in his mid-fifties, by Perry's guess, but dressed for eternity in a mangy brown sports coat with leather patches at the elbow and leather edges to the cuffs. The shapeless grey flannels could have been Perry's own. So could the battered Hush Puppy shoes. The artless, horn-rimmed spectacles could have been rescued from Perry's father's attic box.

Finally, but long after time, Hector spoke:

'Wilfred *bloody* Owen,' he pronounced, in a voice that contrived to be both vigorous and reverential. 'Edmund *bloody* Blunden. Siegfried *bloody* Sassoon. Robert *bloody* Graves. Et al.'

'What about them?' the bewildered Perry asked, before he had given himself time to think.

'Your fabulous fucking article about them in the *London Review of Books* last autumn! *"The sacrifice of brave men does not justify the pursuit of an unjust cause. P. Makepiece* scripsit." Bloody marvellous!'

'Well, thank you,' said Perry helplessly, and felt an idiot for not having made the connection fast enough.

The silence returned while Hector continued his admiring inspection of his prize.

'Well, I'll tell you what you are, Mr Perry Makepiece, sir,' he asserted, as if he'd reached the conclusion they had both been waiting for. 'You're an absolute fucking hero, is what you are' – seizing Perry's hand in a flaccid double grip and giving it a limp shake – 'and *that's* not smoke up your arse. We know what you think of us. Some of us think it too, and we're right. Trouble is, we're the only show in town. Government's a fuck-up, half the Civil Service is out to lunch. The Foreign Office is as much use as a wet dream, the country's stony-broke and the bankers are taking our money and giving us the finger. What are we supposed to do about it? Complain to Mummy or fix it?' – not waiting for Perry's answer – 'I'll bet you shitted blood before you came to us. But you came. Just a token' – he had released Perry's hand and was addressing Luke on the subject of malt whisky – 'for Perry, minimal. Lot of water and enough of the hard stuff to loosen his girdle. Mind if I squat next to Luke or are we too much like *when-did-you-last-see-your-father?* Bugger Adam, my name's Meredith. Hector Meredith. We talked on the phone yesterday. Flat in Knightsbridge, wife and two veg, now grown up. Arctic cottage in Norfolk and I'm in the phone book in both places. Luke, who are *you* when you're not being some other swine?'

'Luke Weaver, actually. We live up beyond Gail on Parliament Hill. Last posting Central America. Second marriage, one common son aged ten just got into University College School, Hampstead, so we're thrilled to bits.'

'And no tough questions till the end,' Hector ordered.

Luke poured three minuscule shots of whisky. Perry sat sharply down again and waited. A-list Hector sat directly opposite him, B-list Luke a little to one side.

'Well, *fuck*,' said Hector happily.

'Fuck indeed,' Perry agreed, bemused.

*

But the truth was, Hector's rallying cry could not have been more timely or invigorating for Perry, nor his ecstatic entry better calculated. Consigned to the black hole left by Gail's enforced departure – enforced by himself, never mind the reasons – his divided heart had abandoned itself to every shade of self-anger and remorse.

He should never have agreed to come here, with or without her.

He should have handed over his document and told these people: 'That's it. You're on your own. I *am*, therefore I don't spy.'

Did it *matter* that for a whole night long he had pounded the threadbare carpet of his Oxford digs, debating the step he *knew* – but didn't wish to know – he was bound to take?

Or that his late father, low churchman, freethinker and embattled pacifist, had marched, written and raged against all things evil, from nuclear arms to the war on Iraq, more than once ending up in a police cell for his trouble?

Or that his paternal grandfather, a humble mason by trade and avowed Socialist, had lost a leg and an eye fighting on the Republican side in the Spanish Civil War?

Or that Irish colleen Siobhan, the Makepiece family treasure of twenty years and four hours a week, had been bullied into making deliveries of the contents of his father's wastepaper basket to a plain-clothes detective of the Hertfordshire constabulary? – a burden that had weighed so heavily on her that one day in floods of tears she had confessed all to Perry's mother, never to be seen near the house again, despite his mother's entreaties?

Or that only a month ago Perry himself had composed a full-page advertisement in the *Oxford Times*, endorsed by a hastily assembled body of his own creation calling itself 'Academics against Torture', urging action against Britain's Secret Government and the assault-by-stealth on our most hard-fought civil liberties?

Well, to Perry these things had mattered immensely.

And they had continued to matter on the morning after his long night of vacillation when, at eight o'clock, with a ring-bound lecture notebook jammed under his armpit, he had willed himself to set course across the quadrangle of the ancient Oxford college he was shortly to leave for ever, and ascend the worm-eaten wooden staircase leading to the rooms of Basil Flynn, Director of Studies, Doctor of Law, ten minutes after requesting a quick word with him on a private and confidential matter.

*

Only three years divided the two men, but Flynn, in Perry's judgement, was already the ultimate university committee whore. 'I can squeeze you in if you come at once,' he had said officiously, 'I've a meeting of Council at nine, and they tend to last.' He was wearing a dark suit and black shoes with polished side-buckles. Only his carefully brushed shoulder-length hair separated him from the full-dress uniform of orthodoxy. Perry had not considered how he would begin his conversation with Flynn, and his opening words, he would now concede, were hastily chosen:

'Last term you solicited one of my students,' he blurted, barely across the threshold.

'I did *what*?'

'A half-Egyptian boy. Dick Benson. Egyptian mother, English father. Arabic speaker. He wanted a research grant but you suggested he might like to talk to certain people you knew in London instead. He didn't grasp what you meant. He asked my advice.'

'Which was?'

'If the certain people in London were who I thought they were, tread carefully. I wanted to tell him not to touch them with a bargepole, but didn't feel I could say that. It was his choice, not mine. Am I right?'

'What about?'

'That you recruit for them. You talent-spot.'

'Them being who, exactly?'

'The spies. Dick Benson didn't know which lot he was up for, so how should I? I'm not accusing you. I'm asking you. Is it true? That you're in touch with them? Or was Benson fantasizing?'

'Why are you here and what do you want?'

At this point Perry nearly left the room. He wished he had. He actually turned and headed for the door, then stopped himself and turned back.

'I need to be put in touch with your certain people in London,' he said, keeping the crimson notebook under his arm and waiting for the question 'why?'

'Thinking of joining them? I know they take all sorts these days but Christ, *you*?'

Again Perry nearly headed for the door. Again he wished he had. But no, he checked himself and took a breath and this time managed to find the right words:

'I have stumbled by chance on some information' – with his long, uneasy fingers administering a tap to the notebook, which emitted a ping – 'unsolicited, unwanted and –' he hesitated a long time before using the word – 'secret.'

'Who says so?'

'I do.'

'Why?'

'If true, it could put lives at risk. Maybe save lives as well. It's not my subject.'

'Neither is it mine, I'm glad to say. I talent-spot. I baby-snatch. My certain people have a perfectly good website. They also put cretinous advertisements about themselves in the heritage press. Either route is open to you.'

'My material is too urgent for that.'

'Urgent as well as secret?'

'If it's anything at all, it's very urgent indeed.'

'The nation's fortunes hang by a thread? And that's the *Little Red Book* you're clutching under your arm, presumably.'

'It's a document of record.'

They surveyed each other in mutual distaste.

'You're not seriously proposing to give it to me, are you?'

'I am. Yes. Why not?'

'Dump your urgent secrets on Flynn? Who will stick a postage stamp on them and send them to his certain people in London?'

'Something like that. Why should I know how you people operate?'

'While you go off in search of your immortal soul?'

'I'll do what I do. They can do what they do. What's wrong with that?'

'Everything is wrong with it. In this game, which isn't a game at all, the messenger is at least half as important as the message, and sometimes he's the whole message on his own. Where are you off to now? I mean, this minute?'

'Back to my rooms.'

'Do you have a mobile telephone?'

'Of course I bloody do.'

'Write the number down for me here, please' – handing him a piece of paper – 'I never commit anything to memory, it's insecure. You have a satisfactory signal for your mobile telephone in your rooms, I trust? The walls are not too thick or anything?'

'I get a perfectly good signal, thank you.'

'Take your *Little Red Book*. Go back to your rooms and you will receive a call from somebody calling himself or herself *Adam*. A Mr or Ms Adam. I shall need a soundbite.'

'Need *what*?'

'Something to make them horny. I can't just say, "I've got a Bollinger Bolshevik on my hands who thinks he's stumbled on a world conspiracy." I've got to tell them what it's about.'

Swallowing his outrage, Perry made his first conscious effort to produce a cover story.

'Tell them it's about a crooked Russian banker who calls himself Dima,' he said, after other routes had mysteriously failed him. 'He wants to cut a deal with them. It's short for Dmitri, in case they don't know.'

'Sounds irresistible,' said Flynn sarcastically, picking up a pencil and scribbling on the same piece of paper.

Perry had been back in his room only an hour before his mobile was ringing, and he was listening to the same skittish, slightly husky male voice that had this minute addressed him here in the basement room.

'Perry Makepiece? Marvellous. Name of Adam. Just got your message. Mind if I ask you a couple of quickie questions to make sure we're both worrying at the same bone? No need to mention our chum's name. Just need to make sure he's the same chum. Does he have a wife by any chance?'

'He does.'

'Fat, blonde party? Barmaid sort of type?'

'Dark-haired and emaciated.'

'And the precise circumstances of your bumping into our chum? The when and how?'

'Antigua. On a tennis court.'

'Who won?'

'I did.'

'Marvellous. Third quickie coming up. How soon can you get up to London on our tab, and how soon can we get our hands on this dodgy dossier of yours?'

'Door to door, about two hours, I suppose. There's also a small package. I've pasted it inside the dossier.'

'Firmly?'

'I think so.'

'Well make sure you have. Write ADAM on the outside cover in large black letters – use a laundry marker or something. Then wave it around at reception till somebody notices you.'

Laundry marker? The voice of an old bachelor? Or a sly reference to Dima's dubious financial practices?

*

Enlivened by the presence of Hector lounging four feet from him, Perry was speaking swiftly and intensely, not into the middle air where academics find their traditional refuge, but straight into Hector's eagle-eyed face; and less directly to dapper Luke, seated to attention at Hector's side.

With no Gail to restrain him, he felt free to relate to both men. He was confessing himself to them as Dima had confessed himself to Perry: man to man and face to face. He was creating a synergy of confession. He was retrieving dialogue with the accuracy with which he retrieved all writing, good or bad, not pausing to correct himself.

Unlike Gail, who loved nothing better than to take off people's voices, he either couldn't, or some foolish pride wouldn't let him. But in his memory he still heard Dima's clotted Russian accents; and in his inner eye saw the sweated face so close to his own that, any nearer, the two of them would have been banging foreheads. He was smelling, even as he described them, the fumes of vodka on Dima's rasping breath. He was watching him refill his glass, glower at it, then pounce and empty it at a swallow. He was feeling himself slide into involuntary kinship with him: the swift and necessary bonding that comes of emergency on the cliff face.

'But not what we'd call *rat-arsed*?' suggested Hector, taking a sip of his malt. 'More your social drinker at the top of his form, you'd say?'

Absolutely, Perry agreed: not muddled, maudlin, slurred, just *comfortable*:

'If we'd been playing tennis next morning, I'll bet he'd have played his usual game. He's got a huge engine and it runs on alcohol. He's proud of that.'

Perry sounded as if he was proud of it too.

'Or if we misquote the Master' – Hector, it turned out, was a fellow devotee of P. G. Wodehouse – 'the kind of chap who was born a couple of drinks below par?'

'*Precisely, Bertie,*' Perry agreed in his best Wodehousian, and they found time for a quick laugh, supported by B-list Luke who with Hector's arrival had otherwise assumed the role of silent partner.

*

'Mind if I interject a question here regarding the immaculate Gail?' Hector inquired. 'Not a tough one. Medium soft.'

Tough, medium soft – Perry was on his guard.

'When you two arrived back in England from Antigua,' Hector began – 'Gatwick, wasn't it?'

Gatwick it was, Perry agreed.

'You parted company. Am I right? Gail to her legal responsibilities and her flat in Primrose Hill, and you to your rooms in Oxford, there to pen your immortal prose.'

Also correct, Perry conceded.

'So what sort of deal had the two of you struck between

you at this point – *understanding* is a prettier word – as regards the way forward?'

'Forward to what?'

'Well, to *us*, as it turns out.'

Not knowing the purpose of the question, Perry hesitated. 'There wasn't any actual *understanding*,' he replied cautiously. 'Not an explicit one. Gail had done her part. Now I would do mine.'

'In your separate stations?'

'Yes.'

'Without communicating?'

'We communicated. Just not about the Dimas.'

'And the reason for that was . . . ?'

'She hadn't heard what I'd heard at Three Chimneys.'

'And was therefore still in Arcadia?'

'Effectively. Yes.'

'Where, so far as you're aware, she remains. For as long as you can keep her there.'

'Yes.'

'Do you regret that we asked that she attend this evening's meeting?'

'You said you needed both of us. I told her you needed both of us. She agreed to come along,' Perry replied, as his face began to darken in irritation.

'But she *wanted* to come along, presumably. Otherwise she would have refused. She's a woman of spirit. Not someone who obeys blindly.'

'No. She's not,' Perry agreed, and was relieved to be met by Hector's beatific smile.

*

Perry is describing the tiny space where Dima had taken him to talk: a crow's-nest, he calls it, six by eight, stuck on the top of a ship's staircase leading up from a corner of the dining room; a gimcrack turret of wood and glass built on the half-hexagon overlooking the bay, with the sea wind rattling the clapboards and the windows shrieking.

'It must have been the noisiest place in the house. That's why he chose it, I suppose. I can't believe there's a microphone in the world that could have heard us over that din.' And in a voice that is acquiring the mystified tone of a man describing a dream: 'It was a really *talkative* house. Three chimneys and three winds. And this box we were sitting in, head to head.'

Dima's face no more than a hand's width from mine, he repeats, and leans across the table to Hector as if to demonstrate just how close.

'For an age we just sat and stared at each other. I think he was doubting himself. And doubting me. Doubting whether he could go through with it all. Whether he'd chosen the right man. And me wanting him to believe he had, does that make sense?'

To Hector, all the sense in the world apparently.

'He was trying to overcome an immense obstacle in his mind, which I suppose is what confession's all about. Then finally he rapped out a question, although it sounded more like a demand: "You are spy, Professor? English spy?" I thought at first it was an accusation. Then I realized he was assuming, even hoping, I'd say yes. So I said no, sorry, I'm not a spy, never have been, never will be. I'm just a teacher, that's all I am. But that wasn't good enough for him:

'"Many English are spy. Lords. Gentlemen. Intellectual. I *know* this! You are fair-play people. You are country of law. You got good spies."

'I had to tell him again: no, Dima, I'm not, repeat not, a spy. I'm your tennis partner and a university lecturer, on the point of changing my life. I should have been indignant. But what was *should have*? I was in a new world.'

'And absolutely *hooked*, I'll bet you were!' Hector interjects. 'I'd have given *anything* to be in your shoes! I'd even take up bloody tennis!'

Yes. *Hooked* is the word, Perry agrees. Dima was compulsive viewing in the half-darkness. And compulsive listening above the wind.

*

Hard, soft or medium, Hector's question was delivered so lightly and kindly that it was like a voice of comfort:

'And I suppose that, despite your well-founded reservations about us, you rather wished for a moment that you *were* a spy, didn't you?' he suggested.

Perry frowned, scratched awkwardly at his curly head of hair, and found no immediate answer.

*

'You know Guantánamo, Professor?'

Yes, Perry knows Guantánamo. He reckons he has campaigned against Guantánamo every which way he knows. But what's Dima trying to tell him? Why is Guantánamo suddenly so *very important, very urgent, very critical for Great Britain* – to quote Tamara's written message?

'You know secret planes, Professor? Goddam planes

those CIA guys hire, ship terrorist guys Kabul to Guantánamo?'

Yes, Perry is familiar with these secret planes. He has sent good money to a legal charity that intends to sue their parent airlines for breaches of human rights.

'Cuba to Kabul, these planes got no freight, OK? Know why? Because no fucking terrorist ever fly Guantánamo–Afghanistan. But I got *friends*.'

The word *friends* seems to trouble him. He repeats it, breaks off, mutters something in Russian to himself, and takes a pull of vodka before resuming.

'My *friends*, they talk these pilots, do deal, very private deal, no comebacks, OK?'

OK. No comebacks.

'Know what they fly in these empty planes, Professor? No customs, freight on board, direct to buyer, Guantánamo–Kabul, cash up front?'

No, Perry has no suggestions for a likely cargo out of Guantánamo bound for Kabul, cash up front.

'Lobster, Professor!' – slapping his hand on his great thigh in a fit of savage laughter. 'Couple thousand goddam lobster from Bay of Mexico! Who buy goddam lobster? Crazy warlords! From warlords, CIA buy *prisoners*. To warlords, CIA sell *goddam lobsters*. Cash. Maybe also a few K heroin for prison guards at Guantánamo. Best grade. 999. No shit. Believe me, Professor!'

Is Perry supposed to be shocked? He tries to be. Is this really sufficient reason to drag him to a rickety lookout bombarded by the wind? He doesn't believe so. Neither, he suspects, does Dima. The story sounds more like some kind of sighting shot for whatever lies ahead.

'Know what my *friends* do with this cash, Professor?'

No, Perry does not know what Dima's *friends* do with the profits from smuggling lobsters from the Bay of Mexico to Afghan warlords.

'They bring this cash to *Dima*. Why they do that? Because they are *trusting* Dima. Many, many Russian syndicate trust Dima! Not only Russian! Big, small, I don't give a shit! We take *all*! You tell your English spies: you got dirty money? Dima wash it for you, no problem! You wanna save and conserve? Come to Dima! Out of many little roads, Dima make one *big* road. Tell *this* to your goddam spies, Professor.'

*

'So how are you *reading* the bugger at this stage?' Hector asks. 'He's sweating, bragging, drinking, joking. He's telling you he's a crook and a money-launderer and he's boasting about his bent chums – what are you really *seeing* and *hearing*? What's going on inside him?'

Perry considers the premise as if it has been set for him by a higher examiner, which is how he is beginning to see Hector. 'Anger?' he proposes. 'Directed at a person or persons yet to be defined?'

'Keep going,' Hector orders.

'Desperation. Also to be defined.'

'How about honest-to-God hatred, always good?' Hector insists.

'To come, one suspects.'

'Vengeance?'

'Is somewhere in there, definitely,' Perry agrees.

'Calculation? Ambivalence? Animal cunning? Think harder!' – spoken in jest, but received in earnest.

'All of the above. No question.'

'And *shame? Self-disgust?* None of that about?'

Taken aback, Perry ponders, frowns, peers about him. '*Yes,*' he concedes in a long-drawn-out voice. '*Yes.* Shame. The *apostate's* shame. *Ashamed* to be dealing with me at all. *Ashamed* of his treachery. That's why he had to boast so much.'

'I'm a goddam clairvoyant,' says Hector with satisfaction. 'Ask anyone.'

Perry doesn't need to.

*

Perry is describing the long minutes of silence, the conflicting grimaces of Dima's sweated face in the half-darkness, how he pours himself another vodka, chucks it back, mops his face, grins, glowers indignantly at Perry as if questioning his presence, reaches out and grabs him by the knee in order to hold his attention while he makes a point, relinquishes it, and forgets him again. And how finally, in a voice of deepest suspicion, he growls out a question that must be squarely answered before any other business can be conducted between them:

'You see my Natasha?'

Perry has seen his Natasha.

'She beautiful?'

Perry has no difficulty assuring Dima that Natasha is indeed very beautiful.

'Ten, twelve book a week, she don't givva shit. Read them all. You wanna get a few student like that, you be goddam happy.'

Perry says he would indeed be happy.

'Ride horse, dance ballet. Ski so beautiful like goddam

bird. Wanna know something? Her mother. She got dead. I loved this woman. OK?'

Perry makes noises of regret.

'Maybe I fuck too many women once. Some guys, they need a lotta women. Good women, they wanna be the only one. You screw around, they go a bit crazy. That's a pity.'

Perry agrees it's a pity.

'*Jesus God*, Professor!' He is leaning forward, stabbing at Perry's knee with his index finger. 'Natasha's mother, I *love* that woman, I love her so much I explode, hear me? Love like make your guts on fire. Your prick, balls, heart, brain, your soul: they live only for this love.' He makes another pass of the back of his hand across his mouth, mutters 'like your Gail, beautiful', takes a shot of vodka and continues. 'Her bastard husband kill her,' he confides. 'Know *why*?'

No, Perry does not know why Natasha's mother's bastard husband killed Natasha's mother, but he is waiting to discover, just as he is waiting to discover whether he really is in a madhouse.

'Natasha she *my* child. When Natasha's mother tell this to him because she cannot lie, the bastard kill her. One day, maybe I find this bastard. Kill him. Not with gun. With these.'

He holds up his improbably delicate hands for Perry's inspection. Perry dutifully admires them.

'My Natasha go to Eton School, OK? Tell this to your spies. Or no deal.'

For a brief moment, in a violently rotating world, Perry feels himself on firm ground.

'I'm not absolutely sure that Eton takes girls yet,' he says cautiously.

'I pay good. I give swimming pool. No problem.'

'Even so, I don't think they'll change the rules for her.'

'So where she go?' Dima demands recklessly, as if it's Perry and not the school who is making the difficulties.

'There's a place called Roedean. It's supposed to be the girls' equivalent of Eton.'

'Number one for England?'

'People say so.'

'Kids of intellectuals? Lords? *Nomenklatura?*'

'It's a school for the high end of British society, put it that way.'

'Cost lotta money?'

'A great lot.'

Dima is only half appeased.

'OK,' he growls. 'When we make deal with your spies. Number-one condition: *Roedean School.*'

*

Hector's mouth is wide open. He gawps at Perry, then at Luke beside him, then at Perry again. He passes his hand through his unkempt mop of white hair in frank disbelief.

'Holy fucking cow,' he murmurs. 'How about a commission in the Household Cavalry for his twin sons while he's about it? What did you tell him?'

'I promised I'd do my absolute best,' Perry replies, feeling himself drawn to Dima's side. 'It's the England he thinks he loves. What else was I supposed to say to him?'

'You did *marvellously*,' Hector enthuses. And little Luke agrees, *marvellous* being a word they share.

*

'You remember *Mumbai*, Professor? Last November? The crazy Pakistani guys, kill the whole goddam world? Take orders over their cells? The goddam café they shoot up? The Jews they kill? Hostages? The hotels, train stations? The goddam kids, mothers, all dead? How the fuck they do that, those crazy bastards?'

Perry has no suggestions.

'My kids cut a finger, bleed a bit, I wanna throw up,' Dima protests indignantly. 'I done enough death in my life, hear me? Whadda they wanna do that for, the crazy fucks?'

Perry the unbeliever would like to say 'for God' but says nothing. Dima steels himself, then takes the plunge:

'OK. You tell this once to your goddam English spies, Professor,' he urges with another lurch into aggression. 'October two thousand eight. Remember the fucking date. A *friend* call me. OK? A *friend*?'

OK. Another *friend*.

'Pakistani guy. A syndicate we do business with. October 30, middle of the goddam night, he call me. I'm in Berne, Switzerland, very quiet city, lot of bankers. Tamara she's asleep beside me. Wakes up. Gives me the goddam phone: *for you*. It's this guy. Hear me?'

Perry hears him.

'"Dima," he tell to me. "Here is your *friend*, Khalil." Bullshit. His name's Mohamed. Khalil, that's a special name he got for certain cash business I'm connected with, who givva shit? "I got hot market tip for you, Dima. Very big, very hot tip. Very special. You guys gotta remember it was me who tell you this tip. You remember for me?" OK, I say. Sure. Four o'clock in the goddam morning, some piece shit about the Mumbai stock market. Never mind. I tell him,

OK, we remember it's you, Khalil. We got good memory. Nobody stiff you. What's your hot tip?

"'Dima, you gotta get the fuck outta the Indian stock market or you catch big cold." "*What?*" I say, "*what*, Khalil? You fucking crazy? Why we gonna catch a big cold in Mumbai? We got a shitload respectable business in Mumbai. Regular, squeaky-fucking-clean investments, took me five years I clean – services, tea, timber, hotels so fucking white and big the Pope could hold a mass in them." My friend don't listen. "Dima, hear me, get the fuck outta Mumbai. Maybe a month after, you take strong position again, make a few million. But first you get the fuck outta those hotels.'"

A fist again passes across Dima's face, punching away the sweat. He whispers *Jesus God* to himself and stares around their tiny box for help. 'You gonna tell this to your English apparatchiks, Professor?'

Perry will do what he can.

'Night October 30 two thousand eight, after this Pakistani arsehole wake me up, I don't sleep good, OK?'

OK.

'Next morning October 31 I call my goddam Swiss banks. "Get me the fuck outta Mumbai." Services, timber, tea, I got maybe thirty per cent. Hotels seventy. Couple week later, I'm in Rome. Tamara call me. "Turn on the goddam television." What do I watch? Those crazy Pakistani fucks shooting the shit outta Mumbai, Indian stock market stop trading. Next day, Indian Hotels are down sixteen per cent to 40 rupees and falling. March this year, they hit 31. Khalil call me. "OK, my friend, now you get the fuck back in. Remember it's me who told you this." So I get the fuck back in.' The sweat is pouring down his bald face. 'End of year, Indian Hotels are 100 rupees. I make twenty million profit cold. The Jews are dead, the hostages are dead and I'm a fucking genius. You tell this to your English spies, Professor. Jesus God.'

The sweated face a mask of self-disgust. The cracking of the rotten weatherboards in the sea-wind. Dima has talked himself to a point of no return. Perry has been observed and tested and found good.

*

Washing his hands in the prettily decked-out upstairs lavatory, Perry peers into the mirror and is impressed by the eagerness of a face he is beginning not to know. He hurries back down the thickly carpeted staircase.

'Another nip?' Hector asks, flapping a lazy hand in the direction of the drinks tray. 'Luke, lad, how's about making us a pot of coffee?'

7

In the road above the basement, an ambulance tears past, and the howl of its siren is like a scream for the whole world's pain.

In the wind-beaten, half-hexagon turret overlooking the bay, Dima is unrolling the satin sleeve from his left arm. By the changeful moonlight that has replaced the vanished sun, Perry discerns a bare-breasted Madonna surrounded by voluptuous angels in alluring poses. The tattoo descends from the tip of Dima's massive shoulder to the gold wristband of his bejewelled Rolex watch.

'You wanna know who make this tattoo for me, Professor?' he whispers in a voice husky with emotion. 'Six goddam month every day one hour?'

Yes, Perry would like to know who has tattooed a topless Madonna and her female choir on to Dima's enormous arm, and taken six months to do it. He would like to know what relevance the Holy Virgin has to Dima's quest for a place at Roedean for Natasha, or permanent residence in Britain for all his family in exchange for vital information, but the English tutor in him is also learning that Dima the storyteller has his own narrative arc and that his plots unfold with indirection.

'My Rufina make this. She was *zek*, like me. Camp hooker, sick from tuberculosis, one hour each day. When she finish, she die. Jesus Christ, huh? Jesus Christ.'

A respectful quiet while both men contemplate Rufina's masterpiece.

'Know what is *Kolyma*, Professor?' Dima asks, still with a husk in his voice. 'You heard?'

Yes, Perry knows what is *Kolyma*. He has read his Solzhenitsyn. He has read his Shalamov. He knows that Kolyma is a river north of the Arctic Circle that has given its name to the harshest camps in the Gulag archipelago, before or after Stalin. He knows *zek* too: *zek* for Russia's prisoners, the millions and millions of them.

'With fourteen I was goddam *zek* in Kolyma. Criminal, not political. Political is shit. Criminal is pure. Fifteen years I serve there.'

'*Fifteen* in *Kolyma*?'

'Sure, Professor. I done fifteen.'

The anguish has gone out of Dima's voice, to be replaced by pride.

'For *criminal prisoner Dima*, other prisoners got *respect*. Why I was in Kolyma? I was murderer. *Good* murderer. Who I murder? Lousy Sovietsky apparatchik in Perm. Our father suicide himself, got tired, drank lotta vodka. My mother, to give us food, soap, she gotta fuck this lousy apparatchik. In Perm, we live in communal apartment. Eight crappy rooms, thirty people, one crappy kitchen, one shithouse, everybody stink and smoke. Kids do not like this lousy apparatchik who fuck our mother. We gotta stand outside in kitchen, very thin wall, when apparatchik come to visit us, bring food, fuck my mother. Everybody stare at us: listen to your mother, she's a whore. We gotta put our hands over our goddam ears. You wanna know something, Professor?'

Perry does.

'This guy, this apparatchik, know where he get his food?'

Perry does not.

'He's a fucking *military administrator*! Distributes food in barracks. Carries a gun. Nice pretty gun, leather case, big hero. You wanna try fucking with a gun belt round your arse? You gotta be big acrobat. This *military administrator*, this *apparatchik*, he take off shoes. He take off his pretty gun. He put gun in shoes. OK, I think. Maybe you fuck my mother enough. Maybe you don't fuck her no more. Maybe nobody gonna stare at us no more like we're whore's kids. I knock on door. I open it. I am polite. "Excuse me," I say. "Is Dima. Excuse me, *Comrade Lousy Apparatchik*. Please I borrow your pretty gun? Kindly look me in my face once. You don't look me, how do I kill you? Thank you so much, Comrade." My mother look me. She don't say nothing. Apparatchik look me. I kill the fuck. One bullet.'

Dima's forefinger rests on the bridge of his nose, indicating where the bullet went. Perry is reminded of the same forefinger resting on his sons' noses in the middle of the tennis match.

'Why I murder this apparatchik?' Dima inquires rhetorically. 'Was for my *mother* who protect her *children*. Was for love of my crazy *father* who suicide himself. Was for honour of *Russia*, I kill this fuck. Was to stop stares they give us in corridor, maybe. Therefore in Kolyma I am *welcome* prisoner. I am *krutoi* – good fellow, got no problems, pure. I am not *political*. I am criminal. I am *hero*, I am *fighter*. I kill military apparatchik, maybe also *Chekist*. Why else they give me fifteen? I have *honour*. I am not –'

*

Reaching this point in his story, Perry faltered, and his voice became diffident:

'I am not *woodpecker*. I am not *dog*, Professor,' he offered dubiously.

'He means informant,' Hector explained. 'Woodpecker, dog, hen: take your pick. They all mean informant. He's trying to persuade you that he isn't one when he is.'

With a nod of respect for Hector's superior knowledge, Perry resumed.

*

'One day, after three years, this good boy Dima will become *man*. How he become *man*? My friend *Nikita* will make him man. Who is *Nikita*? Nikita is also *honourable*, also good *fighter*, big criminal. He will be *father* to this good boy Dima. He will be *brother* to him. He will *protect* Dima. He will *love* Dima. It will be *pure* love. One day, it is very good day for me, proud day, Nikita bring me to *vory*. You know what is *vory*, Professor? You know what is *vor*?'

Yes, Perry even knows what is *vory*. He knows *vor* too. He has read his Solzhenitsyn, he has read his Shalamov. He has read that in the Gulag the *vory* are the prisoners' arbiters and enforcers of justice, a brotherhood of criminals of honour sworn to abide by a strict code of conduct, to renounce marriage, property and subservience to the State; that the *vory* venerate priesthood and dabble in its mystique; and that *vor* is the singular of *vory*, plural. And that the *vory*'s pride is to be Criminals within the Law, an aristocracy far removed from street riff-raff who have never known a law in their lives.

'My Nikita speak to very big *vory* committee. Many big criminals are present for this meeting, many good fighters. He tell to *vory*: "My dear brothers, here is *Dima*. Dima is *ready*, my brothers. Take him." So they *take* Dima, they make him *man*. They make him criminal of honour. But Nikita must still *protect* Dima. This is because Dima – is – his –'

As Dima the criminal of honour hunts for the *mot juste*, Perry the outward-bound Oxford don comes to his assistance:

'Disciple?'

'*Disciple! Yes*, Professor! Like for Jesus! Nikita will protect his *disciple* Dima. This is normal. This is *vory* law. He will protect him *always*. This is *promise*. Nikita has made me *vor*. Therefore he protect me. But he die.'

Dima dabs at his bald brow with his handkerchief, then smears his wrist across his eyes, then pinches his nostrils between his finger and thumb like a swimmer emerging from the water. When the hand comes down, Perry sees that he is weeping for Nikita's death.

*

Hector has called a natural break. Luke has made coffee. Perry accepts a cup, and a chocolate digestive while he's about it. The lecturer in him is in full flood, rallying his facts and observations, presenting them with all the accuracy and precision he can muster. But nothing can quite douse the glint of excitement in his eyes, or the flush of his gaunt cheeks.

And perhaps the self-editor in him is aware of this, and troubled by it: which is why, when he resumes, he selects a staccato, almost offhand style of narrative more in keeping with pedagogic objectivity than the rush of adventure:

'Nikita had picked up a camp fever. It was midwinter. Minus sixty degrees Celsius, or thereabouts. A lot of prisoners were dying. Guards didn't give a damn. The hospitals weren't there to cure, they were places to die in. Nikita was a tough nut and took a long time dying. Dima tended him. Missed his prison work, got the punishment cell. Each time they let him out, he went back to Nikita in the hospital until they dragged him off again. Beating, starving, light deprivation, chained to a wall in sub-zero temperatures. All the stuff you people outsource to less fastidious countries, and pretend you know nothing about,' he adds, in a spurt of semi-humorous belligerence that falls flat. 'And while he was comforting Nikita, they agreed that Dima would induct his own protégé into the *vory* Brotherhood. It was a solemn moment, apparently: the dying Nikita appointing his posterity by way of Dima. A passing of the chalice across three generations of criminals. Dima's protégé – *disciple*, as he was now pleased to call him, thanks to me, I'm afraid – was one Mikhail, alias *Misha*.' Perry reproduces the moment:

'"Misha is man of honour, like me!" I tell to them,' Dima is proclaiming to the *vory*'s high committee of made men. '"He is criminal, not political. Misha love *true* Mother Russia not Soviet Union. Misha respect all *women*. He *strong*, he *pure*, he not woodpecker, he not dog, not military, not camp guard, KGB. He not *policeman*. He *kill* policemen. He despise all apparatchik. Misha my *son*. He your brother. Take the son of Dima for your *vory* brother!"'

*

Perry still determinedly in lecture mode. The following facts for your notebooks, please, ladies and gentlemen. The passage I am about to read to you represents the short version of Dima's personal history, as recounted by him in the lookout of the house called Three Chimneys between slurps of vodka:

'As soon as he was released from Kolyma he hurried home to Perm and was in time to bury his mother. The early 1980s were boom years for criminals. Life in the fast lane was short and dangerous, but profitable. With his impeccable credentials Dima was received with open arms by the local *vory*. Discovering that he had a natural eye for numbers, he quickly engaged in illegal currency speculation, insurance fraud and smuggling. A fast-expanding folio of petty crime takes him to Communist East Germany. Car theft, false passports and currency deals a speciality. And along the way he equips himself with spoken German. He takes his women where he finds them, but his continuing partner is Tamara, a black-market dealer in such rare commodities as women's clothing and essential foods, resident in Perm. With the assistance of Dima and like-minded accomplices she also runs a sideline in extortion, abduction and blackmail. This brings her into conflict with a rival brotherhood who first take her prisoner and torture her, then frame her and hand her over to the police who torture her some more. Dima explains Tamara's *problem*:

'"She don't never squeal, Professor, hear me? She good criminal, better than man. They put her in press-cell. Know what is press-cell? They hang her upside down, rape her ten, twenty time, beat the shit outta her, but she don't never

136

squeal. She tell them, go fuck themselves. Tamara, she big fighter, no *bitch*.'"

Again Perry offered the word with diffidence, and again Hector quietly came to his rescue:

'*Bitch* being even worse than dog or woodpecker. A bitch betrays the underworld code. Dima's getting the serious guilts by now.'

'Then perhaps that's why he stumbled over the word,' Perry suggested, and Hector said perhaps it was.

Perry as Dima again: 'One day the police get so goddam sick of her they strip her naked, leave her in the fucking snow. She don't never squeal, hear me? She go a bit crazy, OK? Talk to God. Buy a lotta icons. Bury money in the fucking garden, can't find it, who givva fuck? This woman got loyalty, hear me? I don't never let her go. Natasha's mother, I loved her. But Tamara, I never let her go. Hear me?'

Perry hears him.

As soon as Dima starts to make serious money he packs Tamara off to a Swiss clinic for rest and rehabilitation, then marries her. Within a year their twin sons are born. Hot upon the wedding comes the betrothal of Tamara's sensationally beautiful, much younger sister, Olga, a high-class hooker greatly prized by the *vory*. And the bridegroom is none other than Dima's beloved disciple Misha, by now also released from Kolyma.

'With the union of Olga and Misha, Dima's cup was full,' Perry declared. 'Dima and Misha were henceforth true brothers. Under *vory* law, Misha was already Dima's son, but the marriage made the family relationship absolute. Dima's children would be Misha's children, Misha's children would be his,' Perry said, and sat back decisively, as if waiting for questions from the back of the hall.

But Hector, who had been observing with some amusement Perry's retreat into his academic skin, preferred to offer his own brand of wry comment:

'Which is a bloody odd thing about these *vory* chaps, wouldn't you say? One minute forswearing marriage, politics and the State and all its works, the next prancing up the aisle in full rig with the church bells ringing. Have another shot of this. Only a teaspoon. Water?'

Business with the bottle and water jug.

'It's who they all were, isn't it?' Perry reflected extraneously, sipping at his very weak whisky. 'All those weird cousins and uncles in Antigua. They were Criminals within the Law who had come to commiserate about Misha and Olga.'

*

Perry's resolute lecture mode again. Perry as capsule historian, and nothing else:

Perm is no longer large enough for Dima or the Brotherhood. Business is expanding. Crime syndicates are forming alliances. Deals are being cut with foreign mafias. Best of all, Dima the *bête intellectuelle* of Kolyma with no education worth a damn has discovered a natural talent for laundering criminal proceeds. When Dima's Brotherhood decides to open up for business in America, it's Dima they send to New York to set up a money-laundering chain based in Brighton Beach. Dima takes Misha as his enforcer. When the Brotherhood decides to open a European arm of his money-laundering business, it's Dima they appoint to the post. As a condition of acceptance, Dima again requests the appointment of Misha, this time as his number two in Rome. Request granted. Now the Dimas and the Mishas are indeed one family, trading together, playing together, exchanging houses and visits, admiring one another's children.

Perry takes another sip of whisky.

'That was in the days of the *old Prince*,' Perry says, almost nostalgically. 'For Dima, the golden age. The old Prince was a true *vor*. He could do no wrong.'

'And the *new* Prince?' Hector inquires provocatively. 'The young fellow? Any take on *him* at all?'

Perry is not amused. 'You know bloody well there was,' he growls. And adds: 'The new young Prince is the bitch of all time. The traitor of traitors. He's the Prince who delivers the *vory* to the State, which is the worst thing any *vor* can do. Betraying a man like that is a duty in Dima's eyes, not a crime.'

*

'You like those little kids, Professor?' Dima asks in a tone of false detachment, throwing back his head and affecting to study the flaking panels of the ceiling: 'Katya? Irina? You *like*?'

'Of course I do. They're wonderful.'

'Gail, she like too?'

'You know she does. She's terribly sorry for them.'

'What they tell her, the little girls, how their father die?'

'In a car smash. Ten days ago. Outside Moscow. A tragedy. The father and mother both.'

'Sure. Was tragedy. Was car smash. Very *simple* car smash.

139

Very *normal* car smash. In Russia we get many such car smash. Four men, four Kalashnikov, maybe sixty bullet, who givva shit? That's a goddam car smash, Professor. One body, twenty maybe thirty bullet. My Misha, my disciple, a kid, forty year old. Dima take him to the *vory*, make him a *man*.'

A sudden outbreak of fury:

'So why do I not protect my Misha? Why I let him go to Moscow? Let bitch Prince's bastards kill him twenty, thirty bullet? Kill Olga, beautiful sister of my wife Tamara, mother of Misha's little girls. Why I not protect him? You are Professor! You tell me, please, why do I not protect my Misha?'

If it was fury, not volume, that gave his voice such unearthly strength, it is the chameleon nature of the man that enables him to put aside his fury in favour of despond-ent Slav reflection:

'OK. Maybe Tamara's sister Olga, she not so goddam religious,' he says, conceding a point that Perry hasn't made. 'I tell to Misha: "Maybe your Olga still look at other guys too much, got beautiful arse. Maybe you don't screw around no more, Misha, stay home once, like me now, take a bit care of her."' His voice falls to a whisper again: 'Thirty goddam bullet, Professor. That bitch Prince gotta pay something for thirty bullet in my Misha.'

*

Perry had gone quiet. It was as if a distant bell had sounded for the end of the lecture period, and he had belatedly become aware of it. For a moment he appeared to surprise himself by his presence at the table. Then with a jerk of his long, angular body he re-entered time present.

'So that's basically about *it* then,' he said, in a tone to wrap things up. 'Dima sank into himself for a while, woke up, seemed puzzled I was there, resented my presence, then decided I was all right, then forgot me again and put his hands over his face and muttered to himself in Russian. Then he stood up, and fished around in his satin shirt, and yanked out the little package I included in my document,' he went on. 'Handed it to me, embraced me. It was an emotional moment.'

'For both of you.'

'In our separate ways, yes, it was. I think it was.'

He seemed suddenly in a hurry to go back to Gail.

'Any instructions to accompany the package at all?' Hector asked, while little B-list Luke beside him smiled to himself over his neatly folded hands.

'Sure. "Take this to your apparatchiks, Professor. A present from World Number One money-launderer. Tell them I want fair play." Exactly as I wrote in my document.'

'Any idea what was *in* the package?'

'Only guesses, really. It was wrapped in cotton wool, then cling-film. As you saw. I assumed it was an audio cassette – from a baby recorder of some kind. Or that's what it felt like anyway.'

Hector remained unpersuaded. 'And you didn't attempt to open it.'

'God no. It was addressed to you. I just made sure it was firmly pasted inside the cover of the dossier.'

Slowly turning the pages of Perry's document, Hector gave a distracted nod.

'He was carrying it against his body,' Perry continued, evidently feeling a need to fend off the gathering silence:

'It made me think of Kolyma. The tricks they must have got up to. Secreting messages and so on. The thing was dripping wet. I had to wipe it dry on a towel when I got back to our cabin.'

'And you didn't open it?'

'I said I didn't. Why should I? I'm not in the habit of reading other people's letters. Or listening to them.'

'Not even before you passed through Customs at Gatwick?'

'Certainly not.'

'But you *felt* it.'

'Of course I did. I just told you I did. What's this about? Through the plastic film. And the cotton wool. When he gave it to me.'

'And when he'd given it to you, what did you do with it?'

'Put it in a safe place.'

'Where was that?'

'I'm sorry?'

'The safe place. Where was it?'

'In my shaving bag. The moment I got back to our cabin, I went straight into the bathroom and put it there.'

'Next to your toothbrush, as it were.'

'As it were.'

Another long silence. Was it as long for them as it was for Perry? He feared not.

'Why?' Hector demanded finally.

'Why what?'

'The shaving bag,' Hector replied patiently.

'I thought it would be safer.'

'When you passed through Customs at Gatwick?'

'Yes.'

'You thought that's where everybody keeps their cassettes?'

'I just thought it would be' – he shrugged.

'Less conspicuous in a shaving bag?'

'Something like that.'

'Did Gail know?'

'What? Of course not. No.'

'I should think not. Is the recording in Russian or English?'

'How on earth do I know? I didn't *listen* to it.'

'Dima didn't tell you which language it was in?'

'He offered no description of it whatever, other than the one I've given you. Cheers.'

He took a last swig of his very thin Scotch, then set his glass heavily on the table, signifying finality. But Hector did not at all share his haste. Quite the contrary. He turned back a page of Perry's document. Then forward a couple.

'So *why* again?' Hector pursued.

'Why what?'

'Why do it at all? Why smuggle a dicey package through British Customs for a Russian crook? Why not chuck it in the Caribbean and forget about it?'

'I'd have thought it was pretty obvious.'

'It is to me. I wouldn't have thought it was for you. What's so pretty obvious about it?'

Perry searched, but seemed to have no answer to the question.

'Well how about *because it's there*?' Hector suggested. 'Isn't that why climbers are supposed to climb?'

'So they say.'

'Load of bollocks, actually. It's because the climbers are

there. Don't blame the bloody mountain. Blame the climbers. Agree?'

'Probably.'

'They're the chaps who see the distant peak. The mountain doesn't give a bugger.'

'Probably not, no' – an unconvincing grin.

'Did Dima discuss your own personal involvement in these negotiations at all, should they transpire?' Hector inquired, after what seemed to Perry an endless delay.

'A bit.'

'In what terms – *a bit*?'

'He wanted me to be present for them.'

'Present *why*?'

'To see fair play, apparently.'

'Whose fair play, for fuck's sake?'

'Well, yours I'm afraid,' said Perry, reluctantly. 'He wanted me to hold you people to your word. He has an aversion to apparatchiks, as you may have noticed. He wants to admire you because you're English gentlemen, but he doesn't trust you because you're apparatchiks.'

'Is that how *you* feel?' – peering at Perry with his oversized grey eyes. 'That we're apparatchiks?'

'Probably,' Perry conceded, yet again.

Hector turned to Luke, still seated strictly at his side. 'Luke, old boy, I rather think you have an appointment. We shouldn't keep you.'

'Of course,' said Luke and, with a brisk smile of farewell for Perry, obediently left the room.

*

The malt whisky was from the Isle of Skye. Hector poured two stiff shots and invited Perry to help himself to water.

'So,' he announced. 'Tough question time. Feel up to it?'

How could he not?

'We have a discrepancy. A king-sized one.'

'I'm not aware of any.'

'I am. It concerns what you have *not* written to us in your alpha-plus essay, and what you have so far omitted from your otherwise flawless *viva voce*. Shall I spell it out, or will you?'

Noticeably ill at ease, Perry shrugged again. 'You do it.'

'Gladly. In both performances you have failed to report a key clause in Dima's terms and conditions as relayed to us in the package you ingeniously smuggled through Gatwick Airport in your shaving bag or, as we oldies prefer to call it, sponge bag. Dima *insists* – not a *bit*, as you suggest, but as a breakpoint – and Tamara *insists*, which I suspect is even more important, despite appearances – that you, Perry, be present at all negotiations, and that the said negotiations be conducted in the English language for your benefit. Did he happen to mention that condition to you in the course of his meanderings?'

'Yes.'

'But you saw fit not to mention it to us.'

'Yes.'

'Was that by any chance because Dima and Tamara also stipulate the participation not merely of *Professor Makepiece* but of a lady they are pleased to describe as *Madam Gail Perkins*?'

'*No*,' Perry said, his voice and jaw rigid.

'*No?* No what? No, you didn't unilaterally edit that condition out of your written and oral accounts?'

Perry's response was so vehement and precise that it was apparent he had been preparing it for some time. But first he closed his eyes as if to consult his inner demons. 'I'll do it for Dima. I'll even do it for you people. But I'll do it alone or not at all.'

'While in the same rambling diatribe addressed to us,' Hector pursued, in a tone that took no account of the dramatic statement of which Perry had just delivered himself, 'Dima *also* refers to a scheduled meeting in Paris this *coming* June. The 7th, to be precise. A meeting not with us despised apparatchiks at all, but with *yourself and Gail*, which struck us as a bit peculiar. Can you account for that by any chance?'

Perry either couldn't or wouldn't. He was scowling into the half-darkness, one long hand cupped across his mouth as if to muzzle it.

'He appears to be proposing a *tryst*,' Hector went on. 'Or more accurately, referring to one that *he's* already proposed and *you* have apparently agreed to. Where's it to be, one wonders? Under the Eiffel Tower at the stroke of midnight and bring a copy of yesterday's *Figaro*?'

'No, it bloody well wasn't.'

'So where?'

With a muttered 'sod it, then' Perry dipped a hand into his jacket pocket, drew out a blue envelope, and slapped it gracelessly on to the oval table. It was unsealed. Picking it up, Hector meticulously drew back the flap with his skinny white fingertips, extracted two pieces of printed blue card, and unfolded them. Then a sheet of white paper, also folded.

'And these tickets are for *where* exactly?' he inquired after a perplexed study that by any normal standards would long ago have given him his answer.

'Can't you read it? Men's Final of the French Open. Roland Garros, Paris.'

'And you came by them how?'

'I was settling our bill at the hotel. Gail was packing. Ambrose handed them to me.'

'Together with this nice note from Tamara?'

'Correct. Together with the nice note from Tamara. Well done.'

'Tamara's note was enclosed in the envelope with the tickets, I take it. Or was it separate?'

'Tamara's note was in a separate envelope, which was sealed, and which I have since destroyed,' Perry said, his voice clotting in anger. 'The two tickets to the Roland Garros Tennis Stadium were in an envelope that was *un*sealed. That is the envelope you are holding in your hand now. I discarded the envelope containing Tamara's letter, and placed her letter *inside* it *with* the tickets.'

'Marvellous. May I read it?'

He did anyway:

'We invite you please to bring Gail for your companion. We shall be happy to reunite with you.'

'For God's sake,' Perry muttered.

'Please be available in Allée Marcel-Bernard of Roland Garros enclosure fifteen (15) minutes before commencement of match. There are many shops in this allée. Please pay particular attention to display of

Adidas materials. It will appear big surprise to meet you. It will appear coincidence ordained by God. Please discuss this matter with your British officials. They will understand this situation.

'Please also accept hospitality at special box of Arena company representative. It will be convenient if responsible person of secret authority of Great Britain will be in Paris at this period for very discreet discussion. Please enable this.

'In God we love you,

'Tamara.'

'Is this all of it?'

'All.'

'And you're distressed. Embittered. Pissed off at having to show your hand.'

'As a matter of fact, I'm pretty fucking furious,' Perry agreed.

'Well, before you explode completely, let me give you a bit of gratuitous background. It may be all you get.' He was leaning forward across the table, his grey, zealot's eyes gleaming with excitement. 'Dima has two vitally important signings coming up at which he will formally pass over his entire, extremely ingenious money-laundering system to younger hands: namely, the Prince and his retinue. The sums of money involved are astronomic. The first signing is in Paris on Monday June 8th, the day after your tennis party. The second and final signing – we may say terminal – takes place in Berne two days later on Wednesday June 10th. Once Dima has signed away his life's work – ergo, post the Berne signing on June 10th – he will be ripe for the same unfriendly treatment dealt out to his friend Misha:

whacking, in other words. I mention this in parenthesis in order to make you aware of the depth of Dima's planning, the desperate straits he's in, and the accrued billions – literally – at stake. Until he's signed, he's immune. You can't shoot your milk-cow. Once he's signed, he's dead meat.'

'So why on earth go to Moscow for the funeral?' Perry objected, in a remote voice.

'Well, you and I wouldn't, would we now?' Hector agreed. 'But we're not *vory*, and vengeance exacts its price. So does survival. For as long as he hasn't signed, he's bulletproof. Can we go back to *you*?'

'If you must.'

'We both must. You mentioned a moment ago that you were pretty fucking furious. Well, I think you've every right to be pretty fucking furious, and with *yourself*, because at one level – the level of normal social intercourse – you are behaving, in admittedly difficult circumstances, like a chauvinistic arsehole. No good bristling like that. Look at the hash you've made of it so far. Gail's not aboard, she's pining to be. I don't know what century you think you're living in, but she's as much entitled as you are to make her own decisions. Were you *seriously* considering doing her out of a free ticket to the Men's Final of the French Open? Gail? – your partner in tennis, as in life?'

His hand once more cupped over his mouth, Perry emitted a stifled groan.

'Quite so. Now for the other level: that of *ab*normal social discourse. *My* level, *Luke's* level. *Dima's*. What you have realized, perfectly correctly, is that you and Gail have wandered by sheer accident into a richly planted minefield. And like any decent person of your stamp, your first instinct is to get Gail the hell out of it, and keep her out of it. You have also worked out, unless I'm mistaken, that you personally, by listening to Dima's offer, by transmitting it to us, and by being appointed umpire or observer or whatever he wants to call it, are by *vory* law, by the reckoning of the people Dima is proposing to blow the whistle on, a legitimate case for the extreme sanction. Agreed?'

Agreed.

'To what extent Gail is potential collateral damage is an open question. You've no doubt thought of that too.'

Perry had.

'So let's count up the big questions. Big question one: are you, Perry, morally entitled *not* to acquaint Gail with the peril she's in? Answer in my view: *no*. Big question two: are you morally entitled to deny her the choice of coming aboard once she has been so acquainted, given that she has an emotional investment in the children of Dima's household, not to mention her feelings for yourself? Answer in my view: again *no*, but we can argue about that later. And *three*, which is a bit toe-curling but we do have to ask: are you, Perry, is she, Gail, are you as a couple, attracted to the idea of doing something *fucking* dangerous for your country, for virtually no reward except what is loosely called the honour of it, on the clear understanding that if you ever bubble about it, even to your nearest and dearest, we'll hound you to the ends of the earth?' He allowed a pause for Perry to speak, but Perry didn't, so he went on:

'You're on record as believing that our green and pleasant land is in dire need of saving from itself. I happen to share that opinion. I've studied the disease, I've lived in the swamp. It is my informed conclusion that we are suffering, as an ex-great nation, from top-down corporate rot. And that's not just the judgement of an ailing old fart. A lot of people in my Service make a profession of not seeing things in black and white. Do not confuse me with them. I'm a late-onset, red-toothed radical with balls. Still with me?'

A reluctant nod.

'Dima is holding out to you, as I am, an opportunity to *do* something instead of bleating about it. You in return are straining at the leash while pretending to do no such thing, a posture I consider fundamentally dishonest. So my strong recommendation is: call Gail *now*, put her out of her misery, and when you get back to Primrose Hill fill her in on every detail, however slight, that you have so far kept from her. Then bring her back here at nine o'clock tomorrow morning. *This* morning, come to think of it. Ollie will collect you. You then sign an even more draconian and illiterate document than the one you both signed today, and we'll tell you as much of the remainder of the story as we can without queering your pitch if you *do* decide between you to take the trip to Paris – and as little as we can get away with if you decide you won't. If Gail wishes to demur separately, that's her business, but I'll give you a hundred to nine she'll stay aboard to the bitter end.'

Perry finally lifted his head.

'*How?*'

'How what?'

'Save England *how*? From what? All right, from itself. What *bit* of itself?'

Now it was Hector's turn to reflect. 'You'll just have to take our word for it.'

'Your Service's word?'

'For the time being, yes.'

'On the strength of what? Aren't you supposed to be the gentlemen who lie for the good of their country?'

'That's diplomats. We're not gentlemen.'

'So you lie to save your hides.'

'That's politicians. Different game entirely.'

8

At midday of a sunny Sunday, ten hours after Perry
Makepiece returned to Primrose Hill to make his peace
with Gail, Luke Weaver renounced his place at the family
lunch table – his wife Eloise having cooked a plump free-
range chicken and bread sauce specially, his son Ben having
invited an Israeli school friend – and with his apologies
ringing in his ears, abandoned the red-bricked terrace house
on Parliament Hill that he could ill afford, and set off for
what he believed was the decisive meeting of his chequered
Intelligence career.

His destination, as far as Eloise and Ben were allowed
to know, was his Service's hideous riverside headquarters
in Lambeth, dubbed by Eloise, who was of aristocratic
French extraction, *la Lubianka-sur-Tamise*. In reality it was
Bloomsbury, as it had been for the last three months. His
chosen mode of transport, either in spite of the tension
brewing in him or because of it, was neither tube nor bus,
but shanks's pony, a habit he had acquired during his stints
in Moscow where three hours of pavement-bashing in all
weathers were standard fare if you were looking to clear a
dead letter box or sidestep into an open doorway for a
thirty-second breathless handover of cash and materials.

To reach Bloomsbury from Parliament Hill on foot, a walk for which Luke customarily allowed himself a good hour, it was his practice, so far as possible, to take a different route each day, the purpose being not to shake off notional pursuers, though the thought was seldom far from his head, but to savour the byways of a city he was keen to get to know again after years of service overseas.

And today, what with the sunshine and the need to clear his head for action, he had decided on a stroll through Regent's Park before swinging eastwards across town; and to that end had added an extra half-hour to his journey. His mood, shot through with anticipation and excitement, was also one of dread. He had slept little if at all. He needed to steady the kaleidoscope. He needed ordinary, unsecret folk to look at, flowers, and the world outside.

'A wholehearted *yes* from him, and a wholehearted *yes, damn you* from her,' Hector had enthused over the encrypted phone. 'Billy Boy will hear us out at two this afternoon and the Lord is in His Heaven.'

*

Six months ago, when Luke was back on home leave after three years in Bogotá, the Queen of Human Resources, disrespectfully known throughout the Service as the Human Queen, had informed him that he was headed for the shelf. He had expected no less. All the same, her message took him a few painful seconds to decode:

'The Service is surviving the recession with its usual proverbial resilience, Luke,' she assured him, in a tone so blithely optimistic that he could have been forgiven for thinking that, far from being thrown out on his ear, he was about to be offered a Regional Directorship. 'Our stock in Whitehall has frankly never been higher, I'm pleased to say, nor our job of recruitment easier. Eighty per cent of our latest intake of young hopefuls have got *First Class Honours degrees* from decent universities and *nobody* talks about Iraq any more. Some of them *Double* Firsts. Would you believe it?'

Luke would believe it, but forbore from saying that he had acquitted himself pretty decently for twenty years on the strength of a modest Second.

The only *real* problem these days, she explained, in the same determinedly upbeat tone, was that men of Luke's calibre and pay grade who had reached their *natural watershed* were becoming harder and harder to place. And some just couldn't be placed at all, she lamented. But what was she to do – tell her – with a *young* Chief who liked his staff to have no Cold War baggage attached to them? It was just *too* sad.

So the very *best* she could manage, she was afraid, Luke, *superb* as he'd been in Bogotá, and terribly brave – and incidentally the way he conducted his private life was *nothing whatever to do with her*, provided it didn't affect his work, which patently it *hadn't* – all spoken in a gabble between brackets – would be a temporary vacancy in Administration until the present incumbent returned from her maternity leave.

Meanwhile, it might be a good idea for him to have a chat with the Service's Resettlement people to see what they had to offer in the big world: which, contrary to all the nonsense he might have read in his newspaper, wasn't all doom and gloom by any means. The terror thing, *and* the threat of civil unrest, were doing *wonders* for the private-security sector. Some of her very best ex-officers were earning twice as much as they'd earned in the Service, and loving it. With a field record like his – and his private life settled, which by all accounts it was, although it was nothing to do with her – she had no doubt at all that Luke would be a hugely desirable asset to his next employer.

'And you're not in need of post-traumatic counselling or one of *those* things?' she asked solicitously, as he was leaving.

Not from you, thank you, thought Luke. And my private life isn't settled.

*

The Administration Section had its dismal being on the ground floor, and Luke's desk was as near to the street as you could get without actually being thrown into it. After three years in the kidnap capital of the world, he did not take easily to such matters as mileage allowance for home-based junior staff, but tried his best. His surprise had been all the greater therefore when a month into his sentence he lifted the phone that hardly ever rang to hear himself being summoned by Hector Meredith to lunch with him forthwith at his famously dowdy London club.

'*Today*, Hector? Christ.'

'Come early and don't tell a fucking soul. Say it's the time of the month or something.'

'What's early?'

'Eleven.'

'Eleven? *Lunch?*'

'Aren't you hungry?'

The choice of time and place turned out to be not quite as outlandish as might have appeared. At eleven on a week-day morning a decaying Pall Mall club resounds to the honk of vacuum cleaners, the singsong chatter of underpaid migrant labourers laying up for lunch, and little else. The pillared lobby was empty save for a decrepit doorman in his box and a black woman mopping the marble floor. Hector, roosting on an old carved throne with his long legs crossed, was reading the *Financial Times*.

*

In a Service of nomads pledged to keep their secrets to themselves, hard information about any colleague was always difficult to come by. But even by these low standards, the sometime Deputy Director Western Europe, then Deputy Director Russia, then Deputy Director Africa & South East Asia and now, mysteriously, Director Special Projects, was a walking conundrum or, as some of his colleagues would have it, maverick.

Fifteen years back, Luke and Hector had shared a three-month Russian-language immersion course conducted by an elderly princess in her ivy-covered mansion in old Hampstead, not ten minutes from where Luke now lived. Come evening, they would share a cathartic walk on the Heath. Hector was a fast mover in those days, physically and professionally. Striding out with his gangly legs, he was a hard fellow for little Luke to keep up with. His conversation, which often went over Luke's head in both senses and was peppered with expletives, ranged from the 'two greatest conmen in history' – Karl Marx and Sigmund Freud – to the crying need for a brand of British patriotism that was consistent with the contemporary conscience – usually followed by a typically Hector U-turn, in which he demanded to know what *conscience* meant anyway.

Only rarely since then had their paths crossed. While Luke's field career followed its predictable course – Moscow, Prague, Amman, Moscow again, with spells of Head Office in between, and finally Bogotá – Hector's rapid ascent to the fourth floor seemed divinely foretold and his remoteness, so far as Luke was concerned, complete.

But as time passed, the turbulent contrarian in Hector showed signs of raising its head. A new wave of Service power-brokers was pressing for a louder voice in the Westminster village. Hector, in a closed address to Senior Officers that turned out to be not quite as closed as it might have been, castigated the Wise Fools of the fourth floor who were 'willing to sacrifice the Service's sacred obligation to speak truth to power'.

The dust had barely settled when, presiding over a stormy post-mortem into an operational cock-up, Hector defended the perpetrators against the Joint Services' planners, whose vision, he claimed, had been 'unnaturally restricted by having their heads stuck up the American arse'.

Then sometime in 2003, not surprisingly, he vanished. No farewell parties, no obituary in the monthly newsletter, no obscure medal, no forwarding address. First his encoded signature disappeared from operational orders. Then it disappeared from distribution lists. Then it disappeared from the closed-circuit email address book, and finally from the encrypted phone book, which was tantamount to a death notice.

And in place of the man himself, the inevitable rumour mill:

He had led a top-floor revolt over Iraq and been sacked for his pains. Wrong, said others. It was the bombing of Afghanistan, and he wasn't sacked, he resigned.

In a stand-up argument, he had called the Secretary to the Cabinet a 'mendacious bastard' to his face. Wrong again, said a different camp. It was the Attorney-General and 'spineless toady'.

Others with rather more hard evidence to go on pointed at the personal tragedy that had befallen Hector shortly before his departure from the Service when his wayward only son Adrian, not for the first time, had crashed a stolen car at high speed while under the influence of class-A drugs. Miraculously, the only victim had been Adrian himself, who suffered chest and facial injuries. But a young mother and her baby had escaped by inches and CIVIL SERVANT'S RUN-AWAY SON IN HIGH STREET HORROR made ugly reading. A string of other offences was taken into account. Broken by the affair, said the rumour mill, Hector had withdrawn from the secret world in order to support his son while he was in gaol.

But while there might have been some merit in this version – it had at least a few hard facts in its favour – it could not have been the whole story, because a few months after his disappearance, it was Hector's own face staring out of the tabloids, not as the distraught father of Adrian but as the doughty lone warrior fighting to save an old-established family firm from the clutches of those he dubbed VULTURE CAPITALISTS, thereby securing himself a sensational headline.

For weeks, Hector-watchers were regaled with stirring tales of this old-established, decently prosperous docklands firm of grain importers with sixty-five long-serving employees, all shareholders, whose 'life-support system has been switched off overnight', according to Hector who also overnight had discovered a gift for public relations: 'The asset-strippers and carpet-baggers are at our gates, and sixty-five of the best men and women in England are about to be tossed on to the rubbish heap,' he informed the press. And sure enough, within a month, the headlines shouted: MEREDITH FIGHTS OFF VULTURE CAPITALISTS – FAMILY FIRM IN TAKEOVER TRIUMPH.

And a year later, Hector was sitting in his old room on the fourth floor, raising a little hell, as he liked to call it.

*

How Hector had talked his way back in, or whether the Service had gone to him on bended knee, and what anyway were the functions of a so-called Director of Special Projects were mysteries Luke could not but ponder as he followed him at a snail's pace up the splendiferous staircase of his club, past the crumbling portraits of its imperial heroes, and into the musty library of books that nobody read. And he continued to ponder it as Hector pulled shut the great mahogany door, turned the key, dropped it into his pocket, unfastened the buckles of an old brown brief-case and, shoving a sealed Service envelope at Luke with no stamp on it, ambled to the ceiling-high sash window that looked out on to St James's Park.

'Thought it might suit you a bit better than pissing

around in Admin,' he remarked carelessly, his craggy body silhouetted against the grimy net curtains.

The letter inside the Service envelope was a printout from the same Queen of Human Resources who only two months ago had passed sentence on Luke. In lifeless prose it transferred him with immediate effect and no explanation to the post of Coordinator of an embryonic body to be known as the Counterclaim Focus Group, answerable to the Director of Special Projects. Its remit would be to 'consider proactively what operational costs may be recovered from customer departments who have significantly benefited from the product of Service operations'. The appointment carried an eighteen-month extension to his contract, to be credited to his length of service for the purpose of pension rights. Any questions, email this address.

'Make sense to you at all?' Hector inquired, from his place at the long sash window.

Mystified, Luke said something about it helping with the mortgage.

'You like *proactive*? Proactive grab you?'

'Not much,' said Luke, with a baffled laugh.

'The Human Queen *adores* proactive,' Hector retorted. 'Gets her horny as a cat. Shove in *focus*, you're home and dry.'

Should Luke humour the man? What on earth was he up to, hauling him off to his awful club at eleven in the morning, giving him a letter that wasn't even his to give, and making pedantic cracks about the Human Queen's English?

'Heard you had a bad time in Bogotá,' Hector said.

'Well, up and down, you know,' Luke replied defensively.

'Bonking your number two's wife, you mean? That sort of up and down?'

Staring at the letter in his hand, Luke saw it start to tremble but by an act of self-control managed to say nothing.

'Or the sort of up and down that comes of being hijacked at machinegun-point by some shit of a drug baron you thought was your joe,' Hector pursued. '*That* sort of up and down?'

'Very probably both,' Luke replied stiffly.

'Mind telling which came first – the hijack or the bonk?'

'The bonk, unfortunately.'

'*Unfortunately* because, while you were being detained at your drug baron's leisure in his jungle *redoute*, your poor dear wife back in Bogotá got to hear you'd been bonking the girl next door?'

'Yes. That's right. She did.'

'With the result that when you escaped from your drug baron's hospitality, and found your way home after a few days of rubbing shoulders with nature in the raw, you didn't get the hero's welcome you were expecting?'

'No. I didn't.'

'Did you tell all?'

'To the drug baron?'

'To Eloise.'

'Well, not *all*,' said Luke, not entirely sure why he was going along with this.

'You confessed to whatever she already knew, or was certain to find out,' Hector suggested approvingly. 'The partial hang-out posing as the full and frank confession. Fair reading?'

'I suppose so.'

'Not prying, Luke, old boy. Not judgemental. Just getting it straight. We stole some good horses together back in better days. In my book you're a bloody good officer and that's why you're here. What d'you think of it? Overall. The letter you're holding in your hand. Otherwise?'

'Otherwise? Well, I suppose I'm a bit puzzled by it.'

'Puzzled by *what* exactly?'

'Well why this urgency, for a start? All right, it's with immediate effect. But the job doesn't exist.'

'Doesn't have to. Narrative's perfectly clear. Cupboard's bare, so the Chief goes to the Treasury with his begging bowl and asks 'em for more cash. Treasury digs its toes in. "Can't help you. We're all broke. Claw it back from all the buggers who've been getting a free ride off you." I thought it played rather well, given the times.'

'I'm sure it's a good idea,' said Luke earnestly, by now more lost than he had been ever since his untriumphant return to England.

'Well, if it *doesn't* play, now's your time to speak up, for Christ's sake. No second chances in this situation, believe you me.'

'It plays, I'm sure. And I'm very grateful, Hector. Thanks for thinking of me. Thanks for the leg-up.'

'The Human Queen's plan is to give you your own desk, God bless her. A few doors along from Finance. Well I can't mess with that. Be ungracious to. But my advice would be to give Finance a wide berth. They don't want you counting *their* beans, and we don't want 'em counting *ours*. Well, do we?'

'I don't expect we do.'

'Anyway, you won't be in the shop that much. You'll be out and about, trawling Whitehall, making a bloody nuisance of yourself with the fat-cat ministries. Check in a couple of times a week, report to me on progress, fiddle your expenses, that'll be your lot. You still buying it?'

'Not really.'

'Why not?'

'Well, why *here*, for a start? Why not email me on the ground floor, or call me up on the internal line?'

Hector had never taken easily to criticism, Luke remembered, and he didn't now. 'All right, dammit. Suppose I *did* email you first. Or called you, what the fuck? Would you buy it *then*? The Human Queen's offer as it stands, for Christ's sake?'

Too late in the day, a different and more heartening scenario was forming in Luke's mind.

'If you're asking me whether I would accept the Human Queen's offer as it has been presented to me in the letter – asking me notionally – my answer is yes. If you're asking me – notionally, again – whether I'd smell a rat if I found the letter lying on my desk in the office, or on my screen, my answer is no, I wouldn't.'

'Scout's honour?'

'Scout's honour.'

They were interrupted by a ferocious rattle of the door handle, followed by a burst of angry knocks. With a weary 'oh *fuck* 'em', Hector gestured to Luke to get himself out of sight among the bookshelves, unlocked the door, and shoved his head round it.

'Sorry, old boy, not today, I'm afraid,' Luke heard him say. 'Unofficial stock-taking in progress. Usual fuck-up.

Members taking out books and not signing for 'em. Hope you're not one of them. Try Friday. About the first time in my life I've been grateful to be Honorary fucking Librarian,' he continued, not much bothering to lower his voice as he closed the door and relocked it. 'You can come out now. And in case you think I'm the ringleader of a Septembrist plot, you'd better read this letter as well, then shove it back at me and I'll swallow it.'

This envelope was pale blue, and conspicuously opaque. A blue lion and unicorn rampant were finely embossed on the flap. And inside, one matching blue sheet of writing paper, the smallest size, with the portentous printed heading: From the Office of the Secretariat.

Dear Luke,
    This is to assure you that the very private conversation you are conducting with our mutual colleague over lunch at his club today takes place with my unofficial approval.
    Ever, –

– then a very small signature which looked as if it had been extracted at gunpoint: William J. Matlock (Head of Secretariat), better known as Billy Boy Matlock – or plain Bully Boy if that was your preference, as it was for those who had fallen foul of him – the Service's longest-standing and most implacable troubleshooter and left-hand man to the Chief himself.

'Load of horseshit, as a matter of fact, but what else can the poor bugger do?' Hector was remarking, as he returned the letter to its envelope and stuffed the envelope into an inside pocket of his mangy sports coat. 'They know I'm right, don't want me to be, don't know what to do if I am. Don't want me pissing into the tent, don't want me pissing out of it. Lock me up and gag me's the only answer, but I don't take kindly to that, never did. Nor did you, by all accounts – why weren't you eaten by tigers or whatever they have out there?'

'It was insects mainly.'

'Leeches?'

'Those too.'

'Don't hover. Take a pew.'

Luke obediently sat down. But Hector remained standing, hands thrust deep in his pockets, shoulders stooped, glowering into the unlit fireplace with its ancient brass tongs and pokers and cracked leather surrounds. And it occurred to Luke that the atmosphere inside the library had become oppressive, if not threatening. And perhaps Hector felt it too, because his flippancy deserted him, and his hollowed, sickly face turned as grim as an undertaker's.

'Want to ask you something,' he announced abruptly, more to the fireplace than to Luke.

'Ask away.'

'What's the most dire, fucking awful thing you've ever seen in your life? Anywhere? Apart from the business-end of a drug lord's Uzi staring you in the face. Pot-bellied starving kids in the Congo with their hands chopped off, barking mad with hunger, too tired to cry? Fathers castrated, cocks stuffed in their mouths, eyeholes full of flies? Women with bayonets stuck up their fannies?'

Luke had never served in the Congo, so he had to assume Hector was describing an experience of his own.

'We did have our equivalents,' he said.

'Such as what? Name a couple.'

'Colombian government having a field day. With American assistance, naturally. Villages torched. Inhabitants gang-raped, tortured, hacked to bits. Everybody dead except the one survivor left to tell the tale.'

'Yes. Well. We've both seen a bit of the world then,' Hector conceded. 'Not wanking around.'

'No.'

'And the dirty money sloshing about, the profits of pain, we've seen that too. In Colombia alone, *billions. You've* seen that. Christ knows what *your* man was worth.' He didn't wait for the answer. 'In the Congo, *billions.* In Afghanistan, *billions.* An eighth of the world's fucking economy: black as your hat. We know about it.'

'Yes. We do.'

'Blood money. That's all it is.'

'Yes.'

'Doesn't matter where. It can be in a box under a warlord's bed in Somalia or in a City of London bank next to the vintage port. It doesn't change colour. It's still blood money.'

'I suppose it is.'

'No glamour, no pretty excuses. The profits of extortion, drug dealing, murder, intimidation, mass rape, slavery. Blood money. Tell me if I'm overstating my case.'

'I'm sure you're not.'

'Only four ways to stop it. *One:* you go for the chaps who are doing it. Capture 'em, kill 'em or bang 'em up. If you can. *Two:* you go for the product. Intercept it before it reaches the street or the marketplace. If you can. *Three:* collar the profits, put the bastards out of business.'

A worrying pause while Hector seemed to reflect on matters far above Luke's pay grade. Was he thinking of the heroin dealers who had turned his son into a gaolbird and addict? Or the *vulture capitalists* who had tried to put his family firm out of business, and sixty-five of the best men and women in England on the rubbish heap?

'Then there's the *fourth* way,' Hector was saying. 'The really bad way. The best tried, easiest, the most convenient, the most common, and the least fuss. Bugger the people who've been starved, raped, tortured, died of addiction. To hell with the human cost. Money's got no smell as long as there's enough of it and it's ours. Above all, think big. Catch the minnows, but leave the sharks in the water. A chap's laundering a couple of million? He's a bloody crook. Call in the regulators, put him in irons. But a few *billion*? Now you're talking. Billions are a *statistic*.' Closing his eyes while he lapsed into his own thoughts, Hector resembled for a moment his own death mask: or so it seemed to Luke. 'You don't have to agree with any of this, Lukie,' he said kindly, waking from his reverie. 'Door's wide open. Given my reputation, a lot of chaps would be through it by now.'

It occurred to Luke that this was a fairly ironic choice of metaphor, since Hector had the key in his pocket, but he kept the thought to himself.

'You can go back to the office after lunch, tell the Human Queen, thanks awfully but you're happier serving out your time on the ground floor. Draw your pension, keep away from drug lords and colleagues' wives, lie on your back and spit at the ceiling for the rest of your life. No bones broken.'

Luke managed a smile. 'My problem is, I'm not very good at spitting at the ceiling,' he said.

But nothing was going to stop Hector's hard sell: 'I'm offering you a one-way street to nowhere,' he insisted. 'If you sign up to this thing, you're fucked all ways up. If we lose, we were two failed whistleblowers who tried to foul the nest. If we win, we'll be the lepers of the Whitehall–Westminster jungle and all stations between. Not to mention the Service we do our best to love, honour and obey.'

'This is all the information I get?'

'For your own preservation and mine, yes. No nookie unless you come to the altar first.'

They were at the door. Hector had produced the key and was about to turn the lock.

'And about Billy Boy,' he said.

'What about him?'

'He's going to put the arm on you. Bound to. Stick-and-carrot stuff. "What's that mad bugger Meredith been telling you? What's he up to, where, who's he hiring?" If that happens, talk to me first, then talk to me again afterwards. Nobody's kosher in this thing. Everyone's guilty till proven innocent. Deal?'

'I've managed pretty well on the counter-interrogation stakes this far,' Luke replied, feeling it was about time he asserted himself.

'All the same,' said Hector, still waiting for his answer.

'Is it *Russian*, by any chance?' Luke asked hopefully, in what he afterwards regarded as an inspired moment. He was a Russophile, and had always resented being taken off the circuit on the grounds of supposed over-affection for the target.

'Could be Russian. Could be *any* fucking thing,' Hector retorted, as his big grey eyes lit up again with his believer's fire.

*

Did Luke ever *really* say yes to the job? Did he ever, now that he looked back, say, 'Yes, Hector, I will come aboard, blindfolded with my hands tied, just the way I was that night in Colombia, and I will join your mystery crusade' – or words to that effect?

No, he did not.

Even as they sat down to what Hector happily described as the second-worst lunch in the world, first prize yet to be awarded, Luke was still, if he was true to himself, entertaining lingering doubts about whether he was being invited to join the sort of private war that the Service was from time to time led into against its better judgement, with disastrous results.

Hector's opening shots at affable small talk did nothing to put these anxieties to rest. Seated in the outer regions of his club's sepulchral dining room, at the table closest to the clatter of the kitchen, he treated Luke to a masterclass in the uses of indirect conversation in public places.

Over the smoked eel, he confined himself to inquiring after Luke's family, incidentally getting the names of his wife and son right, a further sign to Luke that he had been reading his personal file. When the shepherd's pie and school cabbage arrived, on a clanking silver trolley ferried by an angry old black man in a red hunting jacket, Hector passed to the more intimate but equally harmless topic of Jenny's marriage plans – Jenny, it turned out, being his beloved daughter – which she had recently abandoned since, according to Hector, the chap she was involved with had turned out to be the most unmitigated shit:

'Wasn't love on Jenny's part, it was addiction – same as Adrian except, thank God, it wasn't drugs. Chap's a sadist, she's an old softie. Willing seller, docile buyer, we thought. We didn't say anything, you can't. Hopeless. Bought 'em a sweet little house in Bloomsbury, all fitted out. Vulgar bugger needed three-inch-deep wall-to-wall carpets, so Jenny needed 'em too. Hate 'em personally, but what else can you do? Couple of minutes' walk from the British Museum, and just right for Trotsky and her D.Phil. But old Jenny rumbled the little turd, thank God, full marks to her. Good recession price, the landlord was broke, I shan't lose money. Nice garden, not too big.'

The old waiter had reappeared with an incongruous jug of custard. Waved away by Hector, he muttered an imprecation and shuffled off to the next table twenty feet away.

'Got a decent basement too, which you don't often see these days. Pongs a bit. Not offensively. Used to be someone's wine cellar. No party walls. Decent amount of traffic going past outside. Only luck she didn't have a baby by the chap. They weren't taking precautions, knowing Jenny.'

'Sounds a blessing,' said Luke politely.

'Yes, well it could be, couldn't it?' Hector agreed, leaning forward in order to be sure of being heard beneath the din of the kitchen. By now Luke was half wondering whether Hector had a daughter at all. 'I thought you might care to take the place over rent-free for a bit. Jenny won't go near it, understandably, but it does rather need living in. I'll give you the key in a minute. Remember Ollie Devereux, by the way? Son of a White Russian travel agent in Geneva and a fish-and-chip lady in Harrow? Looks about sixteen going on forty-five? Helped you out of a scrape when you fucked up a probe-mike job in that St Petersburg hotel a while back?'

Luke remembered Ollie Devereux well.

'French, Russian, Swiss–German and Italian, if we need 'em, and the best back-door man in the business. You'll be paying him cash. I'll give you some of that too. You start at nine sharp tomorrow morning. Give you time to pack up your desk in Admin and take your pins and paper clips to the third floor. Oh yes, and you'll be shacked up with a nice woman called Yvonne, other names irrelevant: professional bloodhound, butter wouldn't melt, balls of steel.'

The silver trolley reappeared. Hector recommended the club's bread-and-butter pudding. Luke said it was his favourite. And custard would be great this time, thank you. The trolley left in a cloud of geriatric fury.

'And will you kindly consider yourself one of the chosen few, as of a couple of hours ago,' Hector said, dabbing at his mouth with a moth-eaten damask napkin. 'You'd be number seven on the list including Ollie, if there was a list. I don't want an eighth without my say-so. Deal?'

'Deal,' said Luke this time.

So perhaps he had said 'yes' after all.

*

That afternoon, under the stony gaze of his fellow detainees in Administration, and reeling from the effect of vile club claret, Luke gathered together what Hector had called his pins and paper clips and transferred them to the seclusion of the third floor, where a dingy but acceptable room with a door labelled COUNTERCLAIM FOCUS did indeed await its theoretical occupant. He was carrying an old cardigan, and something moved him to hang it over the back of the chair, where it remained to this day, like the ghost of his other self whenever he dropped by of a Friday afternoon to say a cheery something to whomever he happened to bump into in the corridor, or put in his week's fictitious expenses which he later religiously paid back into the Bloomsbury housekeeping account.

And the very next morning – he was just starting to sleep again in those days – he embarked on his first walk to Bloomsbury, exactly as he was walking there now, except that on the day of his maiden voyage, sheets of blinding rain were sweeping across London, obliging him to wear his neck-to-toe waterproofs and a hat.

*

First he had checked out the street – hardly a problem in the deluge, but there are some operational habits you can't change, however much sleep you get and hard walking you do – one pass north to south, another from a side street feeding into the road bang opposite the target house, which was number 9.

And the house itself as pretty as Hector had promised, even in the downpour: a late-eighteenth-century flat-fronted terrace house of London stock brick on three floors with freshly painted white steps leading up to a newly painted door of royal blue with a fan window above it, a sash window either side of it, and basement windows to each side of the front steps.

But no separate outside basement staircase, Luke duly noted as he climbed the steps, turned the key and went inside, then stood on the doormat, first listening, then hauling off his drenched overclothes and extracting a pair of dry slip-ons from their carry-bag under his waterproof.

The hall richly carpeted in screaming deep-pile vermilion: legacy of the little turd that Jenny had rumbled just in time. An antique porter's chair in strident new green hide. A period mirror, lavishly regilded. Hector had meant to do well by his beloved Jenny, and after his successful foray against the Vulture Capitalists, he could presumably afford to. Two staircases above him, also deep-carpeted. He called out 'anyone here?' – and heard nothing. He pushed open a door to the drawing room. Original fireplace. Roberts prints, sofa and armchairs in upmarket close covers. In the kitchen, high-end equipment, distressed pine table. He pushed open the basement door and called down the stone steps: 'Hello there – excuse me' – no reply.

He climbed to the first floor without hearing his own footsteps. At the half-landing, there were two doors, the one on his left reinforced with a steel plate and brass locks either side at shoulder height. The door on his right was just a door. Twin beds not made up, small bathroom off.

A second key was attached to the house key Hector had given him. Addressing the door on his left, he turned the locks and stepped into a pitch-dark room that smelled of woman's deodorant, the one Eloise used to like. He groped for the light switch. Heavy red velvet curtains, barely hung out, tightly drawn and held together with oversized safety pins that haphazardly recalled for him his weeks of recuperation in the American Hospital in Bogotá. No bed. At the centre of the room, a bare trestle table with rotating chair, computer and reading light. On the wall ahead of him, fixed into the angle of the ceiling, four black blinds of waxy cloth reaching to the floor.

Returning to the half-landing, he leaned over the bannisters and yet again called 'anyone there?' and yet again received no answer. Back in the bedroom he released the black blinds one by one, nursing them into their housings on the ceiling. At first he thought he was looking at an architect's plan, wall wide. But a plan of *what*? Then he thought it must be a huge piece of calculus. But calculating *what*?

He studied the coloured lines and read the careful italic handwriting denoting what he at first took to be towns. But how could they be towns with names like Pastor, Bishop, Priest and Curate? Dotted lines beside solid ones. Black lines turning to grey, then vanishing. Lines in mauve and blue, converging on a hub somewhere south of centre, or did they emanate from it?

And all of them with such detours, so much backtracking, so many turns, doublings and switches of direction, up, down and sideways, and then up again, that if his son, Ben, in one of his unexplained rages, had holed up in this same room and seized a tin of coloured crayons and zigzagged his way across the wall, the effect wouldn't have been much different.

'Like it?' Hector inquired, standing behind him.

'Are you sure you've got it the right way up?' Luke replied, determined not to show surprise.

'She's calling it *Money Anarchy*. I reckon it's just about right for the Tate Modern.'

'She?'

'Yvonne. Our Iron Maiden. Does mainly afternoons. This is her room. Yours is upstairs.'

Together, they climbed to a converted attic with stripped beams and dormer windows. One trestle table of the same design as Yvonne's. Hector is no fan of desk drawers. One desktop computer, no terminal.

'We don't use landlines, encrypted or t'other,' Hector said, with the hushed vehemence that Luke was learning to expect of him. 'No fancy hotlines to Head Office, no email connection, encrypted, decrypted or fried. The only documents we deal with are on Ollie's little orange sticks.' He was holding one up: a common memory stick with a number 7 branded on its orange plastic shell. 'Each stick tracked in transit by each of us each end, got it? Signed in, signed out. Ollie runs the shuttle, keeps the log. Spend a couple of days with Yvonne and you'll get the hang of it. Other questions as they arise. Any problems?'

'I don't think so.'

'Nor do I. So lean back, think of England, don't maunder, and don't fuck up.'

And think too of Our Iron Maiden. Professional bloodhound, balls of steel and Eloise's expensive deodorant.

*

It was advice Luke had done his utmost to adhere to for the last three months, and he prayed devoutly that he would do so today. Twice, Billy Boy Matlock had summoned him to the presence, to blandish or threaten him, or both. Twice he had ducked and weaved and lied to Hector's instruction, and survived. It had not been easy.

'Yvonne does not exist either in Heaven or here on earth,' Hector had decreed from Day One. 'Does not, will not. Got it? That's your bottom line. And your top line too. And if Billy Boy straps you by your balls to the chandelier, she *still* doesn't exist.'

Does not exist? A demure young woman in a long dark raincoat and pointed hood standing on the doorstep on the very first evening of his very first day here, no make-up, clutching a baggy briefcase in both arms as if she had just rescued it from the flood, *does not, will not exist?*

'Hi. I'm Yvonne.'

'Luke. Come on in, for Heaven's sake!'

A dripping handshake as they bundle her into the entrance hall. Ollie, the best back-door man in the business, finds a hanger for her raincoat and hangs it in the loo to drip on to the tiled floor. A three-month-long working relationship that does not exist has begun. Hector's strictures about paper did not extend to Yvonne's bulky bag, Luke quickly learned later that same night. That was because whatever she brought in her bag left in it the same day. And the reason for this again was that Yvonne was no mere researcher, she was a clandestine source.

One day her bag might contain a bulky file from the Bank of England. Another, it would be from the Financial Services Authority, the Treasury, the Serious and Organized Crime Agency. And on one momentous Friday evening, never to be forgotten, it was a stack of six fat volumes and a score of audio cassettes, enough to fill the bag to bursting, from the hallowed archives of the Government Communications Headquarters itself. Ollie, Luke and Yvonne spent the whole weekend copying, photographing and replicating the material any way they could, so that Yvonne could return it to its rightful owners at crack of dawn on Monday morning.

Whether she came by her loot licitly or by stealth, whether she filched it or cajoled it out of her colleagues and accomplices, Luke to this day had no idea. He knew only that as soon as she arrived with her bag, Ollie would whisk it to his lair behind the kitchen, there to scan its contents, transfer them to a memory stick, and return the bag to Yvonne: and Yvonne, come end of day, to whichever Whitehall department officially owned her services.

For that too was a mystery, never once revealed in the long afternoons when Luke and Yvonne sat cloistered together comparing the illustrious names of Vulture Capitalists with billion-dollar cash transfers conducted at lightning speed across three continents in a day; or chatting in the kitchen over Ollie's lunchtime soup, tomato a speciality, French onion not bad either. And his crab chowder, which he brought part-cooked in a picnic Thermos and completed on the gas stove, a miracle by common consent. But as far as Billy Boy Matlock is concerned, Yvonne does not and will not ever exist. Weeks of training in the arts of resisting interrogation say so: so does a month of crouching handcuffed in a mad drug lord's jungle *redoute* while your wife discovers that you are a compulsive womanizer.

*

'So what are we looking at here for whistleblowers, Luke?' Matlock inquires of Luke over a nice cup of tea in the comfortable corner of his large office in *la Lubianka-sur-Tamise*, having invited him to drop by for a chat, and no need to tell Hector. 'You're a fellow who knows a thing or two about informants. I was thinking of you only the other day when the question of a new senior trainer in agent-running came up. A nice five-year contract for somebody just your age,' Matlock says in his homespun Midlands drawl.

'To be perfectly honest with you, Billy, your guess is as good as mine,' Luke replies, mindful that Yvonne does not, will not exist, even if Billy Boy straps him to the chandelier by his balls, which was about the one thing the drug lord's boys didn't think of doing to him. 'Hector just conjures up his information out of the fresh air, frankly. It's amazing,' he adds, with appropriate bewilderment.

Matlock seems not to hear this answer, or perhaps not to care for it, for the geniality disappears from his voice as if it had never been.

'Mind you, it's a double-edged sword, is a training appointment like that one. We'd be looking for the veteran officer whose career would serve as a role model to our idealistic young trainees. Male *and* female, I don't have to emphasize. The Board would need to be convinced there were no suggestions of impropriety that might be levelled against the successful candidate. And Secretariat would be tendering that advice, naturally enough. In your case, we might have to be looking at a little creative restructuring of your CV.'

'That would be generous, Billy.'

'It would indeed, Luke,' Matlock agreed. 'It would indeed. And somewhat conditional on your current behaviour too.'

*

Who *was* Yvonne? For the first of those three months, she had driven Luke – he could say it now, he could admit it – just a little bit wild. He loved her demureness and her privacy, which he longed to share. Her discreetly scented body, if she ever allowed it to be revealed, would border on the classic, he could imagine it exactly. Yet they could sit for hours on end, cheek by jowl in front of her computer screen, or poring over her Tate Modern mural, feeling each other's body-warmth, grazing hands by accident. They could share every twist and turn of the chase, every false trail, dead end and temporary triumph: all at a distance of a few inches from each other, in the upstairs bedroom of a secret house that for most of the day they shared alone.

And still nothing: until an evening when the two of them were sitting exhausted and alone at the kitchen table enjoying a cup of Ollie's soup and, at Luke's suggestion, a shot of Hector's Islay malt. Taking himself by surprise, he asked Yvonne point-blank what sort of a life she led apart from *this*, and whether she had anyone to share it with who could support her in her stressful labours – adding, with the old sad smile of which he was instantly ashamed, that after all it was only our *answers* that were dangerous, wasn't it, not the questions, if she saw what he meant?

For a long time her dangerous answer didn't materialize: 'I'm a *government employee*,' she said, in the robotic tone of somebody speaking into camera for a quiz competition. 'My name is not Yvonne. Where I am employed is none of your business. However, I don't think you're asking me that. I'm Hector's discovery, as I assume we both are. But I don't think you're asking me that either. You're asking me about my orientation. And whether, by extension, I wish to go to bed with you.'

'Yvonne, I was asking you nothing of the kind!' Luke protested, truthlessly.

'And for your information, I'm married to a man I'm in love with, we have a three-year-old daughter, and I don't fuck around even with people as nice as you. So let's get on with our soup, shall we?' she suggested – at which, amazingly, they both broke out in cathartic laughter and, with the tension broken, returned peacefully to their separate corners.

*

And Hector, who was he, after three months of him, albeit in sporadic bursts? – Hector of the feverish stare and the scatological tirades against the City crooks who were the source of all our evils? On the Service grapevine it was hinted that in successfully saving the life of his family firm, Hector had resorted to methods honed by half a lifetime in the black arts, and deemed, even by the City's abysmal standards, foul. So was the vendetta against the City's evildoers driven by revenge – or guilt? Ollie, not normally given to gossip, had no doubt: Hector's experience of the City's bad manners – and his own employment of them, said Ollie – had turned him overnight into an avenging angel. 'It's a little vow he's taken,' he confided to them in the kitchen, while they waited for Hector to put in one of his late appearances. 'He's going to save the world before he leaves it if it kills him.'

*

But then Luke had always been a worrier. From infancy he had worried indiscriminately, rather in the way he fell in love.

He could worry as much about whether his watch was ten seconds fast or slow, as about the direction of a marriage that was null and void in every room except the kitchen.

He worried whether there was more to his son Ben's tantrums than just growing pains, and whether Ben was under his mother's orders not to love his father.

He worried about the fact that he was at peace when he was working, and that when he wasn't, even now walking along, he was a mass of unjoined ends.

He worried whether he should have swallowed his pride and accepted the Human Queen's offer of a shrink.

He worried about Gail, and his desire for her, or for some girl like her: a girl with real light in her face instead of the glum cloud that followed Eloise around even when the sun was on her.

He worried about Perry and tried not to be envious of him. He worried about which half of Perry would come out on top in an operational emergency: would it be the intrepid mountaineer or the unworldly university moralist – and anyway, was there a difference?

He worried about the impending duel between Hector and Billy Boy Matlock, and which of them was going to lose his temper first – or pretend to.

*

Leaving the sanctuary of Regent's Park, he entered the throng of Sunday shoppers looking for a bargain. Ease down, he told himself. It'll be all right. Hector's in charge, not you.

He was counting off landmarks. Ever since Bogotá, landmarks had been important to him. If they kidnap me, these are the last things I saw before they put the blindfold on me.

The Chinese restaurant.

The Big Archway nightclub.

The Gentle Readers' Bookshop.

This is the ground coffee I smelled while I was wrestling with my attackers.

Those are the snowy pine trees I saw in the window of the art shop before they sandbagged me.

This is number 9, the house where I was reborn, three steps to the front door and act like any normal householder.

9

There were no formalities between Hector and Matlock, friendly or otherwise, and perhaps there never had been: just a nod and a silent handshake of two veteran belligerents shaping up for another bout. Matlock arrived on foot, having been dropped round the corner by his driver.

'Very nice Wilton carpeting, Hector,' he said, while he took a slow look round that seemed to confirm his worst suspicions. 'You can't beat Wilton, not when it comes to cost versus quality. Good day to you, Luke. It's just the two of you, is it?' – passing Hector his coat.

'Staff are away at the races,' Hector said, hanging it up.

Matlock was a broad-shouldered bull of a man, as his nickname implied, broad-headed, and at first glance avuncular, with a crouch that reminded Luke of an ageing rugby forward. His Midlands accent, according to the ground-floor gossips, had become more noticeable under New Labour, but was receding with the prospect of electoral defeat.

'We're in the basement, if you're comfortable with that, Billy,' said Hector.

'I've no alternative but to be comfortable with it, thank you, Hector,' said Matlock, neither pleasantly nor rudely, leading the way down the stone steps. 'What are we paying for this place, by the by?'

'You're not. This far it's on me.'

'You're on *our* payroll, Hector. The Service is not on *yours*.'

'As soon as you greenlight the operation, I'll be putting in my bill.'

'And I'll be querying it,' said Matlock. 'Taken to drink, have you?'

'It used to be the wine cellar.'

They took their places. Matlock assumed the head of the table. Hector, normally the stubborn technophobe, sat himself on Matlock's left in order to be in front of a tape recorder and a computer console. And to Hector's left sat Luke, thereby providing the three of them with a clear view of the plasma screen that the absent Ollie had erected overnight.

'Did you have time to wade through all the material we bunged at you, Billy?' Hector inquired sympathetically. 'Sorry to interfere with your golf.'

'If *all* is what you sent me, yes, Hector, I did, thank you,' Matlock replied. 'Though in your case, as I have come to learn, the word *all* is somewhat of a relative term. I don't play golf, as a matter of fact, and I'm not enamoured of summaries, if I can avoid them. Specially not yours. I could have done with a bit more raw material and a bit less arm-twisting.'

'Then why don't we offer you some of that raw material now, and make up?' Hector suggested, just as sweetly. 'I take it we're still Russian speakers, Billy?'

'Unless yours has gone rusty while you were out making yourself a fortune, yes, I think we are.'

They're an old married couple, thought Luke, as Hector pressed 'play' on the tape recorder. Every quarrel they have is a rerun of one they've had before.

*

For Luke, the very sound of Dima's voice acted like the start of a full-colour film. Every time he listened to the cassette that Perry the innocent had smuggled in his shaving bag he came away with the same image of Dima crouched in the forests around Three Chimneys, clutching a pocket recorder in his improbably delicate hand, far enough from the house to escape Tamara's real or imagined microphones, but near enough to scurry back if she yelled at him to come and take another phone call.

He could hear the three winds battling round Dima's glistening bald head. He could see the treetops above him shaking. He could hear the crashing of leaves and a gurgle of water, and he knew it was the same tropical rain that had drenched him in the forests of Colombia. Had Dima made his recording in a single session or in several? Did he have to brace himself with shots of vodka between sessions in order to overcome his *vory* inhibitions? Now his Russian bark drops into English, perhaps to remind himself who his confessors are. Now he is appealing to Perry. Now to a bunch of Perrys:

> 'You English gentlemen! Please! You are *fair play*, you have land of law! You are pure! I trust you. You will trust Dima also!'

Then back to his native Russian, but so careful of its grammatical niceties, so prinked and articulated, that in Luke's imaginings he is trying to rid it of its Kolyma stain in preparation for rubbing shoulders with the gentlemen of Ascot and their ladies:

> 'The man they are calling Dima, number one for money-laundering for the Seven Brothers, financial mastermind to the retrograde usurper who calls himself the Prince, presents his compliments to the famous English Secret Service and wishes to make the following offer of valuable information in exchange for trustworthy guarantees by the British government. *Example.*'

Then only the winds speak as Luke imagines Dima mopping away his sweat and tears with a large silk handkerchief – Luke's own gloss, but Perry had repeatedly mentioned a handkerchief – before taking another slug from the bottle and proceeding to the full, irrecoverable act of betrayal.

> '*Example.* Operations of the Prince's criminal organization now known as the Seven Brothers include:
>
> '*One*: importations and rebranding of embargoed oil from Mid East. I know these transactions. Many corrupt Italians and many British lawyers are involved.
>
> '*Two*: injection of black money into multi-billion-dollar oil purchases and revenues. For this my friend Mikhail, called Misha, was specialist for all seven *vory* Brotherhoods. For this purpose he also lived in Rome.'

Another break in the voice, and perhaps a silent toast to the late Misha, followed by an exuberant return to fractured English:

> '*Example three*: black logging, Africa. First we are converting black timber into white timber. Then we are converting

black money into white money! Is normal. Is simple. Many, many Russian criminals in tropical Africa. Also black diamonds very interesting new trade for Brotherhoods.'

Still in English:

'*Example four*: facsimile medicines, made in India. Very lousy, do not cure, make you bring up, maybe kill. Official State of Russia has very interesting relations with official State of India. Also very interesting relations between Indian and Russian Brotherhoods. The one they call Dima knows many interesting names, also English, regarding these vertical connections and certain private financial arrangements, Swiss-based.'

Luke the worrier is undergoing an impresario's crisis of confidence on Hector's behalf:

'Volume all right for you there, Billy?' Hector asks, pausing the tape.

'The volume is very fine, thank you,' Matlock says, with just enough emphasis on *volume* to suggest that the content may be a different matter.

'On we go then,' said Hector, a little too meekly for Luke's taste, as Dima gratefully reverts to his native Russian:

'*Example*: in Turkey, Crete, Cyprus, in Madeira, in many coastal resorts: black hotels, no guests, twenty million black dollars weekly. This money also is laundered by the one they call Dima. Certain criminal British so-called property companies are complicit.

'*Example*: personal corrupt involvement of European Union officials with criminal meat contractors. These meat contractors must certify high quality, very expensive Italian meat for export to Russian Republic. For this arrangement my friend Misha was also personally responsible.'

Hector again pauses the recorder. Matlock has raised his hand.

'How can I help you, Billy?'

'He's reading.'

'What's wrong with him reading?'

'Nothing. As long as we know what he's reading from.'

'Our understanding is that his wife Tamara wrote some of his lines for him.'

'She told him what to say, did she?' said Matlock. 'I don't think I like the sound of that. Who told *her* what to say?'

'Want me to fast forward? It's only stuff about our colleagues in the European Union poisoning people. If it's outside your remit, say the word.'

'Kindly continue as you are proceeding, Hector. I shall henceforth reserve my comments till later in the performance. I'm not sure we have a requirement for Intelligence on meat sales to Russia, in point of fact, but you may rely on me to make it my business to find out.'

*

To Luke, the story Dima was about to tell was truly shocking. Nothing he had endured in life had dulled his senses. But what Matlock made of it was anybody's guess. Dima's weapon of choice is once more Tamara's English:

'Corrupt system is as follows. *First*: Prince arranges through corrupt officials in Moscow that certain meat is called *charity meat*. To be for *charity*, meat must be for needy elements of

Russian society only. Therefore on meat that is corruptly classified for charity, no Russian tax payable. *Second*: my friend Misha who is dead buys many carcasses of meat from *Bulgaria*. This meat is dangerous to eat, very lousy, very cheap. *Third*: my friend Misha who is dead arranges with very corrupt officials in Brussels Union that all Bulgarian meat carcasses will be stamped *individually with European Union stamp of certification identifying meat as very top quality excellent best European Standard Italian meat*. For this criminal service, I, Dima, personally pay one hundred euro per carcass to Swiss account of very corrupt *Brussels* official, twenty euro per carcass to Swiss account of very corrupt *Moscow* official. Net profit to Prince, after deduction of all overheads: one thousand two hundred euro per carcass. Maybe fifty Russian people, also kids, got sick and die from this very bad Bulgarian meat. This is only *estimate*. This information is officially *denied*. The names of these very corrupt officials are known to me, also Swiss bank accounts by number.'

And a stiff postscript, sonorously delivered:

'It is personal opinion of my wife Tamara L'vovna that immoral distribution of bad Bulgarian meat by criminally corrupted European and Russian officials must be of concern to all Christian person of good heart worldwide everywhere. It is God's will.'

The unlikely intervention of God in the proceedings had created a small hiatus.

'Would somebody mind telling me what a *black hotel* is?' Matlock demanded of the air in front of him. 'I happen to take my holidays in Madeira. There never seemed anything very black about *my* hotel.'

Fired by a need to protect the subdued Hector, Luke appointed himself the somebody who would tell Matlock what a black hotel was:

'You buy a bit of prime land, usually on the sea, Billy. You pay cash for it, you build a five-star luxury-hotel resort. Maybe several. For cash. And throw in fifty or so holiday bungalows if you've got the space. You bring in the best furniture, cutlery, china, linen. From then on your hotels and bungalows are full up. Except that nobody ever stays in them, you see. If a travel agent calls: sorry, we're fully booked. Every month a security van rolls up at the bank and unloads all the cash that's been taken in room rentals, bungalow rentals, the restaurants, the casinos, the night-clubs and the bars. After a couple of years, your resorts are in perfect shape to be sold with a brilliant trading record.'

No response beyond a raising of Matlock's avuncular smile to maximum strength.

'It's not only resorts either, actually. It can be one of those strangely empty white holiday villages – you must have seen them, trickling down Turkish valleys to the sea – it can be, well, scores of villas, obviously, it can be pretty well anything that's lettable. Car hire too, provided you can fudge the paperwork.'

'How are you today, Luke?'

'Fine, thanks, Billy.'

'We're thinking of putting you up for a medal, courage beyond the call, did you know that?'

'No, I didn't.'

'Well, we are. A secret one, mind, nothing public.

Nothing you can flash on your chest on Remembrance Day, mind. That wouldn't be secure. Plus it would fly in the face of precedent.'

'Of course,' said Luke, totally confused, now thinking a medal might be the one thing that would get Eloise over her depression, now that it was yet another of Matlock's wiles. Nevertheless, he was about to say something appropriate in reply – express his surprise, gratitude, pleasure – only to find that Matlock had lost interest in him:

'What I'm hearing so far, Hector, if I cut away the guff, which I like to, is in my humble view straight international crookery. All right, granted, the Service has a statutory interest in international crookery and money-laundering. We fought for a piece of it when times were hard, and now we're landed with it. I refer to that unfortunate fallow period between the Berlin Wall coming down and Osama bin Laden doing us the favour of 9/11. We fought for a piece of the money-laundering market the same as we fought for a larger slice of Northern Ireland, and whatever other modest pickings were available to justify our existence. But that was *then*, Hector. And this is *now*, and as of today, which is where we are living, like it or not, your Service and mine has better things to do with its time and resources than get its knickers caught in the highly complex wheels of City of London finance, thank you.'

Matlock broke off, expecting Luke knew not what, unless it was applause, but Hector, to judge by his stony expression, was a long way from providing it, so Matlock drew breath and resumed.

'As of today, furthermore, we also have, in this country,

a very large, fully incorporated, somewhat over-financed sister agency that devotes its efforts, such as they are, to matters of serious and organized crime, which I take it is what you are purporting to be unveiling here. Not to mention Interpol, and any number of competing American agencies falling over each other's very large feet to do the same job while careful not to prejudice the prosperity of that great nation. My point is, Hector – wait till I'm finished, please – my point is, I'm not seeing what I was brought here for at extremely short notice. We all know that what you've got is *urgent*, though to whom I'm less sure. Maybe it's even *true*. But is it *ours*, Hector? Is it ours?'

The question was evidently rhetorical, for he rolled on.

'Or could it be, Hector, that you are trespassing, at your peril, on the highly sensitive preserves of a sister organization with which, over painful months, I and my Secretariat have thrashed out very hard-won lines of demarcation? Because were that to be the case, my advice to you would be this: package up that material you have just played to me, and any other material of the same ilk that is in your possession and, with immediate effect, pass that material to our sister organization with a grovelling letter of apology for trespassing on its sanctified areas of competence. And when you have done that, I suggest you award yourself, and Luke here, and whoever else you've got tucked away in your cupboard, two weeks of well-deserved sick leave.' Had Hector's fabled nerve finally run out? Luke wondered anxiously. Had the strain of bringing Gail and Perry to the water taken too much of a toll? Or was he so driven by the high purpose of his mission that he had lost his grasp on tactic?

Lethargically reaching out a finger, Hector shook his head and sighed, and fast-forwarded the tape.

*

Dima calm. Dima reading, whether Billy Boy likes it or not. Dima powerful and dignified, orating from script in his best ceremonial Russian:

'*Example*. Details of very secret pact in Sochi 2000 between seven bonding *vory* Brotherhoods, signed by the Seven Brothers and called The Understanding. Under this pact, personally brokered by usurper bitch Prince with arm's-length connivance of Kremlin, all seven signatories agree:

'*One*: to avail themselves and make communal all proven and successful money routes designed by the one they call Dima, henceforth number-one money-launderer for all seven Brotherhoods.

'*Two*: all communal bank accounts will be conducted under *vory* code of honour, any deviation will be punished by death of guilty party, accompanied by permanent exclusion of responsible *vory* Brotherhood.

'*Three*: corporate respectability will be created in following six financial capitals: Toronto, Paris, Rome, Berne, Nicosia, *London*. End destination of all laundered monies: *London*. Best centre of respectability: *London*. Best outlook for long-term banking entity: *London*. Best prospect to save and conserve: *London*. This is also agreed.

'*Four*: the task of obscuring origins of black money and directing its passage into safe havens will continue to remain the primary and sole responsibility of *the one they call Dima*.

'*Five*: for all major movements of money, this Dima will have first-signature rights. Each signatory to The Understanding will appoint one clean envoy. This clean envoy will have second-signature signing rights only.

'*Six*: to effect substantive alteration to above system, all seven clean envoys will be simultaneously required to be present under *vory* law.

'*Seven*: the pre-eminence of the one they call Dima as master architect of all money-laundering structures agreed under The Understanding of Sochi 2000 is hereby acknowledged.'

'And amen, as we might say,' Hector murmurs, and once more switches off the recorder and glances at Matlock for a reaction. Luke does too, to be greeted, of all things, by Matlock's indulgent smile.

'D'you know, Hector, I think I could have made that up myself,' he says, shaking his head in what must pass for admiration. 'Beautiful is all I can say. Fluent, imaginative, and puts him right at the top of the heap. How can anyone possibly question the veracity of such a magnificent global statement? I'd give him an Oscar for a start. What does he mean by *clean envoy*?'

'Clean like cleanskin, Billy. No previous convictions, criminal or ethical. Accountants, lawyers, moonlighting policemen and Intelligence officers, any made brother who can travel, sign his name, owes his allegiance to his Brotherhood and knows he'll wake up with his balls in his mouth if he robs the till.'

*

Appearing to Luke more like a careworn family solicitor than his irrepressible self, Hector consults a bit of battered card on which he had apparently scribbled himself a march route for the meeting, and again fast-forwards the tape.

'*Map*,' Dima barks in Russian.

'Bugger it. Too late,' Hector mutters, and runs back a stretch.

'Also conditional upon reliable British guarantees, will be very secret, very important *map*.'

Dima resumes, reading rapidly, as before, from script in Russian:

'In this *map* will be recorded international routes of all black monies under control of the one they are calling *Dima* who is speaking to you.'

At Matlock's bidding, Hector yet again pauses the tape.

'What he's talking about here isn't a map, it's a *link chart*,' Matlock complains, in the tone of a man correcting Dima's inadequate vocabulary. 'And I'll just say this regarding *link charts*, if you'll bear with me. I've seen a few *link charts* in my time. They tend to resemble multicoloured rolls of barbed wire leading in no direction known to man, in my experience. *Useless*, in other words, in my judgement,' he adds with satisfaction. 'I put them in much the same category as pronouncements regarding mythical criminal conferences on the Black Sea in the year 2000.'

You should see Yvonne's link chart, it's absolutely wild, Luke wants to tell him in a fit of miserable hilarity.

Matlock on a winning streak does not lightly let go. He is shaking his head and smiling ruefully:

'You know something, Hector? If I had a five-pound note for every piece of pedlar material from untried sources that our Service has fallen for over the years – not all in my time, I'm glad to say – I'd be a rich man. Link charts, Bilderberg plots, world conspiracies, and that old green shed in Siberia that's full of rusty hydrogen bombs, they're all one to me. Not rich by the standards of their ingenious fabricators, maybe, or your standards either. But for the likes of me, very comfortably off indeed, thank you.'

Why the hell doesn't Hector cut Bully Boy down to size? But Hector appears to have no stomach left for retaliation. Worse still, to Luke's despair, he doesn't bother to play the last section of Dima's historic offer. He switches off the tape recorder, as if to say 'tried that one, didn't work', and with a chagrined smile and a rueful 'Well, maybe you'll be better off with some pictures to look at, Billy', takes up the remote control for the plasma screen and switches off the light.

*

In the gloom, an amateur video camera shakily roams the battlements of a medieval fort, then descends to the sea wall of an ancient harbour crowded with expensive sailing boats. It is dusk, the camera is of poor quality, unequal to the failing light. A ninety-foot luxury yacht in blue and gold lies at anchor outside the harbour walls. It is dressed overall with fairy lights, its portholes are lit. Distant dance music reaches us from across the water. Perhaps someone is celebrating a birthday or a wedding? From its stern hang the flags of Switzerland, Britain and Russia. At its masthead, a golden wolf bestrides a crimson field.

The camera closes on the bow. The ship's name, inscribed in fancy Roman and Cyrillic gold lettering, is *Princess Tatiana*.

Hector is providing a flat, dispassionate commentary:

'Property of a newly formed company called First Arena Credit Bank of Toronto, registered in Cyprus, owned by a foundation in Liechtenstein which is owned by a company registered in Cyprus,' he announces drily. 'So a circular ownership. Give it to a company, then get it back from the company. Until recently she was called the *Princess Anastasia*, which happens to be the name of the Prince's previous squeeze. His new squeeze is called Tatiana, so we may draw our conclusions. The Prince being presently confined to Russia for his health, the SS *Princess Tatiana* is out on charter to an international consortium called, funnily enough, First Arena Credit International, a different entity entirely, registered, you'll be surprised to hear, in Cyprus.'

'What's wrong with him then?' Matlock asks aggressively.

'Who?'

'The Prince. I don't think I'm being stupid, am I? Why's he confined to Russia?'

'He's waiting for the Americans to drop some thoroughly unreasonable money-laundering charges they levelled against him a few years back. The good news is, he won't have to wait long. Thanks to a spot of lobbying in Washington's halls of greatness, it will shortly be agreed that he has no case to answer. Always helpful when you know where influential Americans keep their illegal offshore bank accounts.'

The camera leaps to the stern. Russian-style crew in striped shirts and matelot hats. A helicopter about to land. Camera returns aft, descends uncertainly to sea level as the picture darkens. A speed-launch pulls alongside, passengers aboard. Busy crew in attendance as passengers in their finery cautiously ascend ship's ladder.

Go back to stern. The helicopter has landed but its blades still slowly rotate. Fine lady in billowing skirt descends red-carpeted steps, clutching hat. Followed by second fine lady, then a bevy of fine men in blazers and white ducks, six in all. Fuzzy exchange of hugs. Faint shrieks of greeting over dance music.

Cut back to second speed-launch pulling alongside, delivering pretty girls. Skin-tight jeans, fluttery skirts, many bare legs and shoulders as they ascend ladder. A brace of fuzzy trumpeters in Cossack uniform sound halloos of welcome as pretty girls come aboard.

Pan awkwardly on guests assembled on main deck. There are so far eighteen. Luke and Yvonne have counted them.

Film freezes and becomes a series of clumsily advancing close-ups, much enhanced by Ollie. Caption reads SMALL ADRIATIC PORT NEAR DUBROVNIK JUNE 21 2008. It is the first of many captions and subtitles that Yvonne, Luke and Ollie in committee have superimposed as an accompaniment to Hector's spoken commentary.

The silence in the basement is palpable. It's as if everyone in the room including Hector has drawn in his breath at the same time. Perhaps they have. Even Matlock is leaning forward in his chair, staring fixedly at the plasma screen before him.

*

Two well-preserved, expensively tailored men of affairs are in conversation. Behind them, the bare neck and shoulders of a middle-aged woman with lacquered white bouffant. She has her back turned to us and wears a four-row diamond collar and matching pendant earrings, the cost anyone's guess. At left of screen, an embroidered cuff and white-gloved hand of a Cossack waiter is offering a silver tray laden with glasses of champagne.

Close on the two men of affairs. One wears a white dinner jacket. He is black-haired, heavy-jawed and of Latin appearance. The other wears a very English double-breasted navy blue blazer with brass buttons or, as the British upper echelons prefer to have it – Luke should know, they're where he comes from himself – a boating jacket. By comparison with his partner, this second man is young. He is also handsome in the way that young men of the eighteenth century were handsome in the portraits they donated to Luke's old school when they left it: broad brow, receding hairline, the haughty sub-Byronic gaze of sensual entitlement, a pretty pout, and a posture that manages to look down on you however tall you are.

Hector has still not spoken. The committee's decision was to let the subtitles say what anyone would know from half a glance: that the double-breasted boating jacket with brass buttons belongs to a leading member of Her Majesty's Opposition, a Shadow Minister tipped for stratospheric office at the next election.

It is Hector, to Luke's relief, who ends the awkward silence.

'His remit, according to the Party handout, will be *to put British trade into point position in the international financial marketplace*, if anyone can tell me what that means,' he remarks caustically, with a slight resurgence of his old energy. 'Plus of course putting an end to banking excesses. But they're all going to do that, aren't they? One day.'

Matlock has found his tongue:

'You can't have *business* without making friendships, Hector,' he protests. 'That's not how the world works, as you of all people should know, having dirtied your hands out there. You can't *condemn* a man just for being on someone's boat!'

But neither Hector's tone nor Matlock's implausible indignation can ease the tension. And it is no consolation at all that, according to Yvonne's subtitle, the white dinner jacket belongs to a tainted French marquis and corporate raider with strong ties to Russia.

*

'Anyway. Where did you get this lot from?' Matlock suddenly demanded, after a spell of silent brooding.

'What lot?'

'The film. Amateur video. Whatever it is. Where d'you get it?'

'Found it under a stone, Billy. Where else?'

'Who did?'

'A friend of mine. Or two.'

'What stone?'

'Scotland Yard.'

'What are you talking about? *The Metropolitan Police?* You've been tampering with police evidence, have you? Is that what you've been doing?'

'I would like to think I have, Billy. But I very much doubt it. Would you care to hear the story?'

'If it's true.'

'A young couple from the London suburbs saved up for their honeymoon and took a package holiday on the Adriatic Coast. Walking the cliffs, they happened on a luxury yacht at anchor in the bay and, seeing that there was a spectacular party in progress, filmed it. Examining the footage in the privacy of their home in let us say Surbiton, they were amazed and thrilled to identify certain well-known British public figures from the worlds of finance and politics. Thinking to recoup the cost of their holiday, they sent their prize hotfoot to Sky Television News. The next thing they knew, they were sharing their bedroom with a squad of uniformed gun-toting policemen in full-body armour at four o'clock in the morning, and being threatened with prosecution under the Terrorism Act if they didn't hand over all copies of their film immediately and forthwith to the police, so very wisely they did as they were told. And that's the truth, Billy.'

*

Luke is beginning to realize that he has been underrating Hector's performance. Hector may appear bumbly. He may have only a bit of scruffy old card in his hand. But there is nothing scruffy about the march route he's put together in his head. He's got two more gentlemen to introduce to Matlock and, as the frame widens to include them, it becomes evident that they have all along been party to the conversation. The one is tall, elegant, mid-fifties, and of a vaguely ambassadorial demeanour. He dominates our Minister-of-State-in-Waiting by nearly a head. His mouth is open in jest. His name, Yvonne's caption tells us, is Captain Giles de Salis, RN, retired.

This time, Hector has reserved the job description for himself:

'Leading-edge Westminster lobbyist, influence-broker, clients include some of the world's major shits.'

'Friend of yours, Hector?' Matlock asks.

'Friend of anybody willing to brass up ten grand for a tête-à-tête with one of our incorruptible rulers, Billy,' Hector retorts.

The fourth and last member of the piece, even in fuzzy enlargement, is high society's quintessence of vitality. Fine black piping defines the lapels of his perfect white dinner jacket. His mane of silver-fox hair is dramatically swept back. Is he perhaps a great conductor? Or a great head waiter? His ringed forefinger, raised in humorous admonition, is like a dancer's. His graceful spare hand rests lightly and inoffensively on the upper arm of the Minister-in-Waiting. His pleated shirt-front sports a Maltese Cross.

A *what?* A Maltese Cross? Can he then be a Knight of Malta? Or is it a gallantry medal? Or a foreign order? Or did he buy it as a present to himself? In the small hours of morning, Luke and Yvonne have thought long and hard about it. No, they agreed. He stole it.

Signor Emilio dell Oro, Italian Swiss national, resident in Lugano, reads the subtitle, drafted this time by Luke under strict instructions from Hector to keep the description carbon neutral. *International socialite, horseman, Kremlin power-broker.*

Once again, Hector has awarded himself the best lines:

'Real name, far as we can get it, Stanislav Auros. Polish-Armenian, Turkish antecedents, self-educated, self-invented, brilliant. Currently the Prince's major-domo, enabler, factotum, social advisor and frontman.' And with no pause or alteration in his voice: 'Billy, why don't you take him over from here? You know more about him than I do.'

Is Matlock ever to be outmanoeuvred? Apparently not, for he is back without so much as a second's thought:

'I fear I'm losing you, Hector. Be so kind as to remind me, if you will.'

Hector will. He has revived remarkably:

'Our recent childhood, Billy. Before we become grown-ups. A midsummer's day, as I recall it. I was Head of Station in Prague, you were Head of Operations in London. You authorized me to drop fifty thousand US dollars in small notes into the boot of Stanislav's parked white Mercedes at dead of night, no questions asked. Except that in those days he wasn't Stanislav, he was Monsieur Fabian Lazaar. He never once turned his pretty head to say thank you. I don't know what he earned his money for, but no doubt you do. He was making his way up in those days. Stolen artefacts, mostly from Iraq. Chaperoning rich ladies of Geneva out of their husbands' cash. Hawking diplomatic pillow talk to the highest bidder. Maybe that's what we were buying. Was it?'

'I did *not* run Stanislav *or* Fabian, thank you, Hector. Or Mr dell Oro, or whatever he calls himself. He was *not* my joe. At the time you made that payment to him, I was merely standing in.'

'Who for?'

'My predecessor. Do you mind not interrogating me, Hector? The boot's on the other foot, if you've not noticed. *Aubrey Longrigg* was my predecessor, Hector, as you well know, and come to think of it will remain so for as long as I'm in this job. Don't tell me you've forgotten *Aubrey*

Longrigg, or I'll think Dr Alzheimer has paid you an unwelcome visit. Sharpest needle in the box, Aubrey was, right up to his somewhat premature departure. Even if he did overstep the mark occasionally, same as you.'

In defence, Luke recalled, Matlock knew only attack.

'And believe you me, Hector,' he rode on, gathering reinforcements as he went, 'if my predecessor *Aubrey Longrigg* needed fifty grand paying out to his joe just as Aubrey was leaving the Service to go on to higher things, and if Aubrey requested me to undertake that task on his behalf in full and final settlement of a certain private understanding, which he did, I was not about to turn around and say to Aubrey: "Hang on a minute, Aubrey, while I obtain special clearance and check your story out." Well, was I? Not with *Aubrey*! Not the way Aubrey and the Chief were in those days, hand in glove, hugger-mugger, I'd be off my head, wouldn't I?'

The old steel had at last re-entered Hector's voice:

'Well, why don't we take a look at Aubrey as he is today: Parliamentary Under-Secretary, Member of Parliament for one of his Party's most deprived constituencies, staunch defender of the rights of women, valued consultant to the Ministry of Defence on arms procurement and' – softly snapping his fingers and frowning as if he really has forgotten – 'what else is he, Luke? – *something*, I know.'

And bang on cue, Luke hears himself trilling out the answer:

'Chairman designate of the new parliamentary subcommittee on banking ethics.'

'And not *completely* out of touch with our Service either, I suppose?' Hector suggested.

'I suppose not,' Luke agrees, though why on earth Hector should have regarded him as an authority at that moment was hard to tell.

*

Perhaps it's only right that we spies, even our retired ones, do not take naturally to being photographed, Luke reflected. Perhaps we nurture a secret fear that the Great Wall between our outer and inner selves will be pierced by the camera's lens.

Certainly Aubrey Longrigg MP gave that impression. Even caught unawares in poor light by an inferior video camera hand-held fifty metres away across the water, Longrigg seemed to be hugging whatever shadow the fairy-lit deck of the *Princess Tatiana* afforded.

Not, it must be said, that the poor chap was naturally photogenic, Luke conceded, once more thanking his lucky stars that their paths had never crossed. Aubrey Longrigg was balding, mean and beaky, as became a man famous for his intolerance of lesser minds than his own. Under the Adriatic sun, his unappetizing features have turned a flaming pink, and the rimless spectacles do little to alter the impression of a fifty-year-old bank clerk – unless, like Luke, you have heard tales of the restless ambition that drives him, the unforgiving intellect that had made the fourth floor a swirling hothouse of innovative ideas and feuding barons, and of his improbable attraction to a certain kind of woman – the kind presumably that gets a kick out of being intellectually belittled – of whom the latest example was standing beside him in the person of: *The Lady Janice (Jay) Longrigg, society hostess and fundraiser*, followed by

Yvonne's shortlist of the many charities that had reason to be thankful to Lady Longrigg.

She wears a stylish, off-the-shoulder evening dress. Her groomed raven hair is held in place by a diamanté grip. She has a gracious smile and the royal, forward-leaning totter that only Englishwomen of a certain birth and class acquire. And she looks, to Luke's unsparing eye, ineffably stupid. At her side hover her two pre-pubescent daughters in party frocks.

'She's his new one, right?' Matlock the unabashed Labour supporter suddenly sang out, with improbable vigour, as the screen went blank at Hector's touch, and the overhead light came on. 'The one he married when he decided to fast-lane himself into politics without doing any of the dirty work. Some Labourite Aubrey Longrigg is, I will say! Old *or* new!'

*

Why was Matlock so jovial again? – and this time for real? The last thing Luke had expected of him was outright laughter, which in Matlock was at the best of times a rare commodity. Yet his big, tweedy torso was heaving with silent mirth. Was it because Longrigg and Matlock had for years been famously at daggers drawn? That to enjoy the favour of the one had been to attract the hostility of the other? That Longrigg had come to be known as the Chief's brain, and Matlock, unkindly, as his brawn? That with Longrigg's departure, office wits had likened their feud to a decade-long bullfight in which the bull had put in *la puntilla*?

'Yes, well, always a high-flyer, Aubrey was,' he was

remarking, like a man remembering the dead. 'Quite the financial wizard too, as I recall. Not in *your* league, Hector, I'm pleased to say, but getting up there. Operational funds were never a problem, that's for sure, not while Aubrey was at the helm. I mean, how did he ever come to be on that boat to begin with?' – asked the same Matlock who only minutes ago had asserted that a man couldn't be condemned for being on someone's boat. '*Plus* consorting with a former secret source after departing the Service, which the rule book has some very firm things to say about, particularly if said source is a slippery customer like – whatever he calls himself these days.'

'Emilio dell Oro,' Hector put in helpfully. 'One to remember, actually, Billy.'

'You'd think he'd know better, Aubrey would, after what we taught him, consorting with Emilio dell Oro, then. You'd think a man of Aubrey's somewhat serpentine skills would be more circumspect in his choice of friend. How come he happened to be there? Perhaps he had a good reason. We shouldn't prejudge him.'

'One of those happy strokes of luck, Billy,' Hector explained. 'Aubrey and his newest wife and her daughters were enjoying a camping holiday up in the hills above the Adriatic Coast. A London banking chum of Aubrey's called him up, name unknown, told him the *Tatiana* was anchored near by and there was a party going on, so hurry on down and join the fun.'

'Under canvas? *Aubrey?* Tell me another.'

'Roughing it in a campsite. The populist life of New Labour Aubrey, man of the people.'

'Do *you* go on camping holidays, Luke?'

'Yes, but Eloise hates British campsites. She's French,' he replied, sounding idiotic to himself.

'And when you go on your camping holidays, Luke – taking care, as you do, to avoid *British* campsites – do you as a rule take your dinner jacket with you?'

'No.'

'And Eloise, does she take her diamonds with her?'

'She hasn't got any, actually.'

Matlock thought about this. 'I suppose you bumped into Aubrey quite a lot, did you, Hector, while you were cutting your lucrative swathe in the City, and others of us went on doing our duty? Had the odd jar together now and then, did you, you and Aubrey? The way City folk do?'

Hector gave a dismissive shrug. 'Bumped into each other now and then. Haven't got a lot of time for naked ambition, to be honest. Bores me.'

At which Luke, to whom dissembling these days did not come quite as easily as it used to, had to restrain himself from grasping the arms of his chair.

*

Bumped into each other? Dear Heaven, they had fought each other to a standstill – and *then* gone on fighting. Of all the *vulture capitalists*, asset-strippers, dawn-raiders and *carpet-buggers* that ever stepped – according to Hector – Aubrey Longrigg was the most two-faced, devious, backsliding, dishonest and well-connected.

It was Aubrey Longrigg lurking in the wings who had led the assault on Hector's family grain firm. It was Longrigg who, through a dubious but cleverly assembled network of cut-outs, had cajoled Her Majesty's Revenue & Customs into storming Hector's warehouses at dead of night, slashing open hundreds of sacks, smashing down doors and terrifying the night shift.

It was Longrigg's insidious network of Whitehall contacts that had unleashed Health & Safety, the Inland Revenue, the Fire Department and the Immigration Service to harass and intimidate the family employees, ransack their desks, seize their account books and challenge their tax returns.

But Aubrey Longrigg was not mere *enemy* in Hector's eyes – that would have been too easy altogether – he was an archetype; a classic symptom of the canker that was devouring not just the City, but our most precious institutions of government.

Hector was at war not with Longrigg personally. Probably he was speaking the truth when he told Matlock that Longrigg bored him, for it was an essential pillar of his thesis that the men and women he was pursuing were by definition bores: mediocre, banal, insensitive, lacklustre, to be distinguished from other bores only by their covert support for one another, and their insatiable greed.

*

Hector's commentary has become perfunctory. Like a magician who doesn't want you to look too closely at any one card, he is shuffling swiftly through the pack of international rogues that Yvonne has put together for him.

Glimpse a tubby, imperious, very small man loading up his plate from the buffet:

'Known in German circles as Karl der Kleine,' Hector says dismissively. 'Half a Wittelsbach – which half eludes me. Bavarian, pitch-black Catholic as they say down there;

close ties with the Vatican. Closer still with the Kremlin. Indirectly elected member of the Bundestag – and non-executive director of a clutch of Russian oil companies, big chum of Emilio dell Oro's. Skied with him last year in St Moritz, took his Spanish boyfriend along. The Saudis love him. Next lovely.'

Cut too quickly to a bearded beautiful boy in a glittering magenta cape making lavish conversation with two bejew-elled matrons:

'Karl der Kleine's latest pet,' Hector announces. 'Sentenced to three years' hard labour by a Madrid court last year for aggravated assault, got off on a technicality, thanks to Karl. Recently appointed non-executive director of the Arena group of companies, same lot that own the Prince's yacht – ah, now *here's* one to watch' – flick of the console – '*Doctor* Evelyn Popham of Mount Street, Mayfair; Bunny to his friends. Studied law in Fribourg and Manches-ter. Licensed to practise in Switzerland, courtier and pimp to the Surrey oligarchs, sole partner of his own flourishing West End law firm. Internationalist, bon viveur, bloody good lawyer. Bent as a hairpin. Where's his website? Hold on. Find it in a moment. Leave me alone, Luke. There you are. Got it.'

On the plasma screen, while Hector fumbles and mutters, Dr (Bunny-to-his-friends) Popham continues to beam patiently down on his audience. He is a rotund, jolly gentle-man with chubby cheeks and side-whiskers, drawn straight from the pages of Beatrix Potter. Improbably he sports tennis whites and is clutching, in addition to his racquet, a comely female tennis partner.

The home page of The Dr Popham & No Partners

website, when it finally appears, is mastered by the same cheerful face, smiling over the top of a quasi-royal coat of arms featuring the scales of justice. Beneath him runs his Mission Statement:

> My expert team's professional experience includes:
> - successfully protecting the rights of leading individuals in the international entrepreneurial banking sphere against Serious Fraud Office investigations
> - successfully representing key international clients in matters regarding offshore jurisdiction, and their right to silence at international and UK tribunals of inquiry
> - successfully responding to importunate regulatory inquiries and tax investigations and charges of improper or illegal payments to influence-makers.

'And the buggers can't stop playing tennis,' Hector complains as his rogues' gallery recovers at its former spanking pace.

*

In short order, we're in the sporting clubs of Monte Carlo, Cannes, Madeira and the Algarve. We're in Biarritz and Bologna. We're trying to keep up with Yvonne's captions, and her album of fun photographs plundered from society magazines, but it's hard, unless like Luke you know what to expect and why.

But however swiftly faces and places change under Hector's volatile management, however many beautiful people in state-of-the-art tennis gear whisk by, five players repeatedly assert themselves:

- jocular Bunny Popham, your lawyer of choice for responding to importunate regulatory inquiries and charges of illegal payments to influence-makers
- ambitious, intolerant Aubrey Longrigg, retired spy, Member of Parliament and family camper, with his latest aristocratic and charitable wife
- Her Majesty's Minister-of-State-in-Waiting, and specialist-to-be in banking ethics
- the self-taught, self-invented, vivacious and charming socialite and polyglot Emilio dell Oro, Swiss national and globe-trotting financier, addicted – we are told by a scanned press cutting that you have to be quick as lightning to read – to 'adrenalin sports from bareback riding in the Ural Mountains, heli-skiing in Canada, tennis in the fast lane, and playing the Moscow Stock Exchange', who gets longer than his due, owing to a technical hitch, and finally:
- patrician, urbane public-relations maestro Captain Giles de Salis, Royal Navy, retd., influence-pedlar, specialist in bent peers – presented to the background music of: 'one of the slimiest buggers in Westminster' from Hector.

Light on. Change memory stick. House rules dictate: one subject, one stick. Hector likes to keep his flavours separate. Time to go to Moscow.

10

Hector has for once taken a vow of silence: which is to say that, released from his mawkish technical preoccupations, he is sitting back in his chair and allowing the baritone-voiced Russian news commentator to do his work for him. Like Luke, Hector is a convert to the Russian language – and, with reservations, the Russian soul. Like Luke, each time he watches the film that is running, he is by his own admission awestruck in the presence of the classic, timeless, all-Russian, bare-faced whopping lie.

And the Moscow-based television news service can manage very well on its own, without help from Hector or anybody else. The baritone voice is more than capable of imparting its revulsion at the grisly tragedy it is recounting: this senseless drive-by shooting, this wanton cutting-down of a brilliant and devoted Russian couple from Perm in their very prime of life! Little had the victims known, when they decided to visit their beloved homeland from distant Italy where they were based, that their journey of the soul would end here in the ivy-clad graveyard of the ancient seminary they had always loved, with its onion domes and thuja trees, set on a hillside outside Moscow at the edge of gently swelling forest:

On this dark, unseasonable afternoon in May, all Moscow is in mourning for two blameless Russians and their two small daughters who, by the mercy of God, were not present in the car when their parents were shot to pieces by terrorist elements of our society.

See the shattered windows and bullet-riddled doors, the burned-out carcass of a once-noble Mercedes car tossed on to its side between silver birch trees, the innocent Russian blood mingling in brutal close-up with the fuel oil on the tarmac; and the disfigured faces of the victims themselves.

The outrage, the commentator assures us, has aroused the justified anger of all responsible Moscow citizens. When will this menace end? they ask. When will decent Russians be free to travel their own roads without being gunned down by marauding bands of Chechen desperadoes bent on spreading terror and mayhem?

Mikhail Arkadievich – rising international oil and metals trader! Olga L'vovna – selflessly engaged in procuring charitable food supplies on behalf of Russia's needy! Loving parents of little Katya and Irina! Pure Russians, homesick for the Motherland they will never leave again!

Against the rising tide of the commentator's indignation a crawling column of black limousines escorts a glass-sided hurdy-gurdy up the wooded hillside to the seminary gates. The procession halts, car doors fly open as young men in dark designer suits leap out and form ranks to accompany the coffins. The scene changes to a grim-faced Deputy Chief of Police in full uniform and medals posed rigidly at an inlaid desk surrounded by testimonials and photographs of President Medvedev and Prime Minister Putin:

> Let us take comfort in the knowledge that one Chechen at least has already voluntarily confessed to the crime,

he tells us, and the camera holds his face long enough for us to share his outrage.

We return to the graveyard, and the strains of a Gregorian funeral lament as a choir of young Orthodox priests in flowerpot hats and silky beards proceeds with icons aloft down the seminary steps to a double graveside where the principal mourners are waiting. The picture freezes, then zooms in on each mourner as Yvonne's subtitles surface beneath them:

TAMARA, wife to Dima, sister to Olga, aunt to Katya and Irina: poker upright, under a wide-brimmed beekeeper's black hat.

DIMA, husband to Tamara: his bald, racked face so sickly in its stretched smile that he might as well be dead himself, despite the presence of his beloved daughter.

NATASHA, daughter to Dima: her long hair swept down her back in a black river, her slender body swathed in layers of shapeless black weed.

IRINA and KATYA, children of Olga and Misha: expressionless, each clutching a hand of Natasha.

The commentator is reciting the names of the great and good who have come to pay their respects. They include the representatives of Yemen, Libya, Panama, Dubai and Cyprus. None from Great Britain.

The camera fixes on a grassy knoll halfway up a hillside darkened by thuja trees. Six – no, seven – neatly suited young men in their twenties and early thirties are clustered together. Their beardless faces, some already running to fat, are directed at the open grave twenty metres down the slope beneath them, where the erect figure of Dima stands alone, his upper body tilted backwards in the military manner that he favours as he stares, not into the grave, but at the seven suited men gathered on the knoll.

Is the photograph still or moving? Dima has remained quite motionless, so it's hard to tell. So also have the men gathered on the knoll above him. Belatedly, Yvonne's subtitle appears:

THE SEVEN BROTHERS.

One by one, the camera takes a look at each of them in close-up.

*

Luke has long ago given up trying to judge the world by its face. He has studied these faces numberless times, but still finds nothing in them he wouldn't find across the desk from him in any Hampstead estate agent's office, or in any gathering of black-suited, black-briefcased, business types in the bar of any smart hotel from Moscow to Bogotá.

Even when their long-winded Russian names appear, complete with patronymics, criminal nicknames and aliases, he can't bring himself to see in their owners' faces anything more interesting than another edition of prototypes from the uniformed ranks of middle management.

But keep looking, and you begin to realize that six of them, either by design or chance, form a protective ring round the seventh at their centre. Look still more closely, and you observe that the man they are shielding is not a day older than they are and that his creaseless face is as happy as a child's on a sunny day, which isn't quite the face you expect to meet at a funeral. The face is such a picture of good health, in Luke's view, that you are almost obliged to assume a healthy mind behind it. If its owner were to pop up uninvited on Luke's doorstep one Sunday evening with a hard-luck story to tell, he would have a difficult time turning him away. And his subtitle?

THE PRINCE.

Abruptly, the said Prince detaches himself from his brothers, trots down the grassy slope and, without shortening his stride or reducing his pace, advances with arms outstretched on Dima, who has turned to confront him, shoulders back, chest out, chin thrust proudly forward in defiance. But his curled hands, so fine in contrast to the rest of him, seem unable to leave his sides. Perhaps – it crosses Luke's mind each time he watches – perhaps he is thinking that this is his chance to do to the Prince what he dreamed of doing to the husband of Natasha's mother – 'with *these*, Professor!' If that is so, then wiser and more tactical thoughts finally prevail.

Gradually, if a little late, his hands grudgingly rise for the embrace, which begins tentatively but then, by force of men's desire or mutual detestation, becomes a lovers' clinch.

Slow motion to the kiss: left cheek to left cheek, old *vor* to young *vor*. Misha's protector kisses Misha's murderer.

Slow motion to the second kiss, right cheek to right cheek.

And after each kiss, the little pause for mutual commiseration and reflection, and that choked word of sympathy between grieving mourners which, if spoken at all, is heard by none but themselves.

Slow motion to the mouth-to-mouth kiss.

*

Over the tape recorder that sits between Hector's lifeless hands, Dima is explaining to the English apparatchiks why he is prepared to embrace the man whom, most in the world, he would prefer to strike dead:

> 'Sure we are sad, I tell to him! But as good *vory* we *understand* why was necessary to murder my Misha! "This Misha, he became too greedy, Prince!" we shall tell to him. "This Misha, he stole your goddam money, Prince! He was too ambitious, too critical!" We do not say, "Prince, you are not true *vor*, you are corrupt bitch." We do not say, "Prince, you take orders from State!" We do not say, "Prince, you pay tribute money to State." We do not say, "You make contract killings for State, you betray Russian heart to State." No. We are *humble*. We regret. We accept. We are respectful. We say, "Prince, we love you. Dima *accepts* your wise decision to kill his blood disciple Misha."'

Hector switches the player to pause and turns to Matlock.

'He's actually talking here about a process we've been observing for some time, Billy,' he says, almost apologetically.

'We?'

'Kremlin-watchers, criminologists.'

'And you.'

'Yes. Our team. We too.'

'And what is this process your team has been observing so closely, Hector?'

'As the criminal Brotherhoods draw closer to each other for reasons of good business, so the Kremlin is drawing closer to the criminal Brotherhoods. The Kremlin threw the book at the oligarchs ten years ago: come back inside the tent, or we tax the shit out of you or chuck you into prison, or both.'

'I do believe I read that for myself somewhere, Hector,' says Matlock, who likes to deliver his shafts with a particularly friendly smile.

'Well, now they're saying the same to the Brotherhoods,' Hector continues unruffled: 'Organize yourselves, clean up your act, don't kill unless we tell you to, and let's all get rich together. And here's your irrepressible friend again.'

The news footage restarts. Hector freezes frame, selects a corner and enlarges it. As Dima and the Prince embrace, the man who now calls himself Emilio dell Oro, clad in black ambassadorial overcoat with astrakhan collar, stands midway up the slope, gazing down in approval on the match – while over the tape recorder Dima reads in staccato Russian from Tamara's script:

'The chief arranger for the Prince's many secret payments is Emilio dell Oro, corrupt Swiss citizen of many former identities who by wickedness has obtained the Prince's ear. Dell Oro is the Prince's advisor in many delicate criminal matters for which the Prince being very stupid is not qualified. Dell Oro has many corrupt connections, also in Great Britain. When special payments must be arranged for these British connections, this is done on the recommendation of the viper dell Oro after personal approval by the Prince. After a recommendation is approved, it is the task of the one they call Dima to open Swiss bank accounts for these British persons. As soon as honourable British guarantees are in place, the one they call Dima will also provide names of corrupt British persons who are in high positions of State.'

Hector again switched off the recorder.

'Doesn't he go on then?' Matlock complained sarcastically. 'He's a right tempter, I'll say that for him! Nothing he won't tell us, if we give him everything he wants and then some. Even if he has to make it up.'

But whether Matlock was convincing himself was another matter. Even if he was, Hector's reply must have rung like a death sentence in his ears:

'Then maybe he made this up too, Billy. One week ago today, the Cyprus headquarters of the Arena Multi Global Trading Conglomerate filed a formal application with the Financial Services Authority to establish a new trading bank in the City of London, to operate under the name of First Arena City Trading and to be known henceforth and for all time by the acronym FACT, hence the FACT Bank Limited, or PLC, or incorporated or what-the-fuck. The applicants claim to have the support of three major City banks and secured assets of five hundred million dollars and unsecured assets of billions. Lots of billions. They're coy about just how many billions for fear of frightening the horses. The application is supported by a number of august financial institutions, domestic and foreign, and an impressive line-up of home-grown illustrious names. Your predecessor Aubrey Longrigg and our Minister-of-State-in-Waiting happen to be two illustrious names. They are joined in their representations by the usual contingent of bottom-feeders from the House of Lords. Among the several legal advisors retained by Arena to press its case with the Financial Services Authority is the distinguished Dr Bunny Popham of Mount Street, Mayfair. Captain de Salis, formerly of the Royal Navy, has generously offered himself as the spearhead of Arena's public-relations offensive.'

*

Matlock's big head has fallen forward. Finally he speaks, but still without raising his head:

'It's all right for you, isn't it, Hector, sniping from the sidelines. *And* your friend Luke here. What about the Service's standing where it counts? You're not *Service* any more. You're Hector. What about the outsourcing of our Intelligence requirements to friendly companies, banks by no means excluded? We're not a crusade, Hector. We're not hired to rock the boat. We're here to help steer it. We're a *Service*.'

Meeting little in the way of sympathy in Hector's gaunt stare, Matlock selects a more personal note:

'I've always been a status quo man myself, Hector, never been ashamed of it either. Be grateful if this great country of ours gets through another night without mishap, is me. That doesn't do for you, does it? It's like the old Soviet joke we used to tell each other back in the Cold War: there'll be no war, but in the struggle for peace, not a stone will be left standing. An *absolutist* is what you are, Hector, I've decided. It's that son of yours who gave you so much pain. He's turned your head. Adrian.'

Luke held his breath. This was holy ground. Never once, in all the intimate hours he and Hector had passed together – over Ollie's soups, and malts in the kitchen after hours, huddled together watching Yvonne's stolen film footage or listening yet again to Dima's diatribe – had Luke risked so much as a glancing reference to Hector's errant son. Only by chance had he learned from Ollie that Hector was not to be troubled on a Wednesday or a Saturday afternoon, except in dire emergency, because those were his visiting times at Adrian's open prison in East Anglia.

But Hector appeared not to have heard Matlock's offending words or, if he had, not to heed them. And as to Matlock, he was so fired up with indignation that he was quite likely unaware that he had spoken them at all.

'*Plus another thing, Hector!*' he barks. 'What's *wrong*, when you come down to it, with turning black money to white, at the end of the day? All right, there's an alternative economy out there. A very big one. We all know that. We're not born yesterday. More black than white, some countries' economies are, we know that too. Look at Turkey. Look at Colombia, Luke's parish. All right, look at Russia too. So where would you rather see that money? Black and out there? Or white, and sitting in London in the hands of civilized men, available for legitimate purposes and the public good?'

'Then maybe you should take up laundering yourself, Billy,' says Hector quietly. 'For the public good.'

Now it's Matlock's turn not to have heard. Abruptly he changes tack, a trick he has long perfected:

'And who's this *Professor* we're hearing about anyway?' he demands, talking straight into Hector's face. 'Or *not* hearing about? Is he your *source* for all this? Why am I being fed snippets all the time, no hard data? Why haven't you cleared him with us – or her? I don't remember anything about a professor crossing *my* desk.'

'Want to run him, Billy?'

Matlock gives Hector a long, silent stare.

'Be my guest, Billy,' Hector urges. 'Take him over, whoever he or she is. Take over the whole case, Aubrey Longrigg and all. Hand it to the organized crime people, if you prefer. Call in the Met, the security services and the guards armoured while you're about it. The Chief may not thank you, but others will.'

Matlock is never defeated. Nevertheless, his truculent question has the unmistakable ring of concession:

'All right. Let's do some plain talking for a change. What d'you want? How long for, and how much? Let's have your full bag. Then let's empty it out a bit.'

'I want *this*, Billy. I want to meet Dima face to face when he comes to Paris in three weeks' time. I want to get trade samples out of him exactly as we would from any high-priced defector: names from his list, account numbers, and a sight of his map – sorry, link chart. I want written approval – yours – to take him to first base on the under-standing that if he can provide what he says he can provide, we buy him on the nail, at full market price, and don't piss around while he tries to flog himself to the French, the Germans, the Swiss – or, God help us, the Americans, who will need one quick look at his material to confirm their current dismal view of this Service, this government and this country.' A bony forefinger shoots into the air and stays there as the fervent light once more rises to his wide grey eyes. 'And I want to go *barefoot*. You follow me? That means *no* tipping off the Paris Station that I'm there, and *no* operational, financial or logistical support from you or the Service at any level until I ask for it. Got it? Ditto with Berne. I want the case kept watertight and the indoctrination list closed and locked. No more signatories, no whispering in the corridor to best chums. I'll handle the case *on* my own, *in* my own way, using Luke here and whatever other resources I choose. All right, go on, now have your fit.'

So Hector did hear, thought Luke with satisfaction: Billy Boy hit you with Adrian, and you've made him pay the price.

Matlock's outrage was mingled with frank disbelief. 'Without the Chief's word even? Without fourth-floor approval, at *all*? Hector Meredith flying solo all over again? Taking information from unsymbolized sources on your own initiative for your own ends? You're not in the real world, Hector. You never were. Don't look at what your man's *offering*. Look at what he's *asking*! Resettlement for his whole tribe, new identities, passports, safe houses, amnesties, guarantees, I don't know what he *isn't* asking! You'd have to have the entire Empowerment Committee behind you, *in writing*, before you'd get me signing up to that. I don't trust you. Never did. Nothing's enough for you. Never was.'

'The *entire* Empowerment Committee?' Hector inquired.

'As constituted under Treasury rules. The full Committee of Empowerment, in plenary session, no subcommittees.'

'So a clutch of government lawyers, an all-star cast of Foreign Office mandarins, Cabinet Office, the Treasury, not to mention our own fourth floor. You think you can contain that, do you, Billy? In this context? How about the Parliamentary Oversight lot? They're worth a laugh. Both houses of Parliament, cross-Party, Aubrey Longrigg to the fore, and de Salis's fully paid-up choir of parliamentary mercenaries, all singing from the same hymn-sheet?'

'The size and constitution of the Empowerment Committee is flexible *and* adjustable, Hector, as you very well know. Not all elements have to be present at all times.'

'And this is what you propose before I've even spoken to Dima? You want a scandal before the scandal's broken? Is that what you're pushing for? Go wide, blow the source before you've let him show you what he's got to sell, and sod the consequences? Is that seriously what you're suggesting? You'll let the shit hit the fan before it's even turning, all to save your back? And you talk about the good of the Service.'

Luke had to hand it to Matlock. Even now, he did not relax his aggression.

'So it's the interests of the Service we're protecting at last! Well, well. I'm glad to hear it, late as it may be. What are *you* suggesting?'

'Hold off your committee meeting until after Paris.'

'And in the meantime?'

'Against your better judgement and all you hold dear, such as your own arse, you give me a temporary operational licence, thereby entrusting the whole affair to the hands of a maverick officer who can be disowned the moment the operation goes belly up: me. Hector Meredith has his virtues, but he's an identified loose cannon and he's exceeded his brief. Media please copy.'

'And if the operation *doesn't* go belly up?'

'You assemble the smallest version of the Empowerment Committee that you can get away with.'

'And you'll address it.'

'And you'll be on sick leave.'

'That's not fair, Hector.'

'It wasn't intended to be, Billy.'

*

Luke never knew what piece of paper it was that Matlock was drawing from the recesses of his jacket, what it said and didn't say, whether both signed it or only one, whether there was a copy and if so who kept it and where, because Hector reminded him, not for the first time, that he had an engagement, and he had left the room to keep it by the time Matlock was spreading out his wares on the table.

But he would remember all his life the walk back to Hampstead through the last of the evening sunshine, and wondering whether he might just stop by on Perry and Gail at their flat in Primrose Hill on his way, and urge them to run for their lives while there was time.

And from there his thoughts as so often strayed, with no prompting from him, to the booze-sodden sixty-year-old Colombian drug lord who, for reasons neither he nor Luke would ever understand, decided that instead of providing Luke with Intelligence, which he had done for the last two years, he would lock him up in a stinking jungle stockade for a month and leave him to the tender mercies of his lieutenants, then bring him a set of clean clothes and a bottle of tequila and invite him to find his own way back to Eloise.

Of the many emotions that Gail had expected to feel as she boarded the 12.29 Eurostar from St Pancras Station bound for Paris on a cloudy Saturday afternoon in June, relief was about the last of them. Yet relief, albeit hedged around with every sort of caveat and reservation, was what she felt, and if Perry's face opposite her was anything to go by, so did he. If relief meant clarity, if it meant harmony between them restored, and getting back on track with Natasha and the girls and mopping Perry's brow when he was doing his Land and Liberty number, then Gail was relieved; which didn't mean she'd tossed her critical faculties out of the window, or was one half as enchanted as Perry patently was by his role as master-spy.

Perry's conversion to the cause had come as no big surprise to her, though you had to be a Perry-watcher to know just how far he had moved: from high-minded rejection to outright commitment to what Hector referred to as The Job. Sometimes, it was true, Perry would express residual moral or ethical reservations, even doubts – is this *really* the only way to handle this? Isn't there a simpler route to the same end? – but he was capable of asking himself the same question halfway up a thousand-foot overhang.

The original seeds of his conversion, she now realized, had been planted not by Hector but by Dima, who since Antigua had acquired the dimensions of a Rousseau-esque noble savage in the Perry lexicon:

'Just imagine who *we'd* have been if we'd been born into *his* life, Gail. You can't get away from the fact: it's practically a badge of honour to be selected by him. And I mean, think of those *children*!'

Oh, she thought of the children all right. She thought of them day and night, and most particularly she thought about Natasha, which was one reason why she had refrained from suggesting to Perry that, stuck out on a headland in Antigua with the fear of God in him, Dima mightn't exactly have been spoiled for choice when it came to selecting a messenger, confessor, or prisoner's friend, or whatever it was that Perry had been appointed, or had appointed himself. She'd always known there was a slumbering romantic in him waiting to be woken when selfless dedication was on offer, and if there was a whiff of danger in the air, so much the better.

The only missing character had been a fellow zealot to sound the bugle: until enter on cue Hector, the charming, witty, falsely relaxed, eternal litigant, as she saw him; the archetypal justice-obsessed client who had spent his life proving he owned the land that Westminster Abbey was built on. And probably if her Chambers spent a hundred years on his case he would be proved right and the courts would find for him. But in the meantime the Abbey would remain pretty much where it was, and life would go on as before.

And Luke? Well, Luke was Luke, as far as Perry was concerned, a safe pair of hands, no argument: a good pro, conscientious, savvy. All the same, it had been a comfort to Perry, he had to admit, to learn that Luke was not, as they had at first assumed, the team leader, but Hector's lieutenant. And since Hector could do no wrong in Perry's eyes, this was obviously the right thing for Luke to be.

Gail was not so sure. The more she had seen of Luke over their two weeks of 'familiarization', the more inclined she was to regard him – despite his twitchiness and exaggerated courtesy and the worry-ripples that flitted across his face when he thought nobody was looking – as the safer pair of hands; and Hector, with his bold assurances and ribald wit and overwhelming powers of persuasion, as the loose cannon.

That Luke was also in love with her neither surprised nor discomfited her. Men fell in love with her all the time. There was security in knowing where their feelings lay. That Perry was unaware of this came as no surprise to her either. His lack of awareness was also a kind of security.

What disturbed her most was the passion of Hector's commitment: the sense that he was a man with a mission – the very sense that so enchanted Perry.

'Oh, I'm still on the testing-bench,' Perry had said, in one of his throwaway self-denunciations he was so fond of. 'Hector's the *formed man*' – a distinction he constantly aspired to, and was so reluctant to bestow.

Hector a formed version of *Perry*? Hector the *raw action man* who did the stuff Perry only talked about? Well, who was in the front line now? Perry. And who was doing the talking? Hector,

*

And it wasn't only Hector that Perry was enchanted by. It was Ollie too. Perry, who prided himself on a shrewd eye when it came to deciding who was a good man on a rope, had simply not been able to believe, any more than Gail had, that lumbering, out-of-condition Ollie with his camp ways and single earring and overintelligence, and the buried foreign accent she hadn't been able to trace and was too polite to question, should turn out to be the model of a born educator: meticulous, articulate, determined to make every lesson fun and every lesson stick.

Never mind it was their precious weekends that were being hijacked, or it was late evening after a wearying day in Chambers or in court; or that Perry had been in Oxford all day attending ball-breaking graduation ceremonies, saying goodbye to his students, clearing out his digs. Ollie within moments had them in his spell, whether they were walled up in the basement, or sitting in a crowded café on Tottenham Court Road with Luke out on the pavement and big Ollie in his cab with his beret on, while they tested the toys from his black museum of fountain pens, blazer buttons and tiepins that could listen, transmit, record, or all of the above; and for the girls, costume jewellery.

'Now which ones do we think are *us*, maybe, Gail?' Ollie had asked when it came to her turn to be fitted. And when she replied, 'If you want it straight, Ollie, I wouldn't be seen dead in any of them,' off they had trotted to Liberty's to find something that was more *her.*

Yet the chances of them ever having to use Ollie's toys were, as he was anxious to tell her, virtually zero:

'Hector, he wouldn't *dream* of letting you *near* them for the main event, darling. It's only for the "in case". It's for when all of a sudden you're going to hear something wonderful that nobody was ever expecting, and there's no risk to life or property or such, and all we need is to be sure you've got the necessary know-how to work it.'

With hindsight Gail doubted this. She suspected that Ollie's toys were in reality teaching aids for instilling psychological dependency in the people who were being taught to play with them.

'Your familiarization course will proceed at *your* convenience, not ours,' Hector had informed them, addressing his newly recruited troops on their first evening in a pompous voice she never heard him use again – so perhaps he too was nervous. 'Perry, if you find yourself stuck in Oxford for an unscheduled meeting or whatever, stay stuck and give us a call. Gail, whatever you do at Chambers, don't push your luck. The message is act natural and look busy. Any alteration in either of your lifestyles will raise eyebrows and be counter-productive. With me?'

Next, he reiterated for Gail's benefit the promise he had made to Perry:

'We shall tell you as little as we can get away with, but whatever we do tell you will be the truth. You're a pair of innocents abroad. That's how Dima wants you, and that's how I want you, and so do Luke and Ollie here. What you don't know you can't fuck up. Every new face has got to *be* a new face to you. Every first time has got to *be* a first time. Dima's plan is to launder you the way he launders money. Launder you into his social landscape, make you respectable currency. Effectively, he'll be under house arrest wherever he goes, and will have been since Moscow. That's his problem and he'll have thought hard and long about how to solve it. As ever, the initiative is with the poor bugger in the field. It's Dima's job to show us what he can manage, when and how.' And as a typical Hector afterthought: 'I'm foul-mouthed. Relaxes me, brings me down to earth. Luke and Ollie here are prudes, so it evens out.'

And then the homily:

'This is not, repeat not, a training session. We don't happen to have a couple of years to spare: just a few hours spread over a couple of weeks. So it's familiarization, it's confidence-building, it's establishing trust in all weathers. You in us, us in you. But you are *not* spies. So for Christ's sake don't try to be. Don't even *think* about surveillance. You are *not* surveillance-conscious people. You're a young couple enjoying a spree in Paris. So don't for fuck's sake start dawdling at shop windows, peering over your shoulders or ducking into side alleys. Mobiles are a slightly different matter,' he went on, without a blip. 'Did either of you use your phones in front of Dima or his gang?'

They had used their mobiles from the balcony of their cabin, Gail to call her Chambers concerning *Samson v. Samson*, Perry to call his landlady in Oxford.

'Did anyone in Dima's lot ever hear either of your phones go off?'

No. Emphatic.

'Do Dima or Tamara know either or both of your mobile numbers?'

'*No*,' said Perry.

'No,' Gail replied, if slightly less confidently.

Natasha had Gail's number and Gail had Natasha's. But within the four corners of the question, her reply was truthful.

'Then they can have our encrypted jobs, Ollie,' Hector

said. 'Blue for Gail, silver for him. And you two people please hand over your SIM cards to Ollie and he'll do the necessary. Your new phones will be encrypted for the calls between the five of us only. You'll find the three of us pre-set under Tom, Dick and Harry. Tom's me. Luke's Dick. Ollie's Harry. Perry, you're Milton after the poet. Gail's Doolittle after Eliza. All pre-set. Everything else on the phones functions as per usual. Yes, Gail?'

Gail the barrister:

'Will you be listening to our calls from now on, if you haven't been already?'

Laughter.

'We shall be listening only on the pre-set encrypted lines.'

'No others? Sure?'

'No others. Truth.'

'Not even when I call my five secret lovers?'

'Not even, alas.'

'How about our personal texts?'

'Absolutely no. It's a waste of time and we're not into that stuff.'

'If our pre-set lines to one another are encrypted, why do we need our funny names?'

'Because people on buses earwig. Any more questions from the prosecution? Ollie, where's the bloody malt?'

'Got it right here, Skipper. Actually, I got a new bottle already' – in that irritatingly unplaceable voice.

*

'So your family, Luke?' Gail had asked him over soup and a bottle of red in the kitchen one evening before they went home.

234

It amazed her that she hadn't asked him the question before. Perhaps – dark thought – she hadn't wanted to, preferring to keep him on a hook. It evidently amazed Luke too, because his hand rose sharply to his forehead to comfort a small, livid scar that seemed to come and go of its own accord. A fellow spy's pistol butt? Or an angry wife's frying pan?

'One child only, I'm afraid, Gail,' he said, as if he should be apologizing for not having more. 'Boy. Marvellous little chap. Ben, we call him. Taught me everything I know about life. Beats me at chess too, I'm proud to say. Yes.' Twitch of the stray eyelid. 'Trouble is, we never get around to finishing a game. Too much of *this*.'

This? Did he mean booze? Spying? Or falling in love?

She had briefly suspected him of having a thing with Yvonne, largely from the way Yvonne discreetly mothered him. Then she decided they were just a man and a woman working side by side: until an evening when she caught his eyes staring now at Yvonne, now at herself, as if they were both some sort of higher being, and she thought she'd never seen such a sad face in all her life.

*

It's last night. It's end of term. It's end of school altogether. There will never be another two weeks like these. In the kitchen, Yvonne and Ollie are cooking a sea bass in salt. Ollie is singing from *La Traviata*, rather well, and Luke is doing appreciation, smiling at everyone and shaking his head in exaggerated marvel. Hector has brought a grand bottle of Meursault – actually, two bottles. But first of all, he needs to talk to Perry and Gail alone in the Headmaster's chintzy drawing room. Do we sit or stand? Hector is standing so Perry, ever the formalist despite himself, stands too. Gail selects an upright chair under a Roberts print of Damascus.

'So,' says Hector.

So, they agree.

'Last words, then. Without witnesses. The Job is dangerous. I've told you before but I'm telling you again now. It's *fucking* dangerous. You can still jump ship and no hard feelings. If you stay aboard, we'll wet-nurse you all we can, but we've got no logistical support worth a hoot. Or as we say in the trade, we're going in barefoot. You don't have to say your goodbyes. Forget Ollie's fish. Get your coats from the hall, walk out of the front door, none of it happened. Last call.'

The last of many, if he did but know. Perry and Gail have discussed the same question every night of the last fourteen. Perry was determined she should answer for them both, so she does:

'We're all right. We've decided. We'll do it,' she says, sounding more heroic than she means to, and Perry does a big, slow nod and says, 'Yup, definitely,' which doesn't sound like him either – a thing he must know, because he promptly turns Hector's question back on him:

'So how about *you* people?' he demands. 'Don't *you* ever have doubts?'

'Oh, we're fucked anyway,' Hector replies carelessly. 'That's the point, isn't it? If you're going to be fucked, be fucked in a good cause.'

Which for Perry, of course, is balm to his puritan ear.

*

And to judge by the expression on Perry's face as they pulled into the Gare du Nord, the same balm was still working, because there was a suppressed I-am-Britain look about him that was completely new to Gail. It wasn't till they reached the Hôtel des Quinze Anges – a typical Perry choice: scruffy, narrow, five rickety floors high, tiny rooms, twin beds the size of ironing boards, and a stone's throw from the rue du Bac – that the full impact of what they had signed up to hit them. It was as if their sessions in the Bloomsbury house with its chummy family atmosphere – a cosy hour with Ollie, another with Luke, Yvonne has dropped by, Hector's on his way over for a nightcap – had instilled in them a sense of immunity which, now they were alone, had evaporated.

They also discovered that they had lost the power of natural speech and were talking to each other like an ideal couple in a television commercial:

'I'm *really* looking forward to tomorrow, aren't you?' says Doolittle to Milton. 'I've never seen Federer in the flesh before. I'm really thrilled.'

'I just hope the weather will hold,' Milton replies to Doolittle with a worried glance at the window.

'Me too,' Doolittle agrees earnestly.

'So how's about we unpack this lot and find ourselves a spot of food?' Milton suggests.

'Good idea,' says Doolittle.

But what they're really thinking is: if the match is rained off, what on earth will Dima do?

Perry's mobile is ringing. Hector.

'Hi, Tom,' says Perry idiotically.

'Checked in OK, Milton?'

'Fine, just fine. Good trip. Everything went perfectly,'
Perry says with enough enthusiasm for both of them.
'You're on your own tonight, OK?'
'You said.'
'Doolittle in the pink?'
'Blooming.'
'Call if you need anything. Service round the clock.'

*

In the hotel's minuscule hallway on their way out, Perry
discusses his anxieties about the weather with a formidable
lady named Madame Mère after the mother of Napoleon.
He has known her from his student days and Madame
Mère, if she is to be believed, loves Perry like a son. She
stands four foot nothing in her bedroom slippers and
nobody, according to Perry, has ever seen her without a
headscarf over her curlers. Gail enjoys hearing Perry rattling
away in French, but his fluency has always been a challenge
to her, perhaps because he is not forthcoming about his
early instructors.

At a *tabac* in the rue de l'Université, Milton and Doolittle
eat indifferent steak frites and a tired salad and agree it's the
best in the world. They don't finish their litre of house red,
so take it back to their hotel.

'Just do whatever you'd normally do,' Hector had told
them airily. 'If you've got Paris-based buddies and want to
hang out with them, why not?'

Because we wouldn't be doing what we normally do, is
why not. Because we don't want to be hanging out in a St
Germain café with our Paris-based buddies when we've
got an elephant called Dima sitting in our heads. And

because we don't want to have to lie to them about where we got our tickets for tomorrow's Final.

*

Back in their room, they drink the rest of the red out of tooth-mugs and make deep and adoring love without speaking a word, the best. When morning comes Gail sleeps late out of nervousness, and wakes to find Perry watching the rain spotting the grimy window, and worrying again about what Dima will do if the match is cancelled. And if it's postponed till Monday – Gail's thought now – will she have to call her Chambers with another cock-and-bull story about a sore throat, which is Chambers code for a bad period?

Suddenly everything is linear. After coffee and croissants brought to their bedside by Madame Mère – with an appreciative murmur to Gail of '*Quel titan alors*' – and a vacuous call from Luke asking whether they had a good night and are they feeling fit for tennis, they lie in bed discussing what to do before start of play at 3 p.m., allowing plenty of time to get to the stadium and find their seats and settle in.

Their answer is to take it in turns to use the tiny hand-basin and dress, then march at Perry's pace to the Musée Rodin, where they attach themselves to a queue of school-children, make it to the gardens in time to be rained on, shelter under the trees, take refuge in the museum café and peer through the doorway while they try to work out which way the clouds are moving.

Abandoning their coffees by mutual consent, but for no reason either of them can fathom, they agree to explore the gardens of the Champs-Elysées, only to find them closed on the grounds of security. Michelle Obama and her children are in town, according to Madame Mère, but it's a State secret, so only Madame Mère and all Paris knows.

The gardens of the Marigny Theatre, however, turn out to be open and empty, except for two elderly Arab men in black suits and white shoes. Doolittle selects a bench, Milton approves her choice. Doolittle stares into the chestnut trees, Milton at a map.

Perry knows his Paris and has of course fathomed exactly how they will reach the Roland Garros Stadium – metro to here, bus to there, a fat safety margin to make sure they meet Tamara's deadline.

Nevertheless, it makes sense for him to be burying his face in the map, because what else is there to do if you're a young couple on a spree in Paris and have decided, like a pair of idiots, to sit on a park bench in the rain?

'Everything on course, Doolittle? No little problems we can solve for you?' Luke directly to Gail this time, sounding like the Perkins' all-male family doctor when she was a girl: *Sore throat, Gail? Why don't we have those clothes off and take a look?*

'No problems, nothing you can help us with, thanks,' she replies. 'Milton tells me we'll be hitting the trail in half an hour.' *And there's nothing wrong with my throat either.*

Perry folds his map. Talking to Luke has made Gail feel angry and conspicuous. Her mouth has dried up, so she sucks in her lips and licks them from the inside. How much madder does this get? They return to the empty pavement and set course up the hill towards the Arc de Triomphe, Perry stalking ahead of her the way he does when he wants to be alone and can't.

'What the *fuck* d'you think you're doing?' she hisses into his ear.

He has dodged into an airless shopping mall that is blaring out rock music. He is peering into a darkened window as if his whole future is revealed there. Is he playing spy? – and incidentally flouting Hector's injunction not to look for imaginary watchers?

No. He's laughing. And a moment later, thank God, so is Gail as, arms slung round one another's shoulders, they gaze in disbelief at a veritable arsenal of spy toys: brand-name photographic wristwatches that cost ten thousand euros, briefcase microphone kits and telephone scramblers, night-vision glasses, stun guns in all their glorious variety, pistol holsters with non-slip lap-straps as optional extras, and pick-your-own bullets of pepper, paint or rubber: welcome to Ollie's black museum for the paranoid executive who has nothing.

*

There had been no bus to take them there.

They hadn't ridden on the metro.

The pinch on the bum she'd received from a departing passenger old enough to be her grandfather was non-operative.

They had been wafted here, and that was how they had come to be standing in a queue of courteous French citizens at the left side of the western gate to the Roland Garros Stadium exactly twelve minutes before the time appointed by Tamara.

It was also how Gail came to be smiling her way weightlessly past benign uniformed gatekeepers who were only too happy to smile back at her; then sauntering with the crowd down an avenue of tented shops to the thump-chump of an unseen brass band, the mooing of Swiss alphorns and the unintelligible advice of male loudspeakers.

But it was Gail the cool-headed courtroom lawyer who counted off the sponsors' names on the shopfronts: Lacoste, Slazenger, Nike, Head, Reebok – and which one did Tamara say in her letter? – don't pretend you've forgotten.

'*Perry*' – tugging hard at his arm – 'you promised me *faithfully* you'd buy me some decent tennis shoes. *Look.*'

'Oh, did I? So I did,' agrees Perry alias Milton, as a bubble saying *REMEMBERS!* appears over his head.

And with more conviction than she might have expected of him, he cranes forward to examine the latest thing by – Adidas.

'And it's high time you bought some for *yourself* too, and threw away that stinky old pair with verdigris round the uppers,' bossy Doolittle tells Milton.

'*Professor! I swear to God!* My friend! You don't remember me?'

The voice had come at them without warning: the disembodied voice of Antigua bellowing above the three winds.

Yes, I do remember you, but *I'm* not the Professor.

Perry is.

So I'll keep looking at the latest thing in Adidas tennis shoes, and let Perry go first before I turn my head in an appropriately delighted and highly astonished manner, as Ollie would say.

Perry is going first. She feels him leave her side and turn. She measures the length of time it takes for him to believe the evidence of his eyes.

'Christ, *Dima*! Dima from Antigua! – incredible!'

Not too much, Perry, keep it down –

'What in Heaven's name are *you* doing here! Gail, *look*!'

But I won't look. Not at once. I'm eyeing shoes, remember? And eyeing shoes, I'm always distracted, I'm on a different planet actually, even tennis shoes. Absurdly, as it had seemed to them at the time, they had practised this moment outside a sports shop in Camden Town that specialized in athletics shoes, and again in Golders Green, first with Ollie overplaying the back-slapping Dima and Luke playing innocent bystander, then with their roles reversed. But now she was glad of it: she knew her lines.

So pause, hear him, wake, turn. *Then* be delighted and highly astonished.

'Dima! Oh my *God*. It's *you*! You marvel! This is just totally – this is *amazing*!' – followed by her ecstatic mouse-squeak, the one she uses for opening Christmas parcels, as she watches Perry dissolve into the huge torso of a Dima whose delight and astonishment are no less spontaneous than her own:

'What you *do* here, Professor, you lousy goddam tennis player!'

'But Dima, what are *you* doing?' Perry and Gail together now, a chorus of yaps in different keys, as Dima roars on.

Has he changed? He's paler. The Caribbean sun's worn off. Yellow half-moons under the sexy brown eyes. Sharper downward lines at the corners of the mouth. But the same stance, the same backward lean saying 'come at me if you dare'. The same Henry the Eighth placing of the little feet.

And the man's an absolute natural for the stage, just listen to this:

'You think Federer gonna pussy this Soderling guy the way you pussy *me*? – you think he gonna tank the goddam match because he love fair play? Gail, I swear to God, come here! – I gotta hug this girl, Professor! You married her yet? You goddam crazy!' – as he draws her into his enormous chest, driving his whole body against her, starting with a clammy, tear-stained cheek, then his chest, then the bulge of his crotch until even their knees are touching; then shoves her away from him in order to bestow the obligatory three kisses of the Trinity on her cheeks, left side, right side, left side again while Perry does 'well, I must say this really *is* the most ridiculous, totally improbable coincidence', with rather more academic detachment than Gail thinks appropriate: a little short on spontaneity in her opinion, and she's making up for it with a thrilled gabble of too many questions all at once:

'Dima, *darling*, how are Katya and Irina, for Heaven's sake? I just can't stop thinking about them!' – true – 'Are the twins playing *cricket*? How's *Natasha*? Where have you all *been*? Ambrose said you'd all gone to *Moscow*. Is that where you all went? For the funeral? You look so *well*. How's Tamara? How are all those weird, lovely friends and relations you had around you?'

Did she *really* say that last bit? Yes she did. And while she's saying it, and intermittently receiving bits of answer in reply, she is becoming aware, if only in soft focus, of smartly dressed men and women who have paused to watch the show: another Dima-supporters' club, apparently, but of a younger, slicker generation, far removed from the mossy bunch assembled in Antigua. Is that Baby-Face Niki lurking among them? If so, he's bought himself an Armani summer suit in beige with fancy cuffs. Are the link bracelet and the deep-sea-diver's watch nestling inside them?

Dima is still talking and she is hearing what she doesn't want to hear: Tamara and the children flew straight from Moscow to Zurich – yes, Natasha too, she don't like goddam tennis, she wanna get home to Berne, read and ride a bit. Chill out. Does she also gather that Natasha hadn't been all that well, or was it her imagination? Everyone is conducting three conversations at once:

'Don't you teach goddam *kids* no more, Professor?' – mock outrage – 'you gonna teach *French* kids be English gentlemen once? Listen, where you sitting? Some goddam bird house, top floor, right?'

Followed by, presumably, a rendering of the same witty suggestion over his shoulder in Russian. But it must have got lost in translation, because few of the group of smartly dressed onlookers smile, except for a spruce little dancer of a man at their centre. At first glance, Gail takes him to be a tour guide of some sort, for he is wearing a very visible cream-coloured nautical blazer with an anchor of gold thread on the pocket, and carrying a crimson umbrella which, together with the head of swept-back silvery hair, would have made him instantly findable by anyone lost in a crowd. She catches his smile, then she catches his eye. And when she returns her gaze to Dima, she knows his eye is still on her.

Dima has demanded to see their tickets. Perry makes a habit of losing tickets, so Gail's got them. She knows the numbers by heart, so does Perry. But that doesn't prevent her from not knowing them now, or from looking sweetly vague as she hands them to Dima who lets out a derisive snort:

'You got *telescopes*, Professor? You so fucking high up, you need oxygen!'

Again he repeats the joke in Russian, but again the standing group behind him seems to be waiting rather than listening. Is his breathlessness new since Antigua? Or new for today? Is it a heart thing? Or a vodka thing?

'We gotta goddam hospitality box, hear me? Corporation shit. Young guys I work with from Moscow. Armani kids. Got pretty girls. Look at them!'

A pair of the girls do indeed catch Gail's eye: leather jackets, pencil skirts and ankle boots. Pretty wives? Or pretty hookers. If so, top of the range. And the Armani kids a hostile blur of blue-black suits and sodden stares.

'Thirty number-one seats, food you die for,' Dima is bellowing. 'You wanna do that, Gail? Come join us? Watch the game like a lady? Drink champagne? We got spare. Hey, *come on*, Professor. Why the fuck not?'

Because Hector told him to be hard to get, is why the fuck not. Because the harder he is to get, the harder you'll have to work to get him, and me with him, and the greater will be our credibility with your guests from Moscow. Pushed into a corner, Perry is making a good job of being Perry: frowning, doing his diffident and awkward bit. For a rank beginner in the arts of dissembling, he's putting on a pretty good turn. Time to help him out all the same:

'The tickets were a *present*, you see, Dima,' she confides sweetly, touching his arm. 'A good friend gave them to us, a dear old gentleman. For love. I don't think he'd like us to leave our seats empty, would he? If he found out, he'd be heartbroken' – which was the answer they'd cooked up with Luke and Ollie over a late nightcap of malt.

Dima stares from one to other of them in disappointment while he regroups his thoughts.

Restlessness in the ranks behind him: can't we get this over?

The initiative is with the poor bugger in the field . . .

Solution!

'Then hear me, Professor, OK? Hear me once' – his finger jabbing into Perry's chest – 'OK,' he repeats, nodding menacingly. '*After* the game. Hear me? Soon as the goddam game is over, you gonna come visit us in hospitality.' He swings round to Gail, challenging her to upset his great plan. 'Hear me, Gail? You gonna bring this Professor to our hospitality. And you gonna drink champagne with us. The game don't end when it ends. They gotta do goddam presentations out there, speeches, lotta shit. Federer gonna win easy. You wanna bet me five grand US he don't win, Professor? I give you three to one. Four to one.'

Perry laughs. If he had a god, it would be Federer. No dice, Dima, sorry, he says. Not even at a hundred to one. But he isn't out of the wood yet:

'You're gonna play me tennis tomorrow, Professor, hear me? A *rematch*' – the finger still stabbing at Perry's chest – 'I gonna send someone round find you after the game, you gonna come visit us in hospitality, and we gonna fix a rematch, no pussying. And I'm gonna beat the shit outta you, buy you a massage after. You're gonna need it, hear me?'

Perry has no time for further protestation. Out of the corner of her eye, Gail has observed the tour guide with the silvery hair and red brolly detach himself from the group and advance on Dima's undefended back.

'Aren't you going to introduce us to your friends, Dima? You can't keep a beautiful lady like this all to yourself, you know,' a silken voice says reproachfully in pitch-perfect English with a faint Italian accent. '*Dell Oro*,' he announces. '*Emilio* dell Oro. An old friend of Dima's from way, way back. So pleased.' And takes each of their hands, first Gail's with a gallant downward tip of the head, then Perry's without one, thereby reminding her of a ballroom Lothario called Percy who cut in on her best boyfriend when she was seventeen, and nearly raped her on the dance floor.

'And I'm Perry Makepiece and she's Gail Perkins,' Perry says. And as a light-hearted footnote that really impresses her: 'I'm not really a professor, so don't be alarmed. It's just Dima's way of putting me off my tennis.'

'Then welcome to Roland Garros Stadium, Gail Perkins and Perry Makepiece,' dell Oro replies, with a radiant smile that she is beginning to suspect is permanent. 'So glad we shall have the pleasure of seeing you after the historic match. If there *is* a match,' he adds, with a theatrical lift of the hands and a glance of reproach at the grey sky.

But the last word is Dima's:

'I gonna send someone get you, hear me, Professor? Don't walk out on me. Tomorrow I beat the shit outta you. I love this guy, hear me?' he cries to the supercilious Armani kids with their watery smiles gathered behind him, and having enfolded Perry for a last defiant hug, falls in beside them as they resume their amble.

12

Settling at Perry's side in the twelfth row of the western stand of the Roland Garros Stadium, Gail stares incredulously at the band of Napoleon's Garde Républicaine in their brass helmets, red cockades, skin-tight white breeches and thigh-length boots as they roll out their kettledrums and give their bugles a final blow before their conductor mounts his wooden rostrum, suspends his white-gloved hands above his head, spreads his fingers and flutters them like a dress designer. Perry is talking to her but has to repeat himself. She turns her head to him, then leans it on his shoulder to calm herself, because she's trembling. And so in his own way is Perry, because she can hear the pulse of his body – boom boom.

'Is this the Men's Singles Finals or the Battle of Borodino?' he shouts gaily, pointing at Napoleon's troops. She makes him say it again, lets out a hoot of laughter and gives his hand a squeeze to bring them both down to earth.

'It's all right!' she yells into his ear. 'You did fine! You were a star! Super seats too! Well done!'

'You too! Dima looked great.'

'Great. But the children are already in Berne!'

'What?'

'Tamara and the little girls are already in Berne! Natasha too! I'd have thought they'd all be together!'

'Me too.'

But his disappointment is of a lesser order than hers.

Napoleon's band is very loud. Whole regiments could march to it and never return.

'He's very keen to play tennis with you again, poor man!' Doolittle shouts.

'I've noticed!' Big nods and smiles from Milton.

'Have you got time tomorrow?'

'Absolutely not. Too many dates,' Milton replies, with an adamant shake of his head.

'That's what I feared. Tricky.'

'Very,' Milton agrees.

Are they just being children, or has the fear of God crept into them? Carrying his hand to her lips, Gail kisses it then keeps it against her cheek because, quite unconsciously, he has moved her nearly to tears:

Of all the days in his life that he should be free to enjoy, and isn't! To watch Federer in the Final of the French Open is for Perry like watching Nijinsky in *L'Après-midi d'un Faune*! How many Perry-lectures has she not happily listened to, curled up with him in front of the television set in Primrose Hill, on the subject of Federer, the perfected athlete Perry would love to be? – Federer as *formed man*, Federer the *runner as dancer*, shortening and lengthening his stride to tame the flying ball into providing him with the tiny, hanging extra split second that he needs to find the pace and angle – the steadiness of his upper body whether it's moving back-wards, forwards, sideways – his supernatural powers of anticipation that aren't supernatural at all, Gail, but the summit of eye–body–brain coordination.

'I really want you to enjoy today!' she shouts into his ear like a final message. 'Just put everything else out of your mind. I love you: I said I *love* you, idiot!'

*

She conducts an innocent survey of the spectators next to them. Whose are they? Dima's? Dima's enemies? Hector's? *We're going in barefoot.*

To her left, an iron-jawed blonde woman with a Swiss national cross on her paper hat and another on her ample blouse.

To her right, a middle-aged pessimist in a rainproof hat and cape, sheltering from the rain everybody else is pretending not to notice.

In the row behind them, a Frenchwoman leads her children in a lusty singing of 'La Marseillaise', perhaps under the mistaken impression that Federer is French.

With the same insouciance Gail scans the crowd on the open terraces opposite them.

'See anyone special?' Perry yells into her ear.

'Not really. I thought *Barry* might be here.'

'*Barry?*'

'One of our silks!'

She is talking nonsense. There is a silk called Barry in her Chambers but he loathes tennis and loathes the French. She's hungry. Not only did they leave their coffees behind in the Rodin Museum. They actually forgot lunch. The realization prompts memories of a Beryl Bainbridge novel in which the hostess of a difficult dinner party forgets where she has put the pudding. She shouts to Perry, needing to share the joke:

'How long is it since you and I actually *lost the lunch*?'

But for once Perry doesn't get the literary reference. He's staring at a row of picture windows halfway up the stands on the other side of the court. White tablecloths and hovering waiters are discernible through the smoked glass, and he's wondering which window belongs to Dima's hospitality box. She feels the pressure of Dima's arms round her again, and his crotch pressing against her thigh with childlike unawareness. Were the fumes of vodka last night's, or this morning's? She asks Perry.

'He was just getting himself up to par,' Perry replies.

'*What?*'

'*Par!*'

*

Napoleon's troops have fled the battlefield. A prickly quiet descends. An overhead camera glides on cables across an ugly black sky. *Natasha*. Is she or isn't she? Why hasn't she answered my text? Does Tamara know? Is that why she's whisked her back to Berne? No. Natasha takes her own decisions. Natasha is not Tamara's child. And Tamara, God knows, is nobody's idea of a mother. Text Natasha?

> Just bumped into yr Dad. Watching Federer. RU pregnant? xox, Gail

Don't.

The stadium is erupting. First Robin Soderling, then Roger Federer looking as becomingly modest and self-assured as only God can. Perry is craning forward, lips pressed tensely together. He's in the presence.

Warm-up time. Federer mis-hits a couple of backhands; Soderling's forehand returns are a little too waspish for a friendly exchange. Federer practises a couple of serves, alone. Soderling does the same, alone. Practice over. Their jackets fall off them like sheaths from swords. In the pale blue corner, Federer, with a flash of red inside his collar and a matching red tick on his headband. In the white corner, Soderling, with phosphorescent yellow flashes on his sleeves and shorts.

Perry's gaze strays back to the smoked windows, so Gail's does too. Is that a cream-coloured blazer she sees with a gold anchor on the pocket, floating in the brown mist behind the glass? If ever there was a man not to get into the back of a taxi with, it's Signor Emilio dell Oro, she wants to tell Perry.

But quiet: the match has begun and to the joy of the crowd, but too suddenly for Gail, Federer has broken Soderling's serve and won his own. Now it's Soderling to serve again. A pretty blonde ballgirl with a ponytail hands him a ball, drops a bob, and canters off again. The linesman howls as if he's been stung. The rain's coming on again. Soderling has double-faulted; Federer's triumphal march to victory has begun. Perry's face is lit with simple awe and Gail discovers she is loving him all over again from scratch: his unaffected courage, his determination to do the right thing even if it's wrong, his need to be loyal and his refusal to be sorry for himself. She's his sister, friend, protector.

A similar feeling must have overtaken Perry, for he grasps her hand and keeps it. Soderling is going for the French

Open. Federer is going for history, and Perry is going with him. Federer has won the first set 6–1. It took him just under half an hour.

*

The manners of the French crowd are truly beautiful, Gail decides. Federer is their hero as well as Perry's. But they are meticulous in awarding praise to Soderling wherever praise is due. And Soderling is grateful, and shows it. He's taking risks, which means he is also forcing errors and Federer has just committed one. To make up for it he delivers a lethal drop shot from ten feet behind the baseline.

When Perry watches great tennis, he enters a higher, purer register. After a couple of strokes he can tell you where a rally is heading and who's controlling it. Gail isn't like that. She's a ground-shot girl: wallop and see what happens, is her motto. At the level she plays, it works a treat.

But suddenly Perry isn't watching the game any more. He isn't watching the smoked windows either. He has leaped to his feet and barged in front of her, apparently to shield her, and he's yelling: '*What the hell!*' with no hope of an answer.

Rising with him, which isn't easy because now everyone is standing too and yelling 'what the hell' in French, Swiss German, English or whatever language comes naturally to them, her first expectation is that she is about to see a brace of dead pheasant at Roger Federer's feet: a left and a right. This is because she confuses the clatter of everybody leaping up with the din of panicked birds clambering into the air like out-of-date aeroplanes, to be shot down by her brother and his rich friends. Her second equally wild thought is that it is Dima who has been shot, probably by Niki, and tossed out of the smoked-glass windows.

But the spindly man who has appeared like a ragged red bird at Federer's end of the tennis court is not Dima, and he is anything but dead. He wears the red hat favoured by Madame Guillotine and long, blood-red socks. He has a blood-red robe draped over his shoulders and he's standing chatting to Federer just behind the baseline that Federer has been serving from.

Federer is a bit perplexed about what to say – they clearly haven't met before – but he preserves his on-court nice manners, although he looks a tad irritated in a grouchy, Swiss sort of way that reminds us that his celebrated armour has its chinks. After all, he's here to make history, not waste the time of day with a spindly man in a red dress who's burst on to the court and introduced himself.

But whatever has passed between them is over, and the man in the red dress is scampering for the net, skirts and elbows flying. A bunch of tardy, black-suited gentlemen are in comic pursuit, and the crowd isn't uttering a word any more: it's a sporting crowd, and this is sport, if not of a high order. The man in the red dress vaults the net, but not cleanly: a bit of net-cord there. The dress is no longer a dress. It never was. It's a flag. Two more black-suits have appeared on the other side of the net. The flag is the flag of Spain – L'Espagne – but that's only according to the woman who sang 'La Marseillaise', and her opinion is contested by a hoarse-voiced man several rows up from her who insists it belongs to *le Barça*.

A black-suit has finally brought the man with the flag

down with a rugger tackle. Two more pounce on him and drag him into the darkness of a tunnel. Gail is staring into Perry's face, which is paler than she has ever seen it before.

'*Christ* that was close,' she whispers.

Close to what? What does she mean? Perry agrees. Yes, close.

*

God does not sweat. Federer's pale blue shirt is unstained except for a single skid-mark between the shoulder blades. His movements seem a trifle less fluid, but whether that's the rain or the clotting clay or the nervous impact of the flag-man is anybody's guess. The sun has gone in, umbrellas are opening round the court, somehow it's 3–4 in the second set, Soderling is rallying and Federer looks a bit depressed. He just wants to make history and go home to his beloved Switzerland. And, oh dear, it's a tie-break – except it hardly is, because Federer's first serves are flying in one after the other, the way Perry's do sometimes, but twice as fast. It's the third set and Federer has broken Soderling's serve, he's back in perfect rhythm and the flag-man has lost after all.

Is Federer weeping even before he's won?

Never mind. He's won now. It's as simple and uneventful as that. Federer has won and he can weep his heart out, and Perry too is blinking away a manly tear. His idol has made the history that he came to make, and the crowd is on its feet for the history-maker, and Niki the baby-faced bodyguard is edging his way towards them along the row of happy people; the handclapping has become a coordinated drumbeat.

'I'm the guy drove you back to your hotel in Antigua, remember?' he says, not quite smiling.

'Hello, Niki,' Perry says.

'Enjoy the match?'

'Very much,' says Perry.

'Pretty good, eh? Federer?'

'Superb.'

'You wanna come visit Dima?'

Perry looks doubtfully at Gail: *your turn.*

'We're a bit pressed for time, actually, Niki. We've just got *so* many people in Paris who need to see us –'

'You know something, Gail?' Niki inquires sadly. 'You don't come have a drink with Dima, I think he'll cut my balls off.'

Gail lets Perry hear this instead of her:

'Up to you,' says Perry, still to Gail.

'Well how about just *one* drink?' Gail suggests, doing reluctant surrender.

Niki shoos them ahead and follows, which she supposes is what bodyguards learn to do. But Perry and Gail are not planning to run away. In the main concourse, Swiss alphorns are booming out a heart-rending dirge to a swarm of umbrellas. With Niki leading from the back, they climb a bare stone staircase and enter a jazzy corridor with each door painted a different colour, like the lockers in Gail's school gymnasium, except that instead of girls' names they bear the names of corporations: blue door for MEYER-AMBROSINI GMBH, pink for SEGURA-HELLENIKA & CIE, yellow for EROS VACANCIA PLC. And crimson for FIRST ARENA CYPRUS, which is where Niki pops open the cover of a black box mounted on the doorpost, and taps a number into it, and waits for the door to be opened from the inside by friendly hands.

*

After the orgy: that was Gail's irreverent impression as she stepped into the long, low hospitality box with its sloped glass wall, and the red clay court so near and bright the other side that, if dell Oro would only get out of the way, she could reach her hand through and touch it.

A dozen tables were ranged before her with four or six diners apiece. In total disregard of the stadium's rules, the men had lit up their post-coital cigarettes and were reflecting on their prowess or lack of it, and a few of them were looking her over, wondering if she'd have been a better lay. And the pretty girls with them, who weren't quite so pretty after the amount they'd been made to drink – well, they'd faked it, probably. In their line of work, that was what you did.

The table nearest to her was the largest, but also the youngest, and it was raised above the others to give Dima's Armani kids more status than the humbler tables round it – a fact acknowledged by dell Oro as he shuffled Gail and Perry forward for the pleasure of its seven dull-faced, hard-eyed, hard-bodied managers with their bottles and girls and forbidden cigarettes.

'Professor. Gail. Say hello, please, to our hosts, the gentlemen of the board and their ladies,' dell Oro is proposing with courtly charm, and repeats the suggestion in Russian.

From along the table a few sullen nods and hellos. The girls smile their air-hostess smiles.

'*You! My friend!*'

Who's yelling? Who to? It's the thick-necked one with the crew-cut and a cigar, and he's yelling at Perry.

'You are *Professor*?'

'That's what Dima calls me, yes.'

'You like this game today?'

'Very much. A great match. I felt privileged.'

'You play good too, huh? Better than Federer!' the thick-necked one yells, parading his English.

'Well, not quite.'

'Have a nice day. OK? Enjoy!'

Dell Oro shoos them on down the aisle. On the other side of the sloped glass wall, Swedish dignitaries in straw hats and blue hatbands are making their way down the rainswept steps from the Presidential enclosure to brave the closing ceremony. Perry has taken hold of Gail's hand. It takes a bit of barging to follow Emilio dell Oro between the tables, squeeze past heads and say 'so sorry, whoops, hello there, yes *wonderful* game!' to a succession of mostly male faces, now Arab, now Indian, now all white again.

Now it's a table of Brit males of the chattering classes who need to bounce up, all at once: 'I'm Bunny, how simply *lovely* you are' – 'I'm Giles, hello *indeed*! – you *lucky Professor*!' – all too much to take in, actually, but a girl does her best.

Now it's two men in Swiss paper hats, one fat and content, the other skinny, needing to shake hands: Peter and the Wolf, she thinks absurdly, but the memory sticks.

'Spotted him yet?' Gail calls to Perry – and in the same moment spots him for herself: Dima, hunched at the furthest end of the room, brooding all alone at a table for four, with a bottle of Stolichnaya vodka in front of him; and looming behind him a cadaverous philosopher, with long wrists and high cheekbones, ostensibly guarding the entrance to the kitchen. Emilio dell Oro is murmuring in her ear as if he has known her all his life:

'Our friend Dima is actually a bit *depressed*, Gail. You know about the tragedy, of course, the double funeral in Moscow – his dear friends slaughtered by maniacs – there has been a *price*. You will see.'

She did indeed see. And wondered how much of what she saw was real: a Dima not smiling and barely welcoming, a Dima sunk in vodka-stoked melancholy, not bothering to get up as they approach, but glowering at them from the corner to which he has been relegated with his two minders. For now blond Niki has mounted guard at the cadaverous philosopher's side, and there is something chilling in the way the two men ignore one another, while bestowing their attention on their prisoner.

*

'You come sit here, Professor! Don't trust that goddam Emilio! Gail. I love you. Siddown. *Garçon!* Champagne. Kobe beef. *Ici.*'

Outside on the court, Napoleon's Republican Guard are back at their post. Federer and Soderling are mounting a saluting stand, attended by Andre Agassi in a city suit.

'You talk to the Armani kids at the table up there?' Dima demanded sulkily. 'You wanna meet some goddam bankers, lawyers, accountants? All the guys that fuck up the world? French we got, German, Swiss.' He lifted his head and shouted down the room: 'Hey everybody, say hello to the Professor! This guy pussy me at tennis! She's Gail. He gonna marry this girl. He don't marry her, she marry Roger Federer. That right, Gail?'

'I think I'll just settle for Perry,' said Gail.

Was anybody listening out there? Certainly not the hard-eyed young men at the big table and their girls, who demonstratively huddled closer together as Dima's voice rose. At the tables nearer at hand too, indifference prevailed.

'English too, we got! Fair-play guys. Hey, Bunny! Aubrey! Bunny, come over here! Bunny!' No response. 'Know what *Bunny* means? Rabbit. Fuck him.'

Turning brightly to share the fun, Gail was in time to identify a chubby, bearded gentleman with side-whiskers, and if his nickname wasn't Bunny it ought to be. But for an Aubrey she looked in vain, unless he was the tall, balding, intelligent-looking man with rimless spectacles and a stoop who was heading briskly down the aisle towards the door with his raincoat over his arm, like a man who suddenly remembers he has a train to catch.

Sleek Emilio dell Oro with his gorgeous silver-grey hair had taken the spare seat at Dima's other side. Was his hair real or a piece? she wondered. They make them so well these days.

*

Dima is proposing tennis tomorrow. Perry is making his excuses, pleading with Dima like an old friend, which is what he has somehow become in the three weeks since they have seen him.

'Dima, I *truly* don't see how I can,' Perry protests. 'We've got a flock of people in town we're pledged to see. I've no kit. And I've promised Gail faithfully this time round that we'll take in the Monet water lilies. Truly.'

Dima takes a pull of vodka, wipes his mouth. '*We play*,' he says, stating a proven fact. 'Club des Rois. Tomorrow twelve o'clock. I book already. Get a fucking massage after.'

'A massage in the *rain*, Dima?' Gail asks facetiously. 'Don't tell me you've discovered a new vice.'

Dima ignores her:

'I gotta meeting at a fucking bank, nine o'clock, sign a bunch fucking papers for the Armani kids. Twelve o'clock I get my re-match, hear me? You gonna chicken?' Perry starts to protest again. Dima overrides him. 'Number 6 court. The best. Play an hour, get a massage, lunch after. I pay.'

Suavely interposing himself at last, dell Oro opts for distraction:

'So where are you staying in Paris, if I may inquire, Professor? The Ritz? I do hope not. They have marvellous niche hotels here, if one knows where to look. If I'd known, I could have named you half a dozen.'

If they ask you, don't screw around, tell them straight out, Hector had said. *It's an innocent question, it gets an innocent answer.* Perry had evidently taken the advice to heart, for he was already laughing:

'A place so lousy you wouldn't believe,' he exclaimed.

But Emilio did believe, and liked the name so much that he wrote it down in a crocodile notebook that nestled in the royal blue lining of his crested cream blazer. And having done so, addressed Dima with the full force of his persuasive charm:

'If it's tennis tomorrow that you're proposing, Dima, I think Gail is quite right. You have completely forgotten the rain. Not even our friend the Professor here can give you satisfaction in a downpour. The forecasts for tomorrow were even worse than for today.'

'*Don't fuck with me!*'

*

Dima had smashed his fist on the table so hard that glasses went skittling across it, and a bottle of red burgundy tried to pour itself on to the carpet until Perry deftly fielded it and set it upright. All along the length of the sloped glass wall it was as if everybody had gone deaf from shell-shock.

Perry's gentle plea restored a semblance of calm:

'Dima, give me a break. I haven't even got a *racquet* with me, for pity's sake.'

'Dell Oro got *twenty* goddam racquets.'

'Thirty,' dell Oro corrected him icily.

'*OK!*'

OK what? OK Dima will smash the table again? His sweated face is rigid, the jaw rammed forward as he climbs unsteadily to his feet, tilts his upper body backwards, grabs Perry's wrist, and hauls him to his feet beside him.

'OK, everybody!' he yells. 'The Professor and me, tomorrow, we're gonna play a re-match and I'm gonna beat the shit outta him. Twelve o'clock, Club des Rois. Anyone wanna come watch, bring a goddam umbrella, get lunch after. Winner gonna pay. That's Dima. Hear me?'

Some hear him. One or two even smile, and a couple clap. From the Top Table at first nothing, then a single low comment in Russian, followed by unfriendly laughter.

Gail and Perry look at each other, smile, shrug. In the face of such an irresistible force, and at such an embarrassing moment, how can they say no? Anticipating their surrender, dell Oro seeks to forestall it:

'Dima. I think you are being a little hard on your friends. Maybe fix a game for later in the year, OK?'

But he's too late, and Gail and Perry are too merciful.

'Honestly, Emilio,' says Gail. 'If Dima's dying to play and Perry's willing, why don't we let the boys have their fun? *I'm* game, if you are. Darling?'

The *darlings* are new, more for Milton and Doolittle than themselves.

'OK then. But on one condition' – dell Oro again, fighting for the upper hand now – 'tonight, you come to my party. I have a superb house in Neuilly, you will love it. Dima loves it, he is our house guest. We have our honoured colleagues from Moscow with us. My wife at this very moment, poor woman, is supervising the preparations. How about I send a car to your hotel at eight o'clock? Please dress exactly how you like. We are very informal people.'

But dell Oro's invitation has already fallen on dead ground. Perry is laughing – saying it really is *completely* impossible, Emilio. Gail is protesting that her Paris friends would *never* forgive her, and no, she can't possibly bring them too, they're having their own party and Gail and Perry are the guests of honour.

They settle instead for Emilio's car to pick them up at their hotel at eleven o'clock tomorrow for tennis in the rain, and if looks could kill, dell Oro's would be killing Dima, but according to Hector he won't be able to do that till after Berne.

*

'You two make absolutely *stunning* casting,' Hector cried. 'Don't they, Luke? Gail, with your *lovely* intuition. You, Perry, with your *fucking marvellous* Brain-of-Britain. Not that Gail's exactly thick either. Thanks hugely for coming this far. For being so plucky in the lion's den. Do I sound like a scoutmaster?'

'I'll say you do,' said Perry, stretched out luxuriously on a chaise longue beneath the great arched window overlooking the Seine.

'Good,' said Hector complacently to jolly laughter.

Only Gail, seated on a stool at Perry's head, and running her hand meditatively through his hair, seemed a little distant from the celebration.

It was after supper on the Île St-Louis. The splendid apartment on the top floor of the ancient fortress belonged to Luke's artistic aunt. Her work, which she had never stooped to selling, was stacked against the walls. She was a beautiful, amused woman in her seventies. Having fought the Germans as a young girl in the Resistance, she was at ease with her appointed role in Luke's little intrigue:

'I understand we are old friends from long ago,' she had told Perry a couple of hours ago, delicately touching his hand in greeting, then letting it go. 'We met at the salon of a dear friend of mine when you were a student with an insatiable desire to paint. Her name, if you wish for one, was Michelle de la Tour, now dead, alas. I allowed you to sit in my shadow. You were too young to be my lover. Will that do for you, or do you require more?'

'It will do very well, thank you!' said Perry, laughing.

'For me it does *not* do well. Nobody is too young to be my lover. Luke will provide you with confit of duck and a Camembert. I wish you a pleasant evening. And you, my dear, are *exquisite*' – to Gail – 'and *far* too good for this failed artist of yours. I'm joking. Luke, don't forget Sheeba.'

Sheeba, her Siamese cat, now sitting in Gail's lap.

At the dinner table, Perry – still over-bright – had been the soul of the party, whether breathlessly extolling Federer or reliving the contrived encounter with Dima, or Dima's tour de force in the hospitality room. For Gail, it was like listening to him winding down after a perilous rock climb or a neck-and-neck cross-country run. And Luke and Hector were the perfect audience: Hector, rapt and uncharacteristically silent, interrupting only to squeeze another morsel of description out of them – the possible Aubrey, what sort of height would they say? Bunny, was he tight? – Luke darting back and forth to the enormous kitchen or topping up their glasses with special attention to Gail's, or taking a couple of calls from Ollie, but still very much a member of the team.

It was only now, when the dinner and the wine had worked their therapy, and Perry's mood of high adventure had given way to a sober quiet, that Hector returned to the precise wording of Dima's invitation to tennis at the Club des Rois.

'So we're assuming that the message is in the *massage*,' he said. 'Anyone want to add to that?'

'The massage was practically part of the challenge,' Perry agreed.

'Luke?'

'Sticks out a mile to me. How many times?'

'Three,' said Perry.

'Gail?' Hector asked.

Waking from her distractions, Gail was less confident than the men:

'I just wonder whether it might have stuck out a mile for Emilio and the Armani kids too,' she said, avoiding Luke's eye.

Hector had wondered it too:

'Yes, well, I guess the truth *is*, that if dell Oro *is* smelling a rat, he'll cancel the tennis forthwith, and we're fucked. Game over. However, according to Ollie's latest reports, the signs point the other way, right, Luke?'

'Ollie's been attending an informal meeting of chauffeurs outside the dell Oro chateau,' Luke explained, with his burnished smile. 'Tomorrow's tennis match is being billed by Emilio as a knees-up after the signing. His gentlemen from Moscow have seen the Eiffel Tower and aren't interested in the Louvre, so they're weighing a bit heavy on Emilio's hands.'

'And the message about the massage?' Hector prompted.

'Is that Dima has booked two parallel sessions for Perry and himself for immediately after the match. Ollie has also established that, although the Club des Rois provides tennis for some of the world's most desirable targets, it prides itself on being a safe haven. Bodyguards are not encouraged to traipse after their wards into changing rooms, saunas or massage rooms. They're invited to sit out in the club foyer or in their bulletproof limos.'

'And the club's resident masseurs?' Gail asked. 'What do *they* do while you boys have your powwow?'

Luke had the answer, and his special smile. 'Mondays are their day off, Gail. They only come in by appointment.

Not even Emilio's going to know they're not coming in tomorrow.'

*

In the Hôtel des Quinze Anges, it was one o'clock in the morning and Perry was finally asleep. Tiptoeing down the corridor to the lavatory, Gail locked the door, and by the sickly glow of the lowest-wattage light bulb in the world reread the text message she had received at seven that evening, just before they left for dinner on the Île.

> My father says you are in Paris. A Swiss doctor informs I am nine weeks pregnant. Max is climbing in the mountains and does not respond. Gail

Gail? Natasha signed it with *my* name? She's so demented she's forgotten her own? Or does she mean 'Gail, please, I implore you'? – *that* kind of *Gail*?

Half asleep in one part of her head, she brought up the number and, before she knew what she had done, pressed green and got a Swiss answering service. In a panic, she rang off and, wide awake now, texted instead:

> Do absolutely nothing until we have spoken. We need to meet and talk. Much love, Gail

She returned to the bedroom and climbed back under the horsehair duvet. Perry was sleeping like the dead. To tell him or not to tell him? Too much on his plate already? His big day tomorrow? Or my oath of secrecy to Natasha?

13

Climbing into Emilio dell Oro's chauffeur-driven Mercedes which to Madame Mère's fury had been blocking the road outside her hotel for the last ten minutes – and that halfwit of a driver refusing so much as to lower his window to receive her insults! – Perry Makepiece was prey to anxieties far greater than he was willing to acknowledge to Gail, who for the occasion had dolled herself up to the nines in the Vivienne Westwood outfit with harem pants that she'd bought on the day she won her first case: 'If those high-class hookers are going to be on board, I'll need all the help I can get,' she had informed Perry, as she balanced precariously on her bed to see herself in the mirror over the handbasin.

*

Last night, returning to the Quinze Anges from their supper party, Perry had caught Madame Mère's boot-button eyes peering at him from her den behind the reception desk.

'Why don't you have first run of the facilities and I'll follow you up?' he had suggested, and Gail with a grateful yawn complied.

'Two Arabs,' Madame Mère whispered.

'*Arabs?*'

'Arab police. They spoke Arabic together, and to me French. *Arab* French.'

'What did they want to know?'

'Everything. Where you were. What you do. Your passport. Your address in Oxford. Madame's address in London. Everything about you.'

'What did you tell them?'

'Nothing. That you are an old guest, you pay, you are polite, you are not drunk, you only have one woman at a time, you have been invited by an artist to the Île, and you will be late but you have a key, you are trusted.'

'And our English addresses?'

Madame Mère was a small woman, and her Gallic shrug all the greater for it: 'Whatever you wrote on your fiche, they took. If you didn't want them to have your address, you should have written a false one.'

Extracting a promise that she would say nothing of this to Gail – my God, it would never cross her mind, she was a woman too! – Perry contemplated calling Hector at once but, being Perry, and the better for a significant amount of old calvados, he decided on pragmatic grounds that there was nothing anyone could do that wouldn't be better done in the morning, and went to bed. Waking to the aroma of fresh coffee and croissants, he was surprised to see Gail in her wrap sitting on the end of the bed, examining her mobile.

'Anything bad?' he asked.

'Just Chambers. Confirming.'

'Confirming what?'

'You had it in mind to send me home this evening, remember?'

'Of *course* I remember!'

'Well, I'm not going. I've texted Chambers and they're giving *Samson v. Samson* to Helga to fuck up.'

Helga her *bête noire*? Man-eating Helga of the fishnet stockings who played the Chambers' male silks like a lyre?

'What in Heaven's name prompted you to do that?'

'You, partly. For some reason I don't feel inclined to leave you hanging by your eyebrows on a dangerous ridge. And tomorrow I shall be accompanying you to Berne, which I assume is where you're going next, although you haven't told me.'

'Is that all of it?'

'Why shouldn't it be? If I'm in London, you'll still worry about me. So I might as well be where you can see me.'

'And it hasn't occurred to you I might worry more if you're with me.'

That was unkind of him and he knew it, and so did she. In mitigation he was tempted to tell her about his conversation with Madame Mère but feared it would strengthen her determination to remain at his side.

'You seem to have forgotten the children amid all these grown-up goings-on,' she said, moderating her tone to one of reproach.

'Gail, that's utter nonsense! I'm doing everything I can, and so are our friends, to bring about their –' Better not to finish the sentence. Better talk in allusions. After their two weeks of *familiarization* God alone knew who was listening, when. 'The children are my first concern and always have been,' he said, if not entirely truthfully, and felt himself blush. 'They are why we're here,' he persisted. 'Both of us. Not only you. *Yes*, I care about our friend and seeing the

whole thing through. And *yes*, it fascinates me. All of it.'
He faltered, embarrassed by himself. 'It's about being in
touch with the real world. And the children are part of it.
A huge part. They are now and they will be after you've
gone back to London.'

But if Perry was expecting her to be subdued by this
grandiose claim, he was misjudging his audience.

'But the children aren't here, are they? Or in London,'
she replied implacably. 'They're in Berne. And according
to Natasha, they're in deep mourning for Misha and Olga.
The boys are down at the football stadium all day, Tamara
communes with God, everyone knows something big's in
the air, but they don't know what it is.'

'*According to Natasha?* What on earth are you talking
about?'

'We're text pals.'

'You and Natasha?'

'Correct.'

'You didn't tell me that!'

'And you haven't told me about the arrangements for
Berne. Have you?' – kissing him – 'Have you? For my
protection. So from now on, we'll protect each other. One
in, both in. Agreed?'

*

Agreed only insofar as she would get herself ready while
he went off to Printemps to buy tennis gear in the rain. The
rest of their discussion, as far as Perry was concerned,
emphatically *not* agreed.

It wasn't only Madame Mère's nocturnal visitors who
were nagging at him. It was the awareness of imminent and

unpredictable risk that had replaced last night's euphoria. Drenched with rain in the foyer of Printemps, he called Hector and got engaged. Ten minutes later, with a brand-new tennis bag at his feet containing a T-shirt, shorts, socks, a pair of tennis shoes and – he must have been raving mad when he bought it – a sun visor, he tried again and this time got through.

'Any description of them?' Hector inquired, too languidly to Perry's ear, when he had heard him out.

'Arab.'

'Well perhaps they were Arab. Perhaps they were French police too. Did they show her their cards?'

'Didn't say.'

'And you didn't ask?'

'No I didn't. I was a bit pissed.'

'Mind if I send Harry round to have a chat with her?'

Harry? Ah yes, Ollie. 'I think there's been enough drama already, thanks all the same,' Perry said stiffly.

He wasn't sure how to go on. Perhaps Hector wasn't either:

'No wobble otherwise?' Hector asked.

'Wobble?'

'Doubts. Second thoughts. D-day nerves. The heebies, for Christ's sake,' Hector said impatiently.

'On my part, no wobble at all. Just waiting for my fucking credit card to be cleared.' He wasn't. It was a lie and he couldn't fathom why on earth he'd told it, unless he was asking for the sympathy he wasn't getting.

'Doolittle in good heart?'

'She thinks so. I don't. She's pressing to come on to Berne. I'm absolutely sure she shouldn't. She's played her part – wonderfully, as you said yourself last night. I want her to call it a day, go back to London this evening as planned, and stay there till I come back.'

'Well, she won't, will she?'

'Why won't she?'

'Because she rang me ten minutes ago and said you'd be calling me, and that wild horses weren't going to change her mind. So I rather take that as final and I suggest you do. If you can't beat it, go with it. Are you still there?'

'Not entirely. What did you tell her in reply?'

'I was delighted for her. Told her she was absolutely essential equipment. Given it's her choice and nothing on God's earth is going to change her mind, I suggest you take the same line. D'you want to hear the latest news from the front?'

'Go on.'

'We're on schedule. The gang of seven emerged from their big signing with our boy, everybody looking like thunder, but that may be their hangovers. He's currently on his way back to Neuilly under armed guard. Lunch for twenty booked at the Club des Rois. Masseurs standing by. So no change of plan except that, having returned to London *ce soir*, tomorrow the both of you fly City–Zurich, e-tickets at the airport. Luke will pick you up. Not just you alone, as previously planned. Both of you. With me?'

'I suppose so.'

'You sound grumpy. Are you reeling from the excesses of last night?'

'No.'

'Well, don't. Our boy needs you on top form. So do we.'

Perry had debated telling Hector about Gail's text friend-

274

ship with Natasha, but wiser counsels, if that's what they were, prevailed.

*

The Mercedes stank of stale tobacco smoke. A bottle of leftover mineral water was jammed into the back of the passenger seat. The chauffeur was a bullet-headed giant. He had no neck, just a few lateral red scars in the stubble like slashes of a razor. Gail was wearing her silk trouser-suit outfit that looked as if it was going to fall off her any minute. Perry had never seen her looking more beautiful. Her long white raincoat – an earlier extravagance from Bergdorf Goodman in New York – lay at her side. The rain was rattling like hailstones on the car's roof. The windscreen wipers groaned and sobbed as they tried to keep up.

The bullet-headed giant turned the Mercedes into a slip road, drew up before a fashionable block of flats, and gave a hoot of his horn. A second car pulled up behind them. A chase car? *Don't even think about it.* A rotund, jovial man in a quilted mackintosh and wide-brimmed waterproof hat came skipping out of the entrance hall, plonked himself in the passenger seat, swung round and placed his forearm on the seat back, and his double chin on his forearm.

'Well, who's for tennis, I *will* say,' he declared in a squeaky drawl. '*Monsieur le Professeur* himself, for one. And you are his better half, my dear, of course you are. Even better than yesterday, if I may say so. I propose to hog you for the whole match.'

'Gail Perkins, my fiancée,' said Perry stiffly.

His fiancée? Was she really? They hadn't discussed it. Perhaps Milton and Doolittle had.

'Well, I'm *Dr Popham*, Bunny to the world, walking legal loophole to the revoltingly rich,' he went on, as his little pink eyes slipped greedily from one to other of them, as if deciding which to have. 'You may recall that the bearish Dima had the effrontery to insult me before a cast of thousands, but I flicked him off with my lace handkerchief.'

Perry seemed disinclined to reply so Gail jumped in:

'So what's *your* connection with him, Bunny?' Gail asked merrily, as their car rejoined the traffic.

'Oh, my heart, we're barely connected *at all*, thank the good Lord. Call me an old chum of Emilio, rallying round in support. He will *do* it to himself, poor lamb. Last time it was a batch of retarded Arab princes on a shopping spree. This time it's a squad of dreary Russian bankers, *Armani kids*, I ask you! *And* their dear ladies' – dropping his voice for the confidence – 'and *dearer ladies* I've never seen.' His greedy little eyes settled dotingly on Perry. 'But pity your poor dear Professor here, most of all' – pink eyes tragically on Perry – '*What* an act of charity! You'll be rewarded in Heaven, I shall see to it. But how could you resist the poor bear when he's so cut up by the dreadful killings?' Back to Gail. 'Do you stay long in Paris, Miss Gail Perkins?'

'Oh, I wish we could. It's back to the grindstone, I'm afraid, come wind or weather' – a wry look at the rain pouring down the windscreen. 'How about *you*, Bunny?'

'Oh, I *flit*. I'm a flitter. A little nest here, a little nest there. I alight, but never for long.'

A sign to the CENTRE HIPPIQUE DU TOURING, another to the PAVILLON DES OISEAUX. The rain letting up a bit. The chase car still behind them. A pair of ornate gates appeared on their right-hand side. Opposite the gates was a lay-by, where the chauffeur parked the Mercedes. The ominous car parked alongside. Blackened windows. Perry waited for one of its doors to open. Slowly, one did. An elderly matron got out, followed by her Alsatian dog.

'Cent mètres,' the chauffeur growled, pointing a filthy finger at the gates.

'We *know*, silly,' said Bunny.

Abreast, they walked the *cent mètres*, with Gail sheltering under Bunny Popham's umbrella, and Perry nursing his new tennis bag to his chest, and the rain streaming down his face. They arrived at a low white building.

On the top step under an awning stood Emilio dell Oro in a knee-length raincoat with a fur collar. In a separate group stood three of yesterday's sour young executives. A couple of girls sucked disconsolately at the cigarettes they weren't allowed to smoke inside the clubhouse. At dell Oro's side, dressed in grey flannels and blazer, stood a tall, grey-haired, aggressively British man of the entitled classes, holding out a liver-spotted hand.

'*Giles*,' he explained. 'Met yesterday across a crowded room. Don't expect you to remember me. Just passing through Paris when Emilio nabbed me. Proof one should never call up one's chums on spec. Still, we had quite a shindig last night, I will say. Pity you two chaps couldn't make it' – to Perry now – 'Speak Russian? Fortunately I do a bit. I fear our honoured guests don't have much else to offer in the way of languages.'

They trooped inside, dell Oro leading. A wet Monday lunchtime: not a big day for members. To the left of Perry's frame, a bespectacled Luke crouched at a corner table. He had a Bluetooth device in his ear, and was poring over a sleek, silver laptop, to all the world a man of affairs attending to a spot of business.

If you happen to see somebody vaguely resembling one of us, it'll be a mirage, Hector had warned them last night.

Panic. Lurch of the chest. *Where in Heaven's name is Gail?* With the nausea rising, Perry cast around for her, only to spot her at the centre of the room, chatting with Giles, Bunny Popham and dell Oro. Just stay cool and stay visible, he told her in his mind. Stay *down*, don't overheat, stay calm. Dell Oro was asking Bunny Popham whether it was too early for champagne and Bunny was saying it depended on the vintage. Everyone exploded with laughter, but Gail's was loudest. About to go to her aid, Perry heard the now-familiar bellow of *'Professor, I swear to God!'* and turned to see three umbrellas coming up the steps.

Under the centre umbrella, Dima with a Gucci tennis bag.

To left and right of him, Niki and the man Gail had christened for all time the cadaverous philosopher.

They had reached the top step.

Dima slammed shut his umbrella, shoved it at Niki to take, and strode alone through the swing-doors.

'See the goddam rain?' he demanded belligerently of the whole room. 'See the sky? Ten minutes, we get sun up there!' And to Perry: 'You wanna change into your tennis gear, Professor, or I gonna have to beat the shit outta you in that goddam suit?'

Tepid laughter from the audience. Yesterday's surreal pantomime was about to enjoy its second run.

*

Perry and Dima descend a dark wooden staircase, tennis bags in hand. Dima the club member leads the way. Locker-room smells. Pine essence, stale steam, sweated clothes.

'I got racquets, Professor!' Dima bellows up the stairs.

'Great!' Perry bellows back, just as loud.

'Like six! Fucking Emilio's racquets! The guy plays like shit but got good racquets.'

'Six of his thirty, then!'

'You got it, Professor! You got it!'

Dima's telling them we're on our way down. He doesn't need to know that Luke's already tipped them off. At the foot of the staircase, Perry looks back over his shoulder. No Niki, no cadaverous philosopher, no Emilio, nobody. They enter a gloomy, timber-panelled changing room, Swedish style. No windows. Economy lighting. Through frosted glass, two old men showering. One wooden door marked TOILETTES. Two more marked MASSAGE. Notices saying *occupé* on both door handles. *You knock on the right-hand door, but not till he's ready. Now say that back to me.*

'Had a good night, Professor?' Dima asks as he undresses.

'Great. How was yours?'

'Shit.'

Perry dumps his tennis bag on a bench, unzips it and starts to change. Stark-naked, Dima stands with his back to him. His torso is a snakes-and-ladders board in blue from the back of his neck to his buttocks, inclusive. On the central panels of his back, a girl in a 1940s swimsuit is being assailed by snarling beasts. Her thighs are wrapped round a tree of life that has its roots embedded in Dima's rump, and its branches spread over his shoulder blades.

'I gotta piss,' Dima announces.

'Be my guest,' says Perry facetiously.

Dima opens the door to the toilet and locks it behind him. He emerges moments later, holding a tubular object in his hand. It's a knotted condom with a memory stick inside it. In full-frontal, Dima has the Minotaur's body. His black bush spreads up to his navel. The rest predictably ample. At a handbasin he washes the condom under the tap, takes it to his Gucci tennis bag and with a pair of scissors snips off the end, pulls it free and hands the two pieces of the condom to Perry to lose. Perry puts them into a side pocket of his jacket and has a flash vision of Gail finding them there in a year's time and asking, 'When's the baby?'

At prisoner's lightning speed Dima dons a jockstrap and a pair of long blue tennis shorts, drops the memory stick into the right-hand pocket of the shorts, pulls on a long-sleeved T-shirt, socks, trainers. The process has taken him no more than a few seconds. A shower door opens. A fat, elderly man emerges with a towel round his waist.

'*Bonjour tout le monde!*'

Bonjour.

The fat, elderly man pulls open his locker door, lets the towel fall to his feet, takes out a hanger. The second shower door opens. A second elderly man emerges.

'*Quelle horreur, la pluie!*' the second elderly man complains.

Perry agrees. The rain – a horror indeed. He bangs vigorously on the right-hand massage door. Three short knocks, but good and hard. Dima is standing behind him.

'*C'est occupé,*' the first elderly man warns.

'*Pour moi, alors,*' says Perry.

'*Lundi, c'est tout fermé,*' the second elderly man advises.

Ollie opens the door from inside. They brush past him.

Ollie closes the door, gives Perry a reassuring pat on the arm. He has removed his earring and combed his hair straight back. He wears a medic's white coat. It's as if he's taken off one Ollie and put on another. Hector wears a white coat, but has left it carelessly unbuttoned. He is masseur-in-chief.

Ollie is inserting wooden wedges in the door frame, two at the bottom, two at the side. As always with Ollie, Perry has the feeling he's done it all before. Hector and Dima face each other for the first time, Dima leaning backward, Hector forward, the one advancing, the other recoiling. Dima is an old convict awaiting his next dose of punishment, Hector the governor of his gaol. Hector reaches out his hand. Dima shakes it, then keeps it captive with his left hand while he digs in his pocket with his right. Hector passes the memory stick to Ollie, who takes it to a side table, unzips the massage bag, extracts a silver laptop, lifts the lid and inserts the memory stick, all in a single movement. With his white coat, Ollie is larger than ever, yet twice as deft.

Dima and Hector have not exchanged a single word. The prisoner–governor moment has passed. Dima has recovered his backward tilt, Hector his stoop. His steady grey gaze is wide and unflinching, but also inquiring. There is nothing of possession in it, nothing of conquest, nothing of triumph. He could be a surgeon deciding how to operate, or whether to operate at all.

'Dima?'

'Yes.'

'I'm Tom. I'm your British apparatchik.'

'Number One?'

'Number One sends his greetings. I'm here in his place. That's Harry' – indicating Ollie – 'We speak English and the Professor here sees fair play.'

'OK.'

'Then let's sit down.'

They sit down. Face to face. With Perry the fair-play man at Dima's side.

'We have a colleague upstairs,' Hector continues. 'He's sitting alone in the bar behind a silver laptop like Harry's there. His name is Dick. He's wearing spectacles and a Party member's red tie. When you leave the club at the end of the day, Dick will get up and walk slowly across the lobby in front of you carrying his silver laptop and pulling on his dark blue raincoat. Please remember him for the future. Dick speaks with my authority, and with the authority of Number One. Understood?'

'I understand, Tom.'

'He also speaks Russian on demand. As I do.'

Hector glances at his watch, then at Ollie. 'I'm allowing seven minutes before it's time for you and the Professor to go upstairs. Dick will let us know if you're needed before that. Are you comfortable with that?'

'*Comfortable?* You goddam fucking crazy?'

The ritual began. Never in his dreams had Perry supposed that such a ritual existed. Yet both men seemed to acknowledge its necessity.

Hector first: 'Are you now, or have you ever been, in touch with any other foreign Intelligence service?'

Dima's turn: 'I swear to God, no.'

'Not even Russian?'

'No.'

'Do you know of anyone in your circle who has been in touch with any other Intelligence service?'

'No.'

'No one is selling similar information elsewhere? To anybody – police, a corporation, private individual, anywhere in the world?'

'I don't know nobody like that. I want my kids to England. Now. I want my goddam fucking deal.'

'And I want you to have your deal. Dick and Harry want you to have your deal. So does the Professor here. We're all on the same side. But first you have to persuade us, and I have to persuade my fellow apparatchiks in London.'

'Prince gonna kill me, fuck's sake.'

'Did he tell you that?'

'Sure. At the fucking funeral: "Don't be sad, Dima. Soon you gonna be with Misha." Like joke. Bad joke.'

'How did this morning's signing go?'

'Great. One half my fucking life gone already.'

'Then we're here to arrange the rest of it, aren't we?'

*

Luke knows for once exactly who he is and why he is here. So do the Club authorities. He is Monsieur Michel Despard, a man of means, and he is waiting for his eccentric elderly aunt to arrive and give him lunch, the famous artist nobody has heard of who lives on the Île St-Louis. Her secretary has booked a table for them, but being an eccentric aunt she may not appear. Michel Despard knows that of her; so does the Club, for a sympathetic headwaiter has directed him to a quiet corner of the bar where, it being a wet Monday, he is welcome to wait, and discharge a little business while he is about it – and thank you kindly, sir, thank you very much indeed: with a hundred euros, life becomes a little easier.

Is Luke's aunt really a member of the Club des Rois? Of course she is! Or her late protector the Comte was a member, what's the difference? Or so Ollie has spun it to them in his persona as Luke's aunt's secretary. And Ollie, as Hector has rightly observed, is the best back-door man in the business, and the aunt will confirm whatever is necessary to confirm.

And Luke is content. He is at his calm, unflurried operational best. He may be a mere tolerated guest, tucked into an unsociable corner of the club room. With his horn-rimmed spectacles and Bluetooth earpiece and open laptop, he may resemble any harassed Monday-morning executive catching up on work he should have done over the weekend.

But safely inside himself, he is in his element: as fulfilled and liberated as he will ever be. He is the steady voice amid the unheard thunder of the battle. He is the forward observation post, reporting to HQ. He is the micro-manager, the constructive worrier, the adjutant with an eye for the vital detail that his beleaguered commander has overlooked or doesn't want to see. To Hector, those two 'Arab policemen' were the product of Perry's overheated concerns for Gail's safety. If they existed at all, they were 'a couple of French coppers with nothing better to do on a Sunday night'. But to Luke they were untested operational Intelligence, neither to be confirmed nor dismissed, but stored away till further information is available.

He glances at his watch, then at the screen. Six minutes

since Perry and Dima entered the changing-rooms staircase. Four minutes twenty seconds since Ollie reported them entering the massage room.

Raising his eye-line he takes stock of the scene playing itself out before him: first the Clean Envoys, better known as the Armani kids, sulkily bolting canapés and swilling champagne, not much bothering to talk to their expensive escorts. Their day's work is already over. They have signed. They are halfway to Berne, their next stop. They are bored, hungover and restless. Their women last night were a let-down: or so Luke imagines them to have been. And what is it Gail calls those two Swiss bankers sitting all alone in a corner, drinking sparkling water? Peter and the Wolf.

Perfect, Gail. Everything about her perfect. Look at her now, working the room like a trooper. The fluid body, sweet hips, the endless legs, and the oddly motherly charm. Gail with Bunny Popham. Gail with Giles de Salis. Gail with both of them. Emilio dell Oro, drawn like a moth, attaches himself to their group. So does a stray Russian who can't take his eyes off her. He's the podgy one. He's given up on the champagne and started hitting the vodka. Emilio's eyebrows have risen as he asks a comic question Luke can't hear. Gail comes back with a jokey reply. Luke loves her hopelessly, which is how Luke loves. Always.

Emilio is glancing over Gail's shoulder at the changing-room door. Is that what their joke was about? – Emilio saying, *Whatever are those boys doing down there? Shall I go and break it up?* And Gail replying, *Don't you dare, Emilio, I'm sure they're having a lovely time* – which is what she'd say.

Luke into his mouthpiece:

'Time's up.'

Ben, if only you could see me now. See the best of me, not always the bad stuff. A week ago, Ben had pressed a Harry Potter on him. And Luke had tried to read it, really tried. Coming home dog-tired at eleven at night, or lying wakefully alongside his irretrievable wife, he'd tried. And fallen at the first fence. The fantasy stuff made no sense to him – understandably, he might argue, given that his whole life was a fantasy, even his heroism. Because what was so brave about being caught, and allowed to run away?

'So it's *good*, isn't it?' Ben had said, tired of waiting for his father's response. 'You enjoyed it, Dad. Admit.'

'I did and it's terrific,' Luke said handsomely.

Another lie and they both knew it. Another step away from the person he most loved in the world.

*

'*Stop talking, everybody, at once, please. Thank you!*' Bunny Popham, queen of the roost, is addressing the unwashed. 'Our brave gladiators have finally agreed to grace us with their presence. Let us all immediately adjourn to the *Arena*!' A patter of knowing laughter for *Arena*. 'There are no *lions* today, apart from Dima. No Christians either, unless the Professor is one, which I can't vouch for.' More laughter. 'Gail, my dear, kindly show us the way. I have seen many gorgeous outfits in my day but none, if I may say, so nicely filled.'

Perry and Dima lead. Gail, Bunny Popham and Emilio dell Oro follow. After them, a couple of clean envoys and their girls. How clean can you get? Then the podgy boy all alone except for his vodka glass. Luke watches them into a coppice of trees and out of sight. A shaft of sun lights up the flowered pathway and goes out.

*

It was the Roland Garros all over again: if only in the sense that neither then nor afterwards did Gail have any consecutive awareness of the great tennis-match-in-the-rain that she was so diligently following. Sometimes she wondered whether the players had any either.

She knew Dima won the toss because he always did. She knew that he chose to stand with his back to the advancing clouds rather than serve.

She remembered thinking that the players put up a pretty good show of competitiveness to begin with and then, like actors when their concentration flags, forgot that they were supposed to be engaged in a life-or-death duel for Dima's honour.

She remembered worrying about Perry sliding on the slippery wet tape that marked out the court. Was he going to do something as bloody silly as sprain his ankle? Then about Dima doing the same thing.

And although, like yesterday's sporting French spectators, she was meticulous in applauding Dima's shots as well as Perry's, it was Perry that she kept her eyes glued on: partly for his protection, partly because she had a notion that she might be able to tell by his body language what sort of luck they'd been having down there in the changing room with Hector.

She remembered also the faint squelch of the slowing ball as it slurped into the wet clay, and how now and then she let herself be transported to the last phase of yesterday's Final, and had to relocate in time present.

And how the balls themselves got increasingly ponderous as the game dragged on. And how Perry in his distraction kept playing the slow ball too early, either hitting it out or – a couple of times to his shame – missing it altogether.

And how Bunny Popham at some point had leaned over her shoulder to ask her whether she would prefer to make a run for it now before the next cloudburst, or stay with her man and go down with the ship?

And how she had taken his invitation as an excuse for vanishing to the loo and checking her mobile on the off-chance that Natasha might have expanded on her most recent communication. But Natasha hadn't. Which meant that matters stood where they had stood at nine this morning, in the ominous words that she knew by heart, even while she reread them:

> This house is not bearable Tamara is only with
> God Katya and Irina are tragic my brothers do
> only football we know a bad fate awaits us all I
> shall never look at my father in his face again
> Natasha

Press green to reply, listen to a vacuum, ring off.

*

She was also conscious that, after the second rain break – or was it the third? – gouges began to appear in the sopping clay, which had evidently reached a point where it simply couldn't take any more water. And that in consequence an official gentleman of the Club appeared and remonstrated with Emilio dell Oro, pointing to the state of the court and telling him with sideways brushing movements of the hands 'no more'.

But Emilio dell Oro must have had special powers of persuasion, because he took the official gentleman confidingly by the arm and led him under a beech tree, and by the end of the conversation the official was scurrying back to the clubhouse like a chastened schoolboy.

And amid these scattered observations and rememberings there was the ever-present lawyer in her, at it again, fretting about the *membrane of plausibility* that seemed from the outset to be on the point of breaking, which didn't necessarily signify the end of the free world as we know it, just as long as she was able to get to Natasha and the girls.

And then, while she's having these random thoughts, lo and behold, Dima and Perry are shaking hands across the net and calling it a day: a handshake not of reconciled opponents, to her eye, but of accomplices in a deception so blatant that the last few loyal survivors huddled on the stands should be booing rather than applauding.

And somewhere in the middle of the mix – since there are no limits to the day's incongruities – up pops the podgy Russian man who's been following her around, and tells her he would like to fuck her. In those very words: 'I would like to fuck you,' then waits to hear yes or no: an over-earnest thirty-something city boy with bad skin and an empty vodka glass in his hand and bloodshot eyes. She thought she misheard him first time round. There was hubbub inside her head as well as outside. She actually asked him to repeat himself, God help her. But by then he'd lost his nerve, and confined himself to trailing after her at five yards' distance, which was why she had been content to place herself under the wing of Bunny Popham, the least bad option available to her.

And that in turn was how she came to confess to him that she too was a lawyer, a moment she always dreaded, since it resulted in awkward mutual comparisons. But for Bunny Popham it was just an excuse to be shocking:

'Oh, my *dear*' – lifting his eyes to Heaven – 'I am *overcome*! Well, all I can say is, you can have *my* briefs any time.'

He asked which Chambers, so she told him, which was only natural. What else was she supposed to do?

She had thought a lot about packing. That too, she remembered. Stuff like whether she would use Perry's new tennis bag for their dirty clothes, and equally weighty matters associated with getting out of Paris and on the road to Natasha. Perry had kept on their room for tonight so that they could pack last thing this evening before catching the train back to London, which in the world they had entered was how normal people travelled to Berne when they are potentially under surveillance and not supposed to be going there.

*

The massage room supplied bathrobes. Perry and Dima were wearing them. They were sitting three at the table again, where they had been sitting for the last twelve minutes by Perry's watch. Ollie in his white coat was bowed over his laptop in the corner with his massage bag at his feet, and occasionally he scribbled a note and passed it to Hector, who added it to the pile in front of him. The claustrophobic atmosphere was reminiscent of the Bloomsbury basement without the smell of wine, and there was something similarly reassuring about the noise of real lives near by: the grumble of pipes, voices from the locker room, the flushing of a lavatory, the putter of a faulty air conditioner.

'How much does Longrigg get?' Hector asks, after glancing at one of Ollie's notes.

'One half one per cent,' Dima replies tonelessly. 'On the day Arena get its banking licence, Longrigg get first money. After one year, second money. Year later, finish.'

'Paid to where?'

'Switzerland.'

'Know the account number?'

'Till Berne I don't know this number. Sometimes I get only name. Sometimes only number.'

'Giles de Salis?'

'Special commission. I hear this only, no confirmation. Emilio say to me: de Salis get this special commission. But maybe Emilio keep it for himself. After Berne I know for sure.'

'A special commission of how much?'

'Five million cold. Maybe not true. Emilio is fox. Steal everything.'

'US dollars?'

'Sure.'

'Payable when?'

'Same as Longrigg but cash down, not conditional, two year not three. One half on official foundation Arena Bank, one half after one year trading. Tom.'

'What?'

'Hear me, OK?' The voice suddenly alive again. 'After Berne I get everything. For signing, I gotta be willing party, hear me? I don't sign nothing I'm not willing party to, I gotta right. You get my family to England, OK? I go Berne, I sign, you get my family out, I give you my heart, my life!' He swung round on Perry. 'You seen my children, Professor! Jesus God, who the fuck they think I am any more? They fucking blind or something? My Natasha she go crazy, don't eat nothing.' He returns to Hector. 'You get my kids to England *now*, Tom. Then we make deal. Soon as my family's in England, I know everything. I don't givva shit!'

But if Perry is moved by this appeal, Hector's aquiline features are set in rigid rejection.

'No bloody way,' he retorts. And riding roughshod over Dima's protests: 'Your wife and family stay where they are until after the signing on Wednesday. If they disappear from your house *before* the Berne signing, they put themselves at risk, *you* at risk, and the deal at risk. Do you have a bodyguard at your house, or has the Prince taken him away?'

'Igor. One day we make him *vor*. I love this guy. Tamara love him. Kids too.'

We make him *vor*? Perry repeats to himself. When Dima is sitting in his suburban palace in outer Surrey, with Natasha at Roedean and his boys at Eton, *we* will make Igor a *vor*?

'Two men are guarding you at present. Niki and a new man.'

'For Prince. They gonna kill me.'

'What time is your signing in Berne on Wednesday?'

'Ten o'clock. Morning. Bundesplatz.'

'Did Niki and his friend attend the signing this morning?'

'No way. Wait outside. These guys are stupid.'

'And in Berne, they won't be attending the signing either?'

'No way. Maybe sit in waiting room. Jesus, Tom –'

'And after the signing the bank will hold a reception in honour of the occasion. Bellevue Palace Hotel, no less.'

'Eleven-thirty. Big reception. Everybody celebrate.'

'Got that, Harry?' Hector calls to Ollie in his corner, and Ollie raises his arm in acknowledgement. 'Will Niki and his friend attend the reception?'

If Dima's composure is deserting him, Hector's has acquired a driven intensity.

'My fucking guards?' Dima protests incredulously. 'They wanna come to the reception? You crazy? Prince not gonna whack me in the fucking Bellevue Hotel. He gonna wait a week. Maybe two. Maybe first he whack Tamara, whack my children. What the fuck I know?'

Hector's furious stare remains unchanged.

'So to confirm,' he insists. 'You're confident that the two guards – Niki and his friend – will *not* attend the Bellevue reception.'

With a sag of his huge shoulders, Dima lapses into a kind of physical despair. 'Confident? I'm not confident of nothing. Maybe they come to reception. Jesus, Tom.'

'Assume they do. Just for argument's sake. They're not going to follow you when you take a piss.'

No answer, but Hector isn't waiting for one. Stalking to the corner of the room, he places himself behind Ollie's shoulder and peers at the computer screen.

'So tell me how this plays for you. Whether or not Niki and his friend accompany you to the Bellevue Palace, half-way through the reception – let's say twelve o'clock midday, as near as you can make it – you take a piss. Give me the ground floor' – to Ollie – 'the Bellevue has two sets of lavatories for ground-floor guests. One set is to the right as you enter the lobby, on the other side of the reception desk. Am I right, Harry?'

'Bang on target, Tom.'

'You know the lavatories I mean?'

'Sure I know them.'

'That's the set you *don't* use. For the other set you turn left and descend a staircase. It's in the basement and not much used because it's inconvenient. The staircase is next to the bar. Between the bar and the lift. D'you know the staircase I mean? Halfway down it there's a door that pushes open when it isn't locked.'

'I drink many times in this bar. I know this staircase. But at night-time they lock. Maybe day too sometimes.'

Hector resumes his seat. 'On Wednesday morning the door will not be locked. You go down the staircase. Dick upstairs will be following you. From the basement there's a side exit to the street. Dick will have a car. Where he takes you will depend on the arrangements I make in London tonight.'

Dima again appeals to Perry, this time with tears in his eyes:

'I want my family to England, Professor. Tell this appa-ratchik: you seen them. Send the kids first, I follow. That's OK by me. Prince wanna whack me when my family's in England, who givva shit?'

'*We* do,' Hector retorts vehemently. 'We want you and all your family. We want you safe in England, singing like a nightingale. We want you happy. We're in the middle of the Swiss school term. Have you made any plans for the children?'

'After Moscow funeral, I tell to them, fuck school, maybe

we make holiday. Go back to Antigua, maybe Sochi, fool around, be happy. After Moscow, I tell them any shit. Jesus.'

Hector remains unmoved. 'So they're at home, out of school, waiting for your return, thinking you may be making a move, but not knowing where to.'

'Mystery holiday, I tell them. Like secret. Maybe they believe me. I dunno no more.'

'On Wednesday morning, while you're at the bank and celebrating at the Bellevue, what will Igor be doing?'

Dima rubs his nose with his thumb.

'Maybe go shop in Berne. Maybe take Tamara to Russian church. Maybe take Natasha to horse-school. If she don't be reading.'

'On Wednesday morning, Igor needs to go shopping in Berne. Can you tell that to Tamara over the telephone without making it sound unusual? She should give Igor a long shopping list. Provisions for when you come back from your mystery holiday.'

'Is OK. Maybe.'

'Only maybe?'

'Is OK. I tell Tamara. She's a bit crazy. She's OK. Sure.'

'While Igor's out shopping, Harry here, and the Professor, will collect your family from the house for their mystery holiday.'

'London.'

'Or a safe place. One or the other, depending how quickly arrangements can be made for you all to be brought to England. If, on the strength of the information you have so far given us, I can persuade my apparatchiks to take the rest on trust – particularly the information you are about to obtain in Berne – we shall fly you and your family to

London on Wednesday night by special plane. That's a promise. Witnessed by the Professor here. If not, we shall put you and your family in a safe place and look after you until my Number One says "come to England". That's the truth of the situation as best I understand it. Perry, you can confirm that.'

'I can.'

'At the second signing in Berne, how will you record the new information that you will receive?'

'I got no problem. First I be alone with bank manager. I gotta right. Maybe I tell him, make me copies of this shit. I need copies before I sign it over. He's my friend. If he don't do it, whatta fuck? I got good memory.'

'As soon as Dick gets you out of the Bellevue Palace Hotel, he'll give you a recorder and you record everything you've seen and heard.'

'No goddam frontiers.'

'You'll cross no frontiers until you come to England. I promise you that too. Perry, you heard me.'

Perry has heard him, but for a moment nonetheless he remains lost in thought, long fingers bunched to his brow as he stares sightlessly ahead of him.

'Tom tells the truth, Dima,' he concedes at last. 'He's given me his promise too. I believe him.'

14

Luke picked up Gail and Perry from Zurich-Kloten Airport
at four o'clock on the following afternoon, Tuesday, after
they had spent an uneasy night in the flat in Primrose Hill,
both wakeful, each worried about different things: Gail
mostly about Natasha – why the sudden silence? – but also
about the little girls. Perry about Dima and the unsettling
thought that Hector would henceforth be directing operations from London, and Luke would have command and
control in the field with back-up from Ollie and, by default,
himself.

From the airport, Luke drove them to an ancient village
Gasthof in a valley a few miles to the west of Berne's city
centre. The Gasthof was charming. The valley, once idyllic,
was a depressing development of characterless apartment
blocks, neon signs, pylons and a porno shop. Luke waited
for Perry and Gail to check in, then sat with them over a
beer in a quiet corner of the Gaststube. Soon they were
joined by Ollie, not in a beret any more, but a broad-
brimmed black fedora hat which he wore rakishly over one
eye, but otherwise his irrepressible self.

*

Luke quietly delivered himself of the latest news. His manner towards Gail was taut and distant, the very opposite of flirtatious. Hector's preferred option, he informed the gathering, was a non-starter. After taking soundings in London – he did not mention Matlock in front of Perry and Gail – Hector saw no chance of obtaining clearance to fly Dima and family to England immediately after tomorrow's signing, and had therefore set in motion his fall-back, namely a safe house within Switzerland's borders until he got the green light. Hector and Luke had thought long and hard about where this should be, and concluded that, given the family's complexity, remote was not synonymous with secret.

'And Ollie, I believe that is also your opinion?'

'Completely and totally, Luke,' said Ollie, in his not-quite-right foreign-flavoured cockney.

Switzerland was enjoying an early summer, Luke went on. Better then, on the Maoist principle, to take cover among the many than stick out like sore thumbs in a hamlet where every unknown face is an object of scrutiny – all the more so if the face happens to be that of a bald, imperious Russian accompanied by two small girls, two boisterous teenage boys, a ravishingly beautiful teenaged daughter and a semi-detached wife.

Neither did distance offer any protection in the view of the barefoot planners: quite the reverse, since the small airport at Berne-Belp was ideally suited to discreet departure by private plane.

*

After Luke, it was Ollie's turn, and Ollie, like Luke, was in his element, his style of reporting sparse and careful.

Having examined a number of possibilities, he said, he had settled on a built-for-rent modern chalet on the outer slopes of the popular tourist village of Wengen in the Lauterbrunnen valley, sixty minutes' drive and a fifteen-minute train journey from where they were now sitting.

'And frankly, if *anybody* gives that chalet a second look, I'd be giving them one back,' he ended defiantly, tugging at the brim of his black hat.

The efficient Luke then handed each of them a piece of plain card bearing the chalet's name and address and its landline number for essential and innocuous calls to be made in the event of a problem with mobiles, though Ollie reported that in the village itself reception was immaculate.

'So how long are the Dimas going to be stuck up there?' Perry asked, in his role as prisoners' friend.

He hadn't really expected an informative answer, but Luke was surprisingly forthcoming – certainly more than Hector would have been in similar circumstances. There were a bunch of Whitehall hoops that had to be gone through, Luke explained: Immigration, the Justice Ministry, the Home Office, to name but three. Hector's current efforts were directed at bypassing as many of them as he could until after Dima and family were safely housed in England:

'My ballpark estimate would be three to four days. Less if we're lucky, longer if we're not. After that, the logistics begin to fur up a bit.'

'*Fur up?*' Gail exclaimed incredulously. 'Like a *water pipe*?'

Luke blushed, then laughed along with them, then strove to explain. Ops like this one – not that any two were ever the same – had constantly to be revised, he said. From the moment Dima dropped out of circulation – as of midday tomorrow, therefore, God willing – there would be some sort of hue and cry for him, though what sort was anyone's guess:

'I simply mean, Gail, that from midday tomorrow on, the clock's ticking, and we have to be ready to adapt at short notice according to need. We can do that. We're in the business. It's what we're paid for.'

Urging the three of them to get an early night and call him at any hour if they felt the least need, Luke then returned to Berne.

'And if you're talking to the hotel switchboard, just remember I'm John Brabazon,' he reminded them, with a tight smile.

*

Alone in his bedroom on the first floor of Berne's resplendent Bellevue Palace Hotel with the River Aare running beneath his window and the far peaks of the Bernese Oberland black against the orange sky, Luke tried to reach Hector and heard his encrypted voice telling him to *leave a bloody message unless the roof is falling in*, in which case Luke's guess was as good as Hector's, *so just get on with it and don't moan*, which made Luke laugh out loud, and also confirmed what he suspected: that Hector was locked in a life-and-death bureaucratic duel that had no respect for conventional working hours.

He had a second number to dial in emergency, but there being no emergency he knew of, he left a cheery message to the effect that the roof was thus far holding, Milton and Doolittle were at their posts and in good heart, and Harry was doing sterling work, and give his love to Yvonne. He then took a long shower and put on his best suit before going downstairs to begin his reconnaissance of the hotel. His feelings of liberation were if anything more pronounced than at the Club des Rois. He was barefoot Luke, riding a cloud: no last-minute panic instructions from the fourth floor, no unmanageable overload of watchers, listeners, overflying helicopters and all the other questionable trappings of the modern secret operation; and no cocaine-driven warlord to chain him up in a jungle stockade. Just barefoot Luke and his little band of loyal troops – one of whom he was as usual in love with – and Hector in London fighting the good fight and ready to back him to the hilt:

'If in doubt, *don't* be. That's an order. Don't finger it, just bloody well *do* it,' Hector had urged him, over a hasty farewell malt at Charles de Gaulle Airport yesterday evening. 'I won't be carrying the can. I *am* the fucking can. There's no second prize in this caper. Cheers and God help us.'

Something had stirred in Luke at that moment: a mystical sense of bonding, of kinship with Hector that went beyond the collegial.

'So how is it with Adrian?' he inquired, recalling Matlock's gratuitous intrusion, and wanting to redress it.

'Oh, better, thanks. *Much* better,' said Hector. 'The shrinks reckon they've got the mixture pretty well right now. Six months, he could be out, if he behaves himself. How's Ben?'

'Great. Just great. Eloise too,' Luke replied, wishing he hadn't asked.

At the hotel's front desk, an impossibly chic receptionist informed Luke that the Herr Direktor was doing his usual round of the bar guests. Luke walked straight up to him. He was good at this when he needed to be. Not your back-door artist like Ollie, maybe, more your front-door, in-your-face, sassy little Brit.

'Sir? My name's Brabazon. John Brabazon. First time I've stayed here. Can I just say something?'

He could, and the Herr Direktor, suspecting it was bad news, braced himself to hear it.

'This is simply one of *the* most exquisite, unspoiled art nouveau hotels – you probably don't use the word *Edwardian*! – that I've come across in my travels.'

'You are a hotelier?'

'Afraid not. Just a lowlife journalist. *Times* newspaper, London. Travel section. Totally unannounced, I'm afraid, here on private business . . .'

The tour began:

'So here is our ballroom which we are calling the Salon Royal,' the Direktor intoned in a well-trodden mono-logue. 'Here is our small banqueting room which we are calling our Salon du Palais, and here is our Salon d'Honneur where we are holding our cocktail receptions. Our chef takes very much pride in his finger foods. And here is our restaurant La Terrasse, and actually the *must* rendezvous for all fashionable Berne, but also our inter-national guests. Many prominent persons have dined here including film stars, we can give you quite a good list, also the menu.'

'And the kitchens?' Luke asked, for he wished nothing to be left to chance. 'May I just take a peep if the chefs don't object?'

And when the Herr Direktor, somewhat exhaustively,

had shown him all there was to be shown, and when Luke had duly swooned and taken copious notes, and for his own pleasure a few photographs with his mobile if the Herr Direktor didn't mind, but of course his paper would be sending a real photographer if that was acceptable – it was – he returned to the bar, and having treated himself to an improbably exquisite club sandwich and a glass of Dôle, added a few necessary final touches of his own to his journalistic tour, which included such banal details as the lavatories, fire escapes, emergency exits, car-parking facilities and the projected rooftop gymnasium presently under construction, before retiring to his room and calling Perry to make sure all was well their end. Gail was asleep. Perry hoped to be any minute. Ringing off, Luke reflected that he had been as near to Gail in bed as he was ever likely to get. He rang Ollie.

'Everything just lovely, thank you, Dick. And the transport's tickety-boo, in case you were worrying at all. What did you make of those Arab coppers, by the way?'

'I don't know, Harry.'

'Me, neither. But never trust a copper, I say. All well otherwise, then?'

'Till tomorrow.'

And finally Luke phoned Eloise.

'Are you having a good time, Luke?'

'Yes, I am really, thank you. Berne's a really beautiful city. We should come here together sometime. Bring Ben.'

That's how we always talk: for Ben's sake. So that he has the full advantage of happy, heterosexual parents.

'Do you want to speak to him?' she asked.

'Is he up? Don't tell me he's still doing his Spanish prep?'

'You're an hour ahead of us over there, Luke.'

'Ah yes, of course. Well, yes please, then. If I may. Hello, Ben.'

'Hello.'

'I'm in Berne, for my sins. Berne, Switzerland. The capital. There's a really fantastic museum here. The Einstein Museum, one of the best museums I've seen in my life.'

'You went to a *museum*?'

'Just for half an hour. Last night when I arrived. They were doing a late opening. Just across the bridge from the hotel. So I went.'

'Why?'

'I felt like it. The concierge recommended it, so I went.'

'Just like that?'

'Yes. Just like that.'

'What else did he recommend?'

'What d'you mean?'

'Did you have a cheese fondue?'

'Not much fun if you're on your own. I need you and Mum. I need you both.'

'Oh, right.'

'And with any luck I'll be back for the weekend. We'll go to a movie or something.'

'I've got this Spanish essay, actually, if that's all right.'

'Of course it's all right. Good luck with it. What's it about?'

'Don't know really. Spanish stuff. See you.'

'See you.'

What else did the concierge recommend? Did I hear that right? Like *is the concierge sending you up a hooker?* What's Eloise been saying to him? And why in God's name did I tell him that

I'd been to the Einstein Museum simply because I saw the brochure lying on the concierge's desk?

*

He went to bed, turned on the BBC World News and switched it off again. Half-truths. Quarter-truths. What the world really knows about itself, it doesn't dare say. Since Bogotá, he had discovered, he no longer always had the courage to deal with his solitude. Maybe he had been holding too many bits of himself together for too long, and they were starting to fall apart. He went to the mini-bar, poured himself a Scotch and soda, and put it beside his bed. Just the one and that's it. He missed Gail, and then Yvonne. Was Yvonne burning the midnight oil over Dima's trade samples, or lying in the arms of her perfect husband? – if she had one, which he sometimes doubted. Maybe she'd invented him to fend Luke off. His thoughts went back to Gail. Was Perry perfect too? Probably was. Everyone except Eloise has a perfect husband. He thought of Hector, father to Adrian. Hector visiting his son in prison every Wednesday and Saturday, six months to go with luck. Hector the secret Savonarola, as somebody clever had called him, fanatical about reforming the Service he loved, knowing he will lose the battle even if he wins it.

He'd heard that the Empowerment Committee had its own war room these days. It seemed appropriate: somewhere ultra, ultra secret, suspended from wires or buried a hundred feet underground. Well, he'd been in rooms like that: in Miami and Washington when he was trading Intelligence with his *chers collègues* in the CIA or the Drug

Enforcement Agency or the Alcohol, Firearms & Tobacco Agency and God knew what all the other agencies had been. And his measured opinion was that they were places that guaranteed collective insanity. He'd watched how the body language changed as the Indoctrinated Ones abandoned themselves and their common sense to the embrace of their virtual world.

He thought of Matlock, who took his holidays in Madeira and didn't know what a black hotel was. Matlock cornered by Hector, pulling Adrian's name out of his pocket and firing it at point-blank range. Matlock sitting at his picture window overlooking Father Thames and droning out his elephantine subtleties, first the stick, then the carrot, then both together.

Well, Luke hadn't bitten and he hadn't bowed either. Not that he had much guile, as he was the first to admit: *insufficiently manipulative* one of his annual confidential reports had run, and he was secretly rather pleased with it. He did not regard himself as a manipulator. Obstinacy was more his thing. Holding out. Clinging to the one note through thick and thin: *no* – whether you're chained up in a stockade or sitting in the other armchair of Matlock's comfortable office at *la Lubianka-sur-Tamise*, drinking his whisky and parrying his questions. A man could drift off into his own thoughts, just listening to them:

'A three-to-five contract down at training school, Luke, nice housing thrown in for your wife, which will help things along after the troubles I needn't refer to, a relocation allowance, nice sea air, good schools in the neighbourhood . . . You wouldn't have to *sell* your London house if you didn't want to, not while prices are down . . . Rent it out is *my* advice, enjoy the income. Have a little chat with Accounts on the ground floor, say I told you to drop by . . . Not that we're in *Hector's* league for property, few are.' A pause for decent anxiety. 'Hector's not dragging you in out of your depth, I trust, Luke, you being somewhat promiscuous in your loyalties, if I may say so? . . . They do tell me Ollie Devereux's fallen under his spell, incidentally, which I wouldn't have thought prudent of him. Full time, would you say Ollie was? Or more in the line of casual labour . . . ?'

Then repeating it all for Hector's benefit an hour later.

'Is Billy Boy for us or against us by now?' Luke had asked Hector over the same farewell drink at Charles de Gaulle Airport, when they had moved gratefully to less personal topics.

'Billy Boy will go wherever he thinks his knighthood is. If he's got to choose between the gamekeepers and the poachers, he'll choose Matlock. However, a man who hates Aubrey Longrigg as much as he does can't be all bad,' Hector added as an afterthought.

In other circumstances Luke might have questioned this happy assertion but not now, not on the eve of Hector's decisive battle with the forces of darkness.

*

Somehow Wednesday morning had arrived. Somehow Gail and Perry had slept a little, and risen bright and ready for breakfast with Ollie, who had then gone off in search of their royal coach, as he called it, while they made a list and went shopping for the children in the local supermarket. Unsurprisingly, they were reminded of a similar expedition they had made to St John's on the afternoon

Ambrose set them on the overgrown wood path to Three Chimneys, but their selections this time were more prosaic: water, still and fizzy, soft drinks – and oh, all right, let them have Coca-Cola (Perry) – picnic foods – kids in general prefer savoury to sweet even if they don't know it (Gail) – small backpacks for everybody, never mind they're not Fair Trade; a couple of rubber balls and a baseball bat which was the nearest they could hope to get to cricket but, if needs must, we'll teach them rounders – or more likely, since the boys are baseball players, they'll teach us.

Ollie's royal coach was an old twenty-foot green horse-box with wooden sides, a canvas roof and spaces for two horses in the back with a partition between them, and cushions and blankets on the floor for human beings. Gail sat herself down cautiously on the cushions. Perry, pleased at the prospect of riding rough, sprang in after her. Ollie put up the ramp and bolted it into place. The purpose of his wide-brimmed black hat became clear: he was Ollie the merry Roma, off to the horse show.

They drove for fifteen minutes by Perry's watch, and stopped with a jolt on soft ground. No hanky-panky and no peeking, Ollie had warned them. A hot wind was blowing and the canvas roof above them billowed like a spinnaker. By Ollie's calculation they were ten minutes from target.

*

Luke Alone, his teachers had called him at his preparatory school, after the derring-do hero of some long-forgotten adventure novel. It struck him as a bit unfair that, at the age of eight, he should have manifested the same sense of solitude that haunted him at forty-three.

But Luke Alone he had remained, and Luke Alone he was now, wearing horn-rimmed spectacles and a red-hot Russian tie, tapping away at a silver laptop as he sat under the splendidly illuminated glass canopy of the great lobby of the Bellevue Palace Hotel, with a blue raincoat slung conspicuously over the arm of a leather chair pitched midway between the glass entrance doors and the pillared Salon d'Honneur, the scene of a midday *apéro* presently being hosted by the Arena Multi Global Trading Conglomerate, see the handsome bronze signpost pointing guests the way. It was Luke Alone, keeping an eye on arrivals by way of the many elegant door mirrors, and waiting to exfiltrate single-handed a red-hot Russian defector.

For the last ten minutes, he had looked on in a kind of passive awe as first Emilio dell Oro and the two Swiss bankers, immortalized by Gail as Peter and the Wolf, made their deliberately inconspicuous entrances, followed by a clutch of grey suits, then two young Saudis, by the look of them, then a Chinese woman and a swarthy man with broad shoulders whom Luke had arbitrarily appointed Greek.

Then in a single bored flock the Armani kids, the Seven Clean Envoys, unprotected save by Bunny Popham with a carnation in his buttonhole, and the languidly charming Giles de Salis with a silver-handled walking stick to go with his offensively perfect suit.

Aubrey Longrigg, where are you now they need you? Luke wanted to ask him. Keeping your head down? Wise fellow. A safe seat in Parliament and a free ticket to the French Open is one thing, so is a multi-million offshore kickback and a few more diamonds for your witless wife, not to speak of a non-executive directorship in a fine new City bank with billions of freshly laundered money to play with. But a full-dress, front-line signing in a Swiss bank with the spotlights on you is a bit too rich for your blood: or so Luke was thinking as the lank, bald-headed, ill-tempered figure of Aubrey Longrigg, Member of Parliament, came stalking up the steps – the man himself, no longer a picture – with Dima, the world's number-one money-launderer at his side.

As Luke buried himself a little deeper in his leather chair, and raised the lid of his silver laptop a little higher, he knew that if there had ever been such a thing as a Eureka moment in his life, it was here and now, and there would never be another like it, while once more thanking the gods he didn't believe in that in all his years in the Service he had never once set eyes on Aubrey Longrigg, and nor had Longrigg, so far as he knew, on him.

Even so, it was not until the two men were safely past him on their way to the Salon d'Honneur – Dima had almost brushed against him – that Luke dared raise his head and take a quick reading of the mirrors and establish the following nuggets of operational Intelligence:

Nugget One: that Dima and Longrigg weren't talking to each other. And probably they hadn't even been talking as they arrived. They had simply happened to be close to each other as they came up the steps. Two other men were following – sound, middle-aged Swiss-accountant types – and it was more likely, in Luke's view, that Longrigg had been talking to one or both of them, rather than to Dima. And although the point was tenuous – they *could* have been talking to one another earlier – Luke was cautiously consoled, because it's never comfortable to discover, just as your operation is reaching fruition, that your joe has a personal relationship with a main player that you didn't know about. Otherwise, on the subject of Longrigg, he had no further thoughts above the exultant, blindingly obvious: *he's here! I saw him! I am the witness!*

Nugget Two: that Dima has decided to go out with a bang. For his great occasion he sports a custom-built blue pinstripe double-breasted suit; and for his delicate feet a pair of black calf Italian slip-ons with tassels – not ideal, in Luke's teeming mind, for making a dash for it, but this isn't going to be a dash, it's going to be an orderly withdrawal. Dima's manner, for a fellow who reckons he's just signed his own death warrant, struck Luke as improbably carefree. Perhaps it was the foretaste of vengeance he was enjoying: of an old *vor*'s pride soon to be restored, and a murdered disciple atoned for. Perhaps, amid all his anxieties, he was glad to be done with the lying, ducking and pretending, and was already thinking of the green-and-pleasant England that awaited him and his family. Luke knew that feeling well.

The *apéro* is getting under way. A low baritone burble issues from the Salon d'Honneur, starts to grow, and drops again. Some honourable Salon guest is making a speech, first in Russian blur, now in English blur. Peter? The Wolf? De Salis? No. It's the honourable Emilio dell Oro; Luke recognizes his voice from the tennis club. Handclapping. Church silence while an honourable toast is drunk. To Dima? No, to honourable Bunny Popham, who is responding; Luke knows that voice too, and the laughter confirms it. He looks at his watch, takes out his mobile, presses the button for Ollie:

'Twenty minutes if he's on time,' he says, and once more settles to his silver laptop.

Oh, Hector. Oh, Billy Boy. Wait till you hear who I bumped into today.

*

Mind a bit of off-the-cuff pontification before I go, Luke? Hector is asking, draining his malt at Charles de Gaulle Airport.

Luke doesn't mind a bit. The topics of Adrian, Eloise and Ben are behind them. Hector has just passed judgement on Billy Boy Matlock. His flight is being called.

In operational planning, there are two opportunities only *for flexibility – with me, Lukie?*

With you, Hector.

One, when you draw up your plan. We've done that. Two, when the plan goes belly up. Until it does, stick like glue to what we've decided to do, or you're fucked. Now shake my hand.

*

So here was the question in Luke's mind as he sat staring at a lot of gobbledegook on the screen of his silver laptop and, with zero minutes to go, waited for Dima to emerge alone from the Salon d'Honneur: did the memory of Hector's parting homily come to him *before* he saw the baby-faced Niki and the cadaverous philosopher taking up their positions in the two tall-backed chairs either side of the glass doors? Or was it instigated by the shock of seeing them there?

And who first called him the *cadaverous philosopher* anyway?

Was it Perry or Hector? No, it was Gail. Trust Gail. Gail has all the best lines.

And why was it that, *precisely* at the moment when he spotted them, the burble in the Salon d'Honneur swelled into a babble, and the great doors opened – actually only one of them, he now saw – to disgorge Dima alone?

Luke's confusion was not only one of time, but of place. While Dima was approaching from behind him, Niki and the cadaverous philosopher were rising to their feet in front of him, leaving Luke hunched at mid-point between them, not knowing which way to look.

A furious bark of Russian obscenities from over his right shoulder informed him that Dima had drawn to a halt beside him:

'What the fuck d'you want with me, you shit-ants? You want to know what I'm doing, Niki? I'm taking a piss. You want to watch me piss? Get out of here. Go piss on your bitch Prince.'

Behind his desk, the concierge's head discreetly lifted. The impossibly chic German receptionist, showing no such discretion, swung round to take a look. Determinedly deaf to all of it, Luke tapped meaninglessly at his silver laptop. Niki and the cadaverous philosopher remained standing. Neither had stirred. Perhaps they suspected Dima was about to make a straight dash for the glass doors and the street. Instead, with a subdued *'fuck your mothers,'* he resumed his walk across the lobby and into the short corridor leading to the bar. He passed the lift and drew up at the top of the stone staircase that led to the basement lavatories. By then he was no longer alone. Niki and the philosopher were standing behind him, and a few feet behind Niki and the philosopher stood meek, unnoticed little Luke with his laptop under his arm and his blue rain-coat over it, needing to go to the loo.

His heart is no longer beating vigorously, his feet and knees feel good and springy. He is hearing and thinking clearly. He is reminding himself that he knows the terrain and the bodyguards don't, and that Dima knows it too, which gives extra incentive to the bodyguards, if they ever needed it, to be behind Dima rather than in front of him.

Luke is as astonished by their unscripted appearance as Dima patently is. It defeats him, as it does Dima, that they should be harassing a man who is of no further use to them, and will by his own reckoning and probably theirs shortly be dead. Just not here and now. Just not in broad daylight with the entire hotel looking on, and the Seven Clean Envoys, a distinguished British Member of Parliament, and other dignitaries, putting back the champagne and canapés twenty metres away. Besides which, as is well attested, the Prince is fastidious in his killing. He likes accidents, or random acts of terror by marauding Chechen bandits.

But that discussion is for another time. If the plan has *gone belly up*, in Hector's words, then it is a time for Luke to exercise flexibility, a time *not to finger it but to* do *it*, to quote Hector again, a time to remember the stuff that has been dinned into him on successive unarmed combat courses over the years, but he has never been obliged to put into effect except the once in Bogotá, when his performance had been fair to middling at best: a few wild blows, then darkness.

But on that occasion it had been the drug baron's hench-men who'd had the advantage of surprise, and now Luke had it. He didn't have the odd pair of paper scissors handy, or the pocketful of small change, or the knotted bootlaces, or any other of the fairly ridiculous bits of household killing equipment that the instructors were so enthusiastic about, but he did have a state-of-the-art silver-cased laptop and, thanks not least to Aubrey Longrigg, huge anger. It had come over him like a friend in need, and at that moment it was a better friend to him than courage.

*

Dima is reaching out to shove the door in the middle of the stone staircase.

Niki and the cadaverous philosopher stand close behind him, and Luke stands behind them, but not as close as they are to Dima.

Luke is shy. Descending to a lavatory is a man's private business, and Luke is a private person. Nevertheless, he is having a life-moment of spiritual clarity. For once, the initiative is his, and no one else's. For once, he is the rightful aggressor.

The door they are standing in front of is occasionally locked for security reasons, as Dima rightly pointed out in Paris, but today it isn't. It's guaranteed to open, and that's because Luke has the key in his pocket.

Therefore the door opens, revealing the rather poorly lit staircase beneath. Dima is still leading the way but that situation changes abruptly when a truly massive blow from Luke with the laptop sends the cadaverous philosopher clattering without complaint past Dima down the staircase, unbalancing Niki and providing Dima with a chance to seize his hated blond turncoat of a bodyguard by the throat in the manner that, according to Perry, he had fantasized about when describing how he proposed to murder the husband of Natasha's late mother.

With one hand still round his throat, Dima drives Niki's astonished head left and right against the nearside wall until his useless, worked-out body collapses under him, and he lands speechless at Dima's feet, prompting Dima to kick him repeatedly and very hard, first in the groin and then on the side of the head, with the toe of his inappropriate Italian right shoe.

All of this happening quite slowly and naturally for Luke, though somewhat out of sequence, but with a cathartic and mysteriously triumphant effect. To take a laptop in both hands, raise it above his head at full stretch, and bring it down like an executioner's axe on the cadaverous bodyguard's neck conveniently placed a couple of steps beneath him was to repay every slight that had been done to him over the last forty years, from his childhood in the shadow of a tyrannical soldier-father, through the catalogue of English private and public schools that he had detested, and the scores of women he had slept with and wished he hadn't, to the Colombian forest that had imprisoned him, and the diplomatic ghetto in Bogotá where he had performed the most idiotic and compulsive of his life-sins.

But in the end, it was undoubtedly the thought of rewarding Aubrey Longrigg for betraying the Service's trust that, irrational though it might be, delivered the greatest impetus because Luke, like Hector, loved the Service. The Service was his mother and father and his bit of God as well, even if its ways were sometimes imponderable.

Which, come to think of it, was probably how Dima felt about his precious *vory*.

*

Someone should be screaming, but no one is. At the foot of the stairs, the two men slump across one another in seeming defiance of *vory* homophobic code. Dima is still kicking Niki, who is underneath, and the cadaverous philosopher is opening and closing his mouth like a beached fish. Turning on his heel, Luke treads cautiously back up the steps and relocks the swing-door, returns the key to his pocket, then joins the tranquil scene downstairs.

Grabbing Dima by the arm – who must have just one last kick before he goes – Luke leads him past the lavatories, up some steps and across an unused reception area until they arrive at the iron-clad delivery door marked EMER-GENCY EXIT. This door requires no key but has instead a tin green box mounted on the wall, with a glass front and a red panic button inside for emergencies such as fire, flood or an act of terrorism.

Over the last eighteen hours Luke has devoted serious study to this green box with its panic button, and has also taken the trouble to discuss with Ollie its most likely prop-erties. At Ollie's suggestion, he has loosened in advance the brass screws attaching the glass panel to its metal surround, and snipped through a sinister-looking red-clad wire that leads back into the bowels of the hotel with the purpose of connecting the panic button with the hotel's central alarm system. In Ollie's speculative view, the effect of snipping the red wire should be to open the emergency exit without provoking an emergency exodus of staff and guests from the hotel.

Removing the loosened pane of glass with his left hand, Luke makes to push the red button with his right, only to discover that his right hand is temporarily out of service. So he again uses his left hand, whereupon with Swiss efficiency the doors fly open precisely as Ollie has speculated, and there is the street, and there is the sunny day, beckoning to them.

Luke hustles Dima ahead of him and – either out of courtesy to the hotel or a desire to look like a couple of honourable Bernese citizens in suits who happen to be stepping into the street – he pauses to close the door after him, and at the same time establish, with grateful acknowledgements to Ollie, that no siren call for a general evacuation of the hotel is resounding behind him.

Fifty metres across the road from them stands an underground car park called, rather oddly, Parking Casino. On the first level, directly facing the exit, stands the BMW car that Luke has rented for this moment, and in Luke's numb right hand lies the electronic key that unlocks the car's doors before you reach them.

'Jesus God, Dick, I love you, hear me?' Dima whispers through his panting.

With his numb right hand, Luke fishes in the hot lining of his jacket for his mobile, hauls it out, and with his left forefinger touches the button for Ollie.

'The time to go in is *now*,' he orders, in a voice of majestic calm.

*

The horsebox was backing down a hard incline and Ollie was warning Perry and Gail that they were going in. After the wait in the lay-by they had driven up a tortuous hill road, heard cowbells and smelled hay. They had stopped, turned, and backed, and now they were waiting again, but only for Ollie to ratchet up the tailgate, which he did slowly in order to be quiet, revealing himself by stages up to his wide-brimmed black fedora hat.

Behind Ollie stood a stables, and behind it a paddock and a couple of good-looking young horses, chestnuts, which had trotted over to take a look at them, then bounced off again. Next to the stables loomed a large modern house in dark red timber with overhanging eaves. There was a front porch and a side porch, both closed. The front porch faced the road and the side porch didn't, so Perry chose the side porch and said, 'I'll go first.' It had been agreed that Ollie, as the stranger to the family, would stay with the van till summoned.

As Perry and Gail advanced, they noticed two closed-circuit television cameras looking down on them, one from the stables and one from the house. Igor's responsibility, presumably, but Igor has been sent out shopping.

Perry pressed the bell and at first they heard nothing. The stillness struck Gail as unnatural so she pressed it herself. Perhaps it didn't work. She gave one long ring then several short ones to hurry everyone up. And it worked after all, because impatient young feet were approaching, bolts were being shot and a lock was turned, and one of Dima's flaxen-haired sons appeared: Viktor.

But instead of greeting them with a buckwheat grin all over his freckled face, which was what they would have expected, Viktor stared at them in nervous confusion.

'Have you got her?' he demanded, in his internat's American English.

The question was directed at Perry not Gail because by now Katya and Irina had come through the doorway and Katya had grabbed one of Gail's legs and was squeezing her head against it, and Irina was reaching up her arms to Gail for an embrace.

'My sister. *Natasha!*' Viktor shouted impatiently at Perry, suspiciously eyeing the horsebox as if she might be hiding in it. *'Have – you – seen – Natasha, for Christ's sakes?'*

'Where's your mother?' Gail said, breaking free of the girls.

They followed Viktor down a panelled corridor that smelled of camphor into a low-beamed living room on two levels with glass doors leading to a garden and the paddock beyond. Crammed into the darkest part of the room between two leather suitcases sat Tamara, wearing a black hat with a piece of veil round it. Advancing on her, Gail saw beneath the veil that she had dyed her hair with henna and rouged her cheeks. Russians traditionally sit down before a journey, Gail had read somewhere, and perhaps that was why Tamara was sitting down now, and why she remained sitting when Gail stood in front of her, staring down at her rouged, rigid face.

'What's happened to Natasha?' Gail demanded.

'We do not know,' Tamara replied, to the void before her.

'Why not?'

Now the twins took over, and Tamara was temporarily forgotten:

'She went to riding school and didn't come back!' Viktor

insisted, as his brother Alexei clattered into the room after him.

'No, she *didn't*, she only *said* she was going to riding school. She only *said*, asshole! She lies, you know she does!' – Alexei.

'*When* did she go to riding school?' asked Gail.

'This morning. Early! Like eight o'clock!' Viktor yelled, before Alexei could get his word in. 'She had a date there. Some kind of demo lesson on dressage! Dad had called like ten minutes earlier, said we'd gotta be ready midday! Natasha says she's got this date at riding school. Gotta go there, an *unbreakable deal*!'

'So she went?'

'Sure. Igor took her in the Volvo.'

'Bullshit!' – Alexei again. 'Igor took her to *Berne*! They never fucking *went* to riding school, you idiot! Natasha *lied* to Mama!'

Gail the lawyer forced her way back: 'Igor dropped her in *Berne*? Where did he take her to?'

'The *train station*!' Alexei shouted.

'*Which* train station, Alexei?' said Perry severely. 'Calmly now. At which train station in Berne did Igor drop Natasha?'

'Berne *main station*! The international train station, Jesus Christ! It goes all over. Goes to Paris! Budapest! Goes to Moscow!'

'Dad *told her to go there*, Professor,' Viktor insisted, lowering his voice in deliberate counterpoint to the hysterical Alexei's.

'*Dima* did, Viktor?' – Gail.

'Dima told her to go to the train station. That's what Igor said. You want I call Igor again and you talk to him?'

'He *can't*, you asshole! The Professor don't speak Russian!' – Alexei, by now nearly in tears.

Perry again, firmly as before: 'Viktor – in a minute, Alexei – Viktor, just say that to me again – slowly. *Alexei*, I'll be yours just as *soon* as I've listened to Viktor. Now, Viktor.'

'It's what Igor says she told him, and that's why he dropped her at the main station. "My dad says, I gotta go to the main train station."'

'And Igor's an asshole too! He don't ask why!' Alexei shouted. 'He's too fucking stupid. He's so frightened of Dad he just drops Natasha at the station and goodbye! He don't ask why. He goes shopping. If she never comes back it's not his fault. Dad told him to do it, so he did it, so it's not his fault!'

'How d'you know she didn't go to the riding demo?' Gail asked, when she had weighed their testimony this far.

'Viktor, please,' Perry said quickly, before Alexei could butt in again.

'First the riding school calls us, where's Natasha?' Viktor said. 'It's a hundred and twenty-five an hour, she hasn't cancelled. She's supposed to do this dressage shit. They got the horse all saddled and waiting. So we call Igor on his cell. Where's Natasha? At the train station, he says, Dad's orders.'

'What was she wearing?' – Gail, turning to the distraught Alexei out of kindness.

'Loose jeans. And like a Russian smock. Like a *kulak*. She's into totally shapeless. Says she don't like boys looking at her ass.'

'Has she any money?' – still to Alexei.

'Dad gives her whatever. He spoils her *totally*! We get like a hundred a month, she gets like *five* hundred. For books, clothes, shoes she's nuts about; last month Dad bought her a violin. Violins cost like millions.'

'And you've all tried calling her?' – Gail to Viktor now.

'Repeatedly,' says Viktor, who by now has cast himself as the calm, mature man. 'Everyone has. Alexei's cell, my cell, Katya's, Irina's. No answer.'

Gail to Tamara, remembering her presence: 'Have you tried to call her?'

No answer from Tamara either.

Gail to the four children: 'I think you should please all go to another room while I talk to Tamara. If Natasha rings, I need to speak to her first. Agreed everyone?'

*

There being no other chair in Tamara's dark corner, Perry pulled up a wooden bench supported by two carved bears, and the two of them sat on it, watching Tamara's tiny, black eyes move between them without engaging.

'Tamara,' said Gail. 'Why is Natasha frightened to meet her father?'

'She must have a child.'

'Has she told you that?'

'No.'

'But you've noticed.'

'Yes.'

'How long ago did you notice?'

'It is immaterial.'

'But in Antigua already?'

'Yes.'

'Have you discussed it with her?'

'No.'

'With her father?'

'No.'

'Why have you not discussed it with Natasha?'

'I hate her.'

'Does she hate you?'

'Yes. Her mother was whore. Now Natasha is whore. It is not surprising.'

'What will happen when her father finds out?'

'Maybe he will love her more. Maybe he will kill her. God will decide.'

'Do you know who the father is?'

'Maybe it is many fathers. From the riding school. The ski school. Maybe it is the postman, or Igor.'

'And you have no idea where she is now?'

'Natasha does not confide in me.'

*

Outside in the stable yard it had come on to rain. In the paddock the two handsome chestnut horses were playfully head-butting each other. Gail, Perry and Ollie stood in the shadow of the horsebox. Ollie had spoken to Luke on his mobile. Luke had had a problem talking because he had Dima with him in the car. But the message that Ollie now relayed brooked no argument. His voice remained calm but his flawed cockney became a tangle in the tension:

'We're to get the hell out of here right now. There's been serious developments and we can't hold up the convoy for one single ship no more. Natasha's got their mobile numbers, and they've got hers. Luke don't want us to run into Igor, so we bloody don't do that. He says you got to get everybody aboard now, please, Perry, and we hightail it *now*, got it?'

Perry was halfway back to the house when Gail drew him aside:

'I know where she is,' she said.

'You seem to know quite a lot I don't.'

'Not that much. Enough. I'm going to get her. I want you to back me up. No heroics, no little-woman stuff. You and Ollie take the family, I'll follow you with Natasha when I find her. That's what I'm going to tell Ollie, and I need to know I've got your support.'

Perry put both his hands to his head as if he'd forgotten something, then let them fall to his sides in surrender: 'Where is she?'

'Where's Kandersteg?'

'Go to Spiez, take the Simplon railway up the mountain. Have you got money?'

'Plenty. Luke's.'

Perry looked helplessly at the house, then at big Ollie in his fedora waiting impatiently beside the horsebox. Then back at Gail.

'For God's sake,' he breathed in bewilderment.

'I know,' she said.

15

In an emergency Perry Makepiece was known to his fellow climbers as a clear-headed thinker and a decisive man of action, and he prided himself on seeing little difference between the two. He was apprehensive for Gail, aware of the precariousness of the operation, appalled by Natasha's pregnancy and by the thought that Gail should have found it necessary to keep it from him. At the same time he respected her reasons and blamed himself for them. The image of Tamara sickened out of her wits by jealousy of Natasha, like some harridan in a Dickensian novel, was disgusting to him and compounded his feelings of concern for Dima. His last sight of him in the massage room had moved him beyond an understanding of himself: an unreformed, lifelong criminal, confessed murderer and number-one money-launderer is my responsibility and friend. Much as he respected Luke, he wished that Hector hadn't had to leave the field to his second-in-command at the moment when the operation was heading either for goal, or meltdown.

Yet his response to this perfect storm was the same as it might have been if the rope had broken under him on a bad rock face: stay steady, assess the risk, look after the weakest players, find a way. Which was what he was doing now, crouching in the horsebox with Dima's natural and adopted children spread around him in one compartment, and Tamara's unbiddable shadow in strips between the slats of the partition. *You have two small Russian girls and two adolescent Russian boys and one mentally unstable Russian woman in your charge and your task is to get them to the top of the mountain without anyone noticing. What do you do?* Answer: you get on with it.

Viktor in a rush of gallantry had demanded to accompany Gail wherever she was going, he didn't care, just anywhere. Alexei had mocked him, insisting that Natasha only wanted her father's attention and that Viktor only wanted Gail's. The little girls hadn't wanted to go anywhere without Gail. They would stay in the house and protect it till she came back with Natasha. Igor would look after them in the meantime. To their entreaties, Perry the born group leader had repeated the same patient but emphatic answer:

'Dima's wish is that you come with us immediately. No, it's a mystery tour. He told you that. You'll know where we're going when we've got there, but it's an exciting place and you haven't been there before. Yes, he'll be joining us tonight. Viktor, you take these two suitcases, Alexei those two. No need to lock up, Katya, thank you, Igor will be back any minute. And the cat stays. Cats love places more than people. Viktor, where are your mother's icons? In the suitcase. Good. Whose is that teddy bear? Well, he needs to come with us too, doesn't he? Igor doesn't need a bear, and you do. And everybody please go to the toilet now, whether or not you want to.'

Inside the horsebox, the girls were at first mute, then

suddenly noisy and quite jolly, largely on account of Ollie and his broad-brimmed black fedora, which he solemnly doffed as he bowed them into his royal coach. Everyone had to shout above the din. Rattly horseboxes are not insulated for sound.

Where are we going? – the girls yelled.

Fucking Eton School – Viktor.

Secret – Perry.

Whose secret? – the girls.

Dima's, silly – Viktor.

How long will Gail be?

Don't know. Depends on Natasha – Perry.

Will they be there before us?

Shouldn't think so – Perry.

Why can't we look out the back?

'Because it's *completely* against Swiss law!' Perry shouted, but the girls still had to lean forward to hear him. 'The Swiss have laws for everything! Looking out of the back of a moving horsebox is a particularly grave offence! People who do it go to prison for a very long time! Better find out what Gail's put in your rucksacks!'

The boys were less amenable:

'Have we got to play with this kids' stuff?' Viktor bawled incredulously over the wind-rush, pointing at a Frisbee poking out of a toggle bag.

'That's the plan!'

'I thought we were going to play *cricket*' – Viktor again.

'So we can go to Eton School!' – Alexei.

'We'll try!' – Perry.

'Then we're not going to the mountains!'

'Why not?'

'You can't play cricket in the fucking mountains! No flat places! Farmers get pissed off. So we're going somewhere *flat*, right?'

'Did Dima *tell* you it was somewhere flat?'

'Dima's like you! Mysterious! Maybe he's in deep shit! Maybe the cops are after him!' Viktor shouted, apparently very excited by the idea.

But Alexei was incensed:

'You don't ask that! It's not cool. It's fucking *shaming* to ask a thing like that about your father, *asshole*. At Eton they're gonna *kill* you for that!'

Viktor pulled out the Frisbee and, deciding to have second thoughts about it, affected to test its balance in the through-draught.

'OK, so I didn't ask the question!' he yelled. 'I revoke it totally! Our dad is not in deep shit and the cops love him. The question is hereby revoked, OK? The question was never asked. It is an *ex-question*!' – which, for all its banter, left Perry speculating whether the boys had been smuggled before: perhaps back in the killing time in Perm, when Dima was still clawing his way up.

'Can I ask you two gents something?' he said, beckoning them forward until they were crouching beneath him. 'We're going to be spending a bit of time together. OK?'

'OK!'

'So maybe you could drop the *shits* and *fuckings* in front of your mother and the kids? Gail too.'

They consulted each other, shrugged. OK. Be like that. See if we care. But Viktor wasn't deterred. He was cupping his hands and whisper-shouting into Perry's ear so that the girls didn't hear:

'The big funeral, OK? The one we just did in Moscow? The tragedy? Thousands mourned, OK?'

'What about it?'

'It began as a road wreck, OK? *Misha and Olga were killed in a road wreck.* Bullshit. It was *never* a road wreck. It was a *shooting.* So who shot them? A bunch of crazy Chechen who didn't steal anything and spent a fortune on Kalashnikov bullets. Why? Because they hate Russians. Bullshit. It was *never* the fucking Chechen!'

Alexei was pummelling him, trying to put his hand over Viktor's mouth, but Viktor shoved it away.

'Ask anyone in Moscow who knows anything. Ask my friend Piotr. Misha was *whacked.* He was up against the *mob.* That's why they took him out. Olga too. Now they're gonna try and take out Dad before the cops get him. Right, Mom?' He was yelling at Tamara through the slats. 'What they call a *little warning* to show everyone who's boss! Mom knows all that stuff. She knows *everything.* She did two years in Perm police gaol for blackmail and extortion. Questioned for seventy-two hours non-stop, five times. Beaten shitless. Piotr's seen her record. *Harsh methods were employed.* Official. Right, Mom? That's why she don't *say* nothing any more to anyone except to God. They beat it out of her. Hey, *Mom*! We love you!'

Tamara recedes further into the shadows. Perry's mobile rings. Luke, crisp and very guarded:

'All well?' Luke asks.

'So far, yes. How's our friend?' – Perry asks, meaning Dima.

'Happy and *sitting right here beside me in the car. Sends his best.*'

'Reciprocated,' Perry replies cautiously.

'From now on, whenever there's a chance, we do smaller

groups. They're easier to move and harder to identify. Can you dress the boys up a bit?'

'How?'

'Just make them look a bit different from each other. So they're not such identical twins.'

'Sure.'

'And take a crowded train up. Maybe spread people around. A boy to each carriage, you and the girls in another. Get Harry to buy your tickets for you in Interlaken so that you're not all queuing up at the same desk. Understood?'

'Understood.'

'Any word from Doolittle?'

'Too soon. She only just left.'

It was the first time they'd spoken directly of Gail's defection.

'Well, she's doing the right thing. Don't let her think otherwise. Tell her that.'

'I will.'

'She's a godsend and we need her to be successful.' Luke speaking in riddles. He has no choice. Dima is sitting '*right here beside me in the car*'.

Clambering past the girls, Perry taps Ollie on the shoulder and shouts appropriate instructions into his ear.

*

Katya and Irina have found their cheese rolls and crisps and are head to head, munching and humming to each other. Now and then they turn round to look at Ollie's hat and burst out giggling. Once Katya reaches out to touch it, but loses her nerve. The twins have settled for a game of pocket chess and their bananas.

'Next stop, Interlaken, boys and girls!' Ollie yells over his shoulder. 'I'll be parking at the railway station and taking the first train up with Madam and the luggage. You lovelies have a nice walk and a sausage, maybe, and follow me up the hill in your own sweet time. Happy as agreed, Professor?'

'All very happy as agreed,' Perry confirms, having consulted the girls.

'Well, *we're* not happy *at all*!' Alexei yelps in protest, and flops back on to the cushions with his arms out. 'We are expletive *miserable*!'

'Any particular reason?' Perry inquires.

'*Every* particular reason! We are going to *Kandersteg*, I know it! I will *not* go to Kandersteg again, *ever*! I will not *rock climb*, I am not a fucking *fly*, I have vertigo and I do *not* enjoy the companionship of Max!'

'Wrong on all counts,' says Perry.

'You mean we're *not* going to Kandersteg?'

'I do.'

But Gail is, he thinks again, glancing at his watch.

*

By three o'clock, thanks to a timely train connection in Spiez, Gail had found the house. It wasn't difficult. She'd asked at the post office: does anyone know a ski teacher called Max, a private instructor, not official Swiss Ski School, parents run a hotel? The large lady at the *guichet* wasn't certain so she consulted the thin man at the sorting desk, who thought he knew but for safety's sake consulted the boy loading parcels into the big yellow trolley, and the answer came back down the line: the Hotel Rössli along the high street on the right-hand side, his sister works there.

The high street was dizzy with unseasonably early sunshine and the mountains either side were shrouded in haze. A family of honey-coloured dogs basked on the pavement or sheltered under shop awnings. Holidaymakers with sticks and sunhats peered into windows of souvenir shops, and on the terrace of the Hotel Rössli a scattering of them sat at tables eating cake and cream and drinking iced coffee through straws out of long glasses.

An overworked red-headed girl in Swiss costume was the only person serving, and when Gail tried to talk to her she told Gail to sit down and wait her turn, so instead of walking straight out again, which would have been her normal reaction, she had meekly sat down, and when the girl came she first ordered a coffee she didn't want, then asked whether by any chance she was the sister of Max, the great mountain guide, at which the girl broke into a radiant smile and had all the time in the world.

'Well, not a *guide* yet, actually, not *officially*, and *great*, I don't know! First he must make the exam, which is rather difficult,' she said, proud of her English and grateful to practise it. 'Unfortunately Max began a bit late. Before, he wanted to be an architect but he didn't like to leave the valley. He's quite a dreamer actually, but fingers crossed, now he is settled down at last, and next year he will qualify. We *hope*! Maybe he is in the mountains today. Do you want me to call Barbara?'

'Barbara?'

'She's actually *very* nice. We say she has completely converted him. It was *high* time, I must say!'

Blüemli. Max's sister wrote it down for Gail on a double page torn from her notepad:

'In Swiss German this means a *little flower* but it also can mean *big* flower, because Swiss people like to call anything they are fond of small. The last new chalet on the left side after you pass the school. Barbara's father built it for them. Actually, I think Max has been *very* lucky.'

Blüemli was a young couple's idyll built in spanking-new pine with window boxes with red flowers, red gingham curtains in the windows and a red chimney pot to match, and a hand-carved inscription under the roof in Gothic letters thanking God for his blessings. The front garden was a patch of fresh-mown new lawn with a new swing and a brand-new inflatable paddling pool and a new barbecue, and chopped-up firewood faultlessly stacked beside the seven-dwarfs front door.

If it had been a virtual house instead of a real one, Gail would not have been surprised, but nothing was surprising her. The case had not turned on its head, it had simply become worst case: but not worse than the many cases she had put together on her journey here by train, and was putting together now as she pressed the bell and heard a woman call cheerfully, 'En Momänt bitte, d'Barbara chunt grad!' which, though she had neither German nor Swiss German, told her that Barbara would be there in a moment. And true to her word Barbara was: a tall, groomed, fit, handsome, thoroughly pleasant woman only a little older than Gail.

'Grüessech,' she said and, catching Gail's apologetic smile, switched a little breathlessly to English: 'Hello! Can I help you?'

Through the open doorway Gail heard the plaintive grizzle of a baby. She took a breath, and smiled.

'I hope so. I'm Gail. Are you Barbara?'

'Yes. Yes, I am!'

'I'm looking for a tall girl with black hair called Natasha, a Russian girl.'

'Is she *Russian*? Well, I didn't know. Maybe that explains something. Are you a doctor, maybe?'

'I'm afraid not. Why?'

'Yes, well, she's here. I don't know why. Can you come in, please? I have to look after Anni. She has a first tooth.'

Stepping briskly after her into the house, Gail smelled the sweet, clean smell of powdered baby. A row of felt slippers, with bunny's ears, hanging from brass hooks, invited her to remove her grubby outdoor shoes. While Barbara waited, Gail pulled on a pair.

'How long's she been here?' Gail asked.

'One hour already. Maybe more.'

Gail followed her to an airy living room with French doors opening on to a second small garden. At the centre of the room stood a playpen, and in the playpen sat a very small girl with golden ringlets and a dummy in her mouth and an array of brand-new toys around her. And against the wall on a low stool sat Natasha with her head down and her face hidden in her hair, leaning over her folded hands.

'Natasha?'

Gail kneeled to her and put a hand to the back of her head, cupping it. Natasha winced, then let the hand stay where it was. Gail spoke her name again. To no effect.

'It was lucky you came, I must say,' said Barbara in garrulous Swiss sing-song, picking Anni up and putting her over

335

her shoulder to wind her. 'I was going to call Dr Stettler. Or maybe the police, I didn't know. It was a problem. Really.'

Gail was stroking Natasha's hair.

'She rings the bell, I am feeding Anni, not bottle but the best way. We have a *lens* in the door now because *these days* you never *know*. I looked, I had Anni at my breast, I thought well, fine, that's a normal girl on my doorstep, quite beautiful actually I must say, she wants to come in, I don't know why, maybe to make an appointment with Max, he has many clients, specially young, because he is so interesting naturally. So she comes in, she looks, she sees Anni, she asks me in *English* – I didn't know she was Russian, one doesn't think of that although one should these days, I think maybe she is Jewish or Italian – "Are you Max's sister?" And I say no, I am not his sister, I am Barbara his wife, and who are you please, and how can I help you? I am a busy mother, you can see. Do you wish to make an arrangement with Max, are you a climber? What is your name? And she says she is Natasha, but actually I am beginning to wonder already.'

'Wonder what?'

Gail pulled up another stool and sat at Natasha's side. With her arm across her shoulder, she gently drew Natasha's head in to her until their temples were pressing hard against each other.

'Well *drugs* actually. The young today, I mean one simply doesn't know,' said Barbara, speaking indignantly like someone twice her age. 'And frankly with foreigners, specially English, the drugs are *everywhere*, ask Dr Stettler.' The baby gave a scream and she calmed it. 'With Max also, his young ones, my God, even in the mountain huts, they are taking drugs! I mean alcohol I understand. Not cigarettes naturally. I offered her coffee, tea, mineral water. Maybe she didn't hear me, I don't know. Maybe she is having a *bad trip*, as the hippies say. But with the baby frankly one doesn't like to say it, but I was a little bit *afraid* even.'

'But you didn't call Max?'

'In the mountains? When he has *guests*? That would be terrible for him. He would think she was ill, he would come immediately.'

'He would think *Anni* was ill?'

'Well naturally!' She paused and reconsidered the question, which was not, Gail suspected, a thing she did often. 'You think Max would come for *Natasha*? That's completely ridiculous!'

Taking Natasha's arm, Gail lifted her gently to her feet, and when she was fully upright, she embraced her, then took her to the front door, helped her change back into her outdoor shoes, changed her own, and walked her across the perfect lawn. As soon as they were through the gate, she called Perry.

She'd called him once from the train, and once when she reached the village. She'd promised to call him practically by the minute because Luke couldn't talk to her himself, he had Dima sitting on top of him somewhere, so please use Perry as the cut-out. And she knew things were very fraught, she could hear it in Perry's voice. The more calm he was, the more fraught she knew things were, and she assumed an episode of some sort. So she spoke calmly herself, which probably conveyed the same signal to him in reverse:

'She's all right. Fine, OK? I've got her here with me, she's alive and well, we're on our way. We're walking towards the station now. We need a little time, that's all.'

'How much time?'

Now it was Gail who was having to watch her words, because Natasha was clinging to her arm.

'Enough to repair our souls and powder our noses. One other thing.'

'What?'

'Nobody needs to be asked where they've been, all right? We had a small crisis, it's over now. Life goes on. It's not just about when we arrive. It's from then on: no questions of the affected party. The girls will be fine. The boys I'm not sure.'

'They'll be fine too. I'll see to it. Dick will be over the moon. I'll tell him at once. Hurry.'

'We'll try.'

*

On the crowded train back to the valley there had been no opportunity to speak, which didn't matter because Natasha showed no inclination to; she was in shock, and at times seemed unaware of Gail's existence. But on the train from Spiez, under Gail's gentle coaxing, she began to wake. They were sitting side by side in a first-class carriage and looking straight ahead of them, just as they had been in the tent at Three Chimneys. Evening was falling fast and they were the only passengers.

'I am so –' Natasha broke out, grabbing Gail's hand, but then couldn't finish the sentence.

'We wait,' Gail said firmly, to Natasha's downturned head. 'We have time. We put our feelings on hold, we enjoy life, and we wait. That's all we need to do, either of us. Are you hearing me?'

Nod.

'Then sit up. Don't give me my hand back, just listen. In a few days you'll be in England. I'm not sure whether your brothers know that, but they know it's a mystery tour, and it's going to begin any day now. There's a short stop-over in Wengen first. And in England we'll find you a really good woman doctor – mine – and you'll find out how you feel, and then you'll decide. OK?'

Nod.

'In the meantime, we don't even think about it. We just wipe it out of our minds. You get rid of this silly smock you're wearing' – plucking affectionately at her sleeve – 'you dress slim and gorgeous. Nothing shows, I promise you. Will you do that?'

She will.

'All the decisions wait till England. They're not *bad* decisions, they're sensible ones. And you make them calmly. When you get to England, not until. For your father's sake, as well as yours. Yes?'

'Yes.'

'Again.'

'Yes.'

Would Gail have spoken in the same way if Perry hadn't said it was the way Luke wanted her to speak? – that this was the absolute worst moment for Dima to be hit with shattering news?

Fortunately, yes, she would. She'd have made the same speech word for word, and she'd have meant it. She'd been there herself. She knew what she was talking about. And

she was telling herself this as their train pulled into Interlaken Ost Station for their connection along the valley to
Lauterbrunnen and Wengen, when she noticed that a Swiss
policeman in smart summer uniform was walking down
the empty platform towards them, and that a dull-faced
man in a grey suit and polished brown shoes was walking
beside him, and that the policeman was wearing the kind
of rueful smile that, in any civilized country, tells you that
you haven't got much to smile about.

'You speak English?'

'How did you guess?' – smiling back.

'Maybe your complexion actually,' he said – which she
reckoned quite pert for your ordinary Swiss policeman.
'But the young lady is *not* English' – glancing at Natasha's
black hair and slightly Asian looks.

'Well, actually she could be, you know. We're all everything these days,' Gail replied in the same sporty tone.

'Do you have British passports?'

'I do.'

The dull-faced man was also smiling, which chilled her.
And his English was a little too good too:

'Swiss Immigration Service,' he announced. 'We are
conducting *random checks*. I'm afraid that these days with
open borders we find certain ones who should have visas
and do not. Not many, but some.'

The uniform was back:

'Your tickets and passports, please. You mind? If you mind,
we take you to the police station and we make a check there.'

'Of course we don't mind. Do we, Natasha? We just wish
all policemen were so polite, don't we?' said Gail brightly.

Delving in her handbag, she unearthed her passport and

the tickets and gave them to the uniformed policeman, who examined them with that extra slowness that policemen all over the world are taught to exhibit in order to raise the stress level of honest citizens. The grey suit looked over the uniformed shoulder, then took her passport for himself, and did the same thing all over again before handing it to her and turning his smile on Natasha, who already had her passport ready in her hand.

And what the grey suit did then was, in Gail's later account to Ollie and Perry and Luke, either incompetent or very clever. He behaved as if the passport of a Russian minor were of less interest to him than a British adult's passport. He flipped to the visa page, flipped to her photograph, compared it with her face, smiled in apparent admiration, paused a moment over her name in Roman and Cyrillic, and handed it back to her with a light-hearted 'thank you, madam'.

'You stay in Wengen long?' the uniformed policeman asked, returning the tickets to Gail.

'Just a week or so.'

'Depending on the weather maybe?'

'Oh, we English are so used to the rain we don't notice!'

And they would find their next train waiting for them on platform 2, departure in three minutes, the last connection up tonight, so better not miss it or you have to stay in Lauterbrunnen, said the polite policeman.

It wasn't till they were halfway up the mountain on the last train that Natasha spoke again. Until then she had brooded in seeming anger, staring at the blackened window, misting it over with her breath like a child, and angrily wiping it clean. But whether she was angry with Max, or the policeman and his grey-suited friend, or herself, Gail could only guess. But suddenly she raised her head and was staring Gail straight in the face:

'Is Dima criminal?'

'I think he's just a very successful businessman, isn't he?' the deft barrister replied.

'Is that why we're going to England? – is that what the *mystery tour*'s all about? Suddenly he tells us we're all going to great English schools.' And receiving no reply: 'Ever since Moscow the whole family has been – has been completely *criminal*. Ask my brothers. It's their new obsession. They talk only of crime. Ask their big friend Piotr who says he works for KGB. It doesn't exist any more. Does it?'

'I don't know.'

'It's the FSB now. But Piotr still says KGB. So maybe he is lying. Piotr knows everything about us. He has seen all our records. My mother was criminal, her husband was criminal, Tamara was criminal, her father was shot. For my brothers, anyone coming from Perm is completely criminal. Maybe that's why the police wanted my passport. "Are you from Perm, please, Natasha?" "Yes, Mr Policeman, I am from Perm. I am also *pregnant*." "Then you are *very* criminal. You cannot go to English boarding school, you must come to prison immediately!"'

By then, her head was on Gail's shoulder, and the rest of what she said was in Russian.

*

Dusk was falling over the cornfields and it was dusk in the BMW hire car as well, because by mutual consent they were allowing themselves no lights, inside or out. Luke had provided a bottle of vodka for the journey and Dima had drunk the half of it, but Luke wasn't giving himself as much as a sniff. He had offered Dima a pocket recorder to record his memories of the Berne signing while they were fresh, but Dima had brushed it away:

'I know all. Got no problem. Got duplicates. Got memory. In London, I remember everything. You tell that to Tom.'

Since their departure from Berne, Luke had used only side roads, driving a distance, finding a place to lie up while his pursuers if they existed went ahead of him. There was definitely something wrong with his right hand, he still seemed to have no feeling in it, but provided he used the strength of his arm and didn't think about the hand, the driving wasn't a problem. He must have done something to it when he coshed the cadaverous philosopher.

They were talking Russian in low voices like a pair of fugitives. Why are we keeping our voices down? Luke wondered. But they were. At the edge of a pine forest he again parked, and this time handed Dima a labourer's blue tunic, and a thick black woollen ski cap to cover his bald head. For himself he had bought jeans, anorak, a bobble hat. He folded Dima's suit for him and put it in a suitcase in the boot of the BMW. It was by now eight in the evening and turning cold. Approaching the village of Wilderswil at the mouth of the Lauterbrunnen Valley, he yet again stopped the car while they listened to the Swiss news and he tried to read Dima's face in the half-darkness because to his frustration Luke had no German.

'They found the bastards,' Dima growled in a Russian

343

undertone. 'Two drunk Russian assholes had a fight at the Bellevue Palace Hotel. Nobody know why. Fell down some steps and hurt themselves. One guy in hospital, the other one OK. The hospital guy pretty bad. That's Niki. Maybe the fucker choke. Told a bunch of stupid lies the Swiss police don't believe, each guy different lies. Russian Embassy want to fly them home. Swiss police are saying, "Not so goddam fast, we want to know a couple more things about these assholes." Russian Ambassador's pissed off.'

'At the men?'

'The Swiss.' He grinned, took another pull from the vodka bottle and waved it at Luke, who shook his head. 'Wanna know how it works? Russian Ambassador calls the Kremlin: "Who are these crazy fucks?" Kremlin call the bitch Prince: "What the fuck are your assholes doing beating the shit out of each other in fancy hotel in Berne, Switzerland?"'

'And the Prince says?' Luke demanded, not sharing Dima's levity.

'The bitch Prince call Emilio. "Emilio. My friend. My wise advisor. What the fuck my two nice guys doing, beating the shit out of each other in fancy hotel in Berne?"'

'And Emilio says?' Luke persisted.

Dima's mood darkened: 'Emilio says: "That shithead Dima, world number-one money-launderer, he disappeared off the fucking planet."'

No great intriguer himself, Luke was doing his sums. First the two so-called Arab policemen in Paris. Who sent them? Why? Then the two bodyguards at the Bellevue Palace: why had they come to the hotel after the signing? Who sent them? Why? Who knew how much when?

He called Ollie.

'All quiet, Harry?' – meaning, who's arrived up there at the safe house and who hasn't? Meaning, am I going to have to deal with a missing Natasha too?

'Dick, our two stragglers clocked in just a couple minutes back, you'll be pleased to hear,' Ollie said reassuringly. 'Found their own way here without any bother much, and everything hunky-dory. Ten-ish over the other side of the hill about right for you? Nice and dark by then.'

'Ten o'clock is fine.'

'Grund Station car park. A nice little red Suzuki. I'll be first right as you drive in and as far from the trains as we can get, then.'

'Agreed.' And when Ollie didn't ring off: 'What's the problem, Harry?'

'Well there's been quite a police presence at Interlaken Ost railway station, I'm hearing.'

'Let's have it.'

Luke listened, said nothing, returned the mobile to his pocket.

*

By *the other side of the hill*, Ollie was referring to the village of Grindelwald, which lay at the opposing foot of the Eiger massif. To reach Wengen from the Lauterbrunnen side by any means except mountain railway was impossible, Ollie had reported: the summer track might be good enough for chamois and the odd foolhardy motorcyclist, but not for a four-wheeled vehicle with three men aboard.

But Luke was determined – as Ollie was – that Dima, in whatever garb, should not be subjected to the glances of railway officials, ticket inspectors and fellow passengers as he approached the place of his concealment: least of all at this late hour of evening, when railway passengers were fewer and more conspicuous.

Reaching the village of Zweilütschinen, Luke took the left fork that led by a winding river road to the edge of Grindelwald. The Grund Station car park was packed with the abandoned cars of German tourists. Entering it, Luke saw to his relief the figure of Ollie in a quilted anorak and peaked cap with earflaps, seated at the wheel of a stationary red Suzuki jeep with its sidelights on.

'And here's your rugs for when it gets nippy,' Ollie announced in Russian as he bundled Dima in beside him, and Luke, having handed Ollie the luggage and parked the BMW under a beech tree, settled himself in the back. 'The forest track is forbidden, but not for locals with business to do, like plumbers and railway workers and such. So if it's all the same to you, I'll do the talking if we're checked. Not that I'm a local, but the jeep is. And its owner told me what to say.'

Which *owner* and *what to say* was Ollie's alone to know. A good back-door man is not forthcoming about his sources.

*

A narrow concrete road led upward into the blackness of the mountain. A pair of headlights descended towards them, stopped, and pulled back into the trees: a builder's lorry, unladen.

'Whoever's coming from the top reverses,' Ollie pronounced approvingly under his breath. 'Local rule.'

A uniformed policeman stood alone in the centre of the

road. Ollie slowed down for him to peer at the triangular yellow sticker on the Suzuki's windscreen. The policeman stepped back. Ollie raised his hand in leisurely acknowledgement. They passed a settlement of low chalets and bright lights. Woodsmoke mingled with the smell of pine. A fluorescent sign read BRANDEGG. The road became an unmade forest track. Rivulets of water ran towards them. Ollie turned on the headlights and shifted gear levers. The engine took on a higher, plaintive drone. The track was pitted by heavy lorries and the Suzuki was hard-sprung. Perched on its back seat with the luggage, Luke clutched the sides as it bounced and swung. In front of him rode the swathed figure of Dima in his woollen hat, the blanket flapping like a coachman's cape round his shoulders in the wind. Beside him, and scarcely any smaller, Ollie leaned tensely forward as he navigated the Suzuki across open meadow and set a pair of chamois scampering for the shelter of the trees.

The air turned thinner and colder. Luke's breath came faster. An icy film of dew was forming on his cheeks and brow. He felt his eyes glistening, and his heart quickening to the scent of pine and the thrill of the climb. The forest closed round them again. From its density, the red eyes of animals flashed at them, but whether they were large or small Luke had no time to find out.

They had passed the tree-line and again broken free. Light cloud covered a starry sky, and at the very centre towered a black starless void, pressing them into the mountainside, then squeezing them out on to the world's edge. They were passing beneath the overhang of the Eiger North Face.

'You been to Ural Mountains, Dick?' Dima yelled at Luke in English, swinging round.

Luke nodded vigorously and smiled yes.

'Like Perm! Perm we got mountains like this! You been Caucasus?'

'Just the Georgian part!' Luke yelled back.

'I love this, hear me, Dick! I *love*! You too, huh?'

Briefly – although he was still worrying about that policeman – Luke was able to love it: and continued to love it as they climbed towards the saddle of the Kleine Scheidegg and slipped through the arc of orange lights shed by the great hotel that mastered it.

They began their descent. To their left, bathed in moonlight, rose the sinewy blue-black shadows of a glacier. Far away across the valley, they glimpsed the lights of Mürren, and now and then, through the density of the forest as it took them back, the fickle lights of Wengen.

16

For Luke, the days and nights in the little Alpine resort of Wengen were mysteriously preordained, now beyond bearing, now filled with the lyrical calm of an extended gathering of family and friends on holiday.

The ugly, built-to-let chalet that Ollie had selected lay at the quiet end of the village on a triangle of land between two footpaths. In the winter months it was rented out to a lowland German ski club, but in the summer it was available to anyone who could pay, from South African Theosophists to Norwegian Rastafarians to poor children from the Ruhr. A disparate family of incompatible ages and origins was therefore exactly what the village expected. Not a head turned among the flocks of summer tourists that trudged past it: or so said Ollie, who spent many spare minutes keeping watch from behind the curtained upper windows.

From inside, the world was almost unimaginably beautiful. Look downward from the top floor and you had a view of the fabled Lauterbrunnen Valley; look upward, and the Jungfrau massif rose glistening before you. Behind you lay unspoiled pastures and forested foothills. Yet from outside the chalet was an architectural void:

cavernous, characterless, anonymous, and sympathetic to nothing around it, with white stucco walls and rustic grace notes that only emphasized its suburban aspirations.

Luke too had watched. When Ollie was out foraging for provisions and snippets of local gossip, it was Luke the habitual worrier who kept lookout for the suspicious passer-by. But watch as he might, no inquisitive eye lingered on the two small girls in the garden practising with their new skipping ropes to Gail's direction, or picking cowslips on the meadow bank behind the house, to be preserved for all time in jam jars of dry sago bought by Ollie from the supermarket.

Not even the rouged and powdered little old lady in weeds and dark glasses sitting motionless as a doll on the balcony with her hands in her lap attracted comment. Swiss resorts have been receiving such people ever since the tourist trade began. And should any passer-by chance, of an evening, to glimpse between the curtains a big man in a woollen ski cap bowed over a chessboard opposite two adolescent opponents – with Perry as referee and Gail and the girls in another corner watching DVDs bought from Photo Fritz – well, if that house hadn't had a family of chess-fiends before, it had had everything else. Why should they know or care that, pitched against the combined intellect of his precocious sons, the world's number-one money-launderer could still outsmart them?

And if the same adolescent boys were seen next day, in their carefully different outfits, scrambling up the precipitous rock path that ran from the back garden all the way up to Männlichen ridge, with Perry out ahead urging them on, and Alexei vowing that he was going to break his neck any fucking minute, and Viktor insisting that he'd just stared down a full-grown stag, even if it was only a chamois – well, what was so remarkable about that? Perry even roped them together. He found a handy bit of overhang, hired boots and bought ropes – ropes, he explained severely, being for a mountaineer both personal and sacrosanct – and taught them how to dangle over an abyss, even if the abyss was only twelve feet deep.

As to the two young women – one sixteen-ish and the other maybe ten years older, both beautiful – stretched out on deck-chairs with their books under a spreading maple tree that had somehow escaped the developer's bulldozer – well, if you were a Swiss male, perhaps you'd look and then pretend you hadn't looked, or if you were an Italian, you might have looked and applauded. But you wouldn't have rushed to the tele-phone and whispered to the police that you had seen two suspicious women reading in the shade of a maple tree.

Or so Luke told himself, and so Ollie told himself, and so Perry and Gail as co-opted members of the neighbour-hood watch agreed – how could they do otherwise? – which didn't mean that any of them, even the small girls, ever quite got rid of the notion that they were in hiding and living against the clock. When Katya asked at breakfast over Ollie's pancake, bacon and maple syrup, 'Are we going to England today?' – or Irina, more plaintively, 'Why haven't we gone to England yet?' – they were speaking for everyone round the table, starting with Luke himself, the hero of the party by virtue of having his right hand in plaster after falling down the steps of his hotel in Berne.

'You gonna sue that hotel, Dick?' Viktor demanded aggressively.

'I shall be consulting my lawyer on the subject,' Luke replied with a smile for Gail.

As to precisely *when* they were going to London: 'Well, perhaps not today, Katya, but maybe tomorrow, or the next day,' Luke assured her. 'It's just a question of when your visas come through. And we all know what apparatchiks are like, even English ones, don't we?'

*

But when, oh when?

Luke asked himself the same question every waking and half-sleeping hour of the day or night as Hector's breathless bulletins piled in: now a couple of cryptic sentences between meetings, now a whole jeremiad in the small hours of another endless day. Bewildered by the barrage of contradictory reports, Luke at first resorted to the officially unforgivable sin of keeping a written log of them as they came in. With the lurid fingertips of his right hand poking from the plaster, he scribbled away painstakingly in his own quaint shorthand on single sheets of A4 bought by Ollie from the village stationer's, one side only.

In the approved training-school manner, he purloined the glass from a picture frame to press on, wiping it clean after each page, and caching the product behind a water tank against the remote possibility that Viktor, Alexei, Tamara or Dima himself might take it into their heads to search his room.

But as the speed and complexity of Hector's messages from the front began to overwhelm him, he prevailed on

Ollie to get him a pocket recorder, much like Dima's, and connect it to his encrypted mobile – another mortal sin in the eyes of Training Section, but a godsend when he was lying wakefully in bed waiting for the next of Hector's idiosyncratic bulletins:

— It's a knife-edge, Lukie, but we're winning.
— I'm bypassing Billy Boy and going straight to the Chief. I've said it's got to be hours not days.
— The Chief says talk to the Vice-Chief.
— The Vice-Chief says if Billy Boy won't sign off on it, nor will he. He won't sign off on it alone. He's got to have the whole fourth floor behind him or it's no deal. I've said bugger that.
— You're not going to believe this but Billy Boy's coming round. He's kicking like hell, but even he can't stay away from the truth when it's rammed up his hooter.

All this within the space of the first twenty-four hours after Luke had sent the cadaverous philosopher spinning down the staircase, a feat Hector initially greeted as sheer genius, but on reflection said he didn't think he'd be bothering the Vice-Chief with it for the time being.

'Did our boy actually *kill* Niki, Luke?' Hector inquired, in the most casual of tones.

'He hopes he did.'

'Yes. Well, I don't think I heard any of that, did you?'

'Not a sound.'

'It was two other blokes, and any similarity is purely coincidental. Deal?'

'Deal.'

By mid-afternoon on day two, Hector sounded frustrated but not yet downhearted. The Cabinet Office had ruled that a quorum of the Empowerment Committee must after all be convened, he said. They were insisting that Billy Boy Matlock must be fully apprised – repeat *fully* – of all operational details that Hector had hitherto held close to his chest. They would settle for a four-man working party comprising one representative each from the Foreign and Home offices, Treasury and Immigration. Excluded members would be invited to ratify the recommendations *post facto*, which the Cabinet Office predicted would be a formality. With every kind of reluctance, Hector had accepted their terms. Then quite suddenly – it was in the evening of the same day – the weather changed, and Hector's voice rose a notch. Luke's illicit recorder played the moment back to him:

H: The buggers are ahead of us somehow. Billy Boy's just had the tip-off from his City sources.

L: Ahead of us *how*? How can they be? We haven't made a move yet.

H: According to Billy Boy's City sources, the Financial Services Authority is shaping to block the Arena application to open a major bank and we're the boys who've put the knife in.

L: *We?*

H: The Service. All of it. The big City institutions are screaming foul. Thirty cross-bench MPs on the oligarch payroll are drafting a rude letter to the Secretary to the Treasury accusing the Financial Services Authority of anti-Russian prejudice and demanding that all unreasonable obstacles to the application be removed forthwith. The usual suspects in the House of Lords are up in arms.

L: But that's utter bullshit!

H: Try telling that to the Financial Services Authority. All *they* know is, the central banks are refusing to lend to each other despite the fact that they've been given billions of public money to do exactly that. Now, lo and behold, along comes Arena to the rescue on its white horse, offering to put hundreds of bloody billions into their hot little hands. Who gives a shit where the money comes from? [*Is this a question? If so, Luke has no answer to it.*]

H [*sudden outburst*]: There aren't any *unreasonable obstacles*, for fuck's sake! Nobody's even begun to *erect* any unreasonable obstacles! As of last night, Arena's application was rotting in the FSA's pending tray. They haven't met, they haven't conferred, they've hardly started their regulatory inquiries. But none of that has stopped the Surrey oligarchs from beating their war drums, or the financial editors being briefed that if Arena's application is rejected, the City of London will end up a poor fourth behind Wall Street, Frankfurt and Hong Kong. And whose fault will that be? The Service's, led up the garden path by one Hector bloody Meredith!

Another silence followed – so long that Luke was reduced to asking Hector whether he was still there, for which he received a snappish 'where the fuck d'you think I am?'

'Well at least Billy Boy's aboard for you,' Luke suggested, by way of offering comfort that he didn't share.

'A total turnaround, thank God,' Hector replied devoutly. 'Don't know where I'd be without him.'

Luke didn't know either.

*

Billy Boy Matlock, Hector's *ally* suddenly? Hector's convert to the cause? His newfound comrade-in-arms? A total turnaround? *Billy?*

Or Billy Boy buying himself a little reinsurance on the side? Not that Billy Boy was *bad*, not bad like wicked, not bad like Aubrey Longrigg, Luke had never thought that of him – not your devious mastermind, your double or triple agent, sidling between conflicting powers. That wasn't Billy at all. He was too obvious for that.

So when precisely might this great conversion have occurred, and why? Luke marvelled. Or might it be that Billy Boy had already covered his back elsewhere, and was now ready to offer Hector his ample front, thereby becoming privy to the most closely guarded secrets in Hector's treasure chest?

What, for instance, had been in Billy's head that Sunday afternoon when he walked out of the Bloomsbury safe house, smarting from his humiliating put-down? Love of Hector? Or serious concerns for his own position in the future scheme of things?

What great City eminence might Billy Boy, in the days of painful rumination following that meeting, have invited to lunch – famously parsimonious though he might be – and sworn to secrecy, knowing that in the great eminence's book a secret is what he tells one person at a time? Knowing also that he has gained himself a friend should events take a tricky turn?

And of the many ripples that might fan out from this one little pebble tossed into the City's murky waters, who knew which of them might lap against the super-sharp ear of that distinguished City insider and rising parliamentarian, Aubrey Longrigg?

Or Bunny Popham?

Or Giles de Salis, ringmaster of the media circus?

And of all the other sharp-eared Longriggs, Pophams and de Salises waiting to jump on the Arena roundabout the minute it begins to turn?

Except that, according to Hector, the roundabout *hasn't* begun to turn. So why jump?

Luke wished very much that he had someone to share his thoughts with, but as usual there was nobody. Perry and Gail were outside the circle. Yvonne was off-air. And Ollie was – well, Ollie was the best back-door man in the business, but no Einstein when it came to the cut and thrust of high-stakes intrigue.

*

While Gail and Perry were performing sterling work as proxy parents, troupe leaders, Monopoly players and tour guides to the children, Ollie and Luke had been counting off the warning signs, and either dismissing them or adding them to Luke's ever-growing worry list.

In the course of one morning, Ollie had observed the same couple pass the house twice on the north side, then twice on the south-west side. Once the woman wore a yellow headscarf and a green Loden coat, once a floppy sunhat and slacks. But the same boots and socks, and carrying the same alpine walking stick. The man wore shorts the first time and baggy leopard-spot pants the second, but the same peaked blue cap and the same way of walking with his hands at his sides, barely moving them with his stride.

And Ollie had taught observation at training school, so it was hard to gainsay him.

Ollie had also been keeping a wary eye on Wengen railway station in the wake of Gail's and Natasha's encounter with Swiss authority at Interlaken Ost. According to a servant of the railway with whom Ollie had had a quiet beer in the Eiger Bar, the police presence in Wengen, normally restricted to resolving the odd punch-up, or conducting a half-hearted quest for drug pushers, had been increased over the past few days. Hotel registers had been checked out, and the photograph of a broad-faced, balding man with a beard had been surreptitiously shown to ticket clerks at the train and cable-car stations.

'I don't suppose Dima ever grew a beard at all, did he, back in the days when he was opening his first money laundromat in Brighton Beach?' he inquired of Luke during a quiet walk in the garden.

Both a beard and a moustache, Luke conceded grimly. They were part of the new identity he assumed in order to get himself to the States. Didn't shave them off till five years ago.

And – call it coincidence, but Ollie didn't – while he was at the railway news-stand, picking up the *International Herald Tribune* and the local press, he had spotted the same suspicious pair that he had seen casing the house. They were sitting in the waiting room and staring at the wall. Two hours and several trains going in both directions later, they were still there. Ollie could offer no explanation for their behaviour except cock-up: the relief surveillance team had missed the train, so the two were waiting while their superiors made up their minds what to do with them, or – taking into account their chosen position overlooking platform 1 – waiting to see who got off trains arriving from Lauterbrunnen.

'Plus the nice lady at the cheese shop asked me how many people I thought I was feeding, which I didn't like, but she *may* have been referring to my somewhat oversized tummy,' he ended, as if to lighten Luke's load, but humour wasn't coming easily to either of them.

Luke was also fretting about the fact that the household included four children of school age. Swiss schools were running, so why weren't *our* children at school? The medical nurse had asked him the same question when he went to the village surgery to have his hand checked. His lame reply to the effect that the International Schools were having a half-term had sounded implausible even to himself.

*

So far, Luke had insisted on confining Dima indoors, and Dima out of indebtedness had grudgingly submitted. In the afterglow of the scuffle on the staircase of the Bellevue Palace, Luke at first could do no wrong in Dima's eyes. But as the days crawled by and Luke had to find one excuse after another for the apparatchiks in London, Dima's mood turned to one of resistance, then revolt. Tiring of Luke, he put his case to Perry with characteristic bluntness:

'If I wanna take Tamara a walk, I gonna take her,' he growled. 'I see a beautiful mountain, I wanna show her. This isn't fucking Kolyma. You tell this to Dick, hear me, Professor?'

For the shallow climb up the concrete path to the benches that overlooked the valley, Tamara decided she needed a wheelchair. Ollie was sent off to find one. With her hennaed hair, splurged lipstick and dark glasses, she resembled some necromancer's artefact, and Dima in his boiler suit and woollen ski cap was no prettier. But in a community inured to every kind of human aberration, they made some sort of ideal elderly couple as Dima pushed Tamara slowly up the hill behind the house to show her the Staubbach Falls and Lauterbrunnen Valley in all their glory.

And if Natasha accompanied them, which she sometimes did, it was no longer as the hated love-child sired by Dima and inflicted on Tamara after she was ejected half-mad from prison, but as their loving and obedient daughter, whether natural or adopted was no longer relevant. But mostly, Natasha read her books or sought out her father when he was alone, blandishing him, stroking his bald head and kissing it as if he were her child.

Perry and Gail too were integral parts of this newly constituted family that was forming: with Gail forever thinking up new activities for the girls, introducing them to the cows in the meadows, marching them off to watch Hobelkäse being planed in the cheese shop, or looking for deer and squirrels in the woods; while Perry played the boys' admired team leader and lightning-rod for their surplus energy. Only when Gail proposed an early-morning four at tennis with the boys did Perry uncharacteristically demur. After the match from hell in Paris, he confessed, he needed time to recover.

*

The concealment of Dima and his troupe was only one of Luke's accumulating anxieties. Waiting out the nights in his upper room for Hector's random bulletins, he had too much time to assemble the evidence that their presence in the village was attracting unwelcome attention, and, in his many sleepless hours, to concoct conspiracy theories that, when morning came, had an uncomfortable ring of reality.

He worried about his identity as Brabazon, and whether the Bellevue's diligent Herr Direktor had by now made the connection between Brabazon's inspection of the hotel's amenities and the two battered Russians at the foot of the staircase; and whether from there, with police assistance, investigations had progressed to a certain BMW parked under a beech tree at Grindelwald Grund railway station.

His most drastic scenario, prompted in part by Dima's light-hearted reconstruction in the car, ran as follows:

One of the bodyguards – probably the cadaverous philosopher – manages to haul himself up the staircase and hammer on the locked door.

Or perhaps Ollie's speculative reading of the emergency door's electronics was a little too speculative after all.

Either way, the alarm is raised and news of the fracas reaches the ears of the better-informed guests at the Arena *apéro* in the Salon d'Honneur: Dima's bodyguards have been attacked, Dima has vanished.

Now everything is in motion at once. Emilio dell Oro alerts the Seven Clean Envoys, who take to their mobiles and alert their *vory* brothers, who in turn alert the Prince in his castle.

Emilio alerts his Swiss-banker friends, who in turn alert *their* friends in high places in the Swiss administration, not excluding the police and security services, whose first duty in life is to preserve the integrity of Switzerland's hallowed bankers, and arrest anyone who impugns it.

Emilio dell Oro further alerts Aubrey Longrigg, Bunny Popham and de Salis, who alert whomever they alert, see below.

The Russian Ambassador in Berne receives urgent instructions from Moscow, fuelled by the Prince, to demand the release of the bodyguards before they can sing, and more specifically to track down Dima and return him post-haste to his country of origin.

The Swiss authorities, who until now have been happy to provide sanctuary for Dima the wealthy financier, insti-gate a nationwide manhunt for Dima the fugitive criminal.

But there is a twist even to this lugubrious tale and, try as he may, Luke cannot unravel it. *By what trail of circumstance, suspicion or hard Intelligence, did the two bodyguards present them-selves at the Bellevue Palace Hotel after the second signing? Who sent them? With instructions to do what? And why?*

Or put a different way: *did the Prince and his brethren already have reason to know, at the time of the second signing, that Dima was proposing to break his unbreakable vory oath and become the bitch of all time?*

But when Luke ventures to air these concerns to Dima – albeit in diluted form – he sees them brushed carelessly aside. Hector himself is no more receptive:

'Go that route, we're fucked from day one,' he almost shouts.

*

Move house? Do a night flit to Zurich, Basel, Geneva? For what, finally? To leave a hornet's nest behind? – mystified traders, landlords, the letting agents, the village gossip mill?

'I could get you a few *guns*, if you're interested,' Ollie suggested, in another vain effort to cheer Luke up. 'According to what *I* hear, there's not a household in the village isn't bristling with them, whatever the new regulations say. It's for when the Russians come. These people don't know who they've got here, do they?'

'Well, let's hope not,' Luke replied, with a brave smile.

*

For Perry and Gail there was something idyllic in their day-to-day existence, something – as Dima would say wistfully – pure. It was as if they had been landed in a far outpost of humanity, with the mission of exercising a duty of care towards their charges.

If Perry wasn't out scrambling with the boys – Luke having urged him to take out-of-the-way paths, and Alexei having discovered that he did not, after all, suffer from vertigo, it was just that he didn't like Max – he was strolling with Dima in the dusk, or sitting beside him on a bench at the edge of the forest, watching him glower into the valley with the same intensity that, crammed into the pepper-pot crow's-nest at Three Chimneys, he had broken off his monologue and glowered into the darkness, wiped the back of his hand across his mouth, taken a pull of vodka and gone on glowering. Sometimes he demanded to be alone in the woods with his pocket recorder while Ollie or Luke kept covert watch from a distance. But he kept the cassettes to himself as part of his insurance policy.

The days, however many there had been, had aged him, Perry noticed. Perhaps the enormity of his betrayal was coming home to him. Perhaps, as he stared into the eternity, or murmured secretively into his tape recorder, he was searching for some kind of inner reconciliation. His demonstrative tenderness towards Tamara seemed to suggest this. Perhaps a revived *vory* instinct towards religion had paved his way to her:

'My Tamara, when she die, God gonna be deaf already, she pray so fucking hard to him,' he remarked proudly, leaving Perry with the impression that, regarding his own redemption, he was less sanguine.

Perry marvelled also at Dima's forbearance towards him, which seemed to grow in inverse proportion to his contempt for Luke's half-promises, no sooner made than regretfully withdrawn.

'Don't you worry, Professor. One day we all be happy, hear me? God gonna fix the whole shit,' he declared, strolling along the footpath with his hand resting proprietorially on his shoulder: 'Viktor and Alexei think you're some kinda fucking hero. Maybe one day they make you *vor*.'

Perry was not deceived by the roar of laughter that followed this suggestion. For days now he had seen himself increasingly as the inheritor of Dima's line of deep male friendships: with the dead Nikita, who had made him a man; with the murdered Misha, his disciple, whom to his shame he had failed to protect; and with all the fighters and men of iron who had ruled over his incarceration in Kolyma and beyond.

*

Perry's improbable appointment as Hector's midnight confessor, by contrast, came out of the blue. He knew, and Gail knew – Luke did not need to tell them, the daily prevarications were enough – that things were not going as smoothly in London as Hector had anticipated. They knew from Luke's body language that, conceal it as he tried, the emotional strain was telling on him also.

So when Perry's mobile chimed its encrypted melody in his ear at one in the morning, causing him to sit immediately upright, and Gail, without waiting to know who the caller was, to hurry down the corridor and check on the sleeping girls, his first thought on hearing Hector's voice was that he was about to ask Perry to bolster Luke's spirits, or – more wishfully – to play a more active role in spiriting the Dimas to England.

'Mind if I chat with you for a couple of minutes, Milton?'

Was this really Hector's voice? – or a recorder, and the batteries were running down?

'Chat ahead.'

'Polish philosopher chap I read from time to time.'

'What's his name?'

'Kolakowski. Thought you might have heard of him.'

Perry had, but didn't feel a need to say so. 'What about him?' Was the man drunk? Too much of his malt whisky from the Isle of Skye?

'Very stern views on good and evil – which I'm tending to share these days – Kolakowski had. Evil is evil, period. Not rooted in social circumstance. Not about being deprived or a drug addict or whatever. Evil as an *absolutely* and *entirely* separate human force.' Long silence. 'Wondered whether you had a take on that?'

'Are you all right, Tom?'

'I dip into him, you see. At bleak moments. Kolakowski. Surprised you haven't come across him. He had a law. Rather a good one in the circumstances.'

'What's bleak about *this* moment?'

'The Law of Infinite Cornucopia, he called it. Not that Poles do a definite article. Not *indefinite* either, which tells you something, but there you are. Nub of his Law being, that there are an infinite number of explanations for any single event. Limitless. Or put in language we both understand, you'll never know which bugger hit you or why. Rather comfortable words, I thought, in the circumstances, don't you?'

Gail had returned and was standing in the doorway, listening.

'If I knew the circumstances, I could probably form a better judgement,' Perry said – talking to Gail as well now. 'Is there anything I can do to help you, Tom? You sound a bit fragged.'

'Think you've done it, Milton, old boy. Thanks for your advice. See you in the morning.'

See you?

'Has he got anyone with him?' Gail asked, getting back into bed.

'Not that he mentioned.'

According to Ollie, Hector's wife Emily had ceased to live with him in London after Adrian's crash. She preferred the arctic cottage in Norfolk, which was nearer to the prison.

*

Luke stands stiffly beside his bed, encrypted mobile to his ear and Ollie's lash-up connecting it to the recorder parked on the side of the handbasin. It is four-thirty in the afternoon. Hector hasn't called all day and Luke's messages have gone unanswered. Ollie is out shopping for fresh trout, and Wienerschnitzel for Katya, who doesn't like fish. And home-made chips for everyone. Food is a big topic these days. Meals are taken ceremoniously, since each one may be their last together. Some are preceded by a long grace in Russian, whispered by Tamara to many crossings of the breast. At other times, when they look to her to do her piece, she declines, apparently to indicate that the company is out of divine favour. This afternoon, to fill the empty hours before dinner, Gail has decided to take the small girls down to Trümmelbach to see the terrifying waterfalls that tumble down the inside of the mountain. Perry is less than happy with the plan. Agreed, she will have her mobile with her, but deep inside the mountain, what kind of signal is she going to get?

Gail doesn't care. They're going anyway. Cowbells are chiming in the meadow. Natasha is reading under the maple tree.

'So here it is,' Hector is saying in a rock-steady voice. 'The whole, dismal fucking story. You listening?'

17

Luke listens. Half an hour turns to forty minutes. Dismal fucking story is right.

Then, because there is no point in hurrying, he listens again, for another forty minutes, lying on the bed. It is a short story. It is a play complex in itself, whether comedy or tragedy to be revealed in due course. At eight o'clock this morning, Hector Meredith and Billy Matlock were arraigned before a kangaroo court of their peers in the Vice-Chief's suite of rooms on the fourth floor. The charge against them was then read out. Hector paraphrased it, sauced with his own expletives:

'The Vice said the Secretary to the Cabinet had summoned him and put a certain proposition to him: to wit, one Billy Matlock and one Hector Meredith were jointly conspiring to besmirch the fine reputation of one Aubrey Longrigg, Member of Parliament, City mogul and arse-licker to the Surrey oligarchs, in return for the perceived injuries that the said Longrigg had inflicted on the accused: i.e., Billy getting his own back for all the shit Aubrey had made him eat while they were at daggers drawn on the fourth floor; and me for when Aubrey tried to bankrupt my family fucking firm, then buy it for a French kiss. There was a perception in the mind of the Cabinet Secretary that our *personal involvement was clouding our operational judgement.* Still listening?'

Luke is. And to listen even better, he now sits up on the edge of the bed, his head in his hands, and the tape recorder on the duvet beside him.

'I am then, as the prime instigator of the conspiracy to shaft Aubrey, invited to explain my position.'

'Tom?'

'Dick?'

'What on earth has shafting Aubrey – even if that's what you two were up to – got to do with getting our boy and his family to London?'

'Good question. I will answer it in the same spirit.'

Luke had never heard him quite so angry.

'Word is abroad, according to the Vice, that our Service is proposing to put on to the public stage a supergrass who will effectively discredit the banking aspirations of the Arena Conglomerate. Do I need to dilate on what the Vice-Chief was pleased to call the *linkage* here? A shining White Knight Russian bank, billions of dollars on the table and many more where they came from, with a promise not only to release these many more billions on to a cash-strapped money market but to invest in some of the great dinosaurs of British industry? And just when the good will of the said White Knights is about to reach fruition, along come us Intelligence wankers wanting to upset the apple-cart by spouting a lot of moralistic candyfloss about the profits of crime.'

'You said you were invited to explain your position,' Luke hears himself remind Hector.

369

'Which I did. Rather well, I must say. Gave it to him with everything I'd got. And what I didn't give him, Billy did. And bit by bit – you'd be amazed – the Vice began to prick his ears up. Not an easy role for a chap to play when his boss is putting his head in the sand, but by the end of the day he came through like a lady. Cleared the room of everybody except the two of us, and heard us out all over again.'

'You and Billy?'

'Billy now being *inside* our tent and pissing vigorously out. A Damascene conversion, better late than never.'

Luke doubts this, but charitably decides not to express his doubt.

'So where do we stand now?' he asks.

'Back where we started. Official but unofficial, with Billy aboard and the charter plane on my tab. Got a pencil poised?'

'Of course not!'

'Then listen up. Here's how we go from here, no looking back.'

*

He listens up twice, then realizes that he is waiting for the courage to ring Eloise, so he does. It looks as though I could be home quite soon, maybe even late tomorrow, he says. Eloise says that Luke must do whatever he thinks right. Luke asks after Ben. Eloise says Ben is fine, thank you. Luke discovers he has a nosebleed and gets back on the bed until it's time for supper, and a quiet word with Perry, who is in the sun room practising climbing knots with Alexei and Viktor.

'Got a minute?'

Luke leads Perry to the kitchen, where Ollie is wrestling with an obstinate deep fryer that refuses to achieve the desired heat for the home-made chips.

'Mind giving us a minute, Harry?'

'No problem, Dick.'

'Great news at last, thank God,' Luke began, when Ollie had departed. 'Hector's got a small plane standing by at Belp from eleven p.m. tomorrow GMT, Belp–Northolt. Cleared for take-off and landing and a clean walk both ends. God knows how he's swung it, but he has. We'll jeep Dima over the mountain to Grund once it's dark, then drive him straight to Belp. As soon as he touches down in Northolt they'll take him to a safe house, and if he delivers what he says he'll deliver, they'll officially land him, and the rest of the family can follow.'

'*If* he delivers?' Perry repeated, tilting his long head quizzically to one side in a way that Luke found particularly irksome.

'Well he will, won't he? We know that. It's the only deal on the table,' Luke went on when Perry said nothing. 'Our masters in Whitehall won't have the family round their necks until they know Dima's worth his salt.' And when Perry still failed to respond: 'It's as far as Hector can get them to move without due process. So I'm afraid that's it.'

'*Due process*,' Perry repeated at last.

'That's what we're dealing with, I'm afraid.'

'I thought it was people.'

'It is,' Luke retorted, flaring. 'Which is why Hector wants *you* to be the person who tells Dima. He thinks it's best coming from you rather than me. I fully agree. I suggest you don't do it now. Early tomorrow evening will be quite soon enough. We don't need him brooding all night. I suggest six-ish, to give him time to make his preparations.'

Has the man no *give* in him? Luke wondered. How long am I supposed to meet this lopsided stare?

'And if he *doesn't* deliver?' Perry inquired.

'Nobody's got that far. It's step by step. That's the way these things are played, I'm afraid. Nothing's a straight line.' And letting himself slip, and instantly regretting it: 'We're not academics here. We do action.'

'I need to talk to Hector.'

'That's what he said you'd say. He's standing by for your call.'

*

Alone, Perry walked up the path to the woods where he had walked with Dima. Reaching a bench, he swept away the evening dew with the flat of his hand, sat down, and waited for his thoughts to clear. In the lighted house below him, he could see Gail, the four children and Natasha squatting in a ring on the floor of the sun room with the Monopoly board at their centre. He heard a squawk of outrage from Katya, followed by a bark of protest from Alexei. Dragging his mobile from his pocket he stared at it in the twilight before touching the button for Hector and immediately hearing his voice.

'You want the dolled-up version, or the hard truth?'

This was the old Hector, the one he relished, the one who had berated him in the safe house in Bloomsbury.

'The hard truth will do fine.'

'Here it is. If we bring our boy over, they'll listen to him and they'll form a judgement. It's the best I can get out of them. As of yesterday they weren't prepared to go that far.'

'*They?*'

'The *authorities*. The *them*. Who the fuck d'you think? If he doesn't measure up, they'll throw him back in the water.'

'What water?'

'Russian probably. What's the difference? The point is, he *will* measure up. *I* know he will, *you* know he will. Once they've decided to keep him, which won't take more than a day or two, they'll buy into the whole catastrophe: his wife, kids, his pal's kids, and his dog if he's got one.'

'He hasn't.'

'The nub of it is, they've accepted the whole package in principle.'

'What principle?'

'D'you mind? I've been listening to over-educated arse-holes from Whitehall splitting hairs all morning and I don't need another. We've got a deal. As long as our boy comes through with the goods, the rest of them follow with due expedition. That's their promise, and I've got to believe them.'

Perry closed his eyes and took a breath of mountain air.

'What are you asking me to do?'

'No more than you've done from day one. Compromise your noble principles for the greater good. Soft-soap him. If you tell him it's a maybe, he won't come. If you tell him we accept his terms without qualification, but there will be a short delay before he's reunited with his loved ones, he will. Are you still there?'

'Partly.'

'You tell him the truth, but you tell it selectively. Give

him half a chance to think we're playing dirty on him, he'll grab it. We may be fair-play English gentlemen, but we're also perfidious Albion shits. Did you hear that or am I talking to the wall?'

'I heard it.'

'Then tell me I'm wrong. Tell me I'm misreading him. Tell me you know a better plan. It's you or nobody. This is your finest hour. If he won't believe you, he won't believe anyone.'

*

They lay in bed. It was after midnight. Gail, half asleep, had barely spoken.

'It's been taken away from him somehow,' Perry said.

'Hector?'

'That's how it feels.'

'Perhaps it was never his in the first place,' Gail suggested. And after a while: 'Have you decided yet?'

'No.'

'Then I think you have. I think no decision's a decision. I think you've decided, and that's why you can't sleep.'

*

It was the next evening, quarter to six. Ollie's cheese fondue had been enjoyed and cleared away. Dima and Perry remained alone in the dining room, standing face to face under a multi-coloured metal alloy chandelier. Luke was taking a tactful stroll in the village. The girls, with Gail's encouragement, were watching *Mary Poppins* again. Tamara had removed herself to the sitting room.

'It's all the apparatchiks can offer,' said Perry. 'You go

374

ahead to London tonight, your family follows in a couple of days. The apparatchiks insist on that. They have to obey the rules. Rules for everything. Even this.'

He was using short sentences, watching for the smallest change in Dima's features, for a hint of softening, or a glimmer of understanding, even of resistance, but the face before him was unreadable.

'They want I go alone?'

'Not alone. Dick will be flying to London with you. As soon as the formalities are completed, and the apparatchiks have satisfied their rules, we all follow you to England. And Gail will look after Natasha,' he added, hoping to allay what he imagined would be Dima's first concern.

'She *ill*, my Natasha?'

'Good Lord no. She's not *ill*! She's young. She's beautiful. Temperamental. Pure. She'll need a lot of looking after in a strange country, that's all.'

'Sure,' Dima agreed, nodding his bald head to confirm this. 'Sure. She beautiful like her mother.'

Then jerked his head abruptly sideways, then downwards, as he stared into some dark gulf of anxiety or memory to which Perry was not admitted. Does he *know*? Has Tamara, in a fit of spite or intimacy or forgetfulness, *told* him? Has Dima, contrary to all Natasha's expectations, taken her secret and pain upon himself instead of tearing off in search of Max? What was certain to Perry was that the outburst of fury and refusal that he had anticipated was giving way to a prisoner's dawning sense of resignation in the face of bureaucratic authority; and this realization disturbed Perry more deeply than any violent outburst could have done.

'A couple days, huh?' Dima repeated, making it sound like a life sentence.

'A couple of days is what they say.'

'Tom say that? *Couple days?*'

'Yes.'

'He's some good fellow, Tom, huh?'

'I believe he is.'

'Dick too. He nearly kill that fucker.'

They digested this thought together.

'Gail, she look after my Tamara?'

'Gail will look after your Tamara very carefully. And the boys will help her. And I'll be here too. We'll all look after the family until they come over. Then we'll look after all of you in England.'

Dima reflected on this, and the idea seemed to grow in him.

'My Natasha go Roedean School?'

'Maybe not Roedean. They can't promise that. Maybe there's somewhere even better. We'll find good schools for everyone. It'll be fine.'

They were painting a false horizon together. Perry knew it and Dima seemed to know it too, and welcome it, for his back had arched and his chest had filled, and his face had eased into the dolphin smile that Perry remembered from their first encounter on the tennis court in Antigua.

'You better marry that girl pretty quick, Professor – hear me?'

'We'll send you an invitation.'

'Wortha lotta camels,' he muttered, and pulled a smile at his own joke – not a smile of defeat in Perry's eyes, but a smile for time gone by, as if the two of them had known each other all their lives, which Perry was beginning to think they had.

'You play me Wimbledon once?'

'Sure. Or Queen's. I'm still a member there.'

'No pussying, OK?'

'No pussying.'

'Wanna bet? Make it interesting?'

'Can't afford it. Might lose.'

'You chicken, huh?'

'Afraid so.'

Then the embrace he dreaded, the prolonged imprisonment in the huge, damp trembling torso, on and on. But when they separated, Perry saw that the life had drained from Dima's face, and the light from his brown eyes. Then, as if to order, he turned on his heel, and headed for the living room where Tamara and the assembled family were waiting.

*

There never had been any possibility that Perry would fly to England with Dima, on that evening or any other. Luke had known it all along, and had hardly needed to float the question with Hector to get the flat answer 'no'. If the answer had for some unforeseeable reason been yes, Luke would have contested it: untrained, enthusiastic amateurs flying escort with high-value defectors simply didn't fit into his professional scheme of things.

So it was less out of sympathy for Perry and more out of sound operational sense that Luke conceded that Perry should accompany them on the journey to Berne-Belp. When you are whisking a major source from the bosom of

377

his family and consigning him with no hard guarantees to the care of your parent Service, he reasoned grudgingly, well yes, then it is prudent to provide him with the solace of his chosen mentor.

But if Luke had been anticipating heart-wrenching scenes of departure, he was spared them. Darkness came. The house was hushed. Dima summoned Natasha and his two sons to the conservatory and addressed them while Perry and Luke waited out of earshot in the front hall and Gail purposefully continued to watch *Mary Poppins* with the girls. For his reception by the gentlemen spies of London, Dima had donned his blue pinstripe suit. Natasha had pressed his best shirt, Viktor had polished his Italian shoes, and Dima was worried about them: what if they should get dirty on the walk to the place where Ollie had parked the jeep? But he was reckoning without Ollie who, as well as blankets, gloves and thick woollen hats for the ride over the mountain, had a pair of rubber overshoes of Dima's size waiting for him in the hall. And Dima must have told his family not to follow him, because he appeared alone, looking as sprightly and unrepentant as he had when he made his appearance through the swing-doors of the Bellevue Palace Hotel with Aubrey Longrigg at his side.

At the sight of him, Luke's heart rose higher than it had risen since Bogotá. Here is our crown witness – and Luke himself will be another. Luke will be witness A behind a screen, or plain Luke Weaver in front of it. He will be a pariah, as Hector will. And he will help nail Aubrey Longrigg and all his merry men to the mast, and to hell with a five-year contract at training school, and a quality house close to it, with sea air and good schools for Ben near by and an enhanced pension at the end of the line, and renting not selling his house in London. He would cease to mistake sexual promiscuity for freedom. He would try and try with Eloise until she believed in him again. He would finish all his games of chess with Ben, and find a job that would bring him home at a sensible hour, and real weekends to bond in, and for Christ's sake he was only forty-three and Eloise wasn't even forty yet.

So it was with both a sense of ending and beginning that Luke fell in next to Dima, and the three of them fell in behind Ollie, for the walk down to the farmstead and the jeep.

*

Of the drive, Perry the devoted mountaineer had at first only a distracted awareness: the furtive ascent by moonlight through forest to the Kleine Scheidegg with Ollie at the wheel and Luke beside him in the front seat, and Dima's great body lurching soggily against Perry's shoulders each time Ollie negotiated the hairpin bends on sidelights, and Dima didn't bother to brace himself unless he really had to, preferring to ride with the blows. And yes, of course, the spectral black shadow of the Eiger North Face drawing ever closer was an iconic sight for Perry: passing the little way station of Alpiglen, he gazed up in awe at the moonlit White Spider, calculating a route through it, and promising himself that, as a last throw of independence before he married Gail, he would attempt it.

About to crest the Scheidegg, Ollie dowsed the jeep's lights altogether, and they slunk like thieves past the twin hulks of the great hotel. The glow of Grindelwald appeared below them. They began the descent, entered forest and saw the lights of Brandegg winking at them through the trees.

'From now on, it's hard track,' Luke called over his shoulder, in case Dima was feeling the effects of the bumpy ride.

But Dima either didn't hear or didn't care. He had thrown his head back and thrust one hand into his breast, while the other arm was stretched along the back seat behind Perry's shoulders.

Two men at the centre of the road are waving a hand torch.

*

The man without the torch is holding up his gloved hand in command. He is dressed for the city in a long overcoat, scarf and no hat although he is half bald. The man with the torch is wearing police uniform and a cape. Ollie is already yelling cheerfully at them as he draws up.

'Hey, you boys, what's going *on* here?' he demands, in a sing-song Swiss-French *argot* that Perry hasn't heard him speak before. 'Somebody fallen off the Eiger? We haven't even seen a rabbit.'

Dima's a rich Turk, Luke had said at the briefing. He's been staying at the Park Hotel and his wife's been taken seriously ill in Istanbul. He left his car in Grindelwald, and we're a couple of English fellow guests playing good Samaritan. It won't stand checking but it may just work for one-time use.

'Why didn't the rich Turk take the train from Wengen to Lauterbrunnen and go round to Grindelwald by cab?' Perry had asked.

'He won't be reasoned with,' Luke had replied. 'This way he reckons, by taking a jeep over the mountain, he saves himself an hour. There's a midnight flight to Ankara from Kloten.'

'Is there?'

The policeman is shining his torch at a purple triangle stuck to the jeep's windscreen. The letter G is printed on it. The man in city clothes is hovering behind him, blacked out by the glare of the torch. But Perry has a shrewd feeling he is taking a very close look at the jovial driver and his three passengers.

'Whose jeep is this?' the policeman asks, resuming his inspection of the purple triangle.

'Arni Steuri's. Plumber. Friend of mine. Don't tell me you don't know Arni Steuri from Grindelwald. He's on the main street, next to the electrician.'

'You drove down from Scheidegg tonight?' the policeman asks.

'From Wengen.'

'You drove *up* from *Wengen to Scheidegg*?'

'What do you think we did? Fly?'

'If you drove *up* from Wengen to Scheidegg, you must have a second vignette, issued from Lauterbrunnen. The vignette on your windscreen is for Scheidegg–Grindelwald *exclusively*.'

'So whose side are *you* on?' Ollie says, still with dogged good humour.

'Actually, I come from Mürren,' the policeman replies stoically.

*

A silence follows. Ollie begins humming a tune, which is another thing Perry hasn't heard him do before. He is humming, and with the help of the beam of the policeman's torch he is hunting among the papers jammed into the pocket of the driver's door. Sweat is running down Perry's back, although he's sitting quite motionless at Dima's side. No difficult peak or Serious Climb has ever made him sweat while he's sitting down. Ollie is still humming while he searches, but his hum has lost its cheeky edge. I'm a guest at the Park Hotel, Perry is telling himself. Luke's another. We're playing good Samaritan to a deranged Turk who can't speak English and his wife is dying. It may work for one-time use.

The plainclothes man has taken a step forward and is leaning over the side of the jeep. Ollie's humming is becoming less and less convincing. Finally he sits back as if defeated, a rumpled piece of paper in his hand.

'Well maybe this will do you,' he suggests, and shoves a second vignette at the policeman, this one with a yellow triangle instead of a purple one, and no letter G superimposed on it.

'Next time, make sure both vignettes are fixed to the windscreen,' the policeman says.

The torch goes out. They are driving again.

*

The parked BMW seemed to Perry's inexpert eye to repose peacefully where Luke had left it – no wheel clamps, no rude notices wedged under the wipers, just a parked saloon car – and whatever Luke was looking for as he and Ollie walked gingerly round it and Perry and Dima remained as instructed in the back seat of the jeep, they didn't find it, because now Ollie was already opening the driver's door and Luke was beckoning to them to hurry over, and inside the BMW it was the same formation again: Ollie at the wheel, Luke up front beside him, Perry and Dima in the back. All through the stop and search, Perry realized, Dima hadn't moved or made a sign. He's in prisoner mode, Perry thought. We're transferring him from one gaol to another, and the details are not his responsibility.

He glanced at the wing mirrors for suspicious following lights, but saw none. Sometimes a car would seem to be trailing them, but as soon as Ollie gave over, it drove past. He glanced at Dima beside him. Dozing. He was still wearing the black woollen cap to hide his baldness. Luke had insisted on it, pinstripe suit or no. Now and then, as Dima lolled against him, the oily wool tickled Perry's nose.

They had reached the autobahn. Under the sodium lights, Dima's face became a flickering death mask. Perry looked at his watch, not knowing why, but needing the comfort of the time. A blue sign indicated Belp Airport. Three lines – two lines – turn right *now* into the slip road.

*

The airport was darker than any airport had a right to be. That was the first thing about it that surprised Perry. All right, it was after midnight, but you'd have expected a lot more light, even from a small on-off airport like Belp that has never quite had its full international status confirmed.

And there were no formalities: unless you counted as a formality the private word Luke was having with a weary, grey-faced man in blue overalls who seemed to be the only official presence around. Now Luke was showing the man a document of some kind – too small for a passport, for sure, so was it a card, a driving licence, or perhaps a small stuffed envelope?

Whatever it was, the grey-faced man in blue overalls needed to look at it in a better light, because he turned and hunched himself into the beam of the downlight behind him, and when he turned back to Luke, whatever it was that he'd had in his hand wasn't in his hand any more, so either he'd hung on to it, or slipped it back to Luke, and Perry hadn't seen him do it.

And after the grey man – who had disappeared without a word in any language – there came a chicane of grey screens, but nobody to watch them negotiate it. And after the chicane, an immobile luggage carousel, and a pair of heavy electric swing-doors that were opening before they reached them – are we *airside* already? Impossible! – then an empty departure lounge with four glass doors leading straight on to the tarmac: and still not a soul to scan their luggage or themselves, make them take their shoes and jackets off, scowl at them through an armoured-glass window, snap fingers at them for their passports, or ask them deliberately unnerving questions about how long they had been in the country and why.

So if all this privileged non-attention they were getting was the result of private enterprise on Hector's part – which Luke had implied to Perry, and Hector himself had effectively confirmed – then all Perry had to say was: hats off to Hector.

The four glass doors to the open tarmac looked closed and bolted to Perry's eye, but Luke the good man on a rope knew better. He made a beeline for the right-hand door, and gave it a little tug and – behold! – it slid obediently into its housing, allowing a sprightly draught of cooling air to dance into the room and run its hand over Perry's face, which he was duly grateful for, because he felt unaccountably hot and sweaty.

With the door wide open and the night beckoning, Luke placed a hand – gently, not proprietorially – on Dima's arm and, guiding him away from Perry's side, led him unprotesting through the doorway and on to the tarmac where, as if forewarned, Luke made a sharp left turn, taking Dima with him and leaving Perry to stalk awkwardly behind them, like somebody who's not quite sure he's invited. Something about Dima had changed. Perry realized what it was. Stepping through the doorway, Dima had removed his woollen hat and dropped it into a handy rubbish bin.

And as Perry turned after them, he saw what Luke and Dima must already have seen: a twin-engined plane, with no lights and its propellers softly rotating, parked fifty yards away, with two ghostly pilots barely visible in the nose-cone.

There were no goodbyes.

Whether that was something to be pleased or sad about, Perry didn't know, either at the time or later. There had been so many embraces, so many greetings, real or contrived, there had been such a feast of goodbyes and hellos and declarations of love, that in the aggregate their meetings and partings were complete, and perhaps there was no room for another.

Or perhaps – always perhaps – Dima was too full to speak, or to look back, or to look at him at all. Perhaps tears were pouring down his face as he walked towards the little plane with one surprisingly small foot in front of the other, as neat as walking the plank.

And from Luke, a pace or two behind and apart from Dima now, as if leaving him to enjoy the absent limelight and the cameras, not one word to Perry either: it was the formed man ahead of him that Luke had his eyes on, not Perry standing alone behind him. It was Dima with his dignity on parade: bare-headed, the backward lean, the suppressed but stately limp.

And of course there was tactic in the way Luke had positioned himself in relation to Dima. Luke wouldn't be Luke if there wasn't tactic. He was the clever, darting shepherd in the Cumbrian hills where Perry had climbed when he was young, urging his prize ewe up the steps into the black hole of the cabin with every ounce of mental and physical concentration he possessed, and ready any time for him to shy or bolt or simply stop dead and refuse.

But Dima didn't shy, bolt or stop dead. He strode straight up the steps and into the blackness, and as soon as the blackness had him, little Luke was skipping up the steps to join him. And either there was someone inside to close the door on them or Luke did it for himself: an abrupt sigh of hinges, a double clunk of metal as the door was made fast from inside, and the black hole in the plane's fuselage disappeared.

Of the take-off, Perry also had no particular memory: only that he was thinking he should call Gail and tell her that the Eagle had Departed or some such phrase, then find himself a bus or cab, or maybe just walk into town. He was a bit hazy about where he was in relation to Belp centre, if there was one. Then he woke to Ollie standing beside him, and remembered that he had a lift back to Gail and the fatherless family in Wengen.

The plane took off, Perry didn't wave. He watched it rise and tip sharply, because Belp Airport has a lot of hills and small mountains to contend with and pilots have to be nippy. These pilots were. A commercial charter, by the look of it.

And there was no explosion. Or none that reached Perry's ears. Later, he wished there had been. Just the thump of a gloved fist into a punchball and a long white flash that brought the black hills rushing at him, then absolutely nothing, either to look at or to hear, until the ta-too-ta-toos of police and ambulances and fire brigades as their flashing lights began to answer the light that had gone out.

*

Instrument failure is the semi-official verdict at present. Engine failure another. Laxity on the part of unnamed maintenance staff is widely touted. Poor little Belp Airport has long been the experts' whipping boy and its critics aren't sparing the rod. Ground control may also have been to blame. Two committees of experts have failed to agree. The insurers are likely to withhold payment until the cause is known. The charred corpses continue to mystify. On the face of it the two pilots were no problem: charter pilots true, but plenty of flying experience, sober fellows, both married, no trace of illegal substances or alcohol, nothing adverse in their records and their wives on neighbourly terms with one another in Harrow, where the families lived. Two tragedies, therefore, but as far as the media was concerned, only worth a day. Why on earth a former official from the British Embassy in Bogotá should have been sharing the plane of a 'dubious Russian Swiss-based minigarch', even the red-top press was at a loss to explain. Was it sex? Was it drugs? Was it arms? For want of a shred of evidence it was none of them. Terror, the great catch-all these days, has also been considered, but rejected out of hand.

No group has claimed responsibility.

Acknowledgements

My heartfelt thanks to Federico Varese, Professor of Criminology at Oxford University and author of seminal works on the Russian mafia, for his creative and ever-patient counsel; to Bérengère Rieu, who took me backstage at the Roland Garros Stadium; to Eric Deblicker, who gave me the tour of an exclusive tennis club in the Bois de Boulogne not so dissimilar to my Club des Rois; to Buzz Berger for correcting my tennis shots; to Anne Freyer, my wise and faithful French editor; to Chris Bryans, for his advice on the Mumbai stock market; to Charles Lucas and John Rolley, bankers of probity, who sportingly advised me on the practices of less scrupulous members of their profession; to Ruth Halter-Schmid, who spared me many wrong turnings on my journeying through Switzerland; to Urs von Almen, for guiding me through the wilder byways of the Bernese Oberland; to Urs Bührer, Direktor of the Bellevue Palace Hotel in Berne, for allowing me to stage an embarrassing episode in his peerless establishment; and to Vicki Phillips, my invaluable secretary, for adding proofreading to her countless skills.

And to my friend Al Alvarez, the most generous and astute of readers, homage.

John le Carré, 2010

JOHN LE CARRÉ

THE PIGEON TUNNEL

'Out of the secret world I once knew, I have tried to make a theatre for the larger worlds we inhabit. First comes the imagining, then the search for reality. Then back to the imagining, and to the desk where I'm sitting now.'

From his years serving in British Intelligence during the Cold War, to a career as a writer that took him from war-torn Cambodia to Beirut on the cusp of the 1982 Israeli invasion, to Russia before and after the collapse of the Berlin Wall, John le Carré has always written from the heart of modern times.

In this, his first memoir, le Carré is as funny as he is incisive – reading into the events he witnesses the same moral ambiguity with which he imbues his novels. Whether he's writing about the parrot at a Beirut hotel that could perfectly mimic machine-gun fire, or visiting Rwanda's museums of the unburied dead in the aftermath of the genocide, or celebrating New Year's Eve with Yasser Arafat, or interviewing a German terrorist in her desert prison in the Negev, or watching Alec Guinness preparing for his role as George Smiley, or describing the female aid worker who inspired the main character in his *The Constant Gardener*, le Carré endows each happening with vividness and humour, now making us laugh out loud, now inviting us to think anew about events and people we believed we understood.

Best of all, le Carré gives us a glimpse of a writer's journey over more than six decades, and his own hunt for the human spark that has given so much life and heart to his fictional characters.